About the Author

Robert's first book, *The Ascension of Karrak*, was published in March of 2017 and this is the second instalment of an enthralling trilogy, not a bad result for an inaugural publication. Winged creatures, slimy beasts and magnificent dragons have always dwelled in his thoughts, and he wants to share them all with you.

Harbouring the typical self-doubt that lies within most of us, Robert delayed penning his ideas for far too long, choosing instead to pursue a 35-year career in the retail furniture trade. What a waste!

Originally writing this story for his wife, Jane, in an attempt to raise her spirits whilst she was seriously ill, it never crossed his mind to submit it to a publisher. She, however, despite her ill-health, believed in him far more than he believed in himself.

If this is your first venture into Robert's world, enjoy. If you've read his first book, *Welcome back*.

Ben!

Robert J Marsters

THE BANE OF KARRAK

ASCENSION TWO OF THREE

Time For Part Two

Robert J. Marsters

AUSTIN MACAULEY PUBLISHERS™

LONDON • CAMBRIDGE • NEW YORK • SHARJAH

A CIP catalogue record for this title is available from the British Library.

ISBN 9781788238328 (Paperback)
ISBN 9781788238335 (E-Book)
www.austinmacauley.com

First Published (2017)
Austin Macauley Publishers Ltd™
25 Canada Square
Canary Wharf
London
E14 5LQ

Acknowledgements

To my wife Jane, for her continued support, as always. Thank you, I love you.

To Nick Berriman, my faithful test-pilot, you survived again. Thank you, my friend.

To Lucy James and Kenny Andrew, of The Studio Tettenhall. Thank you for yet another stunning book cover design.

To David Berriman, for sharing his wealth of experience and giving his valuable time so freely. Thank you, David.

To everyone at Austin Macauley, for their diligence and professionalism in setting me on the right path. I feel honoured to be accepted as one of your featured authors.

Finally, to all of my friends, well-wishers and people who have purchased either the first, second or both of my books, a huge, huge thank you.

CHAPTER 1

Burying his face in his hands, Emnor collapsed to his knees. The destruction of Reiggan Fortress and the slaughter of countless friends and colleagues were too much for him to comprehend. Raising his head, he stared, a glazed look in his eyes as he surveyed the corpses of fallen wizards all around him. Karrak, it seemed, had spared no one. From learned seniors, similar in age to himself, to young novices, barely in their teenage years, all had been butchered mercilessly by either Karrak himself or one of his followers.

Each face Emnor gazed upon brought a memory, a memory of a discussion, a collaboration or even an argument that had taken place decades, if not centuries, before.

Hannock stood behind him and placed his hand on the old wizard's shoulder. "Why, why would Karrak do this? Surely, the artefact can't be that important to him?" he asked.

"His mind was consumed by the thought of possessing The Elixian Soul, Captain. This is only the beginning of the atrocities, he truly is insane. You forget that I have faced him, I saw the madness in his eyes. He will not stop until he dominates the entire world," replied Emnor.

"This may sound like a stupid question, Emnor, but is there anything I can do to help?"

Emnor sighed, "I think it best that you return to Jared and your companions. The danger has passed here. These were *our* friends, it seems only fitting that we should be the ones to lay them to rest."

Hannock nodded and turned away.

Harley, having heard the entire conversation, approached him, "I'll take you back to Cheadleford Village. We'll rejoin you later," he said quietly.

***

Harley returned almost immediately to find that Emnor, having composed himself, was instructing Xarran, Alex and Drake on their next, woeful course of action. As difficult as it would be for all concerned, the bodies of the fallen would have to be dealt with. However, with so many dead, they would not receive the proper ceremony they deserved. Emnor stood in the centre of the courtyard, chanting quietly, offering a prayer to the various gods in which his friends had believed. He raised his arms and looked to the skies as a huge, bright green, magical flame appeared before him. This was no mere bonfire, no heat came from the fuel-less inferno.

For many hours they toiled. Wrapping each corpse tightly within its own robes, one by one the victims were levitated into the heart of the flame. There was no smoke or separate flame from the cadavers; they simply evaporated silently, Emnor speaking the name of each individual as his body vanished.

With the cremations seemingly complete, Harley approached Emnor. He could see in his master's eyes that the proceedings had taken their toll on him, more mentally than physically, although he hid it well.

"Master Emnor," he began, "there is nothing more for us to be concerned with at the moment. Why don't you rest?"

Emnor shook his head vaguely, "No. No time, Harley. There may be survivors! We must begin a search of Reiggan immediately. I should have thought of it before. What if there are some of our friends locked in rooms or trapped in the basements?"

"Alright, Master," replied Harley, quickly, "we'll start right away, but you wait here. We can squeeze through gaps more easily than you, and if there are any survivors who find their way here, you will be here to greet them."

"No, I should come with you," insisted Emnor.

"And should anyone find their own way out and discover the courtyard empty? They may flee, thinking that they are alone," urged Harley. "You *must* stay here, Master."

"Stop treating me as if I am some sort of frail old man, Harley. I have seen worse horrors than this!" snapped Emnor.

"Alright, here's the truth of it," said Harley, snapping back at his master, "If Karrak comes back while we're in there, you'll be able to defend us! I don't want him creeping up behind us while we are searching in the darkness! Only you are strong enough to face him, we're not, and I don't want to die today!"

***

"Xarran, give me a hand to move some of this rubble, would you?"

"Don't you have any muscle at all, Alex?" asked Drake.

"Not as much as you Drake, and it's Alexander."

Xarran moved across the room toward Alex, attempting to find gaps amongst the masonry in which to position his feet. "Have you found something?" he asked.

"I'm not entirely sure," replied Alex. "There seems to be a hollow space between here and the wall."

Drake joined them and together they carefully moved the larger pieces of rock. "Hang on…" said Drake, "… what's that?"

Xarran pushed past him and reached into the gap. His head dropped. "It's a boot, and it still contains a foot." They had recovered the bodies of a few victims, half-buried amongst the devastation so far, but none that were completely entombed.

"Look, I know it might not be the nicest thing to do, but I think you should just grab it and see if you can pull him out of there. It's not as if you're going to hurt him, and I don't mean that disrespectfully."

Xarran disliked the idea as much as the others but realised that Drake, on this occasion, was right. Taking a firm grip on the heel of the boot, he pulled as hard as he could.

"Aaarrrgghhh…!"

The boys recoiled at the scream. Whoever it was, was still alive.

***

"Master Emnor, we've found a survivor!" yelled Alex.

The two larger boys had fervently resumed their digging and sent Alex to fetch Emnor, who now came charging into the room. "Who is it?" he asked warily.

"Not sure, master, he hasn't spoken since I tried to drag him out," replied Xarran.

"Move away, boys, it may not be a friend," said Emnor, pointing his staff toward the rock pile.

"Sorry, master, but if he is a friend, he won't last much longer under this lot. I'm getting him out and if he kills me… you can punish me later," yelled Drake, not even turning to face him.

With the aid of Emnor who, with the use of magic, threw larger pieces of rubble to the side, they unearthed the survivor. His face was smeared with blood and dirt and was swollen, making him unrecognisable to any of them.

"We'll get him cleaned up and attend to his wounds, but for now, I want his hands bound and he must be watched until he regains consciousness. That is, of course, assuming that he survives," ordered Emnor.

He was cared for by Drake who, despite his faults, had become quite skilful, mostly due to the regularity of patching up self-inflicted wounds during his wand-testing exploits. "Mostly cuts and bruises, Master Emnor, must have had a bang on the head though, to knock him out like that. The worst is his leg, it's broken."

"Well, we'll just have to wait for him to wake up then, Drake. Then perhaps we'll find out who he is," said Emnor.

"Yellodius Tarrock, you silly old fool!" muttered the old man, suddenly. "I must be in a bad way if you don't recognise me, Emmy."

Emnor rushed to the man's side, and leaning down, grabbed his hand. "Yello, is it really you? I thought you were halfway across the world. *What are you doing here?"*

"Heard about some upstart brat prince who needs a lesson in manners, thought you could use some help. I only returned yesterday, but now I'm starting to wish I'd stayed where I was." Yello attempted to sit up, but the pain very quickly quelled his enthusiasm. "Ooh, I say, that twinges a bit…" he said with a chuckle, "… I feel like I've had a fortress dropped on me."

"Just stay still, old friend. You're in a bad way, not too bad, nothing life-threatening," assured Emnor.

Yello raised his arm to study the bandage on it. "Who put this on me? They've done a really good job."

"You're welcome, Master Tarrock," said Drake, looking rather pleased with himself.

"Just call me Yello, dear boy, everybody else does. Now where's my staff?" Emnor smiled as the boys all turned to face Yello. "Don't look at me like that, stupid traditionalists, a good staff can become your best friend, boys, trust me."

Harley stepped forward without a word and handed Emnor his staff.

"I say…" said Yello, "… we have been busy, haven't we, Emnor?"

"Well, not me personally, old friend, I had a little help."

Drake gave an indignant cough and looked around the room in a veiled attempt to disguise it.

Emnor smiled as he glanced at him. "Well, to be completely honest, Yello, a lot of help," he added.

"And from the look on his face I'd say the help was from this young fellow here," said Yello.

Drake began polishing his nails against his chest and inspecting them whilst trying not to look too smug.

"One source…" replied Emnor, "… but every one of these fine young men helped in the staff's creation. Drake here plays the most dangerous role I believe, he's the chief tester, and he has the scars to prove it."

"Please, Master Emnor…" implored Xarran, "… don't say any more, we'll never get his head through the door as it is."

"Do you not think he should be proud of such death-defying feats?" asked Yello.

Xarran opened his mouth to offer an answer but could think of no suitable reply. He had never really contemplated just how dangerous the testing of a wand, let alone a staff, could actually be. Turning away, he looked at Drake. "Sorry, Drake, I'd never thought of it like that," he said.

"I too must apologise, Emnor," said Yello, "I think I've just turned one of your boys into a man."

Drake could sense the tension in the air and decided to relieve it in his own inimitable way. "Alright," he said, "enough of this crap, are you going to lie on that floor all day, Yello?"

"I'd rather not, my backside's frozen. Has anybody seen my bag?" he laughed.

The group searched the room and found Yello's staff and, digging through the debris, eventually discovered his carpet bag.

"Is this it?" asked Harley.

"That's the one. Do me a favour, would you? Inside, there's a green vial. Pass it here, there's a good chap."

Harley rummaged through the bag, a look of disgust on his face; chicken's feet, raven's wings, dead frogs, *what on earth are all these for*, he wondered. He took out the vial and passed it to Yello.

"Excellent, dear boy, thank you," he said. Removing the stopper, there was a faint hissing as a green vapour puffed into the air. Yello sniffed it and pulled a face. "That smells disgusting," he announced and, holding his nose, drank half of the contents. He coughed and spluttered, his skin briefly glowing a similar green to that of the vial. "Good grief, it tastes even worse," he gasped through a twisted smile.

"What is that?" asked Alex, pulling a face similar to Yello.

"Abigail's Mercy," replied Yello.

"What does it do?" asked Xarran.

"Well, it dulls the pain initially, then it speeds up the healing process. Wonderful thing Abigail's Mercy, despite the smell."

"So why haven't we heard of it before?" asked Alex.

"Rare ingredients, dear boy, *very* rare."

Yello gestured for his staff to be passed to him and began to gently wave it back and forth over his broken leg. A faint glow appeared as Yello braced himself, sucking air through his teeth.

"What are you doing now, Master Yello?" asked Harley.

"I can't walk on a broken leg, so I'll have to fix it, can't do it as well as a Vikkery admittedly, but I can get it most of the way."

"You know a Vikkery?" asked Harley slowly.

"No, I know *the* Vikkery, lovely folk, so pleasant," replied Yello through gritted teeth, but only because of the pain. Within a few minutes, he was on his feet. A combination of magic and Abigail's Mercy had helped with his injury, but he was still limping badly. Using his staff as a makeshift crutch, he insisted that he was fine and would accept no aid in walking. Slinging his bag over his shoulder, he accompanied the others to the courtyard.

Yello gasped as he witnessed the devastation and gently took Emnor by the arm. "How many, how many survived?" he asked with pleading eyes.

"You were the only one, my friend," Emnor replied quietly.

"Who did this? What mind could be warped enough to do such a thing?"

"Wait there, Yello. Let me speak to the boys and then I'll tell you everything you need to know about Karrak Dunbar."

Leaving the solemn duty of the few remaining cremations in the capable hands of the boys, Emnor guided Yello into one of the relatively undamaged chambers within Reiggan. "You said that you had heard rumours, Yello, exactly what did you hear?"

"Nothing too detailed, just that some prince discovered his magical abilities and started throwing his weight around."

"It's a bit more than that I'm afraid, as you can see," said Emnor pointing at the ruins around them.

"So, who is this…?" Yello began asking.

"Karrak Dunbar, son of Tamor, King of Borell. He now calls himself Lord Karrak, as do his followers."

"His followers? How many *followers*?" Yello asked slowly.

"I'm not quite sure, maybe dozens, maybe hundreds. All I know is that he won't find it difficult to enlist more, now that he has what he came here for," Emnor sighed.

"And what did he come here for?" Yello sat forward, not entirely sure that he wanted to hear the answer.

Emnor sighed heavily, "Do you remember the prophecies of the Peneriphus Scroll?"

"Oh, not that again, Emnor!" exclaimed Yello. "You've been banging on about that blasted scroll for the last four centuries. Peneriphus was just an old lunatic who thought he could predict the end of the world. We've had this conversation time and time again and you know my thoughts on it better than anyone; it's *hogwash*. I'm just amazed that you're sober, you usually start ranting about it when you're in the wine, mind you, two glasses and *you're* hammered. That's why I usually disappear after your first glass."

Emnor folded his arms and crossed his feet, "Have you finished?" he asked calmly.

"That depends, Emnor, have you?"

"I know exactly how you feel on the subject, Yello. Just give me five minutes to explain what I have to say and I promise that if you're not convinced, I will never mention it again."

"Five minutes?" asked Yello, sceptically.

"I promise," vowed Emnor.

Yello shook his head, disbelieving that he was about to allow himself to be subjected to a debate about something he had decried so many times before. He nodded and sat down. "You have five minutes," he said.

"Do you remember the tales of Tamor's queen?" asked Emnor.

"Of course I do, you've told me enough times. She was a witch, went mad and sacrificed some young girls in the dungeon and then tried to kill Tamor himself."

"But Karrak, as an infant, was there when they were tortured and murdered. His body absorbed their souls at the moment of death. In a way, he consumed them."

"So what does this have to do with a thousand-year-old scroll?" asked Yello.

"The scroll predicted it exactly as it happened. The number of sacrifices, the attempt on the king's life, the fact that she would not succeed and the way in which she would be destroyed with a golden crossbow bolt through her temple. They were all written in the scroll."

"How could you possibly know what was written in the scroll, Emnor? Come on, *how*?"

"I had always suspected what was written, Yello, but now I know it to be true. I am the Head of the Administration now and nothing is off limits to me. I have read the scroll myself."

Yello stood up slowly. "You've actually read it? You have held and read the Peneriphus Scroll?"

"I have, and it also predicts the ascension of a member of a royal house as one of the most powerful and cruel sorcerers that shall ever live, but it also suggests that he can be stopped."

"What do you mean, *suggests?*"

"If one reads the scroll, that which has already happened and that which is in the near future are printed boldly and easily visible. Strangely, as one reads further and further, the print fades until eventually, it disappears completely. The size and weight of the scroll never alter, as you unroll it, it never diminishes. It's as if its chronology is endless."

Yello was unaware of his own intrigue. Few were his intellectual equal, but it seemed to Emnor that despite his cynicism, at last, he was beginning to believe. "Do you think it possible that the prediction of his defeat would become visible the closer we were to its reality?" he asked.

"I'm convinced that it will, but there is a dark side to the scroll," replied Emnor.

"And that is…?" asked Yello, slowly.

"That we must not allow ourselves to intervene in any of the predictions. It will be more difficult for me than it will for you, Yello."

"What would be difficult about destroying an evil sorcerer?"

"Many of the Borellians and their companions are my friends. The young men outside are now my charges, one, my apprentice. How would it be if the scroll were to predict the death of any one of them? Would we allow that to happen if it resulted in Karrak's defeat?" Emnor probed.

"It's a tough question I admit, but it's all hypothetical really if Karrak has the scroll," replied Yello.

"That's the thing, Yello, *Karrak doesn't have the scroll,*" whispered Emnor.

"*What*? But you said he got what he came for."

"And he did," replied Emnor, "but he never came here for the scroll; he came for the Elixian Soul."

"He took the Soul?" exclaimed Yello.

"Yes, but he thinks that the Soul is just a magnification stone to enhance his powers. Only if he obtains the scroll can he fulfil the prophecy of world domination."

"So where is the scroll, Emnor? Is it here in Reiggan?"

"All I am prepared to tell you, old friend, is that it's safe. The secret of its location is known only to me."

"And you're positive that Karrak doesn't know its content?"

"I'm unsure as to whether he even knows of its existence, and if not, we must keep it that way," insisted Emnor.

"I doubted you for so long, Emnor. Can you forgive me?" asked Yello, smiling at his lifelong friend.

"In the words of a little friend of mine…" said Emnor laughing, "… *get stuffed.*"

***

Harley entered the room with his head bowed. "Forgive my intrusion, Master Emnor, but I believe our task is complete." As he had approached, he had pondered how to say this to Emnor, but there was no subtle way of explaining that you had finished burning the dead bodies of so many friends.

"Very well, Harley. I think we should stay a while and see if we can make a few of the rooms habitable. We'll fetch Jared and the others in order to plan our next move."

"I'll help as much as I can, Emnor," said Yello, "but you know me, better at blowing things up than rebuilding them."

"In that case, do me a favour, would you*?"* urged Emnor. *"Stay away from Drake."*

CHAPTER 2

"It was horrific, Jared, they killed them all. Some were burned alive, others eviscerated or crushed by falling debris, they never had a chance by the looks of things."

"There were scores of them though, Hannock. Were there any of the enemy amongst the fallen?"

"Hard to tell with the state they were all in. I think that some were unrecognisable to *any* of the wizards."

"It begs the question though, Hannock. If that many wizards couldn't stop Karrak, *what chance do we have?*"

Hannock picked up the golden crossbow. "Get me within a hundred yards of him and I'll show you," he replied.

"Perhaps it would be better if I were to take the shot," suggested Faylore.

Queen Faylore was a seven-foot-tall Thedarian with pointed ears, sparkling white skin and long blond hair. Whenever she spoke, it was always with fairness or good intention. However, there was always an air of pomposity in her tone when asking questions or offering opinions.

Thedarians believed that they were inherently correct about everything.

Hannock looked up at her, "Oh no, Your Majesty, that honour will be mine. I want to see the look in his eyes when the bolt goes through his skull. I just hope he realises it was I who pulled the trigger."

"I know how much you want your revenge, Charles, but I never miss my mark. Can you say the same?"

"Karrak will die by my hand. Nobody, and I mean *nobody*, is going to take that away from me," he replied.

Lawton and Poom, the two Gerrowliens, were watching from the trees where they were perched.

The Gerrowliens, a feline race, were covered with gold and black striped fur. They walked upright when travelling slowly, but when the need for haste came, they would drop to all fours becoming just a blur to most eyes. "You know something, Lawton, his thirst for vengeance could prove to be his downfall."

"Indeed it could, Poom, but would you be any different in his situation?" asked Lawton.

"I would never be in his situation. I'd have already killed the git," replied Poom.

"Nevertheless, we must make it our duty to protect the captain, from himself."

"Why do you care? He's just a soldier. He's cocky and sarcastic and his sense of humour could drive you mad. Personally, I think he's a bit of a prat."

"Oh, really? I quite like him, he reminds me of somebody I know," said Lawton.

"Does he? Who's that then?" asked Poom.

Lawton sighed and stroked his chin, a slight grin on his face.

***

"Didn't you say you don't like shiny things, Grubb?" asked Lodren.

Lodren was a Nibby. Part of a nomadic race, he had wandered the lands quite happily until fate brought about his chance meeting with Jared, Hannock and Faylore. He stood five-foot-tall and had a huge head with saucer-like, bright green eyes. His short, stout body was not unusual, but the same could not be said about his arms. They were colossal, with massive biceps and triceps as hard as steel. Surprisingly, he was the gentlest of all the companions and their allies. His only habit, not a bad one, was his love of cooking. To refer to him as a gourmet chef would be an understatement and he seized every opportunity to grab his pots and pans so as to begin the preparation of a delicious meal. He needed no special occasion, the mere mention of hunger sent him into a frenzy of culinary creation.

"What you on about?" asked Grubb.

Grubb was the strangest individual of the bunch. He was a Vikkery. A two-foot-tall, red-headed (and bearded) shapeshifter who Jared, Hannock, Faylore and Lodren had come across on their journey through the caverns of the Muurkain Mountains. One would not have expected one so small in stature to have as bad an attitude as his, but it was there, and he didn't care who saw it. He was, possibly, the most surly and irascible creature you could meet until you got to know him. For deep down, he had the kindest of hearts.

"Back in Borell, when the king offered you a reward for helping Jared, you said you don't like shiny things and that's why you chose Buster."

"I said I don't like gold, too glinty. But what's that got to do with my Buster?"

"Well, for someone who thinks that gold it too *glinty*, you do a lot of polishing."

"Lodren, what are ye talking about?" asked Grubb.

"That," said Lodren, pointing at the dagger that Hannock had given Grubb as a gift.

Grubb blushed, "It's a poor deal when a Vikkery can't go about his business without bein' spied on. Go on, *bugger off*, keep your nose out."

"I just thought it very sweet of you to take care of the generous gift you were given, I didn't mean to pry Grubb, I'm terribly sorry."

"Well, you can stick your sorry," snapped Grubb and stormed off toward Buster, who was always his excuse for escaping awkward moments.

Lodren smiled to himself. *He really is a lovely Vikkery,* he thought.

It was getting late in the day and the companions were becoming a little concerned for Emnor and the boys.

"They should be back by now," said Hannock as he paced back and forth.

"The disposal of so many bodies will be very time-consuming, my friend, even if one uses magical flame," said Jared.

"All the same, they should have…"

But Hannock never finished his sentence. A dart, similar to the one which Faylore had used to sedate him when he was affected by her simbor (a Thedarian form of puberty), struck the cart beside him. A puff of blue vapour came from it as it hissed and began to rot the wood.

"Get inside, *now!*" roared Poom as he leapt from his branch and swiftly grabbed Lodren under one arm. Lawton too sprang into action as he snatched up Grubb, and in the blink of an eye, both Gerrowliens crashed through the door of the tavern. "Stay here, keep down," panted Poom as both he and Lawton dashed back outside.

Faylore entered moments later, alone, but was followed almost immediately by the other four.

"What was that all about, you great furball!" exclaimed Hannock, straightening his tunic.

"Hissthaar," replied Lawton.

"So what? Let's just go out there and kill them."

"You won't be killing anyone if one of those darts hits you, you'll be dead," said Poom.

"From a little dart, I don't think so," protested Hannock.

"No, you wouldn't, Captain, not from the dart, but you *would* die from the poison it's been dipped in," said Lawton.

"Have a peek outside at the cart, but be careful," suggested Poom.

Hannock peered through the window. The cart had begun to smoulder where the dart had hit it, literally melting the immediate area and causing it to drip, mud-like globules onto the ground.

"Imagine what it would have done to *you*, Captain," said Poom.

Hannock pulled at his tunic again and cleared his throat. "You have my thanks, I didn't realise…" he began.

"Ooohh, I bet it really hurt to say that," laughed Poom.

Hannock smiled at Poom. "You have no idea, Poom…" he replied, "… but I mean it, thank you."

"Oh, give it a rest, it'll be cuddles next," snorted Grubb.

Faylore stepped to the side and raised her bow. Stringing an arrow, she paused for a moment, then let it fly. A screech was heard in the distance as the arrow had obviously found its mark. She turned to face Hannock. "As I said, I *never* miss," she said quietly.

"Now if you can do that a few dozen more times, Faylore, our dilemma should be resolved," said Lawton.

"Why weren't we able to smell them?" Poom asked Lawton.

"Pemimberry, this place is full of it," Lawton replied.

"Pemim… what?" asked Jared.

"Pemimberry. It's a pungent fruit, they rub it on themselves to disguise their scent, and as you've seen, it works perfectly," said Lawton.

"And why didn't we hear them approaching?" asked Poom.

"Well, there are only two possible reasons. One, they were already here when we arrived…" began Lawton.

"And two?" asked Poom.

"…Or two, forgive my speaking whilst you're interrupting… you're getting old, going deaf."

"What do you mean, getting old? I'm the same age as you!" exclaimed Poom.

"Oh, are you? So why do you keep telling everyone you're two hundred and sixty?" hissed Lawton.

Poom suddenly looked a little sheepish. "There's no time for this…" he said, "… we need to decide how we're going to get out of here without being dissolved."

"Jared, how good are you with fire magic?" asked Lawton.

Jared held out his hand and he began to juggle three fireballs that had appeared. "I don't think anyone would want to test me," he replied.

"Now we know Faylore is an excellent shot, Captain Hannock, do you have any ordinary bolts for that crossbow? Using gold ones would seem such a waste."

"Well, I do, but they're on the cart," replied Hannock.

"Anyone want to just nip out and fetch them, just remember to dodge the poison bolts on your way ba…" There was a brief gust of wind and before Grubb could finish his sentence, Poom was standing in front of Hannock, arm outstretched, his bloody, clawed hand clutching the bolts.

"Sorry about that …" he said, retracting them, "… managed to get two of the buggers on the way back."

Lawton placed his hands on his hips, "How can we work out a battle-plan if you keep dashing out like that? Pay attention, Poom, if you're going to do something, tell me first."

"But you said he needed the bolts," shrugged Poom.

"I get it, now…" said Hannock realising Lawton's plan, "… set the bolts and arrows alight before we release them."

"And in the confusion, Poom and I can make our way around and flank them. We'll kill the ones at the rear and you shoot the ones at the front."

"There is one slight flaw to your plan though, isn't there, Mr Gerrowlien?" Everyone looked at Lodren.

"Which is?" asked Lawton.

"All those poison darts flying around. You or Mr Poom might just get stung by one of them. One of them… *hissy*… things might get a lucky shot."

"It's a chance we are willing to take," said Lawton staunchly.

"Is it? What's this *we* crap? I'm not getting shot with one of those flesh-melters," snorted Poom.

"What's wrong, Poom? Scared?" Lawton knew exactly what to say to Poom in order to achieve the correct response.

"*Me? Scared?* Tell you what, don't bother with the fire, let's just go out there by ourselves. *Come on, right now!*" he growled.

"I appreciate your enthusiasm, Poom, but let's just stick to the plan, eh?" suggested Lawton.

They approached the doorway and nodded in agreement, but none uttered a single word. Jared conjured the fireball in his hand. Faylore and Hannock leaned forward, ready to light their projectiles, but before they could, heard an almighty commotion amongst the trees outside. They heard screeches, screams and yelps, heard twigs and branches snapping and cracking but could see no reason why. Slowly, one by one, they crept through the doorway and, in the distance, saw bushes shuddering as unseen bodies brushed past or hurtled between them. The furore lasted a few minutes but not once did they see a hissthaar or any other being. Then suddenly, a deathly silence fell. Confused looks passed between them as none was sure of exactly what had just happened.

"Have they gone?" asked Lodren, peering around from behind Faylore's leg.

"Poom, get your best sprinting paws on and go and have a look, would you?" asked Lawton.

"Won't be long," Poom replied, and as quick as a flash, he was gone again. He leapt into the nearest tree and traversed silently from branch to branch as he travelled deeper into the dense forest. Nothing seemed untoward at first, more trees, bushes and shrubs, just as a forest should look. He paused momentarily, staring at a particular tree, it didn't look right, and he should know having lived amongst them his entire life. This one seemed twisted, warped in some way. The trunk seemed to be split in two as if it had legs and it only had two branches that bent at a peculiar angle. But the strangest thing of all could be seen higher on the trunk. A burr was growing, but it was almost pointed. Above it were two indentations and below, a small hollow. Poom shuddered, it looked like a grotesque face. He pondered for a moment, shaking his head as if to dismiss the thought that had just entered it, but then he saw another tree very similar to the first, and then another. Pouncing from tree to tree, he saw more and more of the strange growths. He turned and hurtled back toward the inn. "I think we may have a bit of a problem," he announced as he hurled himself through the doors of The Hangman's Noose.

"Jendilomin?" asked Lawton.

"The very same," replied Poom.

"And what are Jendilomin?" asked Jared.

"Not a what. A *she*," replied Poom quietly, "and she's far more dangerous than the hissthaar."

"This just keeps getting better and better!" exclaimed Hannock. "First Karrak and his mob, then the Dergon, then the hissthaar and now somebody else wants to kill us, or eat us, or both."

"Jendilomin doesn't want to kill you, Charles, and she doesn't want to eat you either, she wants you to be her friend." The statement by Faylore took everyone by surprise, most of all the Gerrowliens.

"So you've heard of her then?" asked Poom.

"Of course, I've heard of her…" replied Faylore, matter of factly, "… she's my sister."

***

Yello's rapid recovery appeared quite miraculous and although far from being in perfect health, he insisted on assisting as much as his disabilities would allow. He had, once again, tried to improve the healing of his broken leg, with very little effect. Craftily, he took another sip of

Abigail's Mercy, but not craftily enough for it to go unnoticed by his old friend, Emnor.

"Take care with that, Yello. I doubt that we have the correct ingredients for you to brew more, should you run out."

"Don't you worry about me, Emmy," replied Yello. "I've been through worse without the help of this," he continued, holding up the green vial.

Emnor, his young apprentice, Harley, and the others had begun to survey the extent of the damage to Reiggan. Yello joined them and, surprisingly, was more knowledgeable regarding construction than he had given himself credit for. His input was priceless when instructing the young wizards on how to properly erect walls and repair masonry with the use of magic. Throughout, however, he insisted that he had far more love for demolition than construction. Harley and Drake were working with Emnor as Yello was guiding Alex and Xarran's efforts.

"I'm sure it would be easier if you were to just show us, Master Yello," suggested Alex.

"Me? Build something?" laughed Yello as he limped around. "I'd have what's left of Reiggan flattened if I tried, Alexander. I am far better suited to tuition when it comes to reconstructive magic. Now if you want something blown up or demolished, trust me, I'm your man."

Xarran laughed, "Well, we won't be calling you very often then, we've got Drake for that."

"Yes, Emnor mentioned something about that earlier. I take it he's not a very talented wizard then, your young friend?"

"On the contrary, sir, he's a bloody genius!" replied Xarran.

"So why did Emnor suggest that I stay clear of him?" enquired Yello.

"Because Master Emnor realises how talented he is. He also realises that Drake can be a little… *overzealous*. He thinks his skills need tempering in order for him to achieve his full potential," said Alex, "without blowing himself up in the process, of course!"

"I know that feeling well," chuckled Yello. "I was just like him when I was a lad, have a go at anything and damn the risks, but that, of course, was a very long time ago," he added, smiling at the boys.

***

The restoration of Reiggan Fortress was going well. Many thoughts ran through Emnor's mind as they toiled. The young wizards were keen to help, following every instruction to the letter, but Emnor felt that with what may lie ahead, this may not be enough. He needed them to think and start making decisions for themselves. The time may come when he would not be in a position to give them advice or instructions. He needed someone who had a similar amount of experience and knowledge as he. "Yello, might I have a word?"

The two senior wizards ambled into one of the repaired chambers within Reiggan. Waving his staff, Emnor righted a desk that had been tipped over and then, with another wave, he placed two large armchairs either side of it, gesturing for Yello to take a seat.

"Don't mind if I do," said Yello, as he limped toward it, rubbing his leg as he lowered himself onto the sumptuous padding. "Now what can I do for you, old friend?" he asked.

"Nothing, Yello. Nothing at all. You've done quite enough already. You must be exhausted."

"Don't give me that crap, Emnor! Something's going on beneath that mangled mane of yours. Spit it out. What's your problem?"

Emnor smiled as he noticed the twinkle in his friend's eye, a twinkle he recognised from their younger days. Like Emnor, he too was over a thousand years old but still had his youthful sense of adventure. "There's no fooling you, is there?" laughed Emnor.

"Get on with it, you old crock, we don't have all day," mumbled Yello.

"Very well. I think it only fair to explain exactly what our situation is, Yello. Karrak may appear to be just a spoilt brat, and he was. He was an obnoxious child, an annoying teenager and an absolute tyrant as an adult. Realising his magical ability, he tried to kill his brother Jared. The spell he used was pathetic but it was his first attempt. Luckily Hannock, Jared's best friend, cracked a pikestaff on the back of Karrak's skull before he could do any real harm. Ruined Jared's shirt though, *apparently*," said Emnor, frowning.

"So why was he allowed to roam free?" asked Yello. "You said he even has followers now."

"He wasn't *allowed* to roam free. He was locked up here in Reiggan," replied Emnor.

"For a failed spell! A bit harsh, isn't it, Emnor?"

"There *were* other events. The body of a guard was discovered and Jared thought that Karrak had murdered him. But there were no witnesses, no evidence and no proof of Karrak's guilt."

"So, was the guard killed with magic?" asked Yello.

"No, his neck was broken. Twisted until his head was facing backwards," replied Emnor.

"So why would they think that Karrak was the murderer?"

"The guard had prevented him from killing an innocent, a barkeep by the name of George. Lovely chap. Lost one of his eyes due to the unprovoked beating that Karrak gave him."

"It would take immense strength, Emnor, to twist someone's head like that."

"You haven't seen the size of Karrak. Six-and-a-half-foot-tall and almost as wide. He's a monster, *in more ways than one*."

"And you say he was locked up here?" asked Yello.

"After the attack on Jared, King Tamor decided it best. Thought he could be rehabilitated and allowed to re-enter polite society. I wouldn't have anything to do with Karrak or his incarceration, I believed the prophecies of the Peneriphus Scroll, you see?"

"So how did he get out? Did he escape or did he have help?" asked Yello.

"Barden Oldman. He even tried to acquire the Elixian Soul for Karrak," replied Emnor.

"What!" exclaimed Yello. "Barden? But he's been here forever. What would cause him to do such a thing?"

"I think he believed that resisting Karrak would be futile. So, resigned to that futility, he thought he'd be joining the winning side, as it were."

"So what happened to Barden?" asked Yello. "Did he go with Karrak?"

"Not exactly. Barden used a relocation spell to get Karrak out, but not before they killed Dane Fellox and one of the young novices."

"So what now? We know he has the Elixian Soul but not the knowledge to access its full potential. We suspect that he is in league with Barden, so that doesn't bode well…"

"He's not in league with Barden," interrupted Emnor.

"How do you know?"

"Because, Yello, Barden knew of the scroll's existence. If he were still alive, so would Karrak."

"Do you think he was keeping it as a kind of insurance?"

"Possibly, but I don't think he was ever given the chance to play his trump card."

"And what about those boys out there, are we going to take them somewhere out of harm's way?" said Yello, more as a suggestion than a question.

"You read my mind. I'm sure they would have survived against Karrak before all this, but now that he has the Soul, I'm not convinced," replied Emnor.

The two wizards entered the courtyard and beckoned the boys to join them. Drake suspected what was about to be proposed but held his tongue.

"Boys," began Emnor, "I have no doubt where your loyalties lie, and to date your courage and dedication to the rectification of the plight of House Borell, Reiggan and myself have been nothing but selfless, but I fear that you must now abandon…"

Drake had a short fuse, and it had just burnt out. He went red in the face and began to rant. "Stuff that, we've worked our arses off for you. Who gave you the most powerful staff in the world? Who followed you and never asked a single question? Who trusts you more than anyone else? *We do!* Now old hop along turns up and you don't need us any more. Is that what you think? You aren't the only wizards left in this world. *Our* friends died as well as yours. Now you think you can palm us off like a bunch of kids? There are six wizards here, *six*, and you need every one of us. Whether we're with you or alone, we're still going after that bloody sorcerer, and when we do, we're going to blow the crap out of him."

Emnor was stunned and said nothing. Neither did Yello.

Harley sighed. Raising his hand, he pointed at Drake. "Erm, what he said," he smirked.

CHAPTER 3

Karrak stared at the Elixian Soul. Mounted on a golden skeletal hand-shaped stand, it stood on the altar before him. He and his followers had now invaded the monastery that, only hours before, had been inhabited by more than fifty monks. Karrak slaughtered most of them immediately before twisting the remainder into forms similar to that of Barden, who Karrak kept close at hand so he could continue his ceaseless torture of him. The Elixian Soul had proven its worth. No more did Karrak have to waste time enslaving his victims singularly, he could enslave a dozen or so easily, as a collective. He had no real need of the beasts that now yelped and whined outside the walls, but it had the desired effect he wished to convey to his followers: Obey him without question, or test him and suffer the consequences.

The only member of Karrak's loyal clan that dared to speak freely was Darooq. He was, nonetheless, under no illusion that he was indispensable and remained cautious when passing comments or answering questions put to him by his lord. Entering the room, he bowed his head. "I must congratulate you on your acquisition, my lord."

Karrak's gaze never left the Elixian Soul as he answered. "Why should I be congratulated for obtaining something that is mine by right? Something that it was my destiny to possess, according to Barden," he asked. His voice was different now, deeper, monotone and sinister. The words left his lips, but simultaneously seemed to have a different source, a strange echoing as if they had come from a cavernous space before passing through *him*.

"I beg your forgiveness, my lord..." continued Darooq, "... I merely meant that you must be pleased to have at last received your prize."

"I like you, Darooq, I enjoy your company, and your counsel, but do not take me for a fool. What is it that you actually want to know?"

"What is our next move, my lord?" asked Darooq.

"Our next move. *Our* next move. Don't you mean *my* next move, Darooq?"

"As we are loyal to you, my lord, *your* next move shall also be *ours*. We have sworn to serve, and that fealty remains intact."

"Do you believe that I still need you? A rabble of second-rate conjurors and tricksters, now that I have *this*," Karrak raised the Soul, complete with its stand, from the altar.

Darooq stepped back nervously as Karrak turned to face him. "My lord, you cannot guard every hall and courtyard by yourself. Surely, we could at least offer that protection? Every one of your followers..."

"Silence..." barked Karrak, hurrying toward Darooq and throwing his arm around his shoulders. "... Calm yourself, my friend," he continued. "As I said, *you are safe,* Darooq. *You* shall remain as you are. The others, however, may need a little… *adjustment*."

"Adjustment, my lord? In what way?" asked Darooq, not entirely sure that he wanted to hear the answer to his question.

"I mean to destroy royal bloodlines, overthrow kingdoms and take lands and fortunes that have been passed down for generations. In short, I mean to rule this world. Avarice and petty jealousy will eventually corrupt the minds of many of those who follow me, Darooq. The only way to prevent that from happening is to ensure their absolute servitude, and sooner rather than later. If one fears that the beast may bite in the future, one must extract the teeth in the present."

"And am I to be amongst those who shall have their teeth removed, my lord?"

Karrak caressed the Elixian Soul. "No, not you, Darooq," he whispered. "Summon the others. I shall deal with them."

***

"Tell me, Faylore, why is Jendilomin so dangerous?" asked Jared.

"Emotions. Well, *one* emotion anyway," she replied.

"And that emotion is…?" asked Hannock.

"Love," replied Faylore.

"*Love?* How can love be dangerous?" asked Hannock.

"Well, for someone as primitive as you, Charles, it can't. For a Thedarian, it can be devastatingly so."

The look on Hannock's face was priceless. The combination of being called primitive along with Faylore's notion that love could be devastatingly dangerous had rendered him speechless.

"No matter how you flower it up, Faylore, she turns people into trees. Not even the hissthaar are safe," said Poom.

"She merely befriends them," sighed Faylore.

"By turning them into trees!" exclaimed Poom.

Jared and the others were now completely confused. "Faylore, please enlighten us. What does turning people into trees have to do with love?" he asked, innocently.

"As you know, Jared," she began, "we Thedarians are a superior race…"

"Oh yes, and don't forget humble, and modest," interrupted Hannock.

"… A simple fact, Charles," she continued. "As I was saying, my sister was always one of the most intelligent of our kind. Even as a child she would only converse with the more learned and enlightened of our people. Jendilomin matured very quickly, no Thedarian female is known to have reached the simbor at such a young age..."

Jared snorted as he attempted to subdue a laugh, as he remembered the events that had taken place in the cave on their first journey to Reiggan. Hannock glanced at him, having no recollection of the embarrassing incident. Jared couldn't resist the temptation, "Sorry Faylore, swallowed a fly. You alright there, Charles?"

Faylore resumed her explanation, "... Jendilomin became terribly bored with us and had learned the ways of the forest."

"You mean tracking and hunting, that sort of thing?" asked Lawton.

"No, I don't..." she sighed, "... I mean that she had learned to converse with the flora and fauna, but the trees were always her favourite. She found them fascinating."

"You mean, *she can talk to the trees*?" gasped Lodren.

"Yes, my dear Nibby, she can talk to the trees."

"But how is that dangerous?" asked Hannock.

"Well, it wasn't at first, but then she began to wander off for days at a time. That's when she first met the forest nymphs."

"But they're harmless, seen 'em loads o' times, they don't bother anybody. If ye try to get near 'em, they just float away," said Grubb.

"They used to, before they met Jendilomin," said Faylore.

"And she can talk to them too, I presume?" asked Hannock.

"Not at first. Their reaction to her was as it would be if anyone approached them. They tend the forest, they aren't interested in any other life form," replied Faylore.

"So what changed?" asked Poom.

"She started to learn the ways of magic," replied Faylore.

"And there it is. Every bloody time!" exclaimed Hannock. "Magic again. Yet another foe, ready to start blasting away at us!"

"She isn't like that, Charles. She's a white witch, not a sorceress," snapped Faylore in defence of her sibling.

"It doesn't matter. It seems that every time magic is involved, we become the target. We should hang anyone who even thinks about using it!"

"Yeah... thanks for that," said Jared.

"You know what I mean, Jared. I didn't mean you," said Hannock, apologetically.

Lodren, always being the most level-headed, attempted to calm the heated discussion. "Look, if all she wants is to be friends, we'll meet her, introduce ourselves, shake hands politely and be on our way."

"Somehow I get the feeling that it's not going to be that easy, is it Faylore?" asked Jared.

"Indeed..." replied Faylore, "... Jendilomin only regards the trees as her friends, so in order to befriend her, you have to become one."

"How did this all start, Faylore? It's insane," said Hannock.

"To you, Charles, it may seem that way. The sad thing is that Jendilomin's intention is only to create a more peaceful world."

"By turning every living being into a tree?" asked Jared.

"Do trees go to war, Jared? Do you see a tree hunting its brother in order to destroy it? Do you see a tree murdering one of its own to steal its belongings or take a patch of

42

ground that it wishes to possess? Jendilomin has convinced the forest nymphs that the only way for their charges to be safe is to make all living things part of their world, a peaceful world."

"This is wonderful. Her sister's as mad as your brother, Jared. We should introduce them, imagine what their children would be like. Half tree, half insane sorcerer, the possibilities are endless."

"You're not helping, Hannock," sighed Jared.

There was a brief moment of silence before Faylore, resigning herself to their predicament, spoke again. "She will not allow us to leave, I must visit with her... *alone*."

"*Not bloody likely!*" snapped Grubb.

Faylore smiled at him. "Indeed, Master Grubb. What alternative would you suggest?" she asked.

"Easy," Grubb replied, "I'll become a hawk and fly over the forest until I spot her. Then, when I've found her, I'll swoop down and rip her bloody head off."

"How very gallant of you, you wish to murder my sister on my behalf. You must be very proud of yourself."

Grubb lowered his head. "Just trying to look after ye is all. Y*ou're alright , you are*," he muttered.

Faylore leaned down and kissed the top of his tiny head. "You're not so bad yourself, Grubb..."

"Now if you're going, just bugger off," chuntered Grubb, a little embarrassed.

"... *Most* of the time," added Faylore.

The companions watched as Faylore disappeared behind the treeline.

"Strange home you have here, Poom, Shaleford Forest I mean," said Hannock.

"This isn't Shaleford," replied Poom, obviously offended. "Shaleford is a day's walk back the way we came. We crossed its border before we reached here, and of course, I mean a day's walk at your pace. This is Gamlawn. Honestly, *Borellians!* As if *we'd* live somewhere like this!

Hannock looked around him. Trees, bushes, *it's the same,* he thought.

"Right, here we go," said Grubb, and, after transforming into his four-armed alter-ego, he began to climb the side of the inn.

"What's he up to now!?" exclaimed Hannock as Grubb reached the roof.

"Not a clue, but I like it. He obviously has something up his sleeve," said Lawton.

Poom began to laugh as he elbowed Lawton in the ribs. "Or all four of them, eh? All four of them? No? Oh, forget it, I don't know why I bother."

Grubb had now morphed back into his normal state and peered as hard as he could, trying to catch a glimpse of Faylore. "No. No good, I can't see her," he said tetchily.

"She'll be fine, Grubb, come down before you fall down," said Jared.

"In your dreams," replied Grubb and immediately changed shape again, this time into the raptor that they had seen before.

"Grubb, Faylore won't like it if you…" Jared's words were wasted as Grubb took flight.

Soaring high above the trees, Grubb's eyesight was keener than ever in this form. He scanned the forest, but strangely, he could not locate Faylore. *She must have come this way,* he thought. He circled lower and lower until, eventually, he saw a faint shimmering. It was no reflection nor heat haze, it was moving. *There you are,* he thought. Swooping down, Grubb landed in a tree ahead of Faylore and watched intently as she reached the small lea just a few yards ahead.

She paused and became visible, then began to speak quietly, "Jendilomin, I know you're here. Will you not speak to me?"

At the farthest edge of the lea, a strange, pale green vapour could be seen. It crept across the ground towards Faylore but she did not seem alarmed by it. On the contrary, she smiled at its appearance, for as it drifted closer and dissipated, it revealed the graceful approach of her sister, Jendilomin. "It gladdens my heart to see you, Sister," she said, smiling. "It has been far too long since last we met."

"Forgive me, Jendilomin, but the affairs of Thedar are now *my* responsibility and they have taken much of my time."

"Such a burden it must be? It is no surprise to me that you now seek my counsel."

"Why do you believe I seek your counsel, sister of mine?" asked Faylore.

"You have no need to fret. It is obvious to me that your existence is mundane, Faylore. It was simply a matter of time before you understood that I was correct," replied Jendilomin.

"Correct?" asked Faylore, cautiously. "About what, exactly?"

"Why, that we should achieve peace across this world."

"I do admit that it would please me greatly to witness a harmonious existence between all races, Jendilomin. You have a kind heart, Sister, and your intentions are guided by it, but your methods must cease. Transforming living beings into trees is wrong, it is not for you to decide the fate of all."

Jendilomin laughed gently. "Look around you. Is this not the most peaceful of places? Many of these trees were once the most horrid of beasts, cruel and violent. Bear witness to their serenity. They are grateful to me, Faylore, they no longer have to suffer the cruel emotions that were once theirs. Avarice, jealousy, anger, sorrow and fear, all have been eradicated."

"Did you give them the choice, Sister?" asked Faylore, sharply. "Did you ask *them* if this was their desire, or was it yours?"

"Corporeal beings are flawed, Faylore, they cannot be trusted to make enlightened decisions. They must be made for them, for their own good. If I were to leave them to follow their own base instincts, they would render themselves extinct."

"That is not for you to decide, Jendilomin," exclaimed Faylore. "You should not interfere with nature."

Grubb continued to watch the Thedarian sisters during their debate. He was so enamoured with their beauty that he failed to notice what was happening around them, or himself for that matter. The edges of the lea had darkened and the strange green mist was now thick and impenetrable by the naked eye. Within the mist lay the real threat, *the forest*

46

nymphs. They were not evil, what they did could not even be classed as cruel. Jendilomin had convinced them that if the trees were to survive, their number must be increased. The nymphs knew no greater love than that of trees and nurtured them as a parent would their child. To have more, to them, seemed idyllic.

A look of horror appeared on Grubb's face as he suddenly noticed the ethereal form directly behind Faylore. It tilted its head to one side and then the other as it studied her. Still deep in conversation with Jendilomin, she was oblivious to its presence. The nymph floated behind her. Although transparent, its features could still be seen, it looked like a young girl. She had piercing blue eyes and a tiny button nose, but the similarity to a normal child ended there, as she had long green hair and a flowing gown that appeared to be made from living leaves. Grubb opened his mouth to warn Faylore, but no words came out. A hawk cannot speak. The screech caused Faylore to look to the trees, unaware that it was actually an alarm call. The nymph stretched out its arm and gently stroked Faylore's platinum blonde hair. Her reaction was instantaneous.

Placing her hand against her chest and struggling to breathe, she stood upright as if she were suddenly being stretched by unseen restraints. Her skin began to darken and appeared scaly momentarily before thickening to resemble the bark of a tree. She stretched out her arms and held them aloft to witness the horror of her predicament. Her fingers grew thinner and seemed to lose all moisture, stretching, now looking more like twigs. Her fingernails sprouting like tiny leaf-like shoots. Her legs grew heavy as, with great effort and difficulty, she looked down to see that they were now a split tree trunk, her feet splayed roots. Her eyes remained clear throughout as she attempted to plead with

47

Jendilomin to remove the heinous curse, but Jendilomin continued to smile back at her, believing that what she was giving her sister was, in fact, a gift. The final part of Faylore's metamorphosis was her hair, her beautiful platinum hair. It stood upright, the sound of crackling heard as it stiffened and turned dark brown, the ends sprouting leaves.

Grubb swooped into the centre of the lea, transforming into his four-armed creature as he landed. He charged toward Jendilomin, one of his four clawed hands raised, ready to tear her apart. A nymph appeared directly in front of him and in the blink of an eye, stroked Grubb's claws.

***

"Hope you don't mind me saying, Jared," said Lawton, "but, you're looking a bit nervous."

"It's bad enough that Faylore went off to face her sister, but with Grubb gone as well... you've seen what his temper's like," replied Jared.

"Want me to go and have another poke around?" asked Poom.

"No. Thank you anyway, Poom. I think we should give them a bit more time. If they're not back soon, we'll all go."

"What if something's gone wrong, Mr Jared?" asked Lodren. "Waiting in here will just give them more of a chance to surround us."

"What do you mean, *them*?" asked Hannock.

"Well, Faylore's sister can't be on her own, can she?" asked Lodren. "There were loads of them hissy things, she can't have attacked them all by herself."

"We don't know that *she* attacked anyone, Lodren. Like I said, *we'll give them a bit more time*."

Hannock strolled across the room and slung his crossbow on his back. "Do what you like, Your Highness, but I've had enough of sitting around, I'm off to find them. Poom, fancy stretching your legs?"

"Thought you'd never ask," replied Poom. "Come on, Lawton, or are you comfortable where you are, your fatness."

Lawton rolled his eyes. "Oh no, you're not in one of *those* moods again, are you, baldy? You do my head in when you're like this."

"Come on, you know you love me really," replied Poom, nudging his friend.

"Is everything a joke to you two?" asked Hannock.

The Gerrowliens looked at one another nodding. "Yeah… pretty much," said Poom.

"Hannock, I order you not to go, now sit down," said Jared.

"I don't want to appear disrespectful in any way, Your Highness, but it's doubtful that I'm going to survive this little adventure of ours anyway. If what's out there doesn't kill me, the butchering brother of Borell probably will, so I might as well get it over and done with. Now if there's the slightest chance that Faylore is in danger and I can help in her rescue before I get sliced, diced, mangled or murdered, I'm going to take it, alright?"

49

Jared sighed as he stood nose to nose with Hannock. He looked his friend up and down before he spoke. "I'll get my stuff," he replied quietly.

***

Poom and Lawton crept through the trees. Occasionally, they would pause and signal the all-clear to the three remaining companions, allowing them to progress in relative safety. Poom suddenly held up his hand for them to halt and made his way across to Lawton. "That big tree wasn't there before," he whispered.

"Which one?" asked Lawton.

"The one with the four branches, the huge one in the middle," replied Poom.

"Have you noticed that a lot of these trees have only two branches? How very odd," said Lawton, looking puzzled.

"And it's not odd for a tree to have only four branches?" asked Poom.

"That's a good point. So, do you think…?" asked Lawton, pointing at the numerous saplings by which they were surrounded. Poom nodded his head exaggeratedly. "My word…" he added, "… she has been busy." Poom's nodding continued throughout Lawton's deduction.

The lea was quiet. The birds were singing and there appeared to be no danger. The Gerrowliens beckoned the companions to come forward. "Does that ring any bells with you?" Lawton asked Jared.

"It looks a bit like that thing that Grubb turns into," replied Jared.

"A lot like it, to be honest," added Hannock.

As before, the vapour had appeared gradually, unnoticed by the group until Jendilomin emerged from it and spoke, "Do not worry, they are at peace now. We shall keep them safe and take care of them."

Startled, they turned to face her. "We want our friends back. Make them better and give them back!" yelled Lodren, nursing his hammer and scowling at Jendilomin.

"But I *have* made them better, can you not see?" she replied.

"All I see is trees," bawled Lodren. "You've got plenty, you don't need them. *So, give them back!*" he growled.

"Please, my dear friend, there is no need for concern. They are content as they are," she cooed.

"I don't want them as they are, I want them as they *were,*" bellowed Lodren, raising his hammer. But it never struck a blow, the nymph reached him first. In turn, the others suffered the same fate; Jared touched by a nymph from behind; Lawton, by one from above; and Poom, by one in mid-air as he attempted to leap into the trees.

Hannock grabbed his crossbow, but realising he was too late, lowered it again, resigned to his fate. A nymph appeared before him and reached out with its hand when unexpectedly Jendilomin spoke, "Not that one," she instructed.

The nymph turned and gently floated away.

Hannock was shocked. He watched his friends as they reached various stages of transformation, wracked with guilt at his inability to save them. But he had been spared. *Why?* He took a deep breath to compose himself. "What do you want, why spare me? Or is it just a stay of execution?" he asked sternly.

"I like the way you look. I like your jewellery, you wear it well," she replied.

"Jewellery? *What jewellery?*"

"Your golden mask. I like it very much. Why do you wear it? Is it vanity?" she asked. "Perhaps something similar may suit me?"

Hannock tried not to think of his reason for wearing the eye-patch. Tried his best to shut out the memory of the pain that Karrak had caused him with the fire spell that struck him in the face, and most of all, the terrible things he wanted to do to Jendilomin that would cause her to wear one the same. "I'm sure something could be arranged," he replied coldly.

"When I lived in Thedar, there were many pretty baubles, but nothing as impressive as that. Who would give you such a gift? Or did you steal it?" she asked.

Hannock understood that he was temporarily powerless and could bring no harm to Jendilomin, *but something about him had peaked her interest. Maybe this was the only weapon that he needed, her curiosity.* "I am no thief, my Lady. This was a gift, presented to me by the King of Borell."

"Why would a king give away such a treasure?" she asked, more intrigued than before.

Hannock had to think fast, had to invent a story to make him appear more saint than soldier. "His youngest son was sick, my Lady," he replied. "The only healers that could save his life were a great distance away, and I, along with his older brother Jared, undertook a pilgrimage to bring him to them."

"A very honourable mission indeed," said Jendilomin, seemingly impressed. "Tell me, how are you called?"

"Beg pardon, my Lady?"

"What is your name?" she asked.

"Hannock, my Lady," he replied bowing. "Captain Charles Hannock."

"Have you eaten today, Captain Charles Hannock?" she asked. "My friends supply me with the most succulent fruits, given freely of course."

Well, you have to give it to her, thought Hannock. *She's the most polite lunatic you've ever met!*

He followed Jendilomin as she led him from the lea into the forest. The trees were much denser here and Hannock shuddered as he looked at the *faces* of them; faces whose wooden, knot-like eyes appeared to watch them as they passed. *How many had she changed, dozens, hundreds, thousands?* He had no idea of the answer, the only number in his head was six, the six that he intended to save from an eternity of solidified torment.

CHAPTER 4

"How's the leg, Yello?" asked Emnor. "Feeling any better?"

"Much better, thank you. Running a bit low on Abigail's Mercy though. I think I'll go and have a rummage through some of the storerooms. You never know, I may get lucky and find some of the more simple ingredients needed to brew some more," he smiled.

"Very well," replied Emnor. "We're almost finished here anyway. Take Harley with you though, just in case," he suggested.

"In case of what?" asked Yello.

"We may not be alone. What if an enemy is hiding somewhere we have not yet thought to look?" asked Emnor.

"I don't need an apprentice to hold my hand! I'm quite capable of taking care of myself!" exclaimed Yello, feeling a little insulted.

"I know that, Yello, but two pairs of eyes are better than one. Harley can help you look for the things you need. Don't underestimate him, Yello, I didn't. That's why I made him my apprentice."

"Alright then…" sighed Yello, "… if you insist." He hobbled from the room, followed closely by his chaperon.

"So when we reach the storeroom, what exactly are we looking for?" asked Harley.

"The ingredients of Abigail's Mercy," replied Yello.

"Which are…?" asked Harley, inquisitively.

"I'll tell you when we get there," mumbled Yello, rather reluctant to share his secret recipe. They reached one of the storerooms and Yello was delighted to find that it was undisturbed. "Right, Harley, you start searching on that side," he instructed, "I'll start on this side."

"Searching for *what*?" asked Harley.

"Oh yes, that would help, wouldn't it?" laughed Yello. "Erm, let's see. See if you can find some Penellerim leaves and some Simfax petals, and I'll look for some Pollum, it's a very rare fungus. The key ingredient of course is Gibbonite hair."

"Gibbonite hair!" exclaimed Harley. "What's Gibbonite hair?"

"The Gibbonite is a wonderful creature that lives in the south, very friendly, provided that you don't spook them. Unfortunately, that's why they're almost extinct. Fascinating to watch. They sing in order to attract a mate, you know, but as there are so few, they're usually unsuccessful."

"So how do you get the hair then? Sneak up and trim a bit off while they're not looking?" asked Harley with a laugh.

"Of course not. They have so much hair that when they travel through bushes and undergrowth, tufts of it get caught on the smaller branches. You can just follow them around and pick it off."

"Who thinks of these potions, Master Yello?" asked Harley. "They must have had far too much time on their hands."

"Keep searching, Harley," urged Yello, "I'm feeling lucky." They checked cupboards, opened drawers and even checked behind desks as they sought the ingredients. Suddenly, Yello let out an exasperated gasp. "*Bolinium root! What's Bolinium root doing in here? It's been forbidden for decades!*" he exclaimed.

Harley ceased his search and turned to face him. "What's Bolinium root?" he asked innocently.

"Something that shouldn't be here. It should have been destroyed. *Bloody alchemists, they should all be roasted!*"

Harley was a little unnerved by Yello's sudden outburst. "What does it do?" he asked, tentatively.

Yello took a deep breath. "Apparently, if you boil it in water, the resulting potion, if ingested, can make one feel extreme elation."

"What's so bad about that?" asked Harley. "I could do with something like that to cheer me up occasionally."

"It can become terribly addictive; you can't survive a day without it. You become depressed and paranoid. Many attacks and suicides have been the result of an addiction to Bolinium root."

"Nasty stuff then?" asked Harley, grimacing.

"The worst," replied Yello, placing it in his bag.

Their hunt was successful. After a while, Yello's small green vial had been refilled with Abigail's Mercy. As there was no one left alive in Reiggan to make use of them, Yello took the liberty of keeping the remainder of the rare ingredients, placing them carefully into his bag. "Come on, Harley, let's get back to the others," he suggested.

***

The idea was simple. Return to Cheadleford, collect Jared and the others and then bring them back to the safety of Reiggan. *Well, that was the plan.*

The wizards gathered in the courtyard of Reiggan and after a short discussion, disappeared.

In an instant, they were standing on the outskirts of the village. It was calm and quiet, maybe a little too quiet. Wandering along the main street, they noticed that the campfire had gone out.

"*Why would they allow the fire to go out?*" asked Emnor.

"A better question would be," said Yello, "*why isn't there anyone on guard duty?*"

They all began to squint as they studied the trees, hoping to catch a glimpse of Faylore or perhaps one of the Gerrowliens.

"Do you think they are just investigating the forest, Master Emnor?" asked Harley.

"The Gerrowliens may do that, but neither Jared nor Hannock would consider it," replied Emnor. "There would be nothing of use to them amongst the trees. No, we'll

57

probably find them inside the tavern, huddled around the fireplace."

They approached The Hangman's Noose. Seeing the doors off their hinges, they were not surprised to find that it too, was deserted. Drake noticed the unusual rotting on the side of the cart and called for Emnor.

"What could do something like that?" asked Xarran, poking at the decomposed wood with a stick.

"Something very potent…" replied Yello, "… but I'm not exactly sure what it was."

Buster and the horses had been securely tethered and although a little skittish, remained unharmed. "If only you could speak," said Harley, stroking Buster's nose.

"Where could they have gone?" asked Drake. "*Why* would they leave the horses?"

"I hate to say this, Emnor old boy, but I think they were attacked."

"Unfortunately, Yello, I have to agree. But there are no fallen, friends or enemies. Surely, a skilled archer such as Faylore could have brought down at least a few of them before they were overrun."

"You mean *like this one?*" Drake had wandered a short way into the shrubs at the side of the road and was now studying the body that lay there, an arrow centrally between its eyes.

"*Hissthaar…!*" exclaimed Yello, "Most uncharacteristic."

"Could you elaborate?" asked Emnor.

"They're ambush predators. More likely to attack someone who is by themselves. They're quite cowardly in their ways and would never risk open combat," replied Yello.

"So why would they attack our allies?" asked Harley.

"Only one reason I'm afraid. *They're starving.*"

"So why didn't they take any of the provisions from the cart?" asked Drake. "It hasn't been touched."

"That is because the hissthaar prefer fresh meat. The intended meal was… *your friends,*" replied Yello.

"You mean, they're all dead?" exclaimed Alex. "These things have eaten them all?"

"No, they're still alive. If they had been eaten, the diners would still be here, digesting their meal," replied Yello.

"I don't understand. Why would that keep them here?" asked Drake.

"They swallow their prey whole and still *alive*. Difficult to move if you've just swallowed a whole person, I should think," suggested Yello.

"*What…!*" exclaimed the boys in unison.

"Yes, disgusting, isn't it?" replied Yello with a shudder.

"I think we should start searching for them, *now,*" said Emnor. They hastily headed toward the treeline.

None of them could be termed as an experienced tracker, but it was obvious that the most knowledgeable of them was Yello when it came to the ways of the wilds. He had travelled extensively during his long life and, without realising it, had picked up a lot of useful tips from the various races he had befriended. A scuff in the dirt where someone had caught their heel; a broken twig where they had squeezed through a tight space; or a scratch on a tree trunk caused by something they carried when doing the same. Unaware of the danger, they grew closer and closer to the lea.

They entered it much the same as the companions had so very recently and, as had their friends, began to study the strange saplings and trees with which they were now surrounded. Within minutes, the pale green vapour began to form. Yello saw it first and smiled as he pointed at it. "Stay away from that stuff, gentlemen. It's obviously there to conceal something, or *someone*," he advised.

"Someone like whom?" asked Drake nervously, "I don't fancy being someone's dinner."

"This isn't the hissthaar, my dear Drake, *I'm afraid this is something far more dangerous.*" Even as he spoke, the mist parted and the mystery was revealed.

"Ah, my dear Jendilomin. S*o, it is you,*" said Yello.

"Yellodius Tarrock. How good to see you, have you too now realised the futility of your existence and come to join my beautiful forest?" she asked.

"Not exactly, Your Highness. I believe you have given your hospitality to some of our friends. We need their aid and I must regretfully insist that you release them."

"You must *insist?*" she asked calmly. "What gives one such as you the right to insist upon anything?"

"I do not mean to appear impertinent, my Lady. I apologise if I have offended you. There is a great threat that hangs over us all and we need our friends, if we are to succeed in its prevention."

"There have been many threats, Yellodius. Not least, the threat of wizards meddling with elements with which one ought not tamper."

"And what of sorcerers, my Lady?" asked Yello. "Are they not a greater threat?"

"You all appear the same to my eyes, Yellodius. The elements are natural, and nature is the way of my folk."

"*Your folk*? Do you mean the abominations that stand around us?" he asked. "Or the forest nymphs that you have coerced into creating them? The very nymphs that, as we speak, are attempting to surround us, hidden in the mist, at your command."

Emnor and the boys watched the mist as it began to thicken, but as yet could see no lifeforms within it. Subconsciously, they closed their ranks, each facing in a different direction, wands and staff raised, apprehensively.

"I do not command them, I merely suggest a more peaceful way of life. A life of complete harmony."

"They are a very trusting race, Jendilomin. They have no ill thought or will, but how would they react should they realise that they are being manipulated?" asked Yello. "How would they feel if they realised that, in time, they will have to neglect their true friends, the real trees, in order to care for your creations?"

Jendilomin suddenly appeared nervous as she spoke again. "*They*, unlike others, understand what it is that I am trying to accomplish."

"Do they?" asked Yello. "They have protected the trees for many a millennia, Jendilomin, and have the ability to transform any who try to harm their wards. They have never needed you before. Why should they need you now?"

Jendilomin was becoming angry. She had never had her ideals questioned before. "Enough of this!" she bellowed. "You *will* become one of us. *Bring them into the fold, my friends,*" she bellowed.

Emnor and the boys whirled this way and that expecting at any moment to see hordes of forest nymphs charging toward them, but something strange happened, *the mist began to dissipate.* They saw *no* nymphs; there was *no* sudden attack; it seemed the threat was over.

Jendilomin held out her arms toward the edges of the lea as if pleading with her unstrung puppets. Her reign, it seemed, had ended.

***

"Where the bloody hell have you been? I've had to listen to this loony for hours!" The sudden break in the silence was, of course, Hannock. For whatever reason, he had been left unchanged by Jendilomin, who had now fallen to her knees and was oblivious to Hannock's insult.

Emnor stood over her, his hand outstretched. "Come, my dear, we must rectify some of your mistakes," he said.

Jendilomin looked up at him with pleading eyes, still convinced that she had done no wrong.

"Will she be able to turn them back, Master Yello?" whispered Harley.

"*She* never changed them in the first place, my boy, it was the nymphs who did that," Yello replied. "Whether either she or one of *us* can convince them to reverse the transformation, is still to be seen."

After consulting Hannock, they were able to identify which *tree* represented which member of the companions, the only obvious one being Grubb. Both Emnor and Yello stood before each in turn, racking their brains in the hope that some ancient spell or incantation would come to their aid as they tried, unsuccessfully, to rejuvenate their friends to their proper state.

"It's no good, Yello, I have no idea what type of magic made them like this. Maybe we could somehow reason with the nymphs and convince *them* to change them back?" suggested Emnor.

Strolling amongst the trees and bushes, each member of the wizarding party tried in vain to approach one of the nymphs. If they spoke to one, they were completely ignored, and if they drew too near, it would float higher into the trees to escape contact. They were not afraid, simply disinterested. Throughout, Jendilomin remained where she had fallen. Emnor tried a few times to draw any insight that she may have that would help them with their predicament, but she offered no aid as she knelt on the ground, staring deeply into it.

Drake watched with interest as the others continued with their failed attempts at befriending the nymphs. A fleeting thought of capturing rather than enticing one of them may be a better plan, but he cast it from his mind almost immediately. Smiling to himself, he looked around him, he needed a tree, a *real* tree, not a *nymph-made* one. *He had an idea.* Choosing his target, he sat at its roots and leaned against it. Stroking its trunk, he began to speak to it.

"Now you're a *proper* tree, aren't you, you're not one of those nasty *imitations*? I have to admit though, some of the ones your friends have made are handsome, they fit in perfectly. There are a few that are absolutely repulsive though, there's no way that they should be allowed to grow anywhere near you. I mean, look at them, they're tiny, stumpy things with only two limbs. How could they ever hope to become as majestic as you? I bet you wish that they could be taken away, it must be awful for you to even have to look at them?" Drake continued to stroke the tree as he spoke.

As the others heard him, they began to approach. Emnor had realised Drake's simple, brilliant plan and shooed them away. "Leave him be, he knows what he's doing," he hissed.

"Yes, he does…" grinned Hannock, "… he's going barmy!"

"Oh no, on the contrary, Captain. That boy's a genius."

"*He's talking to a tree, Emnor!*" exclaimed Hannock.

"I know," said Emnor. "Brilliant, isn't it?"

Drake continued chatting to his tree. "They don't belong here. They should be moved. I'd help if I could but I'm not big enough and even if my friends were to help, their roots are too deep. Oh well, never mind, I suppose they'll have to stay. You'll get used to them I'm sure… but it'll take a long time, you poor thing. Fancy having something as ugly as them in front of you every day, it really doesn't bear thinking about."

Drake noticed movement in his peripheral vision. It seemed that the nymphs had suddenly become interested as three of them now floated toward him. *Had his plan worked or was it about to backfire spectacularly?* Drake took a deep breath as one of them grew closer and hovered, tilting its head and studying him. To anyone who witnessed the scene, it may have seemed alarming, especially when the nymph opened its mouth and the high-pitched screeching began. This was no threat or warning, the nymph was attempting to communicate directly with Drake. The wizards covered their ears, the noise unbearable to them. Drake, however, heard something completely different. To him, it was a serene, ghostly voice that was as soothing to him as a cold, wet towel on a blisteringly hot day. He sighed contentedly at its sound.

"It seems you have much love for our friends, young one," it said.

"Oh yes," replied Drake, "they're so regal and strong, who wouldn't love them?"

"Many have tried to do them harm. Do you not agree that we should protect them?"

"Of course, you should. It would be a terrible world without their beauty," replied Drake.

"So why should there not be more? Jendilomin told us that we should make more to ensure their safety. Do you not find our creations beautiful?"

"Some of them, yes. But Jendilomin lied to you, not everyone wants to harm your friends; they love them the same as we do and would never harm them. The truth is that the transformed would help protect them if they could, but instead they now stand here as part of your forest."

"What would you have us do, young one?" asked the nymph. "Many of these beings bring fire and dismember our friends for their own purpose. Do you believe we should make them as they were?"

"Not the ones that would try to hurt the trees, no, just our friends."

"Scores of beings have joined our forest, young one. How many do you seek to retrieve?"

"Six. Only six. The rest should be left as they are, they're the bad ones," replied Drake, adamantly.

The nymph stared into Drake's eyes. Despite Jendilomin's deception, it still had faith in the goodness of others. "We shall give you this gift. We shall return your friends to you shortly. Show them to my family and it shall be done." The nymph floated away followed by its kin.

Drake joined his fellows, a dozen questions being asked of him at once. "Hang on, hang on, one at a time!"

It was left to Emnor to begin. "What happened? What did they say?" he asked.

"They're going to let them go, all of them," replied Drake.

"*All of them*!?" exclaimed Yello.

"All of our friends," said Drake. "If I point them out, they'll change them back."

"*Well done, my boy, well done…*" began Emnor "… but what gave you the idea?"

"How many times does anyone here listen to me?" asked Drake. "*None*, that's how many. It's become a habit of mine saying, *might as well talk to the wall*. A tree seemed the next logical step."

They watched eagerly as, one by one, their friends were cured by the nymphs, but there were a few tense moments as both Poom and Grubb were reanimated. They were, after all, in the throes of battle when they had been transformed.

Their work done, the nymphs floated away, leaving the companions, the wizards and the Gerrowliens alone, with Jendilomin.

"Time for a vote, I believe…" announced Hannock, "… I vote we chop her head off," he said.

"Me too," agreed Grubb, "keep 'er from doing anythin' like this again."

Faylore had an arrow on her bowstring and was in front of Jendilomin in an instant. "No one shall harm my sister, or they will die this day," she snapped.

"Put the bow down, Faylore…" sighed Jared, "… no one's going to hurt her. You have my word."

"*Your* word, Jared, but what of them?" she asked, nodding at the others.

Drake held up his hand and the bow and arrow flew from Faylore's hands. Drake caught them without even looking, and smiled at her. It seemed his confidence as a wizard had grown immensely. "You have *my* word as well, Your Majesty, but we don't want any accidents. If anyone here tries to harm your sister, *I'll stand beside you.*"

Hannock started laughing as he slapped Drake on the back. "You're alright you are, wizard boy," he said.

"Is that supposed to be a compliment, *soldier boy?*" Drake replied, stretching out his neck as if goading Hannock to make good on his earlier threat.

The most difficult question now was, indeed, *what should be done with Jendilomin?*

Faylore sat with her sister and took her hand, "What burdens you so, Jendilomin? Why are you so sad?"

"I wished to bring peace to the world, that is all I ever wanted. Why did you prevent me from doing this?"

"One cannot intervene with nature's progress, Jendilomin. If one does, it ceases to be *nature.*"

Leaving the sisters alone, Emnor guided Jared and the others to one side. "Jared, I'd like to introduce you to a very old friend of mine, Yellodius Tarrock. Yello, Prince Jared Dunbar, son of Tamor and heir to the throne of Borell."

"When he says *old friend*, I think he means ancient, Your Highness," laughed Yello.

"A pleasure to meet you, Yellodius," replied Jared, shaking Yello by the hand.

"The pleasure is mine, Jared, and just call me Yello, everybody does."

Yello was introduced to the others, who thanked him profusely for their rescue. *No trouble at all* and *any time,* being amongst his replies.

The smiles faded and the mood became sombre as, inevitably, the subject of Jendilomin was raised. They watched Faylore's attempts to calm her sister, who was now sobbing uncontrollably. It seemed that there was no consoling her. She was not evil and meant no harm to any that had been transformed. In her delusion, however, she still could not see that what she had done was wrong.

"Would you mind awfully if I try to help young Faylore?" asked Yello, "I do feel somewhat responsible for her sister's dismay."

"Not at all, I'm sure she'd welcome any suggestions you may have. Oh, and by the way, Yello, it's Queen Faylore," replied Emnor.

Much to their surprise, Yello walked away from them, not toward Faylore and Jendilomin, but in the opposite direction. Reaching the edge of the lea, he disappeared amongst the trees.

"But I thought…?"

"Trust me, Jared, best not to ask. He has something in mind I'm sure, he'll be back soon," said Emnor.

Yello hadn't gone far before he sat on the ground and began to ferret through his trusty bag. Taking out a small stand, he placed it on a flat rock and, muttering a few words, conjured a magical blue flame that appeared beneath it. It was fascinating to watch, for the flame needed no fuel as it hovered beneath the stand. He then produced a small glass jar and half filled it with plain water before placing it above the heat of the flame and, once more, delved into his bag.

Emnor and the others, unsure of exactly what Yello was doing, discussed the grisly events that had taken place in Reiggan. Emnor explained how ruthless the attackers had been and that if Yello had not been interred by rubble, he too would have surely perished. Almost as if he had heard his name, Yello returned.

He passed them without a word and stood over Faylore and Jendilomin, who still remained seated on the ground. "Queen Faylore, I am Yellodius Tarrock, a *friend*. Would you allow my help with your sister's grief?"

"Why would I allow you to help my sister grieve? She can manage it by herself. Go away! *Jared*, make him go away," she called.

"*Oh crap*. What's he said to her?" mumbled Jared as he hurried across to them.

Yello turned to him as he approached. "I…?" he began, but Jared held up his hand, convinced that he already knew how Yello had attempted to begin the conversation with Faylore.

"Just say what you mean. Forget all the 'may I', 'would you' crap. Ask a question bluntly, make a statement blatantly, got it?"

Yello smiled at him. "Got it," he replied.

"He's not going away, Jared! He's still here," said Faylore.

"He wants to help you make Jendilomin feel better."

"Well, why didn't he just say that?" she replied.

With Jared's help, Yello was allowed to administer a tonic and, within minutes, Jendilomin had stopped sobbing and was chatting pleasantly with Faylore. Yello, who had sat on the ground beside Jendilomin, now began to rise, but stumbled slightly, spilling the topmost contents of his bag onto the floor beside him. The only person who noticed was Harley, and what he noticed was the Bolinium root.

Harley intercepted Yello before he could reach Emnor. "I saw that," he said.

"Saw what, Harley?" asked Yello, feigning ignorance.

"The Bolinium root," replied Harley. "Yello, *you never…!*" he gasped.

"Sometimes, very rarely I might add, one has to bend the rules a bit. We don't have time to waste on a weeping white witch, Harley. You'll understand… *when you're a bit older,"* said Yello, patting him on the shoulder and hobbling away as quickly as his wounded leg would allow.

CHAPTER 5

Standing high on the mountainside, Karrak surveyed the view of Merrsdan Castle nestled in the valley far below him. It was a typical construction. High, fortified walls, guard towers with archery slots and a wooden drawbridge that, when lowered, covered the expanse of the deep moat. His victory, it seemed, would be easier than he had anticipated. Normally, the protection offered by the castle's defences would have been quite sufficient to repel any armed invader or usurper. The thickness of the stone and the strength of the timbers, however, would offer little resistance against as powerful a sorcerer as Karrak and a wry grin was upon his lips as he gazed upon, what would be, his greatest conquest to date.

The snow-covered peak on which he stood would provide him with an array of natural projectiles. Surrounded by rock, snow and ice, it would take little effort to use these against his targeted objective. Karrak glanced at Darooq, who bowed his head immediately, unlike the rest of Karrak's followers.

Darooq had herded them into the monastery at Karrak's behest and there they had all been transformed into mindless drones. Not one had resisted, having foolishly trusted both him and their master, Karrak. Now enslaved, they stood silently. Their appearance gave little indication of their mindless enslavement. Karrak's skill in twisting the minds of others had grown immensely, leaving few tell-tale deformities on his victims as testament to the pain they had endured during the process. There was a slight twist of a lip or the drooping of an eye, noticeable on a few, but little more.

The silence around Karrak was broken by the howling wind that whipped the snow flurries around them into a frenzy, causing his transformed, sub-human beasts to whimper as the cold penetrated their hairless hides. As always, Barden, collar still firmly in place, was at the head of the pack.

Conquering the king of the largest castle in the northern territories would, however, send the message that he intended. His domination of the world had begun. After this, all would be given an ultimatum: *Bow down to him, or be destroyed.*

"It is said that the King of Merrsdan has five thousand soldiers at his command, my lord."

Karrak looked deep into Darooq's eyes, "It will not be enough, Darooq. Should I be lenient? Should I offer him the chance to surrender unconditionally?"

"No, my lord," replied Darooq. "Five thousand is too great a number. You cannot ensure loyalty from so many before you have the opportunity to bring them to the fold, the slightest treachery may endanger you."

"But is that not what you want, Darooq? For me to fail?" asked Karrak. "When first we met, it was your belief that my failure was imminent and that once removed, you would seize my power for your own ends. Or am I mistaken?"

"I shall not lie, my lord, it was my intent, initially. But now, having witnessed your power, I believe that it would be beyond my wildest dreams to achieve in a lifetime, that which *you* could, in the blink of an eye."

"Once I would have killed you for such an admission, Darooq..." said Karrak, approaching him, "... but your loyalty is true. I no longer need to torture those around me to attain that loyalty, a wave of my hand is enough." Karrak raised his hand but Darooq never flinched, he simply gazed into the jet-black eyes of his master. His devotion was absolute and he believed with all his heart that if Karrak felt it necessary to enslave him as he had the others, he would embrace his decision without question. Karrak lowered his hand. "No, my friend, you shall remain *Darooq,* trusted and loyal friend of Lord Karrak."

"Thank you, my lord," replied Darooq, bowing again.

Facing the castle, Karrak raised his arms. His followers were now spread equally to either side of him, forming a line. They imitated his actions, causing the wind to grow stronger and the sorcerers' robes to flap wildly around them. Huge chunks of ice began to break away from the mountainside and float above them until the sorcerers threw their arms forward in unison. The frozen missiles were flung through the air as easily as a man would hurl a small pebble, and crashed into the castle below, destroying many of its fortifications and crushing hundreds of soldiers. Karrak lowered his arms and pointed at the castle far below. His followers began to disappear in clouds of smoke or crackles and sparks.

Amid the onslaught, the soldiers ignored them at first as they materialised within the castle walls. They had no idea who had attacked them or why, but within seconds, the realisation was there as the sorcerers, without provocation, resumed their attack. The first troops, unaware of their impending doom, were incinerated before they had time to understand their situation. Others were frozen solid mid-motion before unbalancing and toppling forward or back, shattering into pieces.

Now identifying their enemy, the remainder began to charge at the sorcerers but were literally blown into the air before, moments later, crashing back down to earth, their bodies broken and their lives extinguished. The sorcerers moved forward, instantly killing anyone in their path. Many soldiers accepted the futility of their attempted defence and tried to flee, tried to escape the barbarous insanity, but for them, there was no hope, none were spared. There was no pause during the relentless attack. Incinerations, decapitations and eviscerations continued until every soldier and citizen of Merrsdan was eradicated. The only survivors, the royal family, who were subsequently banished in order that they might spread the word of Karrak's intentions.

Karrak strolled through the castle grounds with Darooq at his heel as he glanced, emotionless, at the numerous corpses that now littered the ground. Making his way to the throne room, he climbed the steps and brushed the dust from the royal seat, then lowered himself slowly into it. "What do you think, Darooq? Does it suit me?" he asked. "Should I appear as a king to my followers? Should I wear royal robes around my shoulders and a crown upon my head?"

"No, my lord," replied Darooq. "Such things are merely the vanity of mortal men. Robes and crowns are to command authority. You have no need of trinkets or finery, your presence is enough."

Darooq looked, once again, into Karrak's black, soulless eyes. His features had begun to change with the influence of the Elixian Soul. His face was darker, his skin no longer showing any natural pigment, appearing more like a shadow... a *living* shadow.

***

Jared woke and raised his hand to his eyes, Gamlawn seemed very different now as the brilliant sunshine flooded the lea. He saw that it would be difficult for anyone to conceive the threat that the entire world would soon face if they were in this serene, idyllic setting. Even the transformed beings that had become trees no longer seemed imposing, less gnarled and twisted, the face-like growths appearing more peaceful and overall, smoother.

"So, what's the plan, Your Highness?"

Jared was in a world of his own as he looked up at Hannock, the question not registering. "Oh... morning Hannock."

"Yes, Jared, it is. So, what's the plan?" repeated his friend.

"I've only just opened my eyes, Hannock. At least allow me to wake up properly. Is everyone okay?"

"Yes, Jared, everyone's fine. Get up. Things to do and all that."

Jared rose slowly. He had slept more soundly than he had in weeks yet, for some strange reason, still felt exhausted.

"Are you alright, Jared?" asked Hannock. "You look a bit wobbly."

"Of course, I'm alright," laughed Jared. "Probably just an aftereffect of being turned into a tree."

Emnor watched the scene closely, "Yello," he muttered, "I think it's time we removed the prince from this place."

Yello knew that there was more to Emnor's statement than it would first appear, but did not question it.

The forest nymphs, conversing through Drake, had insisted that they be allowed to care for Jendilomin. Faylore, convinced that they would allow no harm to come to her sister, agreed with their proposal and joined the others as they headed back toward Cheadleford. Yello, trying his best, limped alongside Emnor but it was not long before the pair fell behind a little.

"What was all the rush to get Jared out of that place, Emnor?"

"Well, you felt the power of it, Yello. He was absorbing it faster than I've ever witnessed," replied Emnor.

"So he has a little help then?" asked Yello. "What is it?"

"The Heart of Ziniphar," replied Emnor.

"Hah, no wonder he went a bit shaky. Is he carrying it?" chuckled Yello.

"On a chain around his neck. Lovely gold setting," replied Emnor. "The boys made it for him."

"But does he know what it truly is, Emnor? Does he know what it's capable of?"

"Good lord, no! If he did, he'd refuse to wear it. He's the sort of fellow who'd say it was an unfair advantage. Noble by nature that one, not simply by birth."

"He may need that advantage if one day he's to face his brother, alone."

Reaching Cheadleford Village, they began to gather their belongings. Jared suggested that they rest for a while, but Emnor would not hear of it, "We shall not linger here for any longer than is necessary, Jared. Get your things together, we leave for Reiggan at once."

The Gerrowliens seemed uneasy. They were wary of magic and its use and had no intention of visiting a wizard fortress. "You obviously have everything in hand," announced Poom. "We'll let you get on with it," he added nervously. "We better head home now, make sure everything's okay. I am sure you understand?"

"Of course, my friends," replied Jared. "Thank you for all your help. Hopefully our paths will cross again," he added, shaking hands with Lawton and Poom.

"If you need our aid, you know where to find us," said Lawton.

In the blink of an eye, the Gerrowliens were gone.

***

Reaching Reiggan, Hannock was amazed at how much restoration the wizards had achieved in such a short space of time. The horrors that had greeted him when they had first entered, however, had not left him. There were still tell-tale bloodstains visible, bloodstains that were either missed, or deliberately omitted.

Emnor approached Jared. "Time to resume your training, Your Highness," he announced.

"Training? I don't have time for training, Emnor," exclaimed Jared. "I need to find Karrak!"

"And when you do, you will also need to be ready to face him. At the moment, you are not," replied Emnor.

"My magic is strong enough, and if all else fails, I have this," said Jared, drawing his sword.

"And we also have this," added Hannock, raising the golden crossbow.

Emnor laughed as he eyed the weapons that the Borellians were now brandishing. "And very pretty they are…" he said, "… if you are able to get close enough to Karrak in order to use them. Drake," he called, glancing across at the young wizard, "take them away, would you, they won't be needed for now."

Drake held out his hands and the weapons were suddenly torn from the hands of Jared and Hannock. Catching them, Drake let out a long, high-pitched whistle. Nestling the crossbow, he looked at Hannock. "Got some weight in it, hasn't it, *soldier boy!"*

"As I said, Jared," reiterated Emnor, "you'll need to be ready."

Jared, Hannock and the others were now safely ensconced in Reiggan. Emnor had secured the stone entrance doors and, despite Jared's protestations, refused to open them until Jared could prove to him that his power would offer him a reasonable defence against Karrak.

Hannock spent his time on target practise with the crossbow; the boys continued with restorations; Lodren kept them fed and Grubb… was Grubb. Faylore it seemed, was the only one who was at ease with her captivity. She wandered the halls of Reiggan, her Thedarian inquisitiveness fuelled by the wonders she discovered and almost drove the boys to distraction. She had resumed her: '*What's this? What's that? What does it do?*' phase. A phase that seemed endless. At one point, Drake forgot he was talking to a queen, giving way to an outburst of frustration. "It's a bloody vase!" he bellowed, before receiving a very loud smack around the back of the head from Yello. "Sorry, sorry… I'm really sorry," he added quickly, attempting to ease the pain by rubbing his scalp vigorously.

Grubb had noticed Yello still limping on his wounded leg. He would not see anyone suffer, and although not overly fond of the old wizard, he sidled over to him. "Might be able to do something with that for ye, if ye want me to, that is."

Yello looked down at Grubb, who was now facing the ground and shuffling his feet. "I don't want to impose, Grubb," replied Yello. "But if you could, I'd be very grateful. I actually said when I tried to fix it myself that a Vikkery could do it far better."

"Sit down," instructed Grubb. "It'll only take a minute or two. And you were right… *we can do it better.*"

Grubb's hands began to glow faintly as he placed them on Yello's wounded leg. His willing patient sighed with the relief that was produced by Grubb's healing touch. The boys looked on in awe. They all had basic healing skills, but nothing as impressive as the natural healing touch of the

Vikkery. Faylore had once been mortally wounded by a zingaard, a huge, ferocious beast, but had been revived from the brink of death by Grubb. She glanced over with disinterest, as Grubb treated Yello.

***

Emnor was attempting to explain to Jared the relocation spell that the wizards so often used, when Faylore approached them, "Jared," she announced, "I need to visit my homeland."

"What! Right now?" asked Jared, a little confused and taken aback by her statement.

"Not immediately," she replied, "I can wait a few minutes." To Faylore, a few minutes was almost a lifetime. She was impatient but never rude and made her opinion known if she was kept waiting. Never voiced, her actions spoke volumes, sighing and tapping her foot being the most obvious signs of her displeasure.

Emnor gave Jared a knowing look. "This can wait, Jared," he said, "I suggest you take care of her Majesty first."

"Can't you wait until tomorrow, Faylore?" asked Jared. "We would be better prepared for the journey if you could."

"*You* won't need to be ready, Jared," she replied. "I'm going alone."

"Faylore, it's not safe…" began Jared.

"I have my bow and my sword. I need no other protection," she sighed.

"How about a bit of company then?" asked Lodren. "I'd love to see your homeland, if you don't mind me tagging along, that is."

"Don't forget me," added Grubb. "Who's gonna patch you up if ye get in another scrape with some beastie?"

It was evident to Faylore that neither of the *volunteers* was about to take 'no' for an answer. She dismissed all objections by Emnor and Jared but did agree that she, Grubb and Lodren would allow themselves to be relocated to the foot of the mountain to save time. The only stipulation came from Grubb; *Buster had to go with them.* There seemed no urgency for Faylore's home visit, but once she had decided, there was no changing her mind. Unsure of how long it would take, she promised that she would contact them within a few weeks. Karrak's whereabouts were a mystery. The trail was cold and, for now, there was nothing to be done but wait for the next rumour of evil goings-on to surface.

They departed for Thedar within the hour and were left at the foot of the Muurkain Mountains by Yello. He wished them the best of luck, smiling at them before vanishing in a cloud of blue smoke.

"I wish I could do that," said Lodren. "You know, just disappear."

"Sometimes I wish ye could, when ye're bein' all nice and mushy like," mumbled Grubb.

Lodren snorted and pulled the straps a little tighter on his backpack. "Just get on your pony and let's get going," he said.

***

Jared, Hannock, Emnor and Yello were discussing their own next move.

"We can't just sit around here waiting for something to happen," said Hannock.

"So in what direction should we begin our search, Captain?" asked Yello.

"I don't know, but we have to do *something,*" replied Hannock.

"We don't know where Karrak is, so it's no good just thrashing around in forests or climbing mountains in order to find him. He'll make a move sooner or later and when he does, we'll be ready for him," said Jared.

"Quite right, Jared," agreed Emnor. "Shall we continue with your instruction?"

"Yes, shortly. I've been thinking though. Do you think that it might be an idea to check on things at home?" suggested Jared. "Now that I know the basic theory of relocation, I could be there and back in no time."

Xarran and the other boys were sitting close by and could be heard sniggering as they eavesdropped on the conversation.

"Did I say something to amuse you?" asked Jared.

"You haven't even gone further than the length of this courtyard and you think you could make it all the way to Borell! That's a good one, that is," laughed Drake.

"Hold your tongue, boy!" snapped Hannock. "You're speaking to a member of royalty and don't you forget it!"

"We're really sorry..." smiled Alex, "... but trust me, within minutes you'd be dead. The slightest change of wind direction and you'd end up halfway into a mountain or up a glamoch's backside. It isn't as easy as you think, Your Highness."

Jared gave a huge sigh.

"I'm afraid they're right, Jared," agreed Yello, reluctantly. "It'll be some time before you're able to travel a greater distance than you can at the moment."

"And how long is 'some time'?" asked Jared, his obvious frustration showing.

"That depends on you, I'm afraid," replied Emnor. "Weeks, perhaps even months."

"Wonderful!" exclaimed Jared. "In that case, can *you* take me to Borell?"

"I have a better idea, Jared," said Yello. "Why don't *I* go to Borell?" he suggested. "You stay here and continue your studies with Emnor. The sooner you get the knack of relocation, the sooner you'll be independent of us having to hold your hand."

Jared sighed again. As frustrating as it was, it made sense.

"Would you like me to leave now, Jared, or will tomorrow do?" Yello chuckled.

"There's no rush. Go tomorrow, or the day after perhaps, I'll leave it up to you," he replied. "Apparently, I'm going nowhere."

The day wore on and, as evening came, thoughts turned to food. Lodren had left with Faylore. *Who was going to do*

84

the cooking? Jared shuddered at the thought of Hannock's past endeavours, to say they were atrocious was an understatement at best, and far too polite. His fears were soon allayed as Drake and Alex volunteered to prepare a meal, which actually turned out to be surprisingly enjoyable, although the boys would not reveal the ingredients.

***

"If he discovers the power too soon, he'll be overconfident. It'll protect him instinctively anyway. The twin sisters cannot be allowed to merge, not until the scroll reveals the time," whispered Emnor.

"But it does say that they *must* merge," hissed Yello. "Is it essential that the time be specific?"

"There is a chance that each would attempt to dominate the other, good versus evil," replied Emnor. "If that happens, there is a chance, however slight, that they would both be destroyed and their bearers along with them. They are equally powerful, Yello, we must take care."

"I wish I'd set fire to that blasted scroll centuries ago," chuntered Yello. "After I'd stuffed it in your beard for good measure."

"So do I, old boy…" whispered Emnor, "… so do I."

The two ancient wizards were far below the ground level of Reiggan Fortress. Emnor, as he had vowed, had not revealed the location of the Peneriphus Scroll to Yello and was merely informing him of its latest content. They were there to search the depths of Reiggan for anything that may yield information or aid them in their plight. An ancient talisman perhaps, or a spell, or incantation that would give them an edge. The briefest of pauses could be the difference between life and death for anyone, if not all of them.

"Here's one that we could use, Emnor. Time dilation, what's *dilation*?"

"It means it slows down time," replied Emnor.

"Well, why not just put that? Why all the fancy words?"

"I wouldn't worry about it, it won't work against the Elixian Soul anyway," replied Emnor.

"I'm keeping it regardless," said Yello, slipping the small scroll into his robes.

"We're wasting our time here, there's nothing of any use. Let's have faith that Jared is who we think he is. We may not need anything else."

"You've never been wrong before, Emmy, I just hope you're not this time."

They headed toward the staircase and were about to ascend when Yello saw a glint as the light caught a small object, partially buried beneath a pile of scrolls. Brushing the scrolls aside, he revealed a silver disc approximately six inches in diameter. The centre was made from an unusual, milky-white, translucent stone that seemed to be alive. The stone seemed to contain a swirling mist.

"Hang on!" said Emnor, excitedly. "Is that what I think it is?"

"It is indeed," replied Yello with a sly grin, "*Tallarans Eye.*"

"But old what's-his-face took that off us years ago. He said he'd destroyed it!"

"But he never found out what it was for, did he?" asked Yello. "He could never figure out how we could find almost anyone in seconds. If only he knew."

"All you had to do was brush something belonging to the owner across it and it would show you where they were," added Emnor.

Both wizards had exactly the same thought at the same time, *Karrak.*

"All we need is something belonging to him and... *bingo!"* said Emnor.

"Bingo? What does *bingo* mean?" asked Yello.

"Oh, sorry. It's a new word all the youngsters are using. Becomes a habit after a while, it just means you get the result you wanted."

"So why not just say that? Honestly, you're gone a couple of years and people start inventing a new language!"

They hurried to the chamber in which Jared and Hannock were sleeping soundly, charging through the door so quickly that it slammed against the wall. Hannock immediately jumped to his feet and, grabbing his sword while still half asleep, began to slash about wildly causing the wizards to retreat rapidly through the still-open doorway. Jared opened one eye and seeing Hannock's antics, thought that it was the result of a bad dream and simply pulled the blanket over his head.

"Hannock, it's only us, you fool!" shouted Emnor. "Put that blasted sword down before you kill someone!"

Hannock squinted at them with his one good eye. "What do you expect when you come charging into a fellow's room

87

in the middle of the night, a bedtime story? What the hell were you thinking, you silly old sods?"

"We may have a way of locating Karrak," they announced.

Jared immediately sat bolt upright. "*How?*" he asked, shaking his head vigorously to rid himself of his drowsiness.

"We discovered this," began Emnor. "It was just a bit of a lark when we were younger, more of a toy than anything else. But it has a *real* use."

"Which is?" asked Hannock.

"It can locate anyone, providing you have something that belongs to them," answered Yello.

Hannock looked across at Jared. "Well?" he asked.

For some strange reason, Jared's mind leapt back to one of his very first confusing conversations with Faylore. He grinned. "Yes, thank you," he replied.

Hannock, didn't get the joke. "I meant, well, have you anything that belonged to Karrak in your possession?"

"I know," laughed Jared.

"Are you actually awake yet, Jared?" asked Emnor. "You're acting very strangely."

"I'm fine, Emnor…" sighed Jared, "… and no, I don't have anything of Karrak's."

"Not to worry," said Yello, "I'll grab something of his when I'm in Borell tomorrow. Then, we'll find the git."

"Are you sure that thing'll work?" asked Hannock.

"Positive!" replied Emnor. "It never let us down once. We even found one of the seniors who had been missing for months. He'd gone a little strange and turned himself into a goat by accident, but we still found him. I never had the heart to tell him he'd eaten my favourite underwear before we had a chance to reverse the spell."

CHAPTER 6

Faylore, Lodren and Grubb had set off at a brisk pace that morning. No real thought had been given to the urgency with which they had departed and the rest of the companions would never dare to question the motives of a queen. Faylore strode ahead of the others and even Buster seemed to be almost trotting to keep up with her.

"How long will it take to reach your home, Your Majesty?" asked Lodren.

"Seven, eight, nine days maybe, it depends on whether you can keep up…" she replied, "… and it's Faylore, not Your Majesty. At least, when we are alone anyway."

"Never took you to be the kind to become homesick," said Grubb.

"Why ever not, my dear Grubb? Our lands are amongst the most beautiful in the world and to be away from them for a single moment can appear, to some of my folk, an eternity."

"I don't doubt it for a minute, Your Majesty. But you said 'some', not 'I'."

"Don't be so pedantic, Grubb. It was merely a figure of speech," she replied.

"So what's it like, your homeland?" asked Lodren.

"Let's see," she replied. "A thousand shades of green, broken by the beiges and browns of the tree trunks and branches, with crystal-blue streams that trickle gently between the foliage."

"Sounds lovely," said Lodren.

"Sounds damp and soggy to me," grumbled Grubb.

"I can assure you, Grubb, it is far from soggy. The sun streams between the leaves and the air is warm and clean," she said, smiling as she pictured it in her mind.

"Why would you ever want to leave if it's that beautiful, I mean?" asked Lodren.

"How could we appreciate its beauty if we have no comparison?" she asked.

"I can understand that," said Grubb. "I liked it in my cavern. Quiet, dark, secluded, just what we Vikkery are used to. But I have to say now that I get to travel with you lot, I have gained a new appreciation for other landscapes."

"How very philosophical of you, Master Grubb," laughed Lodren. "You'll be reciting poetry next."

"Get stuffed, stumpy," snapped Grubb, slightly embarrassed.

"Ignore him, Grubb, I think it's wonderful that you are happy with your altered lifestyle," said Faylore.

"And of course, I wouldn't have Buster if I were still in me cavern, would I?"

"No, you wouldn't, Grubb, and he wouldn't have you taking care of *him* either," added Faylore.

"No, he wouldn't. And this dopey git here would be walking instead of being given a ride. I'll let *you* remind him of that next time he's making fun of me."

"And while we're on the subject of reminding people, Faylore," began Lodren. "Can you remind Grubb that if he doesn't shut his face, *he'll be cooking his own dinner!*"

Less than an hour had passed when it began to rain. It was only a light shower at first, but soon became torrential. Faylore was as sure-footed as she would have been if the ground were bone dry, for poor Buster though, it was a different story. His hooves slid in the mud, and the burden of both Lodren and Grubb on his back soon gave way to the inevitable as he slipped once too often, spilling both riders straight into the muddiest puddle they could have encountered. Grubb scrambled back to his feet to check that his precious pony had not been hurt as Lodren lifted Buster off the ground, allowing Grubb to check his legs.

The mud-spattered, soaking wet pair, combined with the antics of Lodren lifting the pony and Grubb's attempts to check he was alright, was just too much for Faylore, who suddenly burst into hysterical laughter at their antics. Tears ran down her cheeks, disguised by the rain, and she held her sides, her ribs beginning to ache. At first, even *she* thought she must be ill. No Thedarian would ever behave like this. Giving in to emotion was most unseemly, even if that emotion was a form of joy. She attempted to compose herself... but failed dismally.

"Well, I'm glad you think it's funny, Your Majesty," snapped Grubb. "Buster might have been hurt."

"But he's not, is he?" asked Lodren. "He's just dirty, and so are you. I suppose I am as well, so let's just brush the worst of the dirt away and carry on. We can get cleaned up properly when this rain stops."

Faylore had enjoyed their comedic interlude but felt slightly guilty at the same time, not for laughing at them, but because she knew something that they didn't. *Yes, the rain would stop, eventually*. However, in a few days at the very latest, it would start again and they would then have to suffer it for almost a week as they entered the rainforest that she knew so very well. Here, the downpour was ceaseless. So far they had only travelled on even ground. *How would they fare with the peaks and troughs of a rainforest?* she thought.

The ground became more and more treacherous as the day wore on. There was no respite from the rain and less distance seemed to be covered with each hour's passing. At one point, Lodren actually lifted Buster onto his shoulders for fear of him getting bogged down. After an exhausting day, the decision to set camp was a welcome one and just as Lodren was about to light the campfire, the rain stopped.

"Well, that's just flamin' typical!" yelled Grubb.

"I don't do this very often, Grubb…" announced Lodren, "… but I have to agree with you on that one, *typical*. It doesn't stop all day and as soon as *we* do, *it* does."

"At least we'll have a chance to dry our wet things," said Faylore. "I'll show you how. You never know, it may be of some help in the future." She knew, of course, that it was to be in the not-too-distant future. She began to gather branches from the sparse bushes, assembling a small framework that she supported with stones placed around the back of the campfire. Wrapping a cloak around herself, she changed out of her wet clothes and arranged them on the framework to allow the heat from the fire to dry them. "Come on, you two, get out of those wet things. It'll be easier for you, you can hold the cloak for one another."

Lodren blushed and Grubb began muttering under his breath. With a little encouragement from Faylore, they eventually gave in and were now more evenly tempered, enjoying the comfort of their dry clothes.

Later that evening, as they ate, Lodren realised that this was the first time that he had ever had the chance to get to know Faylore properly. They had sat together many times but somehow the conversation was always between Jared, Hannock and herself. He took no offence when this happened, it just seemed *natural*. They were, after all, warriors, despite two of them being of royal blood, and tended to unintentionally gravitate toward one another. Grubb never concerned himself with such things. He understood that he was part of the companions by chance and, having been the last to join, would never make any decisions for them. They listened to his opinions and valued his input, for he had knowledge of things with which they were unfamiliar. The incident with the zingaard being the most memorable.

"Do you enjoy your travels, Faylore?" asked Lodren.

"I enjoy meeting new folk, well, some of them anyway," she replied. "The bad ones are no challenge, but there are few of those. Occasionally one meets a fascinating character, although the most interesting tend to be the most infuriating."

"You mean like Captain Hannock?" asked Grubb.

"Yes, I suppose I do," she said, with a smile.

"We must all seem really stupid to someone like you," said Lodren.

"Not at all, I think *you* are wonderful. You too, Grubb. I bless the days on which I met you both."

Lodren blushed again, and so did Grubb. "And we bless the day we met you, Your Majesty," said Lodren.

"Lodren, what's in this stew?" asked Grubb, prodding at the contents of his bowl.

"Mind your own business, Grubb," replied Lodren. "Just eat it."

A few moments passed before they spoke again, but you could almost hear the questions rattling around inside Lodren's brain. "Maybe we should have brought one of those young wizards along with us. Might have been able to do something about all that rain," he said.

"Oh no, we couldn't do that," replied Faylore. "Thedarians do not approve of the use of magic within our borders."

"But *you* don't seem to have any objection to it. Mind you, I suppose we're not in your lands yet, are we? Is that why?" asked Lodren.

"Not as such, Lodren. It's just that we, as a race, are not synergic with magic, it tends to have a strange effect on us. You saw what happened with Jendilomin."

"You mean it sends you barmy, like Jared's brother," said Grubb.

Faylore glared at him. "My sister is not *barmy,* as you put it, Grubb. She was merely a little *confused.*"

"That's what I said, *barmy,*" repeated Grubb, shrugging his shoulders.

Lodren could see the disapproval on Faylore's face and quickly changed the subject. "What do your people do for pleasure, Faylore?" he asked.

Faylore, despite the fact that her sister had just been so cruelly insulted, composed herself and smiled at Lodren. "Unlike me, very few venture into the outside world. We love poetry, philosophy and craft. Many things occupy our time in Thedar."

"What do you mean by *craft?*" asked Grubb.

"We make everything that we require. Our clothing, treehouses and pottery are all made by hand. But our smiths are exceptional, the most skilled in the world as you will see if you study my sword and bow."

"I have to admit, I don't know much about weapons," said Lodren. "All I know is my hammer."

"And a most impressive hammer it is, my friend," said Faylore.

Lodren had a dreamy look on his face. "Your history must be fascinating. Living in such a beautiful place with no magic, at peace with your surroundings. A real home without petty squabbles."

"It has been chronicled for generations. We have thousands of scrolls and tomes should you wish to read some of them," she offered.

"I'm not the best reader, Your Majesty. Recipes and the like are my kind of thing. Don't think I could read thousands of scrolls."

"Well, the offer's there if you wish to accept, Lodren. A thousand-year-old scroll may be of some interest even to you," she added.

"A thousand-year-old scroll!" exclaimed Lodren.

"We have others that far pre-date that, hundreds of them in fact."

"How do you manage to keep them that long? Don't they dry out and crumble?"

"We have our ways, a process that was first thought of by one of my ancestors, *King Peneriphus*. He wrote everything down. Even in advanced old age, he would urgently demand a quill and parchment. It was a shame for him in the end, apparently most of his texts were thought to be the ramblings of a senile old soul, but no one ever had the heart to destroy them. They're all still in the archives, even his prophecies of doom."

"Do you keep any pets?" asked Grubb.

"No. Beasts roam freely in Thedar, we do not hold with the domestication of any animal."

"I mean horses and ponies and the like?" emphasised Grubb.

"None that you would recognise and none are tame. They aid us should we have need and we compensate them for their trouble."

"Why wouldn't we recognise them?" asked Lodren. "What are they?"

"Well, dragons of course."

***

97

"Should I take the Tallarans Eye with me, Emnor?" asked Yello. "It may save time."

"Oh no, Yello, I know you too well to allow that," replied Emnor. "The minute you lay your hands on one of Karrak's belongings, you'll be off to face him on your own, you silly old fool."

"Who are you calling old…?" laughed Yello, "… I'm younger than you."

"I know, and I'd be a sillier, older fool if I let you take the Tallarans Eye."

"I *hate* the fact that you know me so well, Emmy."

"I know. But it's kept you alive more than once, and for that very reason, you should be grateful."

"Why don't I just go with you?" Jared asked Yello.

"Because Karrak is more likely to attack Borell Castle if he knows that you *and* your father are inside. No, you stay here for now, Jared, where you're safe," interrupted Emnor, not allowing Yello the opportunity to reply.

"Safe?" scoffed Jared. "You do remember what happened here, don't you? A hundred wizards couldn't stop him last time, Emnor. What chance do you think we'll have if he decides to come back?"

"He won't return. He already has what he came for. I don't know where his next target will be, but rest assured, *it won't be Reiggan Fortress.*"

"Have you considered the fact that he may have already attacked Borell Castle?" asked Hannock quietly.

Jared had not only considered it, he had agonised over it from the moment he had entered Reiggan. He had tried to convince himself that now that Karrak had acquired the Elixian Soul, he would no longer be interested in the acquisition of Borell. *Surely, there were far greater riches to be had elsewhere?* But, try as he might, the danger to his father and his subjects haunted his thoughts. "Just be as fast as you can, Yello. Can you be back by nightfall?" he asked.

"I'm not as young as I once was, Jared. It would have taken at least a day even then. Sorry, my friend, I'll be gone for a couple of days at least," he replied.

"Well, perhaps we could send a couple of the younger men. They would be quicker, surely?" Jared suggested.

"And an easier target for any sorcerers who follow Karrak," said Emnor.

Jared gave a sigh. "I suppose you're right. Sorry, I just hate to think of what Karrak is up to while we idle away our time in here."

"We're hardly idling, Jared," replied Emnor. "You need to hone your skills some more. It will be worthwhile, trust me."

"Right, I think I'm all set…" said Yello, "… wish me luck." And with a shimmer, he disappeared.

"I have to say, I'm not really interested in the whole magic thing, but that vanishing trick gets me every time," chuckled Hannock.

Emnor frowned at him. "It is *not* a trick, Captain. It is one of the most difficult spells for any wizard to learn. Something that Jared, you know, *the prince,* is about to discover."

Hannock snorted and marched off. Picking up his crossbow, he aimed at a target at the far end of the courtyard and continued with his archery practise. Squeezing the trigger gently, he released the bolt. It flew toward the target on course for the bullseye, but a split second before it struck, it was turned to ash by a firebolt. Turning quickly, he saw Drake swinging his arms nonchalantly. "I suppose you think that's funny?"

"Who me, Captain Sir…?" Drake replied, grinning, "… I didn't do anything."

Emnor and Jared laughed. Witnessing Drake's devilment was the light relief they had needed. The next few minutes consisted of Hannock berating Drake and Drake vehemently denying any involvement in the destruction of the bolt.

"You're off your rocker, you are. As if I could blast a crossbow bolt out of the air. Who do you think I am, Emnor?" yelled Drake.

Emnor steered Jared away from the verbal duellists so as to allow them to argue uninterrupted. "I trust you are still wearing the talisman I gave you, Jared?" he asked.

"Of course, I am," replied Jared. "You told me never to remove it."

"Good, very good. It will aid you in the days to come."

"I had a feeling that it was more than a simple talisman," said Jared.

"Of course, you did. I wouldn't waste my time on an idiot," snorted Emnor.

"So what does it do?" Jared asked.

"Nothing, but then again, *everything,* " replied Emnor.

100

Jared smiled, "Oh, I remember these, *the barmpot days*. I hold such fondness of their memory."

"You're not ten anymore, Jared, be serious," Emnor said, sternly. "What I meant was, that it has a single purpose. It is a magical enhancement."

"Oh my! The possibilities are endless," said Jared, sarcastically.

"Jared! We are, I mean *you are*, about to attempt your first unaided relocation spell," snapped Emnor. "Concentrate on any point in the courtyard. You must, at *first*, be able to see your destination. Once you feel confident enough, imagine yourself in that place and you will be transported to it. Now, we don't have the time for you to study the technique of others so you're just going to have to try for yourself, understand? Clasp the talisman, it should give you a boost."

Drake was now free of Hannock's abuse and he couldn't help overhearing, well, eavesdropping on, the conversation between Jared and Emnor. He nudged Harley and nodded toward Jared. Harley, in turn, got the attention of Alex and Xarran and they too, now watched in anticipation.

Jared took hold of the talisman and in a split second began to wobble animatedly from side to side. This was followed by twitching and jerking that then developed into him thrashing about violently as if he was being jostled by an invisible, angry mob. Two large grooves were left in the ground as he started to slide forward. Leaning back and digging his heels in had no effect as he gained velocity and was now headed rapidly for the wall at the other side of the courtyard, a cloud of dust pluming behind him. He babbled faster and faster, his words completely incoherent as he zoomed toward his fate. There was a loud thud as he hit the

101

wall. Jared remained there momentarily, twitching slightly and groaning. He stared up at the wall, trying to fathom out what he had done wrong. He turned to face Emnor, still gripping the talisman. He pointed at the wall, grinned, and fell forwards flat on his face, out cold.

Hannock sidled up to Emnor, hands clasped behind his back and nudged the old wizard with his shoulder. "So, tell me something, old chap," he asked, "did that go according to plan?"

***

Faylore, Lodren and Grubb had now been in the rainforest for three days. To Faylore, it was no hardship. She was familiar with the terrain and the horrendous torrential downpours. Sad to say, her friends were not. Yes, they had both been in similar situations with adverse weather conditions before, but not for so prolonged a period. Even the ever-cheerful Lodren was showing signs that he was becoming a little tired of it. Normally, very careful with his pots and pans, he had now begun to slam them down whenever he prepared a meal for them, which was most uncharacteristic. Grubb, however, was his usual self, he always moaned and complained, so the change in him was barely noticeable.

"How much longer have we to put up with this rain, Faylore?" groaned Lodren. "My backpack weighs twice what it should. It's so wet, you could wring it out like a rag."

Sympathy was not something that Faylore offered often, and a little rainwater was hardly the end of the world in her eyes anyway. "Not long now," she replied. "It should clear by this afternoon."

"Good. My Buster hasn't been properly dry for days, poor fella," chuntered Grubb.

As Faylore had suggested, the rain eased off by mid-morning. It was obvious that the trees were thinning, but the air rapidly grew colder as they reached the edge of the forest. A light frost was on the ground and small puddles were covered by ice as the travellers emerged from the dense bushes that grew there. Lodren and Grubb were not prepared for what they were about to see. Before them was a desolate scene, for miles there was nothing. The ground was flat, a white plateau as far as the eye could see, covered with ice.

"I thought you said your homeland was all warm with trees an' sunshine," snapped Grubb.

Faylore looked down at the Vikkery and raised her eyebrows in disapproval at his tone. "And it is," she replied haughtily. "This is not my homeland, we are still weeks away. At least, we would be, were we to walk the rest of the way."

"Well, what do you suggest we do, *fly?*" asked Grubb, sarcastically. "I know I can if I need to, but *you* can't."

"We'll discuss it later, Grubb. For now, let us continue our journey. Two more days and it will be much easier for you both, *and* your beloved Buster, of course."

"Fantastic! First, we nearly drown with all the rain, now we're goin' to freeze to death. I'm so glad I came along, wouldn't have missed this for the world."

"Stop complaining, Grubb…" snapped Lodren, "… why don't you shapeshift into that thing with the four arms? *It's* covered with fur, that'll keep you warm."

"I can't," replied Grubb quietly as he looked down at the ground.

"What do you mean, you can't? Have you forgotten how?" asked Lodren.

"Of course I haven't forgotten, you pillock," snapped Grubb. "It's just that… well… it scares Buster when I change into that."

Lodren was lost for words, he turned away from Grubb and looked up at Faylore, thinking that a change of subject was in order. "So, Your Majesty…" he began, "… if this isn't your home, where are we?" he asked politely.

"This is Ellan-Ouine. It means land of ice," she replied.

"Is that what it's called in your language then, Thedarian language?"

"No, Lodren, my native tongue is the same as yours. It is from the language of dragons. This is *their* homeland."

"You mean… dragons live here, and they can talk?" asked the Nibby, his eyes bigger than ever.

Faylore laughed and smiled at Lodren. "That is precisely what I mean. You seem surprised."

"'ang on a minute!" yelled Grubb in a panic. "If they see Buster, they might try to eat him."

"They don't eat horses or ponies, or sheep, or even cows for that matter," said Faylore, frowning.

"What do they eat then?" asked Lodren.

Faylore paused for a moment as she looked at her two vertically-challenged friends. "Anyone less than five-foot-tall," she sighed.

"That's not funny, Your Majesty," snorted Lodren. "You shouldn't make fun of Grubb like that."

"Would you listen to 'im…" said Grubb, "… you're no six-footer yourself, stumpy."

Acting on Faylore's advice, Grubb wrapped rags around Buster's hooves to allow him more purchase on the ice and they set off across the barren wasteland. Lodren was still eager to hear all there was to learn on the subject of dragons. "Are they friendly?" he asked.

"Not friendly as you would perceive, Lodren, but they leave us in peace, as we leave them. It is just a matter of mutual understanding and respecting one another's borders, nothing more," she replied.

"But what do they do for you?" he asked. "You said before that they help you."

"Our borders are safe, but we allow them to patrol occasionally. It gives them the sense that we are under their protection."

"But you don't really need looking after, do you?" asked Lodren.

"No, of course not. Dragons like to think of themselves as intellectuals. They believe they know best, whatever the subject. We simply allow them that belief."

"You mean they're a bit thick," stated Grubb, abruptly.

"No, Grubb, far from it," Faylore quickly replied. "Why do you think they live here?"

"'Cos they like the cold?" Grubb suggested.

"Quite the contrary," replied Faylore. "They hate the cold. It's the reason they breathe fire, to keep themselves warm in their caves."

"So, why don't they move somewhere warmer?" asked Lodren, baffled by the illogical actions of the dragons. "It's obvious. If you hate the cold, go somewhere warm!"

"They would never be left in peace, Lodren, that's why. Apparently, they have tried to settle in many places. Whenever they are discovered, people want to see them, or even worse, kill them."

"So, they live out here because nobody wants to come out into the frozen lands?" asked Lodren, the realisation dawning on his face.

"Precisely," replied Faylore.

"What a shame for them. All they want is to be left alone," Lodren sighed heavily. "Why would anyone want to kill a dragon? They sound lovely."

"Oh, shut yer face, Lodren! *He's lovely, she's lovely, everybody's bloomin' lovely!*"

106

CHAPTER 7

Yello held his hand to his chest as he struggled for breath. He had not been exaggerating when he had emphasised how strenuous relocation spells were. A strain with which Jared was becoming fully and *painfully* aware. In the distance, Yello could see the towers of Borell Castle. He had hoped to appear right outside the gates, but his failing strength had caused him to fall a little short of his mark.

Sitting on a hillock, he gazed at the impressive façade of the Dunbar Kingdom. Generally, Yello would not be seen in the company of royalty, in fact, he was not the sort who wished to mix with anyone, save one or two of his oldest, closest friends. Emnor being his closest. He smiled as he reminisced, the memories of their youth flashing through his mind. To look at him now one would have believed that he had always been a serious, determined old man. When in reality, in his youth, he had been a bit of a thrill-seeker. Whenever there was a perilous encounter of any kind, from subduing a rogue sorcerer or dangerous beast to a simple tavern brawl, you could rest assured that he was in the thick of things.

The castle was unusually quiet. *Should he walk the remainder or take a brief respite, then appear within the castle grounds*? He decided on the latter, far more impressive for a wizard to appear out of thin air. 'Always put on a bit of a show if you're able' had been the motto of one of his masters centuries before, one he had lived up to whenever possible. Yello's leg ached. Grubb had done a fine job with its repair, but at his age the natural healing process took a little longer than it used to. Reaching into his bag, he drew out the Abigail's Mercy and took a small sip. *Just to take the edge off the pain,* he thought. The potion had the desired effect and, almost immediately, he stood up as his strength began to return. With a deep sigh, he disappeared.

He appeared seconds later, enveloped by a cloud of bright lilac smoke, an effect that he had perfected centuries before. Now, standing in the centre of the castle courtyard, he waited for the cries of the castle guard for him to stand fast and identify himself, or perhaps the cry of someone who had been startled by his appearance, but as the smoke cleared, he found the courtyard completely deserted.

No guards, no squires nor serfs were there to witness his grand entrance. Slightly perplexed, he wandered around for a few moments. *Maybe there was someone in the wooden hut on the far side?* he thought. He entered, but found no one. He headed for the castle. Only then did he realise that something was very wrong. There was no sound, no voices, no noise of everyday life, nothing. Being unfamiliar with the layout of the castle was a problem in itself. *Should he turn left or right? Should he take that passage or the one in the other direction?* Borell was vast, but after half an hour, Yello still found no sign of life.

It was then that he discovered the throne room, and there, sitting in his rightful place, was King Tamor. He was slumped in his throne, his head forward, motionless. Believing Tamor to be dead, Yello approached him slowly and placed his hand on the king's arm. "Who did this to you?" he asked himself aloud. "What am I to tell Jared?"

Yello could feel no real sorrow, this was his first encounter with Tamor and, therefore, he had no real opinion of the man. His son, however, had proven himself to be an honest and honourable man, and informing Jared of his father's passing was not a duty that Yello relished. He lowered his head, contemplating the kindest way of breaking the news to Jared.

"Stay away from me, sorcerer!" roared Tamor, suddenly rising from the throne. Yello reeled backwards, his wounded leg sending him off balance and causing him to fall. "Have you not done enough?" cried Tamor, hysterically.

"Your Majesty, fear not, I am a friend," said Yello, hurriedly. "The danger has passed, I am here to help," he added, trying to calm the panic-stricken king.

"You're one of them! You're here to kill me!" ranted Tamor, shrinking away from Yello, head in hands, obviously terrified and confused.

Yello frantically rummaged through his bag hoping to find something, a potion perhaps, that would calm Tamor. All he had was the Abigail's Mercy and that was more for pain relief from wounds, which at first glance, Tamor had not seemed to have sustained.

The king was becoming more and more agitated, now shouting at the top of his voice, but making little sense.

What if there were still enemies within the castle? Surely, the king's ravings would attract them? Yello could take no chances. His staff pulsed once as he pointed it at Tamor. The king instantly fell to the ground, unconscious.

"My apologies, my liege," muttered Yello. "It was for your own good."

He checked Tamor for wounds, but found none. There was no sign of even the slightest abrasion. It was obvious to Yello that the king's mind had been affected by sorcery.

***

"How are you feeling, Your Highness? Bit of a headache?"

Jared opened his eyes and blinked a few times before he could focus properly on Emnor. "What happened?" he asked. "How long was I out?"

"Oh, not long, just the one day," replied Emnor.

"A day?" exclaimed Jared, immediately grabbing his head and discovering the egg-sized lump on his brow. *"How is a day not long?"*

"I've known wizards who were knocked out for weeks when a spell backfired on them," replied Emnor. "You should think yourself lucky."

"I don't feel very lucky. I feel like I've been slammed into a wall."

"That's because you have, but at least you did the slamming yourself."

"Is that supposed to make me feel better?" asked Jared, frowning.

"No, but at least you won't be looking for revenge on anybody else."

"What? You mean like you, for instance?"

"I'll leave you to rest a while longer. If you need anything, Alexander will get it for you. He'll be your nursemaid, don't worry," and chuckling to himself, Emnor left the room.

"Can I get you anything, Your Highness?" asked Alex. "I've been instructed to take care of you."

"No, thank you, Alexander. I'm fine."

"It's no bother, Jared. How about a drink?"

"On second thoughts, yes. Thank you, I'm parched."

"I can't believe no one ever told you that magic dehydrates your body."

"That's why Drake told Hannock to drink the water that morning then?"

"That's right. I know he winds him up, but he actually likes the captain, you know."

Alex paused momentarily as he handed Jared a glass of fruit juice. "What's it like?" he asked.

"Have some," offered Jared.

"Not the fruit juice! I meant, what's it like being a prince?"

"I've never given it much thought, to be honest," replied Jared. "It's who I am, I don't know any different."

"But it must be fun? I mean nice clothes, a castle, servants, not having to get out of bed if you don't want to, all that stuff."

"You have a very strange idea of what it means to be a member of a royal house, my friend. It's far removed from what you may think."

"But you did have all that stuff when you were growing up, didn't you?" asked Alex.

"Well yes, I suppose I did, but it's also about setting an example. You have a responsibility to be better than your subjects."

"That's what you think, is it?" Alex's tone had changed. "You think you're better than everyone else just because you were lucky enough to be born into a royal family?"

"Not at all. As I said, as a member of the royal house one has to set an example. You have to be more honest; you have to work harder; you have to be more tolerant and forgiving. If you don't have those qualities, you can become a tyrant."

"You mean like Karrak?"

"Mind your tongue, boy. Know your place," yelled Jared, pointing at Alex. "Whatever my brother has done is not something on which you may comment, do I make myself clear?"

"As crystal, Your Highness," replied Alex, bowing to Jared.

Jared sighed, his attack on Alex was unnecessary and, to a degree, uncalled for. "I'm sorry, Alex, you didn't deserve that," he said, quietly. "Must be the bang on the head. Will you accept my apology?"

"Don't worry about it. I had a lot worse said to me when I was growing up, that's for sure."

"I heard your father died when you were very young. It must have been difficult growing up without him?"

"No, he never died, he just didn't hang around. Mum said as soon as he found out I was on the way, he was off."

"That's even worse. Do you know who he was, or *is*?"

"No. Every time I asked Mum about him, she said not to give him a second thought. After all, he never cared about me."

"So, your mother never met anyone else? Someone to take his place, I mean?"

"Not that I remember, but I think I had a brother once. Not a real brother, just somebody else's boy who lived with us for a while. He was older than me but I don't know what happened to him. One day he was just gone."

"You haven't had it easy, have you?" asked Jared, sympathetically.

"Not until I learned the power of magic," replied Alex. "The other boys used to beat me up. As you can see, I'm a bit of a weed. But when I found magic, it all changed. There was this one lad, big fat kid he was, all the other boys were scared of him so they did whatever he told them to do. One day, they caught me in an alley and were punching me in the face as usual when it got really nasty. The fat kid had a knife and I was sure he was going to stab me when, for the first time ever, I lost my temper. I screamed at him at the top of my voice and tried to push him away. He flew across the alley and crashed into the wall, split his head wide open. There was so much blood I thought I'd killed him. But then I realised, I hadn't even touched him, I just pictured him slamming into that wall and it just happened."

"So, what happened after that?" asked Jared, intrigued.

"I legged it, thought I'd done murder, but the fat kid survived. Neither him nor any of his cronies ever bothered me again," replied Alex, laughing.

Jared thought back to when he was a boy in the courtyard of Borell Castle receiving weapons training. He remembered how terrified he had been as one of the guards, who had been ordered to give him a scare, stood over him with his sword raised high in the air. That same guard had flown through the air and crashed through a hay cart without any physical contact being made.

The events that had brought about both his and Alex's awareness of magic were almost identical, save the fact that the threat to Alex's life was far more real than his.

"Do you know something, Alex? I think you and I are going to be very good friends."

Alex chose not to correct Jared, always preferring to be referred to as Alexander. He had antagonised him once and did not wish a repeat. He stayed with Jared, but after a while the prince closed his eyes and drifted back into a restful sleep. Alex stared at him for a while, tilting his head to one side as if studying his patient. His expression changed as he curled his lip.

Turning quietly, he left the chamber. Instead of heading toward Emnor and the others, Alex headed in the opposite direction and began to descend one of the many steep stairways within Reiggan. Looking over his shoulder, he quickly entered the first room he came to. The room itself was not a particular destination, Alex simply wanted to be

114

alone. He pulled a chair toward him, sat on it, and placed his feet on another. He leaned back, rubbing his hands over his face and blowing.

"You really do think you've got them all fooled, don't you?" Strangely, Alex did not react to the sudden voice. "Poor little Alex. His daddy ran off and left him and his mommy all alone. Such a shame," continued the voice, sarcastically.

"I'm not in the mood for your petty ramblings today, Theodore," mumbled Alex. "Can't you go and pester someone else for a change?"

"Funny you should say that, Alex. As a matter of fact, I'd love to. Oops, nearly forgot, I can't, can I? *There's the slight inconvenience of me being dead.*"

"Here we go again. Every day the same thing," groaned Alex. "*I can't do anything, nobody else can see or hear me, I'm dead.*"

"Well, you should know that better than anyone, Alex. After all, *you killed me!*"

"It was a long time ago, Theodore, and I *have* apologised," replied Alex, "I've lost count of how many times."

"*Just let me try my magic on you*, you said. *I won't hurt you, just make you float*, you said. Great for the first few seconds, until your eyes turned black and you started smashing me into the walls before setting me on fire."

"It was an accident, Theodore. I was too young and inexperienced, I thought I could control it, but I was wrong."

"Thought you could control it?" scoffed Theodore. "The more I screamed, the more you enjoyed it. You need to be stopped and I'll find a way, one day," he threatened.

"You have appeared four times in a room full of people when I was present. No matter how loud you shouted or waved your arms about, I was the only one who could see you. What are you going to try next, writing on the walls?"

"I would if I could hold a quill, but you know I can't, so don't make fun of me, Brother."

"I'm not your brother!" snapped Alex. "Don't call me that."

"We had the same father, you prat! Of course, you're my brother!" exclaimed Theodore.

"I only have your word for that. I knew you for barely a year before you died. That does not make us true brothers."

"You mean before you *murdered* me."

"I did not murder you, Theodore. It was an accident."

"So, why did you hide my body and tell your mother that I must have run away?"

"I was a child, Theodore, a scared child! Things would have been different if I'd understood more."

"I watched you when you spoke to your mother, you never even flinched. No sign of emotion came from you, lying came far too easily. You deliberately murdered me, you wanted me out of the way, I'm just not sure why."

"Stick around, you might find out," mumbled Alex under his breath.

"What? So, you admit it!" exclaimed Theodore.

"I admit nothing!" snapped Alex. "Your death was an accident, nothing more. If you were alive right now, however, things would probably be different," Alex stood up and glared at the apparition of the young boy that floated before him. Its features were quite distinct, from the sharp nose to the square jaw and bright blue eyes. "My mother told me that you look far more like our father than I ever did, but that doesn't make you my brother. All you are now is a rotting corpse buried in the woods. Go back there, it's where you belong."

"You should be careful, Alex," warned Theodore. "You can't frighten me and you can no longer harm me. I'm already dead, remember? You may have your new friends fooled for now, but I know you much better than they do, I know how black your heart is. You will pay for what you have done, mark my words."

The ghost vanished.

***

Faylore, as usual, was leading the way. Lodren, despite being much shorter in the leg than her, managed to keep up quite easily, but Grubb, not wanting to morph into his alter-ego for fear of scaring his beloved pony Buster, was now riding him in order to keep pace. Grubb wasn't ordinarily prone to showing off, but when he rode Buster, he took a stance that would resemble any royal astride a magnificent charger, his back straight and his head held high.

"Your neck will freeze like that if you don't drop your chin a bit," said Lodren, laughing.

"Don't know what ye mean by that, I'm just ridin' normal," replied Grubb.

"Take no notice of him, Grubb, you look most impressive, almost regal," smiled Faylore.

"Don't encourage him, Your Majesty. He'd be the first to say something if he saw anyone else riding with their nose in the air like that."

"I have *not* got my nose in the air," snorted Grubb. "It's just more comfortable, is all."

"Just change into Wilf. Buster will soon get used to him," suggested Lodren.

"Wilf?" asked Faylore.

"Every time we talk about Grubb's transformations we refer to it as 'the four-armed alter-ego' or 'the thing with four arms' or whatever. It would be much easier to just give it a name."

"Lodren has a point, Grubb, it would save time and confusion," agreed Faylore.

"Never even thought of givin' it a name before," said Grubb, "but why Wilf?"

"He reminds me of a chap who lived in our village when I was a boy. Bad tempered, old…" Lodren looked across at Faylore and cleared his throat, "… *fellow,* he was always shouting and roaring at anyone who got near to him."

"Was there any reason for his aggressive behaviour?" asked Faylore.

"None at all. Like I said, he was just bad tempered," replied Lodren.

Grubb smiled. "I like it…" he said, "… WILF. It's perfect. When things get dangerous, I'll become a 'Wilf'."

"No, not 'a' Wilf, just Wilf," corrected Lodren.

"Whatever," said Grubb.

The three continued with their journey for the next few hours, making small talk as one does, until Faylore called a halt. "We must tread lightly and speak softly, my friends. A startled dragon could end us before we make ourselves known as friends," she whispered.

"What do you mean 'end us', Your Majesty?" asked Lodren, quietly.

"Destroy us, end our lives," replied Faylore. "They could roast us alive or freeze us solid with their breath."

"I knew a girl like that once," muttered Grubb, "she was 'orrible."

"This is no time for levity, master Grubb, I'm being deadly serious," said Faylore.

"So am I," replied Grubb.

"Stop messing about, Grubb, I don't want to be roasted, or frozen. You'll just have to be quiet, alright?"

Grubb scratched his head, trying to figure out what he had done wrong. He gave up almost immediately, shrugging his shoulders and assuring himself that they just didn't understand him.

"How could we possibly startle a dragon, Your Majesty? They're huge, I'm sure they'll see us well before we reach them. It's not as if we're going to trip over one, is it?" laughed Lodren.

"How much do you know about dragons, Lodren? Have you ever met one? Have you even seen one?" asked Faylore.

"Well no, but the stories…" began Lodren.

"Precisely, my dear Nibby, *stories*. Written or told by folk who have had no dealings with dragons."

"She's got a point, ye know," said Grubb. "You lead the way, Faylore, we'll just do as we're told, I don't fancy getting frazzled either, Lodren."

Faylore led them for mile upon mile across the bleak, seemingly endless tundra. Its glass-like smoothness was a welcome change from the uneven, boggy rainforest. Lodren glanced around as he blindly followed the Thedarian Queen. Ordinarily, he loved exploring new lands. This land, however, held no fascination for the Nibby. To be completely honest, he found it more than a little boring.

Grubb's disinterest was not nearly as great. He cursed the icy ground with every stumble poor Buster made. The wrapping on the pony's legs were a great help but did not completely cure the precarious predicament of his slippery journey. It was a relief to Grubb when finally, the landscape began to change. Small bumps were now visible, nothing drastic at first, admittedly, but it helped Buster's hooves grip and he seemed to be walking far more easily. However, Grubb decided to leave the wrappings in place. It was still bitterly cold. Stretching into the distance, the companions could now see that the ice was formed into small hills, but nothing they could not traverse with ease.

"'Ere," called Grubb, suddenly. "We ain't gonna end up climbing more blasted mountains, are we?"

Lodren tutted as Faylore looked back at Grubb.

"No, master Grubb," she replied, calmly. "We shall encounter no mountains."

"Good," snorted Grubb. "I think Buster has done enough. What with carryin' me and 'im and the provisions as well."

"*'Ere!*" exclaimed Lodren. "*'Ere!* Is that any way to address a queen, you stupid Vikkery? You get ruder by the day, I swear you do."

"I wasn't bein' rude," retorted Grubb. "If you want to 'ear rude, you can f…"

"*Don't you dare!*" snapped Lodren, pointing and pouting at Grubb. "Don't!"

Grubb had a mischievous smile on his face and Faylore could not disguise her laughter as she watched him.

Now amongst the small hills, the temperature appeared less harsh. Whether this was the case or it was because they were shielded from the chilling wind was uncertain, but most welcome.

The light was beginning to fail and Lodren's mind was wandering into 'catering mode'; his only real interest, whatever their circumstances. Grubb was stroking Buster's mane and thinking of nothing in particular when, with a gentle wave of her hand, Faylore brought them to a halt. As Buster stopped, Lodren and Grubb looked up. Ahead of Faylore, the hillocks that she now faced were double that of those around them, and although four distinct peaks could be made out, they seemed fused together as one.

"What is it?" whispered Lodren, glancing at Grubb, who shrugged his shoulders and slid from Buster's back.

"Not sure," he replied. "But it's not that big, we can just go 'round. It'll only take five minutes."

"We do not need to go around, Grubb," advised Faylore, turning to face him. "We need to go *through*."

With this, she moved closer and took a knee, urging her companions to do the same. "My lords," she announced, "forgive my intrusion. Unfortunately, it is unavoidable for I seek your counsel."

Grubb rubbed his brow briskly, "'Ere we go again," he sighed. "First, 'er sister talkin' to trees, now she's talkin' to hills made of ice."

Lodren nudged him and scowled, "Don't say things like that about Faylore," he hissed. "She obviously knows something we don't."

"Well, I hope so. My knees are freezin'," grumbled Grubb.

There were a few moments of silence as Lodren and Grubb looked on with interest, their eyes darting from side to side, dreading what might suddenly appear from behind the ice mounds.

The first noise they heard was a gentle splintering sound, the same as when you drop an ice cube into liquid, and not frightening in the least. The second, however, was the rumbling as the ground began to tremble, and this was mildly unsettling. Then the crackling began, similar to that of a thousand whips being used in unison. Then, the bright, golden light.

The hills before them began to fracture, huge chunks of ice breaking away and rolling down the sides of them. The

122

light was actually emanating from within them until, suddenly, all four peaks exploded.

Lodren and Grubb threw up their arms to protect their faces, expecting to be ripped to shreds by the flying shards of ice. Buster reared up in terror, his whinnying like that of a screaming child. But, unbeknownst to them, they were in no real danger. The ice was reduced to a vapour well before it reached them and, realising their survival, they uncovered their eyes.

Directly in front of them, a huge cloud of mist had appeared and they became more than a little anxious when their eyesight could not pierce it. Only then did they notice Faylore's gaze. Looking over her shoulder, she smiled at them. It was a serene, calming smile to let them know that all was well. The mist cloud began to dissipate. There was a glow from within that pulsed silently and gently. Suddenly, there was a roar as flames rose high into the air. The mist cleared almost immediately. The beings within stretched their wings and stood on their hind legs, their fiery breath illuminating the sky.

They were in the company of dragons.

***

Yello had placed a cushion under Tamor's head and covered him, unusual in itself as Yello was not the type of wizard to pamper anyone. But neither was he a fool. He understood that Tamor was a king and should be treated with respect, if not for that fact alone, then for the fact that he was Jared's father. Placing a goblet of water against Tamor's lips, Yello encouraged the king to sip at it, although he was still quite delirious. "Drink, Your Majesty, it's only water, you seem a little dehydrated, drink."

Tamor's eyes opened wide. It was obvious that despite his rest, he was still terrified, "No more, I can take no more, the pain it's…"

"Be at ease, Your Majesty, nothing will harm you. You are safe now," Yello assured him.

"NO! You don't understand, nobody is safe, not from him. He can invade your mind…" ranted Tamor.

"Who can invade your mind, Sire? Tell me," Yello, despite a lack of tolerance for anyone suffering with any mental affliction, remained calm.

"*The Shadow Lord*," whispered Tamor.

"*The Shadow Lord*? Do you mean Karrak?"

There was an urgency in Tamor's reply. "Do not speak his name. If he hears you, he will return. You will suffer the same fate as the others," he hissed.

"What others? Do you mean your guard?" asked Yello.

Tamor grasped Yello's arm. "Everyone," he replied. "My personal guard, the soldiers, the townsfolk, he took them all."

"What do you mean by 'took them', Your Majesty?"

"He assembled them in the market square, made me watch as he turned some of them into mindless slaves. I did not realise that they were the lucky ones. The rest he turned into twisted, snarling beasts. They screamed in pain as they changed, their faces contorted as their very bones cracked. Their features stretched and sprouted huge teeth and their arms became legs as they writhed on the floor in agony. I was powerless to aid them. My people were destroyed, yet live on as monsters, twisted and mindless."

Yello paused for a moment. *Would pressing the king for more information be wise? Would the added pressure send him beyond the edge of reason?* Unfortunately, he did not have the luxury of sentiment and continued with his questioning, "Was the shadow lord Prince Karrak, Your Majesty? Was it your son?"

Tamor had not released Yello's arm and now tightened his grip as he stared at him with pleading eyes. "Yes," he whispered. "It was Karrak. He was different, his face… it's…" Tamor's voice tailed off, and his gaze now was to the floor.

"Your Majesty," urged Yello, gently shaking the distraught king. "Where did he take them? What became of them?"

Tamor had slipped into a trance of his own. No matter how Yello tried, he could get no reply. *How could he get Tamor back to Reiggan?* It had taken him well over a day to reach Borell whilst he was by himself. With a lunatic in tow, it would be a far more difficult task to get them both back safely. He couldn't leave him behind, he may harm himself. Karrak may return or he could wander off into the forest and be at the mercy of wild beasts. This was going to take some planning. Replacing the cushion, he lay Tamor down and covered him.

He must begin his search, his mission was to find something that belonged to Karrak in order for them to locate him, *but how could he achieve this now?* He did not even know which chambers were Karrak's, let alone what possessions were his. He placed his hand on Tamor's shoulder. Shaking his head, he turned away and headed toward the door. Once through, he ventured toward the stairs, pausing at the foot of them as he looked up. "Oh well, I suppose I have to start somewhere," he said, as he placed his foot on the first step. He drifted from chamber to chamber, unsure of exactly what it was he was looking for. Perhaps a weapon that the prince may have wielded, or if he was really lucky, a tome on the subject of necromancy. He chuckled at his own optimism.

Hours later and still no closer to finding anything obvious, he wandered into yet another chamber. He pawed through chests and closets, but again, found nothing unusual. Feeling slightly fatigued, he sat on the bed and pressed his hands into it, enjoying the luscious, soft feel of the mattress. A piece of cloth rolled down into the dip he had created and settled onto the back of his hand. He flicked it away inadvertently and it landed on the floor by his foot. He scrunched his eyes up, recalling a conversation that he had had with Emnor. *Hannock cracked him across the back of the skull with a pikestaff... took him to his chambers, bound and GAGGED.* Could it possibly be? Had he been fortunate enough to find the very gag that had been placed in Karrak's mouth years before? Would his chambers have been left undisturbed since the day of his departure for Reiggan? It was a bit of a stretch, he had to admit, but optimistically, he snatched the rag from the ground and placed it in his robes. He would continue with his search but, in his heart of hearts, knew that there was no need. This initially insignificant piece of cloth would lead them to Karrak.

His pace quickened as he hurried from chamber to chamber, half-heartedly checking cupboards and chests, convinced that this was unnecessary. He returned to Tamor and held the cloth in front of his eyes. "Do you recognise this?" he asked. "Is this the gag they used to silence

126

Karrak?" he continued, shaking Tamor more violently than before. But it was pointless, Tamor lay motionless and continued to stare into infinity.

***

Jared folded his arms, looking a little impressed with his own achievement.

"What are you looking all smug about?" yelled Xarran. "You only travelled about fifty yards. At that rate, it'd take forever for you to get anywhere."

Emnor raised his arm swiftly as if to stretch it. Xarran let out a yelp, shot forward about six feet and landed face first in a muddy puddle. "Were you saying something, Xarran?" he asked.

Xarran was rubbing the back of his head. "I was just saying how well Prince Jared's relocation spells were coming along, Master," he replied quickly.

"How very polite of you. Now find something of importance to do or I'll find something for you," smiled Emnor. Xarran made himself scarce, followed by Drake, who was, as usual, in fits of laughter at someone else's misfortune. They disappeared into Reiggan.

"He's quite right, of course, you do realise that, don't you, Jared?" asked Emnor.

"He might be," admitted Jared. "It's just not natural, blasting about faster than a bird can fly. It makes my head spin every time I do it."

"Ah, but you are doing it, aren't you, Your Highness?" noted Hannock.

"It doesn't mean I'm enjoying it. I need a bucket every time."

"How positively charming. One can immediately tell that you're royalty, Jared."

"Hannock, if you don't shut it, I'm going to stick my boot up your a…"

"Ah, there you are, Harley," called Emnor. "Would you mind helping out with Prince Jared's lessons?"

"My pleasure, Master Emnor," replied Harley. "How can I help?"

"Relocation sickness, I'm afraid," replied Emnor.

"So, when you said help, you meant bring him some water?"

"Exactly," replied Emnor.

"So, why not just ask me to fetch him some water?" asked Harley.

Hannock marched forward and quickly steered Harley away. "We'll both go," he said.

When they were far enough away, Harley turned to Hannock, obviously annoyed at being asked to perform such a menial task. "Can't your bloody prince get *himself* a drink of water?" he snapped.

"Take a deep breath, Harley. I know exactly how you feel," replied Hannock.

"No, you don't, you have no idea. You're a captain of the guard, how would you?"

"Do you think I was born a captain? Trust me, I've cleaned the boots of thousands of men who didn't even deserve to be wearing a uniform. I've been kicked up the backside, slapped around the head and made fun of more times than you've gotten out of bed," laughed Hannock.

"Sorry, Hannock, I didn't mean to have a go at you. It just feels so unfair some days. I'm supposed to be Emnor's apprentice, not a water-carrier."

"It's all about following orders, Harley. If you can't follow a simple order to fetch some water, it's a bit of a poor deal. It's a mundane task I'll admit, but if you're not willing to do that when you're asked, how will you react if you have to follow an order that could put you or a friend in danger?"

"Hadn't thought of it like that," admitted Harley.

"I've been watching your Master Emnor. He trusts you as much as he trusts himself. There's a valuable lesson to be learned there, young man, I suggest you learn it." Hannock smiled at Harley. If anyone could understand the young wizard's frustration, it was him. He slapped Harley on the shoulder as he handed him the water bucket. "And make sure the ladle's clean," he laughed.

Harley grabbed the bucket and ran to the well. A few moments later he returned and he and Hannock approached Jared.

"Your water, Your Highness," announced Harley, holding out the ladle.

"Bit formal, isn't it, Harley?" asked Jared. "I thought we were all friends here?"

"We are," replied Harley, "but you *are* still a prince."

"And a bit of a prat," shouted Drake, immediately throwing his hands into the air, not wanting to receive the same magical smack in the back of the head as Xarran. "I'm just saying, Master Emnor. We're all entitled to our opinion. With what he has around his neck, he should be zipping across the courtyard and through walls without even feeling it."

Emnor scowled at Drake. He knew, better than any, the power that was at Jared's disposal. A power of which Jared was still unaware. "Hold your tongue, Drake," snapped Emnor. "You should not speak of that which you do not fully understand."

"I'm sorry, Master, but if we're to succeed, Jared has to be told. We don't have the time to waste here. Karrak's out there torturing and murdering at will while we're stuck in here, watching Jared learning first level magic that a five-year-old child is capable of. You can't keep protecting him, *he has to know*."

Jared gave Emnor a puzzled look. "What's he talking about? Emnor, is there something you aren't telling me regarding this?" he asked, holding up the Heart of Ziniphar.

"Only the fact that it's the only way you can defeat your lunatic brother," said Drake.

"Be quiet, Drake! You've already said too much," shouted Harley.

Hannock had heard enough and decided it was time to step in, "I think tempers are becoming a little frayed here. Maybe you should all calm down. It's obvious that there is more to that talisman you gave to Jared than you let on, Emnor. Time to tell us exactly what the secret is, don't you think?"

Emnor lowered his head. Drake was right, of course. Emnor had mentored Jared since he was a boy and had come to think of him as far more than a mere friend. To put him in danger was the last thing he wanted to do. However, he knew that one day, that was precisely what he must do. He had procrastinated, hoping that another solution may arise, one that meant that Jared would not have to face Karrak. He sighed and gave a weak smile. "I think it is about time we sat and talked, Your Highness," he said. Beckoning to the group, Emnor entered Reiggan Fortress.

They gathered in one of the larger chambers. Emnor had sent Drake to inform the others of the meeting, and now they all stood facing the head of the Administration. Emnor cleared his throat, "Please forgive me my friends, but I have not been entirely truthful with you. I would never lie to you, but I have made a few omissions."

Hannock leaned back against a desk and folded his arms. "Such as?" he asked quietly.

"You are all aware of the existence of the Peneriphus Scroll, I presume?"

"The scroll that prophesied the coming of the one sorcerer said to be destined to rule the world?" asked Hannock.

"The very one, Captain," replied Emnor.

"You're saying that there's something in it that you didn't want us to know?" asked Jared.

"There is something in it that I did not want to believe, Jared. Unfortunately, the events that were prophesied have so far been accurate, despite my efforts to bring about any deviation from them."

"Alright, that's enough, Emnor. Time to fill in the blanks," sighed Hannock.

"Of course, Hannock. You all know what Karrak has achieved so far. The evidence is all around us. What you may not know is that he has already taken a kingdom for his own," announced Emnor.

"Borell! You mean Borell," breathed Jared.

"No, Jared, not Borell," replied Emnor. "At least not that I am aware of. He has taken Merrsdan, the largest kingdom of the north, and now sits on the throne."

"He's declared himself a king!" exclaimed Jared.

"I don't believe that to be the case, Jared. I believe he simply took it because he could," replied Emnor.

"How could taking a kingdom that far north affect us?" asked Hannock. "It makes no sense."

"I don't think anyone in this room would accuse Karrak of being sensible, Captain. This is nothing more than a show of strength, a fear tactic. If he can take Merrsdan so easily, surely, all others would surrender unconditionally?"

"How did you discover this, Emnor?" asked Jared. "You've had no contact with the outside world since we arrived here."

"See what I mean about him being a bit of a prat?" laughed Drake.

"Thank you, Maddleton. Please, do not interrupt again," said Emnor, glaring at Drake. "That is not entirely true, Jared. I have, on occasion, had to venture outside the walls."

132

"So, whilst we're asleep, you just nip out and have a bit of a mooch around. Is that how it works, sneaking around in the dark?" asked Hannock, suspiciously.

"Well, I wouldn't have put it quite so bluntly," replied Emnor. "Reconnaissance, would have been a more descriptive term, Captain."

"There's still something you're not telling us, Emnor," said Jared, his frustration showing. "Get to the point. *What does the scroll say?*"

Emnor took a deep breath. There was no easy way for him to say what he needed to. "In order for the second born to be defeated, the firstborn must be consumed by the same flame," he announced.

"What!" exclaimed Hannock, "You mean Karrak and Jared have to be burned to death, together?"

"Of course not, the scroll is not that literal. It means that if Karrak dies, so does Jared," replied Emnor.

"That's preposterous! There must be some other way? Get me close enough and I'll put a golden bolt through his skull before he realises I'm there," ranted Hannock.

"Hannock, you wouldn't get within a mile of him before he detected you, or indeed, any of us," said Emnor.

"Well, I wouldn't announce myself with a fanfare, would I?" Hannock shouted.

"You seem to forget, Captain, I have already faced Karrak once. His power is far greater now that he has the Elixian Soul."

"I don't care, we're not sacrificing Jared. There must be another way."

"Take your own advice, Hannock, calm down and shut your face. Ranting and raving won't help," said Jared calmly.

"There is..." began Emnor, "... if you'll allow me to continue..." he said, glancing sideways at Hannock, "... a weapon at our disposal. One that could turn the tides in our favour."

"Well, spit it out, what weapon?" snapped Hannock.

"Jared himself..." replied Emnor, "...combined with the Heart of Ziniphar."

Drake clapped his hands together, "I knew it. I knew you had something up your sleeve. Or should I say, inside Jared's tunic?"

"Real wizards do not keep things up their sleeves, Maddleton, and by the way, one more interruption from you and I may feel the need to turn you into something nasty." Drake suddenly found the floor very interesting, his eyes darting down to avoid Emnor's gaze.

"So, this is some sort of enhancement?" asked Jared, once again brandishing the Heart, "It's not just a protective talisman, is it?"

"Far from it..." replied Emnor, "... it's the Elixian Soul's twin sister."

"Wait a minute. You mean that thing has as much power as the one that Karrak took from here?" asked Hannock.

"No, not quite. I think it actually has twice the power," replied Emnor.

"If that's the case, won't it send Jared as mad as Karrak?"

Jared shot Hannock a look of disbelief. "Thanks for that," he said.

"You know what I mean, Jared," said Hannock, in dismissal of Jared's feigned indignation.

"It won't send him mad, it's the complete opposite of the Soul. The Soul exists for its own ends, whereas the Heart looks for the good in all creatures. They were once a whole, but somehow became split. To have a pure soul, you must have a pure heart. The scroll says:

> *"With the Heart and Soul combined, one's pure nature is defined*
>
> *If allowed to dwell apart, war will rage 'twixt soul and heart*
>
> *Only death of bearers both, will bring about a new betroth*
>
> *All shall return to endless good, once they re-join in royal blood."*

"So, it seems my fate is sealed," laughed Jared. "I die, Karrak dies. You dip the two halves of this ancient gem into our blood and everybody lives happily ever after. It's just like the stories we had read to us as children, Hannock."

"The stories I used to read ended up with the villain getting his head lopped off and that's how this one's going to end. You said yourself that scroll's ancient. Give me a strong blade or a crossbow and I'll change the details for you."

Alex, unexpectedly, walked toward Jared. Looking up at him and showing no emotion, he spoke, "The only thing that can save you is knowing how to use that…" he said, pointing at the Heart of Ziniphar, "… I think it's time to start your lessons anew."

CHAPTER 8

Karrak was once again walking through the grounds of Merrsdan. He paid no heed to the scores of mindless bodies that shuffled around him as they carried rubble and refuse caused by the destruction of his attack. Darooq sneered at the former citizens and soldiers of Borell. His hatred of them was almost as great as Karrak's had been. Karrak himself no longer gave any thought to such things, hatred and anger were a thing of the past. His only focus now was on power. He had a single-minded obsession to dominate all others and was completely devoid of all emotion.

He turned quickly, his robes parting momentarily, allowing Darooq a brief glimpse of his latest apparel. A glint from the setting in the centre of a newly-forged breastplate revealed his most treasured possession, the Elixian Soul. He had had the breastplate skilfully crafted by a smith of Borell by allowing him his consciousness long enough to complete the intricate design. His task completed, Karrak had granted his freedom by slaughtering him. Now, wherever he went, the Soul was with him, a subconscious addiction over which he had no control.

"My lord…" began Darooq, "… we are running low on provisions. The people you have enslaved need no sustenance, but your beasts are becoming unruly. They are attacking and feeding on anyone who comes near."

"There is meat for them everywhere, Darooq. Can you not see it? Look," Karrak waved his hand and seven of the mindless slaves fell dead. They let out no screams and felt no pain as their lives were extinguished as easily as if Karrak were snuffing out a candle. "Let me know if there is any other way I can waste my time for you, Darooq. I would hate for you to have to think for yourself."

Darooq bowed to his lord. Karrak had now changed beyond recognition. His hood was as far forward as it would reach, completely obscuring his face, or what had been his face. His features had disappeared and now only a shadow that vaguely resembled a human visage existed. Even his robes appeared blacker than they had been.

Once, Darooq had an admiration of Karrak, understanding his thirst for power. That admiration had now turned to fear. To bear witness to Karrak's slaughter of innocents was something that even he could not stomach. In any normal circumstance, an example would be made of one or a few; an example made to bring the others in line. This was no longer the way that Karrak behaved. He destroyed any he deemed inferior and Darooq knew that now, he too, was one of them. He dare not show any sign of weakness. To lower his guard would surely lead to his demise.

Darooq turned away, instructing others to drag the corpses to the pits in which Karrak had commanded his pets be kept, and as he looked on, he gave the slightest shudder. Suddenly, he was lifted from his feet and thrown headlong into a wall. He had no time to gather his thoughts before he was lifted again, spun around and slammed backwards into the wall a second time.

Karrak approached him silently. Even his walk had changed, his robes remaining vertical, as if he were gliding effortlessly. He stood before Darooq and spoke, a deep, echoing, disembodied voice that seemed to fill the entire hallway, "You're not going soft on me, are you, Darooq? Was that compassion I saw? Do you somehow feel sorry for these pathetic beings?"

"No, master," gasped Darooq. "I am unlike them, I feel the cold. It was nothing but a shiver, I assure you."

Karrak tilted his head to one side, studying his only free-thinking follower, "Well, I'd better take care of that for you, hadn't I?"

"Master," begged Darooq. "You said that you valued my opinion, that you would not make me like... *them*. You called me 'friend'."

"I did, and you are. You are my friend still, are you not?"

"Yes, master, and a loyal one," replied Darooq, now struggling to breathe as an immense pressure began to crush his chest.

"That's alright then," Karrak turned away and Darooq fell heavily to the ground. "We'll find you some thicker robes, and maybe some undergarments. Can't have you shivering like a half-starved stray bitch, can we?"

Darooq rose unsteadily to his feet and once again, bowed to his master, "Thank you, my lord. That is most considerate of you."

Karrak stood with his back to Darooq as he spoke again, "Yes, it is. Remember, Darooq, give me no cause to reconsider my decision."

***

Lodren's knees were trembling. Strangely enough, he was unafraid. Something not everyone could honestly say when confronted with the appearance of four fully-grown dragons. His eyes were wide and his mouth open as he gazed upon them. After the initial fire-breathing, they had become completely sedate, Faylore advising that it was an action much the same as you or I clearing our throats before speaking. She now sat facing upwards at the dragons and all were deep in conversation. Grubb, being the wary soul that he always was, had backed away slightly, taking Buster with him. One of the dragons had cast an inquisitive eye over his beloved pony and Grubb decided to remove the temptation of Buster becoming a dragon breakfast.

"What do you think they're talking about?" whispered Lodren.

"Lookin' at the teeth on 'em, probably wondering what we taste like," replied Grubb, sarcastically.

"Don't be stupid," said Lodren. "It's obvious that they know Faylore, I heard one of them call her by name. *And* he knows she's a queen."

"Well, how do I know what they're on about?" asked Grubb. "It's not like I bump into dragons every day."

"Strange, isn't it?" said Lodren. "I've been all over the place. Before I met you and the others, of course. I've been up mountains, followed coastlines and trudged through marshes and bogs that smelt so bad you wouldn't believe me if I told you. You'd have thought in all that time that I would've come across at least one dragon. Look at the size of them, they can't exactly hide, can they?"

"Maybe not," replied Grubb, "but you didn't know these four were 'ere and they were right in front of ye. If Faylore hadn't spoke to 'em, you'd 'ave passed 'em by and been none the wiser."

"My word!" exclaimed Lodren. "You're right. Perhaps I've passed within inches of dragons many times and not even realised it!"

During their discussion, their eyes never left the dragons. One seemed to be speaking with Faylore far more than the rest, he was clearly their leader. Bright gold in colour and slightly larger than the others, he was a most impressive beast. As they watched, Faylore rose and bowed slightly to the dragons before heading toward them. She smiled as Lodren plumped up his half-empty backpack and offered it to her to use as a temporary seat.

"That all seemed very pleasant," he said.

"Yes, and no, I'm afraid," she replied.

"Why? What's the problem?" asked Grubb.

"Not a problem as such, Grubb. I was hoping that they might help us with our predicament concerning Karrak but they have refused to get involved."

"But, why should they?" asked Lodren. "It's none of their business, after all."

"It is more of their business than they realise," replied Faylore. "But they are stubborn. Unless they believe

141

something to be their idea, they can seldom be swayed, once they have made a decision."

"So they won't 'elp us at all?" chuntered Grubb. "Nice friends you've got there."

"I said they won't help us against Karrak, I did not say they would not help us at all. They are allowing us to use the Fenn Immar, which also means we are allowed to enter their home."

"Oh wow! Shall we all clap and 'ave a party? One cave's the same as the next, or 'aven't you noticed?" snorted Grubb.

"You're never grateful, are you, Grubb? If you don't want to go in, you can stay out here in the cold. Queen Faylore and I will see you when we get back," said Lodren, linking his arm through Faylore's.

"Oh no, you don't. If I let you two go off by yourselves and somethin' 'appens to ye, Jared and the others'll blame me. I'd never 'ear the last of it. Where *you* go, *I* go… and Buster o' course."

Faylore smiled again as she turned to face the dragons, "Lord Thelwynn, we are ready. Please, lead on."

Grubb frowned as he nudged Lodren and gripped Buster's reins a little tighter. "Lead on to where?" he whispered. "There's just loads more ice bumps, not a cave in sight."

Lodren shrugged his shoulders. "No idea," he replied, lifting Grubb onto Buster's back.

"Be patient," suggested Faylore, overhearing their conversation.

"You said 'lead on', Your Majesty. Lead on to where? There's nothing here."

"Of course there is, Lodren. If it were not hidden, however, it would make the sentinel's duty far more difficult."

The four dragons stood side by side as they faced one of the ice mounds. Together they breathed, the flames they emitted joining as one and turning illuminous purple. The scene before them shimmered momentarily as the landscape began to change. Incredibly, there was a mountain directly in front of them with a cavernous opening leading deep underground.

Grubb began to laugh. "I'm getting used to all this magic malarkey now. It's good fun," he said, and headed toward the entrance to the cave without waiting for an invitation.

***

Yello lowered himself gently onto the grass verge, panting heavily. Looking across at the comatose Tamor, he shook his head. "This would be much easier if you were well enough to walk without screaming every time something scares you, you know," he said. "What made you think a bramble bush was going to attack you, for pity's sake?"

They had been on the road for three days now. Yello was weary. His leg was aching and the added burden of the confused king was not helping matters. Yello had tried to lighten his load by rousing Tamor. Within seconds, panic took hold of the king. He began to shout and scream as his hallucinations returned once more. Reluctantly, Yello had rendered him unconscious with the use of magic.

Their progress was slow but steady, Yello levitating the king's body behind him as he walked. He would rest briefly at the end of each day and use the last of his energy to perform a relocation spell in order to further their progress.

It must have been one of the most unusual sights to witness. An old man limping along a dirt road with a body hovering behind him, especially as he was prone to talking to it. "Five minutes. If you could just walk for five minutes, that would be enough. Oh no, not you, you're a king. A king who thinks a bush is going to attack you or that a rock somehow may want to eat you. I'll tell you now, if it wasn't for Jared, I'd have left you behind." Opening his flask, Yello shuffled across to Tamor and allowed a trickle of water to pass between the king's lips, "Can't have you dying on me now. Well, not of thirst anyway."

He had decided that although potentially dangerous, the quickest way back to Reiggan would be to travel through Cheadleford. The forest nymphs would pay them no mind, of that he was sure. But there was the possible risk of the hissthaar. *Would they still be in the area? Surely, now that they had been scattered by the nymphs, they would not remain close by?* He had not been present when Emnor and the others had been attacked by the hissthaar, the tale of their misadventures having been explained to him. Subsequently, he had never thought to ask for a description of them. He was, however, a powerful wizard. If he could reach Cheadleford undetected, he was confident that he would have enough strength left to produce a good enough warding spell to protect them overnight. He placed his hand on Tamor's shoulder, and they both vanished.

144

Now at the edge of the village, Yello rolled Tamor's limp body beneath a small hedge, scooted in beside him and began to study the remains of the buildings. The birds were chirping, a good sign that there was no imminent danger nearby. After a few minutes, he crawled from his hiding place, twisting the lower branches of the hedge to camouflage Tamor, and stealthily neared The Hangman's Noose.

Passing the gravesite and still wary of his surroundings, he approached the tavern doorway. Stepping inside he breathed a sigh of relief, it was still deserted. All that remained for him to do was to bring Tamor inside and then he could take a well-deserved rest. He paused in the doorway, the pain in his leg was worsening and he reached into his robes for the Abigail's Mercy. He sipped at it gently, but as he lowered the vial, caught a glimpse of something moving swiftly in the trees ahead. Something *orange*. He replaced the vial in his robes and tightened his grip on his staff, pointing it forwards, prepared for any sudden attack.

"Look, Lawton, another old fellow with a stick. If you throw it, you'll be fetching it back yourself, I'm not a dog, you know."

"Poom, behave yourself. Look at him. He's that old he wouldn't have the strength to throw it."

"Lawton, Poom, is that you? Step out so that I can see you, lads," called Yello.

"Oh yes, of course, we're going to come out into the open," called Poom, slightly taken aback at their being recognised, "so that you can turn us to ash."

"We know who you are," shouted Lawton. "So, why don't you turn around and bugger off? There's nothing left here for you. You've already murdered all the villagers."

"I have murdered no one. I think you are mistaking me for someone else," replied Yello.

"Are we really? An old man who travels alone and dresses like a beggar in order to fool everyone into believing he's vulnerable. Then drops the disguise and tortures them or turns them into beasts," roared Poom. "We know who you are, BE ON YOUR WAY, KARRAK!"

Yello, at first, was astounded by the accusation, the indignation showing on his face. "How dare you! I am not Karrak," he exclaimed, "I am Yellodius Tarrock, second mage of Reiggan. And another thing. What do you mean... dresses like a beggar?"

"Of course, you're not Karrak. My mistake," yelled Poom.

There was a sudden thrashing sound amongst the branches. Yello threw up his hands and roared. The air became very still, there was no longer any noise to be heard. He blinked and stroked his beard. "I say..." he said slowly, "... that was a close one." In his youth, Yello had studied the manipulation of time at length, despite having never referred to it as 'dilation'. He had never needed it in the past, it was simply something he had found interesting and far removed from the mundane elemental magic. He stepped to the side, reaching up to feel the tip of the spear that was perched in mid-air six inches from where his face had been. "I don't know which one of them threw it," he muttered, "but he's a damned fine shot with a spear," he added, clearing his throat nervously.

Limping down the steps, Yello approached Lawton and Poom who, the same as the spear, were now suspended like stringless puppets. He studied them for a moment, "Gerrowliens," he chuntered. "If only they'd believe someone occasionally, without having to point their spears all the time."

It was a bit weird watching the two helpless captives. They could neither move nor speak, but their eyes followed Yello as he paced back and forth before them.

"I wasn't lying to you my fine, furry friends. I am not Karrak Dunbar. You can be forgiven for mistaking me for him. I have heard that he has, in the past, disguised himself as one of advanced years. I do, however, take offence at being told that I dress like a beggar, I should roast you alive simply for that. My friends call me Yello, it would please me should you wish to count yourselves among them. We have met once before, briefly I'll admit, and we were never properly introduced before you departed. Now if you are, like myself, aged and a little forgetful and cannot remember my help in freeing you from Jendilomin's curse, I shall allow the insult to pass. The only alternative is to release you and allow this unfortunate incident to play out to its inevitable conclusion," Yello reached up and gently pinched Poom's cheek. "And I think we all know what that would be," he said, winking at his captive.

With a wave of his hand, Yello turned away and released the two Gerrowliens, who landed silently on their feet behind him.

"Confident old sod, isn't he, Lawton? Turning his back on us like that."

"Oh shut up, Poom, we wouldn't have a chance. He's not like old one-eye Hannock."

Yello turned slowly. "Indeed, I am not, and I would appreciate a slightly more respectful tone toward Captain Hannock," he said, pursing his lips.

The two Gerrowliens began their strange laughter simultaneously. "Oh, but of course, master wizard wouldn't want to insult golden boy," said Lawton.

"You mean golden face, don't you?" said Poom, "The fast one," and they both burst into hysterical, snarling laughter.

"When you have quite finished," said Yello sternly, "I could use a little help."

"What's up, gammy leg giving you some gip again?" said Poom, flicking his brow up and down.

"So, you knew who I was, but still chose to attack," noted Yello.

"If we thought for a second that you wouldn't be able to stop that spear, Poom wouldn't have thrown it," said Lawton.

"Hang on a minute!" protested Poom. "That was your idea. I said all we needed to throw was a stone or something. Oh no, you said throw the spear, it'll be good for a laugh."

"I didn't think you'd actually throw it though," Lawton retorted in mock defence.

"Enough!" snapped Yello, raising his voice in frustration. "I don't care who threw it or whose idea it was. I have the King of Borell hidden beneath a hedge and I'd like to retrieve him before he ends up as worm food, if you don't mind. Now either stop arguing and help me, or go away. I don't really care which at the moment."

The Gerrowliens looked at Yello, shocked at his statement. "You mean, Jared's father?" asked Lawton.

"Yes, Jared's father, but he's not altogether himself," replied Yello.

"Who is he then?" Poom couldn't help himself, he had said it as soon as it entered his head, despite it being in very poor taste.

Lawton glared at him. He kept tight-lipped, despite the many rebukes that he wished to hurl at his friend. Yello turned away and headed toward Tamor's hiding place followed closely by Lawton. Poom was tagging along, apologising profusely for his untimely quip.

Tamor was brought into the tavern and set upon a makeshift bed; a table covered with bracken collected by Poom, by way of apology. A blanket was placed on top of the improvised construction before the king was laid upon it gently, allowing him to rest in relative comfort.

"What's wrong with him?" asked Lawton. "He doesn't seem injured."

"I wish I knew," replied Yello. "His mind is tormented somehow. I've tried everything I can think of but there's no getting through to him."

"Have you tried slapping him across the face?" asked Poom.

"I'll slap you across the face in a minute if you don't…"

"No, he's quite right, Lawton," said Yello, in Poom's defence. "Sometimes a second shock can bring one around from the first. However, it is not the sort of thing one does to a king."

"So? Did you?" asked Poom again.

"Yes, but it didn't work," replied Yello, curling his lip.

"You're as bad as him!" exclaimed Lawton.

"Desperate times, Lawton, desperate times. Anyway, what are you two doing so far from home? Why have you come back here?" asked Yello.

"Hissthaar. There are packs of them moving around here apparently, but we've only seen half a dozen so far," replied Lawton.

"You mean we've only *killed* half a dozen," said Poom, correcting him.

Lawton shrugged his shoulders. "Same thing," he said, smiling.

"What about the forest nymphs?" asked Yello. "I thought their presence would keep the hissthaar away."

"Can't find them," replied Poom. "We've been about five miles in all directions and there's no sign of them. Them *or* Jendilomin."

"So, Faylore's sister is missing as well? Could the hissthaar have killed them?"

"No signs of a battle. No signs of a struggle, they're simply not there," said Poom.

"How odd. It is going to make things a little more difficult for us tonight though," said Yello.

"Us? Tonight?" asked Lawton.

"Well, I was hoping you might stick around until the morning. I'm done in and need to rest. Travelling with the use of relocation spells is hard work enough for an old chap like me, but to have to carry a passenger as well is exhausting," replied Yello.

"Of course, we will, with pleasure," Poom stated adamantly, still feeling a pang of guilt from his earlier, tasteless joke.

Lawton rolled his eyes, "You're pathetic sometimes, Poom."

As dusk came, strange hissing sounds could be heard in the distance, but only by the acute hearing of the Gerrowliens. "Hissthaar," said Poom, growling slightly.

"Are you sure?" asked Yello.

"Positive," replied Poom. "They're still about a mile away, but definitely headed in this direction."

Yello glanced at the open doorway. "Well, that won't do," he said. Kicking the remnants of the doors gingerly between the jambs, he chanted quietly. The broken panels slid towards one another on the floor and began to knit together like a jigsaw puzzle, making crackling and snapping noises. Lifting into the air unaided, perfectly repaired, they gently lowered themselves onto their hinges. The Gerrowliens smiled, fascinated at the ease with which Yello had performed the task. The wizard, however, had not finished and a faint glow appeared, seemingly barring not only the door, but also the windows. "That should do it," he sighed, flopping heavily into the nearest chair.

"Sorry… do what, exactly?" asked Lawton.

"Just a simple barrier. No light can be seen from outside the doors or windows and no sound can be heard. Saves us having to sneak about if they get a bit too close for comfort. They won't even know we're here."

"It hasn't worked though, has it? I can see straight through the glass," said Poom.

"You can see out, but no one can see in. Trust me, we're quite safe," smiled Yello.

***

It was now completely dark outside. Poom and Lawton, despite Yello's assurances, were peering through the windows, aware of every leaf or blade of grass that twitched in the breeze, movements so slight as to go unnoticed by an aged wizard, but not the feline eyes of an alert Gerrowlien. "Here we go," whispered Lawton. "They've arrived, *the hissthaar.*"

"Wonderful!" yelled Yello. "I've been dying to get a closer look at 'em."

"Keep your voice down," urged Poom. "They'll hear you."

"Don't be stupid, they can't hear us, I told you." Yello limped over to the window and started banging against the frame with his staff. "Over here, you ugly bugger. Come on, let's have a look at you," he shouted.

"What are you doing, you mad old fool? Keep the noise down," pleaded Lawton. "If there's more than a dozen, we may be hard pushed to repel them."

But the moment of truth was already upon them. As Lawton turned, he saw one of the hissthaar immediately outside the window. Poom leapt up and grabbed his spear, holding it aloft, ready for a battle.

Yello turned and gave Poom a wry smile. "Watch this," he chuckled. Then, raising his voice again, he began to hurl abuse and insults at the hissthaar that although was not directed at them, made even Lawton and Poom feel uncomfortable. His foul language was colourful to say the least. The creature could neither hear nor see the wizard. It twisted back and forth as if searching for prey but never gave the windows of the inn a second glance.

Yello, although thoroughly enjoying his endless torrent of abuse toward the hissthaar was also fascinated by not only its appearance, but its movement. It was reptilian, of that he was sure, probably descended from a type of giant snake or serpent. It had no legs and slithered along the ground. Its body, almost a yard thick beneath its snake-like hooded head, gradually tapered to a point at the tip of its tail. Its musculature allowed it to stand five-feet-tall but with a further five feet coiled on the ground. It had, obviously over time, developed spindly arms jointed at an elbow halfway and the three fingers on its hands were slightly webbed.

It wore a harness that seemed to be fashioned from a material that resembled leather but was blue, something that Yello had never seen before. Rudimentary weapons were attached to the harness; a hollow cane that could be used as a blowpipe; what appeared to be an axe, just a sharpened or chipped blade of stone lashed to a stick with dried reeds and, further down, a small pouch, made from the same blue leather. The pouch appeared to be steaming, but the steam too was an iridescent blue. Yello grimaced, convinced that whatever the pouch contained was most unpleasant. The apparel, set against the hissthaar's wet, khaki-coloured skin, made its entire surreal appearance even more the stuff of nightmares, but still Yello could not avert his gaze, marvelling at its prehistoric simplicity. He wanted to capture

153

it, to study it, to converse with it in order to understand its needs and desires. As it silently glided away, he came to his senses and yelled at the top of his voice, "And I bet your mother never won any beauty contests either!"

The Gerrowliens were laughing uncontrollably, Lawton snorting and Poom writhing around on the floor in hysterics. Never in their long lives had they witnessed anything as unbelievably insane or amusing. Once they had eventually settled, they began to plan their strategy for the following day. "We will guard you with our lives, Yello, but don't think we're going to accompany you to that awful fortress of yours," said Poom.

"I don't blame you, it's an awfully dismal place. Before all this nonsense with Karrak began, I hadn't been there for about four years," replied Yello.

"But it's where you wizards live, isn't it?" asked Lawton.

"Only the boring ones and of course, the old codgers," he smiled, waiting for any contradiction regarding his age. None was offered.

"So, what's your plan then, stay the night and off at first light?" asked Poom.

"Yes. The only problem is that I won't be able to complete the journey back to Reiggan in one go. I'll need to get a bit closer before the final relocation spell and with those things around..." he replied, gesturing toward the window, "... it'll be difficult to fend them off should they attack, and protect him at the same time," he continued, pointing at the still-comatose Tamor.

"How much closer do you need to get before you can magic him back home?" asked Poom.

"At least another thirty miles," replied Yello.

"Oh, that'll only take a couple of hours then," said Lawton.

Yello laughed. "Maybe for you," he said, "but not for a middle-aged gentleman such as myself."

"Here's a thought. Do you think you could do two of your magic do-dahs in one day if one of them was by yourself?" asked Poom.

"Poom, the spoken word to you is merely an art form with which to be toyed, isn't it? To hear your dulcet tones as they utter such profound understanding is simply breath-taking," said Lawton, sarcastically.

"Shut your face fatty, he knows what I mean."

"And there it is again. Words pouring from your lips as freely as a crystal-clear mountain stream."

"Listen, Lawton, friend or not, if you don't shut your face I swear I'll…"

"I know exactly what you mean, Poom," said Yello, deciding that their banter had lasted long enough, "but what about the king?"

"Easy…" replied Poom, "… Lawton can carry him."

"I don't think so," Yello scoffed. "He's a big man, and if I may say, more than a little overweight. You couldn't carry him thirty miles in two hours."

Lawton raised his eyebrows, a little insulted at Yello's disbelief of his capabilities. Walking across to Tamor, he gently took hold of the front of the king's tunic. In a single, effortless movement he raised the sleeping monarch above his head with one arm.

Poom folded his arms, "You were saying?"

CHAPTER 9

"He's been gone too long, Emnor. Something must have gone wrong."

"What do you suggest we do, Jared, go after him? What if he's not far from here and in our haste we pass him by? No, I'm afraid we must be patient. We'll give him another couple of days and if he hasn't returned then, and only then, we shall set out to find him."

"I think you're all barking mad, if you'll forgive my frankness, Your Highness," said Hannock. "Forget that stupid device you found and let's just go and search for Karrak. I know Yello's a friend of yours, Emnor, but with his wounded leg and the fact that he's at least a million years old, he'll only slow us down if he comes with us anyway."

"You do not hold much faith in wizards do you, Hannock?" asked Emnor.

"In you, I do, and to a point, Jared, but I don't like the idea of a stranger along for the ride," snapped Hannock.

Emnor was sitting with his hands on his knees and the light around him began to dim noticeably as he leaned forward. The air grew cold. A distinct frost appeared across the backs of his hands and the old wizard's breath could be seen leaving his lips as he spoke in a slow, unfamiliar, deep, growling tone, "Tread very carefully, Hannock. Yellodius Tarrock and I have been friends since before you, your father or your grandfather were even thought of. He is the most courageous, honourable, loyal man I have met in over a thousand years. He has fought in battles and destroyed monsters that would haunt your dreams for decades and had wounds that would leave a giant in tears and not complained once. He has saved my life countless times and I his. He is no *stranger*. If he chooses to aid us in our attempt to defeat Karrak, trust me, *we* shall be the passengers."

Hannock, for the first time ever, was fearful of Emnor, and it showed, "Forgive me, I had no right to cast aspersions on a character that is unknown to me. I meant no offence to either you or him."

Emnor sat back, the light returned and the frost on his hands quickly melted and now appeared as beads of water. He rose from his seat, scowled at Jared, and hurried away, staff in hand. Jared glared at Hannock, "Now see what you've done."

Hannock lowered his head, slightly ashamed at having unintentionally insulted Emnor.

A voice spoke quietly from the other side of the courtyard, "Soldier boy, you've outdone yourself this time."

Hannock looked across to see Drake standing, wand in hand, flanked by his three closest friends. They too were holding their wands. "I've warned you before about calling me that, *boy*," he said sternly.

"What makes you think you can warn any one of us, Captain?" asked Harley. "Maybe it's you who should be

158

warned. You use a sword, a crossbow, but mostly your big mouth. Do you think that any of those could possibly defend you against us?"

"Do you think that your standing with House Dunbar has any bearing on events that take place here, in Reiggan?" asked Alex.

"Do you think that you can stand as our guest and under our protection, and be allowed to insult the head of the Administration?" asked Xarran. "That we would not defend the honour of the greatest wizard of his age as you would defend the honour of your beloved Prince Jared?" The four were moving closer, slowly crossing one another as if performing a strangely choreographed, slow-motion dance and asking their questions quietly and methodically.

"Now see here boys, this has gone quite far enough, show a little respect…" but Hannock's defensive stance was interrupted.

"Boys? Is that all you think of us as, *little boys*?" snapped Harley. "Who can be ordered around as easily as your thick-headed soldiers?" he added, twitching his wand and causing Hannock to be thrown to the ground.

Jared stepped forward to shield his friend. "Enough!" he shouted. "We don't want things getting out of hand. Lower your wands and go about your business."

"So, now it's your turn to start barking orders, is it? I don't think so!" Harley slashed the air with his wand causing a firebolt to blast toward Jared. Jared blocked it easily. Holding up one hand, he created a fog that extinguished the firebolt before it reached halfway.

Hannock was horrified. *Had these young wizards gone mad?* Or even worse, *had they changed allegiance? Were*

159

they in support of Karrak? Had he sent them to do his bidding in order to destroy Jared and all who were loyal to him? He attempted to get to his feet but was, once again, felled by the same unseen force that had pushed him to the ground initially. This time, however, he was unsure who was responsible and the effects were slightly different. His limbs were frozen, not cold, but immobilized. He was unable to move and thrashed his head back and forth. He needed to help Jared but, alas, his head was all that he could move as he watched the onslaught with which Jared was having to contend.

Each of the young wizards seemed to take a turn in attacking Jared. Another firebolt flew through the air but was as easily dissipated as the first, followed rapidly by razor sharp shards of ice that were dealt with in much the same way. They were mere feet from Jared as he whirled around, surrounded by green flame, melting the ice instantly.

The attacks were becoming more intense. Two spells at once were now hurtling toward the prince, one a firebolt, the other an ominous-looking green mist that hissed as it travelled through the air. Jared vanished suddenly, appearing a split second later on the other side of the courtyard and beginning an attack of his own. Drake and Xarran were thrown back instantly and slid along the ground as Jared threw up his hands. Harley and Alex were still on the attack but Jared was dealing quite easily with anything that they threw at him.

As the battle continued, Hannock noticed that Jared's body had begun to glow with a pulsating light that seemed to intensify each time he cast a spell or blocked one. If two or more spells were launched at him simultaneously, he would simply disappear again, re-materialising in another part of the courtyard and resuming his own attack. Although there were four of them, it looked to Hannock as if these young wizards were completely outmatched. In unison they grew nearer, each casting a spell of his own choosing. Hannock was expecting Jared to vanish once more, but what he witnessed next astounded him.

Instead of vanishing, Jared actually began to walk toward his enemies, one hand raised in front of him, creating an unseen force-field. The spells struck it and simply fizzled out. It seemed nothing could penetrate it, and throughout, the glow from Jared became brighter. *Would he destroy the youngsters with one counter spell?* Hannock would not allow himself to blink as he watched in awe.

"I think that's enough for today, gentlemen."

The battle stopped abruptly. Hannock recognised Emnor's voice and tried, unsuccessfully, to turn his head far enough to be able see him. "Excellent work, Jared. I think you're almost ready," called Emnor. Jared gave Emnor a wave and nodded his head.

"What!?" shouted Hannock. "What's going on here? Let me up, do you hear me? Let me up!"

Drake hurried across and knelt down in front of him, "Now you *are* going to behave when I release you, aren't you, soldier boy? It was for your own safety. We couldn't run the risk of you getting in the way and ending up frazzled or frozen, could we?"

"Release me now!" shouted Hannock, "I'm going to kick someone's backside from here to Borell once I'm free! Release me."

Eventually, once Jared had managed to calm Hannock down, they gathered with Emnor and the boys to discuss

161

what had happened. "It was a training session, Hannock, that's all," said Jared, smiling.

"Training session or not, you still should have told me," replied Hannock, sternly. "What would have happened if it hadn't gone to plan? I could have run one of the lads through or put a bolt in him."

"Yeah, like that could happen," sniggered Drake.

"Thank you, Drake. Let's not add fuel to any fires, shall we?" advised Emnor.

"I have to be honest, Jared. I've seen the best of the magical world in this place over the last few years, but I've never seen anything that comes close to what you did today. You were brilliant, best I've ever seen." Almost as the last words left his lips, Xarran dropped his head and quickly glanced at Emnor. "Present company excepted, of course," he added.

"Don't worry, Xarran..." chuckled Emnor, "... my pride is not wounded. In fact, I agree with you."

"It wasn't actually me though, was it? It was the Heart. If I hadn't been wearing it, I'd have been as dead as yesterday's fish."

"Of course you wouldn't, Jared... we didn't have fish yesterday," smiled Drake.

Returning his smile, Jared put his arm around Drake's shoulders and gave him a friendly hug, "It's up to you Drake. You can either shut up or I'll cast a spell to pin you to that wall over there for the day." Drake made a gesture of fastening a button on his lip and sat down.

"It's all well and good having a training session, but a real attack wouldn't be like that, would it? Jared knew what spells the lads were going to use, where they were coming from and, of course, that they weren't at full strength."

"Is that what you think, Hannock, that it was all fake?" asked Harley, frowning.

"Of course. You wouldn't really attack a Prince of Borell as an exercise, would you... *would you?* You must be joking. *You mean it was all real!* Jared, what were you thinking? You could have been killed! I bet it was all your idea, wasn't it?" Hannock directed the last question at Emnor, who simply raised his eyebrows.

"Actually, it was my idea," admitted Jared. "It had to be real, Hannock. If I end up facing Karrak, which it seems *is* my fate, I must be able to not only defend myself, but to defeat him, and simply blocking his magic won't do that."

"It's simple. You've all gone mad! Not as mad as Karrak I suppose, but mad nonetheless."

"Nobody has gone mad, Hannock. Can you not see? Jared is our only real hope of defeating Karrak. We may wound him at best, but we could never defeat him alone. Every single one of us would die. And as for the magic not being yours, Jared, you are quite wrong. The Heart of Ziniphar will only bond with the strongest and purest of magical souls. If you were not destined to use it, then yes, I'll admit, you probably would have been killed today, but you weren't, and that's the sign we were looking for. After all, the scroll prophesied it."

"Ah, so you admit that he could have been in danger then? There it is, Jared, now you see the truth. You could have been killed after all!" exclaimed Hannock.

Jared turned to his friend and spoke solemnly, "We've been through a lot recently, Hannock, and I'll admit that there were times when I doubted the prophecy and the tales that went with it. I am a prince. I'm not supposed to be a wizard, at least that's what I thought. Even when Emnor was instructing me as a young man, I thought it was all nonsense. What I felt today, however, was something I was not expecting. It's true, Hannock, all of it. The Elixian Soul; the Heart of Ziniphar; Karrak's rise to power; and the fact that Karrak and I must die in order to end this evil. I have resigned myself to the fact, and you, my dearest friend, must do the same."

Hannock placed his hand on Jared's arm, "Alright," he said quietly, "I'll accept that you're the only one that can defeat him. I'll accept the fact that you're a powerful wizard and I'll accept that we're going to stop the evil that is spreading across these and other lands. But I will not accept that you must die as a consequence. There will be another way and together we *will* find it."

Emnor, despite *his* scepticism of Hannock's *optimism*, felt that it was time to lighten the mood a little, "Are you sure you don't still want to pin Drake to the wall, Jared? Be good for a laugh."

"Oh yeah, great. Forget pin the tail on the donkey, the new game's pin Drake to a wall. I'm so unappreciated. Just remember, we wouldn't have these…" said Drake, waving his wand, "… and you wouldn't have that…" he added, pointing at Emnor's staff "… if it wasn't for me."

"True, true," said Emnor. "But what have you done lately? I mean other than keeping us amused by playing court jester?"

Drake shook his head as they all laughed. "So unappreciated," he repeated.

The day wore on and although he hid it well, Emnor was most concerned by the fact that Yello had still not returned. He made an excuse to the others of having something to attend to in the bowels of Reiggan and wandered into the fortress. Heading through the maze of corridors, Emnor paused occasionally, glancing briefly over his shoulder to ensure that he was not being followed. He rounded yet another corner and, looking up with a start, suddenly found himself confronted by Jared, Hannock and the boys, all with knowing looks on their faces and quite obviously aware of his real intent.

"Off somewhere nice, Emnor?" asked Hannock.

"I told you, I have something to attend to," replied Emnor.

"Wouldn't have anything to do with a certain individual by the name of Tarrock, would it?" asked Jared.

"Not at all, I just have something to take care of downstairs."

"We've all been down there, Emnor. Unless you're going to do a bit of tidying up, there's nothing else down there," said Hannock.

"It is my own personal business. I don't have to explain myself," chuntered Emnor.

"Oh, sorry. If you were on your way to the privy, you should have said. By the way, it's that way," said Hannock, pointing.

"Look here, this is preposterous…"

"Master Emnor," interrupted Harley. "We all have the greatest respect for you, but we also know that you're a devious, stubborn old sod. You were planning on going to look for Yello on your own, leaving us all nice and safe in here. If you want to go, then go, but we're coming with you."

"How dare you," said Emnor, feigning indignation, "I was planning no such thing. I just took a wrong turning, that's all. The privy, this way you say?" He marched away from them, trying to look as innocent as possible.

The assembly followed him at a slower pace, all except one. Alex backed away quietly and slipped down the dark staircase unnoticed. Opening the first door he reached, he entered silently. Sitting on the nearest chair, he began to rub his eyes.

"Going a bit dark again, are they, Brother?" asked the voice.

"Leave me in peace. Please, just go. Why do you insist on haunting me?"

"You know why. I want to be in your company forever, Brother dear. We both know that the only way for that to be accomplished would be for you to die. They don't need you, nobody needs you. Why do you allow your own suffering to go on? A fall from the mountain, a nice short length of rope, or one of your magical fires and you could be at peace. The prince will discover you eventually. Save your suffering and end it all. Once he realises what you are, he'll destroy you anyway, it's only a matter of time, Brother."

Alex jumped to his feet. Grabbing the chair, he hurled it at the ghost. Passing straight through and slightly distorting the apparition, it smashed against the wall, "LEAVE ME ALONE!"

CHAPTER 10

Darooq's mind had become a tormented mess, thoughts racing through it as he paced back and forth until the early hours, in the relative privacy of his own chambers. His frustration grew quickly as he schemed in earnest to facilitate his freedom from Karrak's clutches. He was neither shackled nor incarcerated, but never in his entire life had he felt so utterly vulnerable and helpless. His existence, for that was all his life had become, was completely controlled by Karrak.

In the beginning, Darooq had foolishly underestimated the power that Karrak would possess once he had obtained the Elixian Soul, believing that at any point, he could take everything from the inexperienced prince. Darooq's arrogance and confidence were now things of the past. These emotions had been replaced by fear and loathing. His master was no longer the manic, sadistic individual that he had vowed to follow. Karrak's volatile nature existed no more. He now had a hidden agenda that only seemed to be guided by the wilful destruction of all life, a destruction from which not even his own followers were exempt.

Twice very recently, not only during mid-conversation but mid-sentence, Karrak, for no apparent reason, had glanced at one of his mindless minions and without warning, extinguished their life. He no longer waved his hand, raised an arm or made any gesture that would give warning of his intent, a look and a thought were the only things needed for the shadow lord to end someone's existence.

Darooq had almost convinced himself that his own magic would be enough to subdue Karrak long enough to enable him to take, what appeared to be, the source of the shadow lord's power. The Elixian Soul could be his. His conviction, however, was fleeting. Lasting only until he was, once again, facing his formidable master. After that meeting, Darooq had decided to flee, but his desire for freedom was now overwhelmed by his fear of discovery and retribution. If his escape was unsuccessful, he would undoubtedly be judged by Karrak, an outcome he did not relish, the most favourable result of such judgement being a quick death.

Darooq had used a relocation spell within the walls of Merrsdan, but within a split second of arriving at his predetermined point, Karrak had appeared before him, questioning why he would feel it necessary to use magic. Darooq, somehow, had remained calm and answered that it was merely to save time, but the truth was that it had been a test, the result of which had been exactly as he had predicted. Karrak it seemed, could actually sense the power of magic from any who used it. Surely, there was a limit to Karrak's detection, a boundary one could cross that would be far enough to ensure safety from the shadow lord's reach?

Darooq, now exhausted by the confusion within his own mind, sat heavily on his bunk. Reclining, he folded his arms across his eyes, but sleep would not come to him. His mind ran through endless scenarios until eventually the light of dawn began to show dimly through the small window of his chambers. Resigning himself to yet another sleepless night, he rose and opened the door. He had barely travelled ten yards before the deep, hollow, echoing voice spoke behind him.

"You seem troubled, my friend."

Darooq was now conditioned to such appearances by his lord. There was a time when he would have been startled by such, what he thought to be, a childish action. An action tantamount to sneaking up behind someone and shouting, *boo!* "No, my lord, not at all," replied Darooq, quietly.

Karrak glided from the shadows, the ever-present black mist surrounding him, leaving a vapour trail as he moved forward and stood before Darooq. "You look as if you haven't slept for days. Are you sick? Maybe I could help?"

"I am fine, my lord. I thank you for your concern, it is most kind. But I am sure you must have duties for me to perform."

"And if you drop dead, what then? Return to your quarters, Darooq. I am the only one who decides whether someone should live or die, and today is not your death-day."

Darooq bowed low to Karrak, his eyes drawn to the glow of the Elixian Soul set within his breastplate, a glow that seemed to illuminate the golden embroidered runes of his cloak, "As you wish, my lord." He returned to his quarters, every step watched by Karrak. Lying on his bed, he wept silently. He had to escape.

Karrak stood, staring at the closed door to Darooq's chambers. He tilted his head to one side, the shadow-like features of his face showing no emotion. He looked down and stroked the Elixian Soul, knowing that Darooq, like many others, would give everything to possess it. He drew his robes tightly around him, turned, and silently drifted away.

***

The dragons had taken the lead and the three companions followed willingly. Faylore and Lodren walked but Grubb remained mounted, allowing himself a better view of his surroundings. At first, the entrance to the cavern was much the same as all others, dark and gloomy. All were surprised at how deep they seemed to have travelled without the dimensions of the cave altering in the slightest. Lodren was the first to notice the tiny pinpricks of light in the distance and he pointed to them as he turned to speak to Grubb. "They look like stars," he said.

"Ye don't get stars underground, ye pillock!"

"Well, what are they then, clever clogs?"

"I'm not sure. Could be some sort of metal ore or semi-precious stones, I suppose," replied Grubb.

"You've been down here before, haven't you, Faylore?" asked Lodren. "Have you any idea what they are?"

"Nothing special," she replied. "They're only diamonds."

"Diamonds!" exclaimed Lodren.

"Yes, Lodren. *Diamonds*," repeated Faylore.

"They must be huge! We're still quite a way away from them yet, but they're easily visible."

"What if someone tried to pinch 'em?" asked Grubb.

"What do you mean *pinch?*" asked Faylore.

"He means, steal them," explained Lodren.

"Why would anyone want to steal them?"

"'Cos they're worth a lot of gold," said Grubb.

"So why bother with diamonds? There's plenty of gold on the other side of the mountain," she replied.

"No, Your Majesty. The thing is…" Lodren gave up. "Never mind," he sighed.

The density of the diamonds embedded in the cave walls was increasing. A familiar fungus grew sporadically on the rocky surface. Its bioluminescence glowed dimly, as it was far less dense than they had witnessed before, perhaps the result of many a dragon brushing against the cave walls. However, the little light that it produced was reflected and intensified immensely by the diamonds surrounding the spores and they sparkled like multi-coloured stars on a cloudless summer night.

"How far does this cave go, Faylore?" asked Lodren.

"Quite a way yet, Lodren. When the light appears red, you'll know we're getting close."

"Why will the light turn red?" he asked, scrunching up his face.

"The reflection of the light from the flames, of course," she replied.

As they walked, Lodren could hear a deep throbbing noise. He placed his hand on his chest momentarily believing it to be his own heartbeat, but he was mistaken. He tugged gently at Faylore's sleeve, a habit to which she had become accustomed. She looked down at him.

"Faylore," he said slowly. "Can you hear that throbbing noise?"

"Of course, I can. It is the merrent barndull."

"*What's that*?" he asked, quietly.

"The mountain's breath."

"Mountains don't breathe," he said.

"Do they not?" asked Faylore.

"You mean, the mountain's alive?"

"It is, and if it were not, neither would the dragons be."

Lodren knew when he was beaten. He also knew when to stop asking questions. "Ooh look!" he said suddenly. "I think the light's looking a bit red down there."

***

"How long 'ave we been down 'ere now? Been so long since I lived in a cavern, I tend to lose track of time."

"What's wrong, Grubb, missing your old home? Not enjoying the company of dragons?" asked Faylore.

"I'm not complaining. Big as they are, these dragons, they're very light on their feet so it's surprisingly quiet… and it's nice and dry. Remember that rain? I was soaked to the skin. My bum was that wet when I was sitting on Buster that…"

"GRUBB!" exclaimed Lodren. "You don't use words like that in front of Faylore. How many more times? She's a queen."

"She might be a queen, but we've all got one. And for your information, I could have said ar…"

"Don't you dare, Grubb!" shouted Lodren. "Don't you dare or I'll whack you with my hammer… I'm not kidding."

"Alright! Calm down. I was just saying, it's nice not to be soakin' wet. You really are a touchy sod at times, Lodren."

"And don't say that either," said Lodren, pointing at Grubb. "As a matter of fact, if you can't conduct yourself properly, don't say anything at all."

"S'cuse me for breathin'," mumbled Grubb.

"When are we leaving, Your Majesty?" asked Lodren, rather over-emphasising his polite tone.

Faylore smiled at him and then at Grubb. They were the most unusual pairing and although Grubb could be a little crass and Lodren sometimes behaved like a mother hen, there was an unmistakeable synergy between them. She let out a little laugh before she answered, "Are you in a hurry to leave?"

"Oh no, quite the opposite. I'd stay here forever if they let me," replied Lodren.

"If you were to ask them, Lodren, they would allow it. Or would you prefer that I ask?"

"Neither, thank you. If we didn't have all the problems with stopping Karrak, I'd love to stay for a while. All I'm suggesting is that maybe we should be moving out soon, Jared and the others might need us."

"I need to consult Thelwynn and the others before we can leave. And then there's the eggs to consider," said Faylore.

"Eggs?" asked Lodren, a little confused. "Where am I going to find fresh eggs?"

"She means the dragon eggs, you pillock!" mumbled Grubb.

"I can't do that!" exclaimed Lodren. "I can't cook dragon eggs. Even if we weren't here, I could never cook a dragon egg!"

"Nobody wants you to cook dragon eggs, you berk! Just listen to Faylore and stop interruptin'," said Grubb with a sigh.

Lodren scratched his head. Turning to Faylore, he pushed his head forward and raised his eyebrows, eager for an explanation.

"We have to wait for the eggs that the dragons have laid to be halfway through their development, only then will the dragons open the Fenn Immar."

"And what's the Fenn Immar?" asked Lodren, calmly.

"A stream of fiery rock in which they place the eggs to transport them," replied Faylore.

"Transport them to where?" asked Lodren.

"The borders of my homeland," replied Faylore.

"And why would they want to do that? Surely, they're better here, where they can look after them."

"What does it matter, you annoying Nibby? They just do. Can't you just take that as an answer?"

Lodren gave Grubb a look of disdain, "I'm just interested, that's all. I don't need to know I'll admit, but I would *like* to know."

"It's a wonder your nose hasn't been cut off before now, pokin' it in other people's business. If it was bigger, you probably would've lost it by now."

"It's alright, Grubb. An inquisitive nature is harmless when knowledge is sought for no ill purpose," said Faylore.

Lodren gave a big grin and jokingly poked his tongue out at Grubb.

"They have to move the eggs to allow them a cooler temperature," continued Faylore. "The dragon fire is far too hot for the poor little things."

"So why not just put them into the ice outside?" asked Lodren.

"That would be just as bad I'm afraid, far too cold," replied Faylore.

"It seems as if they're very fragile. Surprising really when you look at how big and tough the parents are," said Lodren.

"Indeed," said Faylore. "That is why we Thedarians help them. They can't keep travelling backwards and forwards to check that the eggs are safe, they might be noticed. We protect the eggs until they begin to hatch. When a shell begins to crack, we send it home so that its parents can be there at the birth."

Lodren leaned forward and whispered, "But how do they know which egg is which? I mean, all eggs look the same, don't they?"

"Oh, not at all. If parents have more than one child they can recognise which is which, can they not?" asked Faylore.

"Well yes, I suppose so, but we're talking about eggs, not people," said Lodren.

"But you must understand Lodren that to a dragon, no two eggs look the same. Those two eggs actually look as different to a dragon as you and I do to Grubb."

"That's fascinating!" said Lodren. "I'll never look at eggs the same way again. To think of all the chicken and duck eggs I've cooked over the years, and they all looked the same to me."

"That's 'cause they were, ye prat! It's only dragon eggs that are different. Weren't ye listenin'?" sighed Grubb.

"That's easy for you to say!" exclaimed Lodren. "They're not your babies. What about all the mommy birds? I bet the eggs don't all look the same to them."

Grubb pretended to bite his fist in order to contain himself.

"I think we're straying a little from the important part of this conversation, Lodren..." said Faylore, once again acting as mediator, "... the subject of how we intend to reach Thedar."

"Yes, sorry, Your Majesty, please continue. Got a little carried away I think."

177

Grubb began to laugh, "Oh, you're going to get carried away alright, just you wait and see. Carried away faster than you've ever been carried before, and much warmer too."

"What do you mean *faster* and *warmer*? Faylore, what's he talking about? Ooh, are the dragons going to take us on their backs? That would be faster."

"But it wouldn't be very warm, would it? Flying through the clouds above a land covered with ice?"

Lodren scowled at Grubb, "It was only a guess," he said.

"Well, it wasn't a very good one," replied Grubb.

"Come with me, Lodren," said Faylore quietly, a mischievous twinkle in her eye. "There's something I want you to see." She began to stroll away and Lodren hurried to her side, sliding his arm under hers as if he was terrified that she would attempt to escape.

"What is it, Faylore? What are we going to see?" he asked.

"If I tell you, it will spoil the surprise. Be patient for a few minutes," she replied. "Trust me, it's worth the wait."

They wandered through the brightly-lit caves for what, to Lodren at least, seemed an age. His height was proving to be a bit of a disadvantage. Occasionally, a dragon would cross their path and completely obscure the way ahead, causing Lodren to duck or stand on tiptoes in order to see either under or over the obstruction. Not once did it cross his mind that dragons were far too honest to hide anything, and far too big. A small space to one of them was a medium-sized field. It had taken no more than ten minutes for them to near the spectacle that Faylore had intended to show the impatient little Nibby. Suddenly, he stopped. "What's that noise?" he asked. In the distance, there was a faint gurgling sound.

"Come along…" said Faylore, "… nearly there."

Their pace quickened and the noise grew louder, resembling the sound of rocks being ground together in a giant machine. Lodren noticed that there were far more dragons here than he had seen together before, at least a dozen in fact. Their demeanour was also different. Closer to the entrance they seemed very relaxed, almost lethargic. Here they seemed far more purposeful and focussed on whatever they were doing. Exactly what that was, Lodren was yet to discover. As usual, it was only a matter of seconds before Lodren's eyes glazed over and the huge silly grin appeared on his face as he watched the numerous wyrms before him.

Faylore nudged his shoulder gently and pointed at one of the dragons. "Watch what she does now," she whispered.

When they had first encountered the lone dragon, it had its back to them and for a brief moment, Lodren could have sworn that it was *singing*. He could hear no words, only a distant melodious cooing. The dragon began to turn slowly as it detected their presence, and only then did Lodren realise why this particular behemoth was behaving in such a peculiar manner. Cradled within its huge, clawed hands, was a freshly-laid egg. Lodren let out a huge sigh and was inexplicably drawn toward, what he assumed to be, the proud mother. To witness a Nibby five-feet-tall approach a dragon thirty-feet-tall that was holding one of its young would, to anyone else, sound like the beginning of a tale that would not end well. Many times, Faylore had held a dragon egg as its mother looked on and she now watched Lodren in a similar way. As Lodren stood at the dragon's feet, it actually reached down to him, proudly displaying her egg.

Lodren reached out and stroked it gently. "We'll all be seeing you very soon," he whispered.

The dragon walked away and Lodren followed, eager to see where her egg was to be put. As he walked, smoke began to drift across his path, thickening with each pace and burning his eyes.

"That's far enough, Lodren, if you go much further, we'll be sweeping up your ashes," called Faylore.

"Sorry!" exclaimed the startled Lodren, suddenly coming out of his trance. "Didn't realise I'd gone this far. Where is this anyway?" he asked, looking around him.

"You were headed for the Fenn Immar," replied Faylore.

"I thought that was where we were supposed to be going."

"Not yet," replied Faylore, "and definitely not without some scales and an eggshell."

Lodren had no idea what Faylore meant by this, and undeterred, resumed his line of questioning, *"Where's she taking her egg? Can we see? Are there any baby dragons here?"*

Faylore, realising that there was no way the Nibby could be fobbed off, grabbed the shoulder of his tunic and marched him toward a natural crack in the cave wall, a rough incline that led upwards, parallel with the Fenn Immar. "You can see all you need to from up here, Lodren," she assured him.

As they climbed, the scene with which they were greeted was awesome. The molten river seemed endless, skirted on both sides by dragons of all colours and sizes, each holding an egg or attending to one that they had already placed in the magma. The Fenn Immar was the fiery causeway on which the eggs would travel, the greatest trust being placed in the hands of the Thedarians, who would nurture them on behalf of the dragons until they were almost due to hatch. Lodren tried his best to not even blink as he looked on in wonder, but a thought crept into his mind as he studied the scene below. Dragons existed in this environment, heat was not an issue but, a Thedarian, a Vikkery, a Nibby and a pony did not. *How were they expected to survive a journey across this river of fire?*

Advising Lodren to mind his step, Faylore left in search of Thelwynn. The Nibby stood in awe of the scene below him and was about to begin his descent when he noticed something that seemed much further away than the cave could reach, but glowed far brighter than any of the jewels embedded within its walls. Lodren held up his hand, physically plotting a course toward the mystery as he waggled his finger in mid-air. He headed down the rough slope, a fervour in his inquisitive Nibby-nature renewed by his mysterious discovery. He weaved between dragon's legs as they crossed his path.

Apologising profusely, he would bow hurriedly before spinning around and resuming his course, only to repeat his actions just a few yards further on. He could now feel the ever-present throbbing in his chest far more intensely than he had so far, and it was obvious to him that his new-found interest had something to do with it. Suddenly, he was facing a tunnel. How he had not seen it before was a mystery to him, when he tried to look down it, the brilliance of the light in the distance made it impossible for him to keep his eyes open for more than half a second. He held his hand up in front of him to shield his gaze from the light's intensity.

"Hypnotic, isn't it?" asked the voice.

Lodren immediately felt an overwhelming sense of contentment. No thought troubled his mind as he stood smiling dreamily down the tunnel. He was no longer covering his eyes, but stared quite openly into the comforting light before him.

"I think that's long enough for one so small," came the voice once again.

Lodren was bathed in shade by the immense figure standing before him. It was Thelwynn.

"Terribly sorry, Thelwynn," chirped Lodren. "Didn't see you there. Was there something I can help you with?"

Leading the way, Thelwynn guided Lodren back to Faylore, the smile on the Nibby's face immoveable.

Seeing Lodren, Faylore turned her inquisitive gaze toward Thelwynn.

"Merrent Barndull," he whispered.

"Ah!" said Faylore, nodding knowingly.

CHAPTER 11

Yello waved his staff across the doorway. Dawn was breaking and neither of the Gerrowliens had seen nor heard any more of the hissthaar. Lawton had insisted on taking first watch, switching with Poom in the early hours and allowing the old wizard to sleep soundly throughout the entire night.

"You should have roused me. I was more than prepared to take my turn," Yello protested.

"What was the point, old chap? After all, your lot are bad enough during the day, what would you hope to see at night?" asked Lawton.

"That's not the point and you know it."

"Listen, Yello," said Poom, reassuringly. "There was a point, that point being that it would be *pointless* you staying awake because you wouldn't be able to see anything at night. It's morning, we're all okay, thanks to your magic and now it's time to leave. You did your bit, and we did ours."

Lawton and Yello looked at one another. Yello opened his mouth, but before he had time to speak Lawton shook his head vigorously, closed his eyes and held his hands out in front of him. "*Don't…*" he urged, "… just… *don't.*"

Yello shrugged his shoulders and chuckled. Stepping into the cool morning air, he stretched himself and gave a loud yawn. "How shall we do this?" he asked. "Should I go on ahead and you catch up, or the other way around?"

"I think it best that you go on ahead, Yello. Don't you agree, Poom?"

"Couldn't care less to be honest, just make a decision..." called Poom, "... and do hurry up, we haven't got all day."

Yello looked at Lawton and smiled. "See you later then," he said and, tapping his staff on the ground three times for effect, vanished.

"Right, he's gone. Now what are you really going to do with that?" asked Poom, pointing at Tamor.

"What do you mean, *what am I going to do with it*, I mean, him?" replied Lawton.

"Well, surely you're not going to follow that old loony for the next two hours carrying a dead king on your shoulder?"

"Yello is not a loony. He is a little eccentric, I'll give you that, but he's not mad. Furthermore, old pal of mine, King Tamor is *not* dead."

"He's doing a bloody good impression of it then. He hasn't so much as twitched since yesterday. Look, easiest thing, we dump old nearly-dead in the river, catch up with the world's wobbliest wizard and tell him we lost the king. We'll just say we must have dropped him somewhere along the way and it would be pointless to go back for him as he'd probably be dead after being left on his own."

"Or better still, Poom, old friend, we could tell him that the king suddenly got better and ran off into the forest, heading for home," suggested Lawton, sarcastically.

"I take it you don't like my idea then?" snorted Poom, indignantly.

"I've heard better... from lunatics!" exclaimed Lawton.

"In that case perhaps we should make a start. We don't want to keep old-wobbly waiting, do we?"

"Do not make the mistake of letting him hear you call him that, Poom. I dread to think what he might turn you in to, something intelligent perhaps."

Poom began to laugh, "I don't think that would be much fun do..." His laughter ceased abruptly as the penny dropped and he scowled at Lawton. Snatching up his spear, he bolted forward. Lawton slung the unconscious king gently over his shoulder and a few seconds later, he too sprinted away leaving the devastated Cheadleford behind.

The Gerrowliens were roughly halfway to their meeting point with Yello. Poom had travelled ahead, acting as scout and ready to alert Lawton of any obstructions or dangers. He was now crouched in a patch of tall grass, waving his arms frantically, indicating that Lawton should approach with stealth. Lawton crept across the ground, his chest and stomach mere millimetres above the earth as he silently joined his friend. Poom pointed at his own eyes, instructing Lawton to look, and then signalled toward a ridge in the distance. Lawton studied the spot that Poom had indicated and immediately saw the band of hissthaar, but he was completely confused by the fact that they were out in broad daylight. Lawton heard a voice. It was not the hissing, high-pitched voice of a hissthaar but a deep eloquent voice that, by the tone, was used to giving orders.

"My friends. As you can see, we mean you no harm. Take me to your chief, your leader. If you do not and he discovers what opportunities have passed him by, he may punish you, and I'm sure you don't want that."

Poom crept closer in an attempt to get a look at the hidden stranger. The hissthaar swayed from side to side, making it difficult for Poom to see. He could see its legs, which ruled it out as being from another hissthaar tribe. Luminous green skin that could mean any one of a dozen races, the voice spoke again, "My name is Ramah…"

Poom backed away. Re-joining Lawton, the two began to whisper.

"Well?" asked Lawton.

"I know *who* it is, I just don't know *what* it is," Poom replied.

"I don't follow," said the puzzled Lawton.

"He actually introduced himself to them," Poom continued. "Said his name's Ramah, but I couldn't get a clear look at his face. I could only see his legs. Green slimy skin, but it's not a snake like the hissthaar. Shall we just go and kill them all? We can always figure out what they are later."

"On any other day, Poom, old friend, we'd already be in the thick of battle, but we have given our word, and that is something we must always keep. We have to get King Tamor safely to the meeting point with Yello. It's for Jared, remember? Even *you* can't deny the fact that you like *him*."

"Do you realise how difficult it is to be as nice as me? It's a curse, you know, Lawton, everyone looking up to you, knowing that they'd be lost without you."

"And do you realise what a shame it is that we Gerrowliens don't like water? If we did, Poom, we could move to the coast and you could be worshipped by the villagers out there as well."

"I'm a legendary warrior who uses a spear, how could I be of any use in water?"

"They could use your fat head as a flotation device!" replied Lawton, still focussing on the ridge.

They crept away, Lawton gently patting Tamor's cheek over his shoulder. "Let's get you back to your son, old man," he mouthed. After what they believed to be a safe distance, they once more began to sprint and before long were re-united with Yello.

"You chaps really can get a wiggle on, can't you? When you don't have an old wizard slowing you down, that is," he called as they approached.

"*Get a wiggle on*?" asked Poom, having never heard the phrase before.

"I think he means we're fast," suggested Lawton, covering his mouth with the back of his hand.

"Well, if that's his idea of a compliment, he can keep it," snorted Poom.

"No problems then?" asked Yello.

"Not as such…" replied Lawton, "… but I need to ask you a question. Have you ever come across the name *Ramah* before?"

187

Yello shook his head, wracking his brains for any distant memory or overheard conversation, "No, doesn't ring any bells I'm afraid. Why, should I have heard of him?"

Lawton and Poom informed Yello of their brief encounter with the hissthaar and the mysterious being who, it seemed, was attempting to befriend them.

"How very odd," said Yello. "The hissthaar never ally with anyone. I'll speak with Emnor, see if *he* knows of our mystery man. When I say man, I obviously mean… oh never mind, you know what I mean."

"I wouldn't bother if I were you. Whoever he is will be dead by the time you come back. *If* you come back here that is," said Poom, calmly.

"Why? Did you see something? Were they about to be attacked?" asked Yello, suddenly intrigued.

"No, but they will be when we get back there," laughed Lawton.

"I don't think that would be wise, my friends. Maybe you could wait a while until I have consulted with Emnor, just a couple of hours. It wouldn't do to draw too much attention to ourselves unnecessarily."

"There won't be any of them left alive to gossip about it, Yello, on that you have my word," said Lawton, showing his claws.

"Of that I have no doubt, my dear sir. However, what if others are awaiting their arrival? If they are missed, a small war band could soon be replaced with an entire tribe, searching for their whereabouts."

"What is this world coming to!" exclaimed Poom. "We're not even allowed to kill the nasty ones for fear of

188

bringing even more. It's ridiculous. I say we go back, kill them as we planned, then kill the ones that come looking for them as well, problem solved."

"Mmm…" said Lawton, "… and if there's a couple of hundred? We could escape easily, but if Emnor or the companions have to come through here again, it's going to make it terribly difficult for them."

Poom drove his spear into the ground. "I might as well trade this in for a fishing rod," he grumbled.

"So, my idea of moving to the coast sounding appealing, is it?" asked Lawton with a big grin.

Yello, *again*, stepped between them, "Can we be serious for a moment? How's King Tamor doing?"

Lawton, once again, patted Tamor's cheek. "Sleeping like a baby," he replied.

Leaning forward, Yello folded Tamor's arms across his chest and pulled his majestic robes tight about his shoulders. "Stay here you two, I shan't be long." Placing the palm of his hand on the king's forehead, he quietly chanted a few words and vanished.

***

He appeared moments later in the main courtyard of Reiggan Fortress. The air around him pulsed, the background rippling like the surface of a pond that had been disturbed by a discarded pebble. Absent for five days and unable to get word to his colleagues in all that time, he was still a little surprised when a ball of flame flew past his head within seconds of his arrival. "It's me, you blasted fools!" he bellowed. Three wands disappeared beneath robes. The culprit, it seemed, wished to remain anonymous. Yello immediately turned away to check on Tamor.

"Tarrock old boy, where have you been? Who's that you've got there? Come on man, speak up," urged Emnor.

"Do be quiet, Emmy," sighed the exhausted Yello. "One thing at a time. Fetch Jared. *Now.*"

Harley, realising that this was no normal request, turned and ran as fast as he could to fetch the prince. "Yello's back, he wants to see you," he panted as he barged into Jared's quarters.

"Alright Harley, calm down. What does he want me for?" asked Jared, rising quickly.

"No idea, but he's brought someone back with him," replied Harley.

"Who?" asked Jared.

"Not a clue, sorry, but whoever he is, he's out cold and floating in mid-air."

Jared shot a look at Hannock, who shrugged his shoulders, then instinctively grabbed his sword and followed the prince.

Jared marched briskly into the courtyard. Glancing across, he could see the body floating and at first was simply intrigued by it, but his intrigue turned to horror as he recognised his father's face. Running to his side, he grabbed Tamor's hand. "Father, what happened to you? *Father!*" he called. It was pointless.

Yello took Jared's arm and steered him away slightly, "He cannot hear you, Jared."

"Why? What has happened to him? Will he live?" pleaded the prince.

"Physically, he is unharmed. Mentally, however, I am unsure. He seems tormented, as if in a perpetual nightmare. Emnor and I shall endeavour to recover his mind, but I am afraid there is little hope that he will again be the man he once was."

"Who did this, Yello? Was it Karrak?" growled Jared.

"I suspect it was, but I have no proof. There was no one left in Borell to question. Soldiers, courtiers, servants, all had disappeared without trace. Not even the slightest damage to any buildings and no bodies of any who may have been murdered."

"He emptied the entire kingdom? Thousands of people just... gone. Why would he want so many prisoners... unless?"

"Unless what, Jared?" asked Emnor.

"Could they have faced the same fate as the villagers in Cheadleford? Could he have turned them all into beasts?"

"Impossible!" scoffed Emnor. "Far too many for a start. He may have somehow enslaved them, but transforming them would serve no purpose, even to a mind as twisted as his."

"He's using them as slave labour to repair Merrsdan. He must have damaged it far worse than he had intended, it's obvious now I come to think of it," said Yello slowly, a strange disbelief in his voice.

191

"I don't care what he's using them for, we've got to stop him!" roared Jared. "We need to find him now, today, and when we do, I'll sever his head from his neck for this. He has done harm to the king and that is blatant treason, the sentence for which is death!"

King Tamor was taken to a secluded room within Reiggan and Alex quickly volunteered to keep an eye on him, lest he wake. Yello assured him that this wouldn't happen, tapping his hand against his bag as if trying to tell Alex something. Alex was far too naïve to realise what that was and even missed the point when Yello winked at him.

"Were you at least successful in finding one of Karrak's possessions, Yello?" asked Jared.

"I'm not entirely sure. I was expecting to encounter someone who could guide me in Borell, but as it was deserted, I could only hazard a guess, I'm afraid." Reaching into his bag, Yello produced the piece of cloth he suspected of being used to gag Karrak. "I thought perhaps this might be of some use."

Jared snatched it from his hand. "You had an entire castle full of belongings and you bring this!" he snapped, "An old piece of rag. How in the name of thunder did you actually come to the conclusion that a scrap of cloth would somehow lead us to my brother?"

"As I said…" began Yello, his tone becoming much sterner, "… I had no idea which chambers were Karrak's or yours or your jelly-brained father's, so don't start bellowing at me, boy. Have I spent time in your castle in the past? *No*. Have I even met a Borellian before being introduced to you? *No*. So how would I have the slightest idea of where to begin searching said entire castle for a random object belonging to someone I've never met? Nice to know you have such gratitude for my endeavours, Your Highness. Now, prince or no prince, I suggest you back off before *I* do something *you'll* regret. Your king would be dead by now, if not for me. I shall, however, not take all the credit. Our friends, the Gerrowliens, also played a part in extricating your father from peril."

Although his main intent was to inform his friends of the events that had taken place, Yello made no attempt to veil his threat toward Jared. His fatigue had made him a little more irascible than he realised and before he could continue with his insults or threats Emnor, wanting to save Yello from himself, spoke quickly, "Do you mean Poom and Lawton?"

Yello smiled. "The very same," he replied, shaking his head. "God, they're infuriating at times."

"What were they doing in Borell?" asked Emnor, slightly confused.

"They weren't in Borell. I met up with them in Cheadleford on the way back. And before you ask, they were investigating rumours of large groups of hissthaar returning to the area."

"Hang on," said Hannock, "I thought they'd all scarpered. Why would they return when Jendilomin and the forest nymphs were still around?"

"That's the problem, they're not, they've disappeared. Poom and Lawton have searched high and low, but can find no trace of them. No signs of battle or anything untoward, they're just… gone," replied Yello, holding up his hands.

"Have Poom and Lawton gone back to Shaleford Forest now?" asked Harley, suddenly.

"No, not yet. They're waiting for my go-ahead actually," replied Yello.

"They're waiting for *you* to tell them it's alright for them to go home?" asked Harley, screwing up his face in confusion.

"Not exactly. They're waiting for me to tell them whether or not to attack a band of hissthaar, well, *them* and a new mystery… 'man'. Well, it may not be a man."

"We could do with a little more clarity, Yello, old chap. Is it a man or not?" asked Emnor.

"Not unless you know any men who have luminous green legs. Poom was spying on them and couldn't get a look at the creature's face, but he did overhear his name. What was it now?" Yello began gently tapping his brow with his fingertips. "Roger? No, that wasn't it. Remus? No, not that either. Ramah!" he suddenly exclaimed. "That was it, Ramah. Ring any bells with anyone?"

"Not the name, no, but the green skin could mean… Hannock, do you remember those things that ambushed us just before we met Faylore for the first time?" asked Jared. "The ones that attacked the local villages? The ones father almost wiped out, the Dergon?"

"Of course, I remember them," replied Hannock. "But King Tamor said there were only a handful left. Surely, they could never pose a threat again?"

"Not alone, no, but if they had allies… And father did say that they had a leader, and was *convinced* that that leader was not amongst the bodies they cremated."

"If he's there and he has other Dergon with him, Poom and Lawton may be biting off more than they can chew. If they have to face the hissthaar as well, I doubt they'll survive. We need to get them out of there, fast." Turning to Emnor, Jared began giving orders. Ordinarily, no wizard would have accepted an order given by any other than a member of the Administration, but this was the beginning of a new age. There was the uncertainty as to whether the present company was indeed the sum of the wizarding world, and if this was the case, all friendships now had to be cherished far more than they had been for countless millennia.

"Take the boys, Emnor, and bring the Gerrowliens back here. Yello, you should rest, but not until you have given Emnor the precise location in which you left our friends. Boys, if you should encounter either the Dergon or the hissthaar, lay low and let them pass. Do not, under any circumstances, engage them. Is that clear?" The young men nodded in understanding. "Hannock, lay out weapons in case any of our enemies manage to get in here, we don't know for sure if they have a mage, necromancer, sorcerer or the like in tow. I know it's unlikely, but we shall not be caught off guard, let's move."

There was suddenly a lot of hustle and bustle as each member of the 'rescue party' took their positions. After a few minutes, Emnor and the boys stood in a circle, watched by Yello, Jared and Hannock. Emnor nodded toward them and as they became transparent, Hannock glimpsed Drake, who winked at him, looked at Jared whilst shaking his head and mouthed, *what a prat*, before disappearing completely.

Moments later they appeared where they had been directed by Yello, but the Gerrowliens, regrettably, were nowhere to be seen. Emnor steered the boys toward the nearest dense shrubs and gestured for them to crouch down.

"Those bloody Gerrowliens can't keep still for a minute, can they!" exclaimed Drake.

"They can't be far away. Probably just camouflaged somewhere," said Emnor.

"Or in the middle of a punch-up with anything that has green skin," suggested Harley.

"Yello asked them to wait until he returned. He wasn't with us more than fifteen minutes. Where could they have gone?" wondered Emnor aloud.

"Have you seen the speed they travel at, Master Emnor?" asked Xarran. "They can cover miles in fifteen minutes."

"Or they could be dead and in a hissthaar's stomach," suggested Alex.

"That's quite enough of that, Alex. They are not dead, they're simply hidden. So well hidden that they don't know we're here. Stay where you are, I'm going to look for them."

"Master Emnor, you can't go alone. Take one of us with you, it'll be safer with two."

"And more noticeable. No, I'll go alone. Don't worry Drake, I'll be back in a few minutes." Without another word, Emnor crept away.

"I'm getting sick of this," hissed Drake. "That silly old sod's going to get himself killed and it'll be our fault. You do realise that, don't you?"

"It is becoming a bit of a theme, isn't it?" said Xarran. "They just see us as a bunch of little kids. What do you think, Drake, time to teach the teacher a lesson?" he asked, grinning.

"If you do this, we all have to do it. Alex, what do you think?" asked Harley.

Alex looked across at Harley, but his eyes were easily drawn away from his friend's face to the one that was directly behind him. Alex was tired, completely exhausted. No one could see or hear what he saw, the ghost of his half-brother, mocking him and calling him a coward. "I'm in," he replied. "Let's go."

They edged through the bushes as silently as was possible, pausing occasionally to take in their surroundings and hoping to catch a glimpse of a familiar face or recognise the sound of a voice. Each time, however, they were disheartened, as neither scenario presented itself. They had now lost all track of time. Unsure of themselves, they quickened their pace slightly, forgetting that stealth was actually their greatest ally as they endeavoured to locate their friends. Drake, as always the adventurer, was leading the procession and seemed quite sure of his route when suddenly, stepping over a few fallen branches, he lost his footing and plunged down a shallow gorge that was hidden by the undergrowth. His friends gasped in horror as he disappeared. Rushing to the point where he had fallen, they could see him below, sitting on the ground with his elbows on his knees, looking totally embarrassed.

"Did you enjoy that?" asked Xarran, in a whisper.

"Very nice, thank you," hissed Drake. "Why don't you give it a try?"

The four stifled their laughter, but their amusement was cut short as they heard twigs snapping nearby, snapping as if they were being trodden on. Drake shuffled to the side and hid beneath the shrubs as, likewise, his friends above sought shelter. As they watched, two figures appeared. Huge muscular figures with luminous green skin that blended into the lush background. So this was what a Dergon looked like.

Eight-foot-tall, musculature that could crush a mule and a face that looked as if the mule had won the first round. The young wizards were out of options. They were in a direct line with the Dergon's route and there was no way that they could move without being discovered. *Should they attack and destroy this formidable foe without giving them the slightest chance to retaliate?* The Dergon, thankfully, paused and the four wizards could see that there were no hissthaar with them. Drake's eyes moved upward. *What had he seen?* Was there a hint of orange in the trees above the Dergon? Drake smiled... it was Poom.

Amazingly, Poom was actually doing the splits between two trees and was holding his spear with two hands, its point directly above one of the green slimy heads. Poom raised his spear and was about to plunge it through the Dergon's skull when a hand wrapped around his wrist from above. If it had been Lawton's hand, it would have been no surprise, but it was Emnor's. The old wizard was floating, cross-legged in mid-air, holding Poom by the wrist and wagging his finger in order to deter the Gerrowlien from his actions. The strangest part of the entire scene was that the Dergon were completely unaware of what was happening directly above them. Emnor, still looking directly into Poom's eyes, pointed out Drake and the others, causing Poom to nod his head and give the 'thumbs-up'.

"This is hopeless, Korbah. Those serpents are the stupidest race I have ever encountered. All they want to do is kill and eat. They have no ambition, I mean, how can one bribe or coerce a being that has no ambition?" Korbah remained silent, as usual. "A few score of them would be enough. Is it too much to want revenge on the sorcerer who killed so many of our kin? A few score to distract Karrak long enough for me to get in close with a blade. It's not a lot to ask for."

"I know, but they said it ain't none o' their business. Why should they let their people die for you to get your own back? They've got a point, you know, chief."

"I know, Korbah… I know."

This was something unexpected, and every wizard was taken aback by the statement of the Dergon chief. Emnor closed his eyes and did something he had never revealed he was capable of; he used telepathy, he actually spoke to his students with his mind. "We're going to capture these two," he said. "Wait until they are near enough and grab them, you only have to hold them for a few seconds whilst you transport them back to Reiggan. Two pairs grab a Dergon each, I'll bring the Gerrowliens."

Not allowing any of the party time to think, he gave his order, "We move on three. Ready, one, two…"

CHAPTER 12

"Now let's just go over this again, just to make sure I'm not missing anything," began Lodren, seeming quite flustered. "You're suggesting that we travel on a molten lava river, in an eggshell? An eggshell lined with dragon scales so that we're not roasted alive."

"Exactly," replied Faylore.

"We're going to be burnt to a crisp," babbled the panic-stricken Nibby. "We'll be nothing but ashes. We'll look worse than my mother's cooking."

"Lodren, I have done this before, so have many of my kin. It is quite safe, the scales protect you from the heat. You won't even get warm," she assured him.

"I bet I won't, I won't have time. One minute I'll be Lodren the Nibby and the next I'll be potash for the garden. I'm sorry, Your Majesty, I just don't like it, not one bit. I know it's going to go horribly wrong."

"Will ye stop bein' such a big scaredy cat, Lodren. Ye faced a zingaard for goodness sake and squashed it with your hammer. Ye weren't scared then," said Grubb.

"The zingaard wasn't trying to set me on fire. He only wanted to eat me."

"Oh, that's perfectly alright then! No need to be afraid if it's only a monster trying to eat ye. Can ye hear yerself? I think you've lost the plot, me friend."

"You won't be saying that when the flames are licking around your bits, Grubb. You'll be wondering why you didn't listen to me. In fact, your last thoughts could be…"

There was a faint, familiar, whistling sound. Lodren's lips continued to move. However, the words he had intended to speak ceased to leave them. Grubb noticed the small green dart that now protruded from Lodren's neck. It seemed that Faylore, despite her new tolerance of people's emotions, still would not permit hysterical ravings from them. Lodren's eyes glazed over as a dopey look swept across his face. Swaying momentarily, he fell slowly backwards to be caught gently by the four arms of Wilf, who had appeared suddenly, lifting the sleeping Nibby as lovingly and easily as a parent would their child. Wilf began to laugh, a deep laugh that boomed in his chest. Seeing Grubb smile, to some, was disturbing enough, but to hear Wilf laugh was positively spine-chilling.

"Have you quite finished!?" snapped Faylore.

Wilf stopped laughing and shrugged his shoulders, "What? I never said a word."

"Don't act innocent with me, Grubb." Faylore refused to refer to Grubb's alter-ego as Wilf. "You know that poor Lodren was a little nervous but instead of trying to help, you mocked him."

Wilf lowered his head and, in an attempt to apologise, started stroking Lodren's brow.

"Now put him into the eggshell, and make sure those scales are arranged properly."

Wilf lowered Lodren into the eggshell. No longer needing four arms or superior strength, his body shivered and shrank until he was back to being Grubb. "I weren't mocking him, Faylore, just tryin' to get his dander up. You know, tryin' to make him a bit braver is all. He's one of the bravest fellas' I know. To be honest, I felt that if I mollycoddled him, 'e would've been insulted. He's one o' my best friends... I'd never mock 'im." Grubb's speech got quieter as his voice tailed off. He had found the scene amusing but he was also sincere about his feelings toward his friend.

"Well, in that case," said Faylore as she knelt down beside the Vikkery, "we'd both better make sure that these scales are arranged properly."

There was the slight detail of Buster to contend with, but Faylore soon took care of, what she saw as, a minor problem. She removed her blowpipe and dart and positioned herself behind Grubb's beloved pony. "Don't worry," she assured him. "He won't feel a thing."

They heard the padding footsteps of a dragon approaching from behind them and turned to see Thelwynn, who seemed fascinated by the fact that one of the travellers was so comfortable within the eggshell that he had actually fallen asleep. "He looks very cosy tucked up in there."

"He'll be fine, Lord Thelwynn. He was a little apprehensive, but as you can see, most at ease with his situation now," said Faylore, winking slyly at Grubb.

"I've never seen any of your kin as keen to get into an eggshell, Your Majesty. May I ask, what species is the little one?" Faylore's mind raced. *Which one did he mean?* The *small* one or the *smallest* one. *Clarify,* she thought, *come along dragon, clarify.* She was saved as Thelwynn now turned to Grubb. "Do *you* know?" he asked.

"He's a Nibby, Lord Thelwynn. They're a bunch of nomads... good manners, really... *pleasant.*" It was obvious that Grubb was unused to paying anyone a compliment, as he squirmed in an attempt to find something nice to say. Faylore cringed, wanting desperately to save him, but at the same time, not wanting to embarrass him.

"Is he really! It's been so long, I wouldn't have known." exclaimed Thelwynn, peering into the eggshell. "Well, well. Anyway, I was wondering..." he continued, "... if you could find it in your heart to do me a favour?"

"Of course, I will, if I can," replied Grubb, sincerely.

"When you are in the company of dragons... be *yourself.* We do not look for eloquent speeches, Grubb, we know what is in your heart. You are a caring soul. A grumpy one I'll admit, but that is my favourite thing about you. To be honest, I love the grumpy ones. You always know where you stand with a grumpy one. Could you do that for me, Grubb, could you simply be yourself?"

Grubb looked up at the magnificent stature of the golden dragon before him and smiled. Taking a deep breath, he shouted up to Thelwynn, "I'll think about it, now bugger off!"

"That's more like it," chuckled Thelwynn as he turned away.

Grubb watched with interest as he approached another of his kin, a ruby-coloured dragon almost as large as Thelwynn himself. Grubb remembered their arrival. The ruby dragon had formed one of the mound that protected the entrance to the dragon's lair and had stood close by as Thelwynn had first greeted Faylore. The two now seemed to be conversing, but Grubb could not hear what their discussion was about.

"Lord Fireweigh," Faylore suddenly whispered.

"Sorry?" replied Grubb. So intent was his study of the two dragons that Faylore's last comment was completely lost on him.

"The ruby dragon. His name is Lord Fireweigh. He's Thelwynn's second," she continued.

"Second what?" asked Grubb.

"Second in command," Faylore replied. "If anything were to happen to Thelwynn, Fireweigh would be his successor."

"Oh! Bit like a king and a prince then?"

"Something like that, Grubb," she replied, smiling.

"I got to admit, Faylore, I don't like the idea o' bein' shut up inside that eggshell for hours, I'm getting' the jitters to be honest. I'll 'ave more space than you two, but it's still gonna be pitch-black an' I can't exactly light a fire, can I? What if I can't breathe?"

"Oh no, it's not like that at all, Grubb," Faylore assured him. "Trust me, you'll be fine. As a matter of fact, I think you'll love it. So will Lodren, when he eventually wakes up, of course."

Two more eggshells had been placed beside the Fenn Immar. *I'll be fine, I'll be fine, I'll be fine*, Grubb kept telling himself. He watched as the dragons themselves lined the two shells with scales, even checking that Lodren was safely insulated before venturing over to speak to him and Faylore.

"Time for you to leave…" urged Fireweigh, "… the eggs are ready for transportation." He ushered them both forward. There was a lot of commotion as dragons dashed around (as much as a dragon is capable of dashing on foot) and began placing the last few 'live' dragon eggs into the river.

Scooping up Faylore and Grubb, Fireweigh hurried to the eggshells and unceremoniously dumped them into them. "Sorry, in a bit of a hurry," he announced as he lowered them into the lava flow. "Remember, do not touch the shell itself and keep the scales beneath you at all times."

Then, something astonishing happened that Grubb had not been expecting. The eggshell was open at the top, as if a piece had been cleanly sliced off with the sharpest of blades, that piece had just been replaced. There was a slight popping noise and a hissing as the top, within seconds, seemed to melt at the edges as it moulded back onto the shell. Grubb, sealed safely inside. His makeshift craft began to rock gently from side to side. *He was moving.* He could feel the motion, like a cork bobbing slowly in tidal waters. He was unnerved, there was no denying, but also a little excited. Then, he got the biggest shock of all.

At first, he thought he must be seeing things, he could have sworn that he saw another egg pass by him. Surely, that was impossible, he couldn't see through the eggshell… *could he*? As he watched from within his cocoon, he realised that, in fact, he could. The whole shell, including the scales upon which he sat, had become transparent. He could see the other eggs around him that had done the same, and he marvelled at the embryonic dragons that wriggled within them. He could see Faylore, and she could see him. He waved to her inadvertently as she smiled at him, before being lost from sight along their predetermined route. It was only then that he realised just how fast they were travelling.

They were hurtling along, more like falling off a waterfall than being swept by a current. All around there were explosions as lava bubbles burst, throwing flame and smoke into the air. Grubb actually recoiled a couple of times as the lava lapped over the top of his safe haven, causing him to laugh with nervous excitement. Faster and faster he went, the egg now completely submerged in the fiery river. Grubb could see the black vertical lines of solidified rock nestled within the lava, whizzing past him at breakneck speeds.

He marvelled at his surroundings. If not for the eggshell, he would have been incinerated within seconds, but as he sat within his protective shell he had never felt safer. Many times, he felt as if he could reach out and touch any part of his volcanic surroundings and had to stop himself as Fireweigh's words of warning came into his head. He reclined and gave in to the fact that his fate, for now, was in someone else's hands. Minutes turned into hours. Occasionally, he would see Faylore and they exchanged waves and smiles.

At one point, all three of the companions were side by side as they drifted along and Grubb took great pleasure in pointing out Lodren still sleeping soundly, oblivious to his surroundings. Grubb stretched and began to yawn, placing his hands behind his head. He was warm and comfortable, feeling more secure here than he had anywhere for some time. He closed his eyes, folded his arms across his chest, and fell into a deep, restful sleep.

Sometime later, but how much later he was unsure, Grubb opened his eyes. A contented smile swept across his face.

It seemed the ride was over. The swaying stopped and Grubb could hear noises outside his now solidified cocoon. Then, the familiar 'pop' as the top was removed. Hands, Thedarian hands, were now reaching in, offering to aid in his exit of the shell.

"I'm fine, thank you. No, really, I'm fine. Faylore!" he called. "Will you tell this lot to leave me alone? Thank you miss, I'm fine. Will you all just bugger off!" he bawled.

Faylore appeared amidst the crowd of people that had gathered to collect the eggs. "Grubb!" she snapped. "Mind your language! There are children present."

Grubb attempted to step from the shell that had somehow been placed on a moss-covered riverbank. No evidence of a lava flow could be seen. Grubb scratched his head as he sat astride the edge of the shell, trying to figure out how they had reached this point. He was so distracted, in fact, that without warning, he suddenly toppled sideways. To save himself from what could have been a nasty fall, he cheated. Transforming into Wilf, his foot hit the ground with a thump and he righted himself and began stretching as if it had been his intention all along.

Faylore burst out laughing, having witnessed his clumsy entrance, "Do pay attention, Grubb. Ooh, on second thoughts, stay like that for a while. You can carry more eggs with four hands."

Grubb lent a hand, well four to be precise, as the dragon eggs were placed in moss beds and covered with turf. Faylore explained that the heat from the sun would be quite sufficient to keep them warm until it was time to return them to their home.

"Don't you think we should wake Lodren now?" asked Grubb.

"Oh, it's such a shame," she replied, "he looks so peaceful."

"He might not look so peaceful when he realises you knocked him out with a tranquiliser dart in his neck," snorted Grubb.

"It was for his own good, Grubb, and *you* know it."

"Yeah, but *he* might not know it. You've seen 'im swing that hammer when he's miffed and if 'e wakes up in a bad mood, something might get broken."

"You may have a point there, Grubb. I think it best to remove any temptation." Turning to a young Thedarian girl, Faylore called to her, "Merralah, could you be a sweetheart and stow that large hammer for me?" The girl attempted to lift Lodren's hammer. She could barely drag it, let alone stow it. "Perhaps you could ask one of the others to help you, dear?" suggested Faylore. "We don't want you hurting yourself, do we?"

The hammer safely stowed, well 'hidden', Faylore turned her attention to the slumbering Nibby. Reaching into her bag, she produced a potion and leaning forward, allowed a trickle of the fluid to fall between Lodren's lips. His eyelids began to flicker as he regained consciousness until eventually, he opened his eyes fully, a huge smile appearing on his face. "Hello Faylore," he sighed dreamily. "Is it morning already?" It appeared that he was blissfully unaware of what had happened. Sitting up, he looked around him. "Where are we?" he asked, looking puzzled, but relaxed.

"We have reached Thedar. My home," replied Faylore.

"How did we manage to get here? I can't remember a thing," uttered the confused Nibby.

"You were exhausted, Lodren. The excitement of seeing the dragons was, perhaps, a little too much for you. You passed out and we decided to allow you to rest. There is no need to concern yourself, we are here and safe. Now gather your thoughts, we are about to attend a meeting with the elders of Thedar. We can't have you meeting them half asleep, can we?" Taking Lodren's hand, she helped him to his feet.

Grubb, seemingly quite comfortable as he leaned back on one of the warm dragon eggs, had a smirk on his face. "Sleep well, did we?" he asked.

"Yes, very well, thank you," replied Lodren.

"We were surprised when you nodded off so fast. Do you do that often?"

"No. As a matter of fact I don't think it's ever happened before," Lodren shook his head, still slightly baffled by the whole affair.

"Let's hope it doesn't keep happenin'. It could become a real pain in the neck for you."

Faylore glared at Grubb, who began chuckling as he rose to join them.

CHAPTER 13

The young wizards and the Dergon appeared in Reiggan Fortress. They were in exactly the same positions as they were when the ambush had taken place. Drake had his arms wrapped around Ramah's leg; Alex clamped tightly around the Dergon chief's neck; Xarran had Korbah in a waist-lock from behind and Harley had grabbed his arm as he reached for his scimitar, not quickly enough apparently, as his hand had almost managed to reach the hilt.

In a cloud of dust, the skirmish continued, but only for a second. Hearing the furore behind them, Jared, Hannock and Yello whirled around. Jared conjured his usual fireball as Hannock raised his crossbow, but both were far slower than the old wizard beside them. Yello simply clicked his fingers and silence ensued.

Unfortunately, for Drake, even this was a moment too late. Ramah had kicked out as hard as he could in an attempt to free his leg. His attempt had been successful, causing Drake to fly through the air like a ragdoll. Startled by his unexpected flight, Drake let out a wail and screwed up his face, bracing himself in anticipation of the inevitable pain that he would feel on his graceless landing. But he had overlooked the presence of Emnor who, with a gentle wave of his hand, swooped the young wizard back into the air, changing his trajectory and allowing him a much softer landing in a pile of hay. Studying the frozen scene before him, Hannock drew his sword and rapidly approached the motionless Dergon. Having witnessed the atrocities performed by them, his mind was set on their demise.

"Just a moment if you please, Captain," said Emnor calmly.

"Not a problem. It'll only take a *moment* to cut their throats," growled Hannock.

"I need them alive, Captain, for now at least. Stay your blade, they may have useful information."

"I don't care!" snapped Hannock. "These… *things*, butchered innocent villagers, even the children. Beheaded them as if it were a noble victory. They're animals, cowardly animals. The sooner they're dead, the better." Hannock was still approaching the Dergon.

"I'm terribly sorry about this… but…" Yello snapped his fingers again and Hannock stopped dead in his tracks. Walking across to him, he placed his hand on Hannock's shoulder before reaching forward and removing the sword from his grasp. "I'm sure you won't hold this against me, Charles."

Now that the fireball was extinguished, Jared approached and stood in front of his friend. "Release him, Yello," he instructed sternly.

Yello looked toward Emnor who nodded his head.

Hannock was immediately released. "How dare you," he roared, "I should…"

"Hannock!" warned Jared, raising his voice slightly. "That's enough. Let's just hear Emnor's explanation. Once we're done with these things, we'll execute them. Until then, I need you to calm yourself."

Hannock cast filthy looks between Emnor and Yello. Not wanting to disobey or insult Jared, he turned on his heel and stormed off toward the doors to Reiggan. "Do not make me regret this, *wizard!*" he shouted.

Jared, without turning, spoke to Emnor, "Whatever your plan is, my friend, it had better be good."

Emnor, flanked by the silent Gerrowliens, explained to Jared the brief conversation they had overheard between the Dergon. One by one, the boys were released and instructed to strip the Dergon of all weapons. This done, their enemies' hands and feet were bound before, eventually, they too were freed from the binding spell.

Ramah immediately went into a rage. "You call us cowards!" he roared. "You outnumber us, use your magic tricks against us, bind our hands and feet before you face us and *we* are branded as cowards. What does that make you?" he sneered.

Jared walked slowly toward Ramah. He looked the proud Dergon in the eye, fingering the ropes around his wrists then, without warning, punched him in the face with all the power he could muster. Ramah, unbalanced by the bindings around his feet, fell backwards and landed heavily. Jared walked around him, no emotion showing as his second blow struck his captive. This time, a heavy kick from his iron-capped boot that struck Ramah in the ribs. He began to speak slowly, "Do you, for one moment, believe that I have a single care about what you think of me?" A second kick struck Ramah, this time to his jaw.

Korbah attempted to shuffle forward in a vain attempt to protect his chief, but he was easily felled by a blow, delivered by Emnor's staff. Jared continued, "You slaughtered innocents, mutilated my people, men, women and children, butchered like cattle. I should have allowed my captain his pleasure, allowed him to gut you as I watched. My friend here…" Jared pointed at Emnor, "… seems to think that you may be of some use to us. I, however, hope that he is wrong," Jared placed his foot on Ramah's throat, applying his full weight and stemming Ramah's breath. "Nothing would give me more pleasure than to hear your screams of agony, dog. And you *will* scream, *that, I will* promise you. Your pride will not allow you to offer us any aid, and if you will not offer it freely, we shall take pleasure from extracting it by any means necessary. If you wish a quick, clean death, I suggest you co-operate. If not, simply nod and I can summon my captain, I'm sure he would relish using his skills to loosen your tongue."

Removing his foot from Ramah's throat, Jared knelt down, glaring into his prisoner's swollen, bloodshot eye, "I see your hatred, Dergon. I can feel your yearning. Oh, how you wish to have a blade in your hand, to strike me down and taste my blood. But I cannot allow that. Perhaps we should remove that temptation." Rising, he turned to Yello. "Amputate its arms," he instructed. "On second thoughts, start with the other one, and make this one watch. Then it can be his turn."

Ramah and Korbah were hauled to their feet with a single wave of Emnor's staff. Korbah resisted with every fibre of his being, trying to wrench his arms free as they were stretched out in front of him. Yello studied Korbah's wrists, pinching at the skin to ascertain its toughness. He crossed to where Hannock had laid out an impressive array of weaponry. First to hand was a sword, which he raised and studied briefly. Glancing over his shoulder, he quickly discarded it before reaching for a large broadaxe. He ran his thumb across the edge of the blade and tutted. "Not very sharp," he muttered, "I suppose it'll do. Might have to hack at it a bit, but it'll get the job done." Reaching down to the ground, he picked up a small stick and offered it to Korbah. "Want to bite down on this?" he asked. "This might sting a bit."

Korbah wriggled and pulled, but it was obvious that no physical force would free him from his invisible, magical bindings. Yello placed the edge of the axe against his wrists, then raised it above his head.

"WAIT!" roared Ramah, "What do you need? Stop this now, I beg of you. Do not mutilate my Dergon brother."

Yello turned his back to the two Dergon and winked at Jared. *Had it all been an elaborate bluff?* Emnor was unsure. Either way, it had worked.

The Dergon were dragged unceremoniously from the courtyard and thrown into a dark room, deep within Reiggan. Jared began their interrogation. "What use would the hissthaar be to you, Dergon?" he asked. *"Why befriend them?"*

"Because your kind have all but rendered my kind extinct. I needed allies."

"For what?" continued Jared. "Two Dergon scum and a few serpents. Hardly an elite fighting force."

"They were not needed as an army, fool. Merely a distraction," Ramah hissed. "A strategy I learned by accident."

"What kind of distraction? Lurking on the outskirts of another defenceless village until the opportunity arises to sneak in and butcher more innocents?"

"We have no interest in attacking villages, Borellian. Our prey is far more substantial."

"And what prey is that?" snarled Jared.

"We seek vengeance on the shadow lord. We were defeated and our differences with your kind are at an end. Our only aim is to destroy the sorcerer *Karrak*!"

Jared was taken aback momentarily but remained staunch. It would not pay to show any emotion in front of his captive. "This… *shadow lord*, this… *Karrak*, what do you know of him?"

"Only what he told us. He is a Prince of Borell and means to usurp his father and brother in order to take the throne."

"Why would that involve you? Were you in his employ in some way?"

"We had declared war on the Borellians but you were too strong for us. Your superior numbers gave you victory. Karrak came to me after the battle and offered his aid in our revenge. He said that all I needed to do was entice the Borellians from the gates of the castle with the few that remained of my army and he would destroy them… but he deceived us."

"You mean he turned his back on you once you had done your part?"

Ramah spoke quietly and slowly, still in disbelief at his own words, "We lured Borell's troops from the castle as Karrak had instructed. He appeared between the open gates as planned, I saw him laughing as my loyal warriors were cut down. Korbah and I were the only ones to escape. My entire army perished."

"Do you expect pity from me, Dergon? Do you believe that your treachery and malice toward my people should be forgiven simply because your planned butchery failed? You and your followers were raiders, vermin that deserved to be eradicated from this world, and you received those just deserts."

"And what of you?" roared Ramah, "Following a fat king who cares more about his own protection than that of his people or lands. A king who, once the battle commenced, sat astride his mount, giving orders, too afraid to join the melee himself. His eldest son, the first Prince of Borell is the greatest coward of all. He never even had the bravery to ride out with his men. Stayed inside the castle, cowering under his bed, no doubt!"

Jared remained calm. The slight toward the heir of Borell was not directed at him but toward an unknown entity, in Ramah's mind. "How would you view the Borellians if I, as one of them, were to deign to release you? Surely, the first thing you would do is seize a weapon and attempt to strike me down?"

"If it were the course I chose to take, there would be no 'attempt'. I could kill you with my bare hands in a fair fight, I would have no need of weapons. But as I have already informed you, my quarrel is now with the shadow lord. Release us. Return us to whence you kidnapped us and our paths will not deliberately cross again. You have my word."

"I shall give it due consideration, but I need more information first."

"What makes you think that I know more?" asked Ramah.

"Why do you refer to your enemy as '*the shadow lord*'?" asked Jared.

Ramah shuffled around, trying to get more comfortable. "When we first met, his features were similar to any other Borellian male. Larger in stature than most I noticed, but much the same as the rest."

"And now?" asked Jared.

"I have not seen him since that day outside the castle walls, but I have heard rumours."

"Rumours? From the hissthaar?" asked Jared.

"Apparently Karrak's features are now disfigured, hidden in some way. Even his gait has changed. His arrogant strut has gone, he moves as if he were floating on the air. It is said that if one is unfortunate enough to see it, his face appears as a sinister black mist. Something to do with his use of dark magic, I would guess," replied Ramah.

"How did the hissthaar find out about Karrak?"

"There are bands of hissthaar everywhere. I'm not sure exactly how they came upon the knowledge. Karrak seized a castle, Merrsdan, slaughtered an entire band of hissthaar with a wave of his hand. He's using the castle as a base, allegedly, and has scores of mindless slaves renovating it."

Jared stared at Ramah. *Could he believe the Dergon?* Ramah offered his hands to his captor and nodded toward his bindings. Jared ignored his plea. Turning swiftly, he marched through the door, followed by Emnor and Yello who promptly locked it behind them.

"Maybe we should discuss this further, upstairs, Jared," suggested Emnor. "Away from prying ears," he added, pointing at the door behind them.

Emnor called everyone together for yet another meeting. Once the tale of Karrak had been shared, each member of the assembly was offered the opportunity to voice their opinion.

Hannock was the first to speak. "Shadow Lord!" he exclaimed. "What a load of crap. They're lying, Jared, making up stories so that you'll release them."

"I'd love to agree with you, my dear Captain but, unfortunately, I cannot. Karrak has the Elixian Soul, and given time, it will destroy and consume its host completely," stated Emnor.

"Why are we hanging around then? Let's just find him and destroy him," Drake had a point, as blunt as it was.

"He's right of course. The sooner we track him down, the sooner we can put an end to his evil," agreed Jared.

"Aren't you forgetting something?" asked Harley. The others glanced across at him, awaiting some sort of revelation. "We have Tallarans Eye. You were supposed to be finding Karrak by using that, remember?"

"If we are to believe what that animal downstairs told us, we already know where he is. All we have to do now is get there and kill him," said Drake.

Emnor began rummaging through his robes. "Here we are," he said. "We shall use the Tallarans Eye to confirm whether or not the Dergon is telling the truth." Placing the mysterious artefact on a bench, he looked across at Yello. "Do you have that piece of cloth with you, old man?" he asked.

"This isn't going to work," scoffed Jared. "That old piece of rag could be anything."

"As a matter of fact…" said Hannock, thoughtfully, "… it isn't. Jared, do you remember that day in the courtyard in Borell, the day I broke the pikestaff across the back of Karrak's head?"

"How could I forget it?" asked Jared. "That was my favourite shirt."

"We gave orders for Karrak to be bound and gagged before being taken to his chambers."

"And?" asked Jared.

"And that was the kerchief I stuffed in your brother's mouth. That was the gag that was used on Karrak."

"But it doesn't belong to him, does it? We needed one of his possessions."

"But doesn't that make it Karrak's?" suggested Emnor. "Hannock, presenting it to him, in whatever circumstance, *makes it his*."

Jared shook his head. "I'm not convinced," he mumbled. "Obviously, I'm not looking at it the same way as you are. Give it a try by all means. What do we have to lose?"

Yello took the Tallarans Eye and wrapped it gently in the kerchief before placing them both in the centre of the bench. He leaned forward expectantly, as did the others, but nothing changed. It was simply an ancient amulet wrapped in a piece of fabric.

Jared gave a sigh, "What were you hoping would happen, Emnor?"

"It should show us a vision of a location or at least a landmark, something that would direct us to Karrak," replied Emnor.

"It's as I feared," said Yello.

"What is?" asked Hannock. "The gag was useless after all?"

"Oh no, the gag would have worked perfectly to find Karrak," replied Yello.

"So why isn't the Eye showing us where he is?" asked Jared.

A knowing look passed between Emnor and Yello, a look that did not go unnoticed by Jared. "What are you not telling us, Emnor? Enough games, out with it!" he snapped.

"I am afraid, Jared..." began Emnor, "... your brother is gone."

"Gone? What do you mean, gone?" asked Jared, frowning.

"All that was Karrak, all that was 'your brother', has been consumed by the Elixian Soul. Your brother's body is now no more than a vessel, a hollow shell that contains nought but pure evil."

"Are you saying my brother is dead?" exclaimed Jared.

"Unfortunately not, Jared," replied Emnor. "He has suffered a far worse fate. He will exist merely as an observer within his own body, but never again will he command it."

Jared lowered his head. He had endured so much pain and anguish as a result of Karrak's ways that he, perhaps, should have felt some sort of relief. But Karrak, despite his faults, had been his brother, and it saddened his heart to think of him as gone. "Is there no hope?" he asked, solemnly. "Can we not, somehow, save him?"

"Sorry, Your Highness, but why would we want to? He's been an absolute nightmare. This is a blessing in disguise, now we won't have to hesitate when we face him. Now that we know he's not your brother," said Drake.

Jared jumped to his feet and glared at the young wizard. He conjured a fireball and pointed at Drake with his free hand. "I've warned you before!" he bellowed.

It seemed that it was not only Jared who was at the end of his tether. Drake was tired of being ordered around by all who were senior to him and, deciding to accept Jared's blatant challenge, he held his hands out in front of him, a swirling white mist distorting their shape. "Come on then, pretty boy. Let's see what you've learned," he yelled.

Jared launched the fireball. Drake laughed as it reached him, holding up one hand and catching the fireball then spinning it in the air like a lasso before sending it straight back toward Jared. Hannock took a step but Emnor grabbed his arm gently and shook his head. They, Yello and the others, retreated to a safe distance. They were going to allow the battle to continue.

Fireballs, ice shards, tsunamis and gale force winds were launched between the warring wizards, but neither could get the better of the other. Drake was suddenly launched into the air, but even as he took flight, a huge chunk of ice flew through the air and hit Jared full-force in the chest as Drake crashed into a distant wall. Both climbed unsteadily to their feet, and try as they might, neither could land another magical blow.

Ten more minutes passed, an eternity for a wizard continually casting spells, spells that were gradually becoming weaker and weaker. Their energy drained, the duellists had collapsed to their knees and were crawling toward one another. Ice spells that were now so pathetic that they were no more than snowballs, and what were tsunamis were now mere splashes of water. As for the fire spells, well, a flint could have produced a brighter spark. Now face to face, they resorted to pushing one another until, with a loud grunt, Drake pushed Jared onto his back before collapsing in a heap. It seemed the battle was over.

Initially, the spectators were a little concerned, but that concern had soon turned to admiration as they began cheering before, eventually, that admiration dwindled to boredom. Hannock turned to Emnor and Yello. "Fancy a glass of wine?" he asked.

"Excellent idea," replied Yello. Beckoning Xarran, Harley and Alex, they all headed indoors, leaving Jared and Drake on the ground, still attempting to shove one another occasionally.

The Gerrowliens, as a race were teetotallers. They had never been interested in the consumption of alcohol. Poom and Lawton, after declining a gracious invitation from Hannock, wandered off to find a secluded area to allow them to do what cats do best… *sleep*.

"I take it…" asked Hannock, "… that either one of you could have stopped that at any time if it became too dangerous?"

"What?" replied Yello, blowing a very loud raspberry. "Get in between that lot? Not bloody likely!"

Needless to say, it was some time before Jared joined them. He limped into the room holding his ribs, followed by Drake, who was nursing a black eye, swollen shut by the bruising.

"Ah, there you are, gentlemen. Have a nice nap, did we?" Hannock received a filthy look from both combatants but didn't seem to care.

The wine had been flowing fairly freely by the looks of things and even the younger members of the group were now sporting silly grins. "I hope… you… {burp} excuse me, I hope you don't mind me ashking, but have you two resolved your… erm… what's the word I'm looking for? … differences? Yes, that was it. Have you resolved your differences?" Harley eventually asked.

"No more for you, Harley," said Yello, taking the goblet from Harley's grasp. "You've had enough, I think." Harley was about to protest and pointed his finger at Yello before hiccoughing, but then his head rolled onto the back of his chair and he began snoring loudly.

Xarran started to laugh. "What a lightweight," he sniggered. "He's only had half a glass."

"Maybe he's had more of a sheltered upbringing than some of us," suggested Emnor, dropping his head and pouting up at Xarran.

"I think you two may benefit from a little of this," said Yello, holding out the familiar vial that contained the Abigail's Mercy.

Jared waved his hand in dismissal, "No, thanks. I've had a lot worse than this."

"I haven't," groaned Drake. "Pass it over, could you? I don't think I can walk any farther."

"That's the trouble with you youngsters," said Hannock. "You can dish it out, but you can't take it."

"O.k. then, soldier boy. You and me, in the courtyard, but you'll have to wait until tomorrow. I might be able to see straight by then," Drake smiled.

Alex, as usual, had dwindled into the background enough for his exit to go unnoticed. Whether the others were engaged in conversation or argument, he had developed a technique that, without actually doing so, seemed to make him invisible to them. He hurried through the doorway and followed the passageway, pausing briefly at the small window and peering through to make sure that the Gerrowliens were still in the courtyard. He screwed up his eyes. The gloom of the passageway was a stark contrast to the bright midday sun. He waited a few moments for his eyesight to adjust to the light but could see neither Poom nor Lawton. Then, something twitched, the tell-tale orange of a Gerrowlien's fur.

It was a tail, a tail that was hanging from the hay cart that had been Drake's saviour a short while ago. The Gerrowliens, having found no other place to lounge, had chosen their comfort spot perfectly and were now sound asleep, it seemed. Alex turned and followed the familiar passage before heading to the room where Tamor slept. Entering, he pulled a chair toward the king's bed and sat staring at Tamor's drawn, haggard features. He glanced around the room, relieved that he was alone. "What happened to you, old man?" he whispered, "What did Karrak do to leave you in such a wretched state?"

The sound of Theodore's disembodied voice drifted in the air. "Does it matter?" he asked. "Look at him, Alexander, a proud king reduced to nothing more than a raving lunatic. You could do him a great service if you were to end his suffering. His, and your own of course."

"Leave me be, Theodore. I refuse to listen to your ramblings. You say the king is a raving lunatic, I suggest that occasionally you listen to your own ravings."

"He is in pain, Alex, tortured by the visions in his mind. You cannot see them but they *are* there."

"I know. We all know, that's why we're going to cure him. Somehow."

"Take the pillow from beneath his head, Alex. Place it over his face. It won't take long before he stops breathing. Once you confess to Jared, he, in turn, can end *your* torment."

"I will not assassinate a king, Theodore, simply for your pleasure at witnessing my execution."

"Think of it another way then, Brother. If you smother the king, the others will believe that he died in his sleep because his mind could take no more. Do not confess, hide away as you always do. Be the coward that you are, at least you'll be one step closer with Tamor gone."

The sound of Theodore's laughter filled the room. Alex's confusion was making him dizzy. The laughter grew louder until deafened by it, he placed his hands over his ears. His eyesight was blurred, he couldn't even focus on the sleeping Tamor, who was mere inches away from him. He couldn't think. He opened his mouth and screamed. The laughter ceased abruptly, Alex hung his head and groaned…

CHAPTER 14

"Oh, Grubb, just look at yourself!" tutted Faylore. "You cannot be allowed to meet my parents looking like that. You're a disgrace."

"OH, SO SORRY, YOUR MAJESTY!" exclaimed Grubb. "Must have something to do with the long road journey, trudging through forests in the pouring rain, or maybe the ice fields, before being stuffed inside a dragon's egg for hours, and shaken up like a bag of dirty washing."

"We've all been through exactly the same, Grubb. Lodren has, at least, tried to give his clothes a brush down. Mind you, it hasn't improved the smell."

"Smell!" exclaimed Lodren. "What smell?"

"It's not your fault, Lodren, I do understand," replied Faylore.

"Understand what?" asked the Nibby.

"That you have had no opportunity to bathe properly, of course," she replied.

"BATHE!" exclaimed Grubb, "What, you mean, like… in water?"

"That's exactly what I mean. I don't wish to insult either of you… but you stink!"

"That's charmin', isn't it?" exclaimed Grubb. "We come all this way to help protect you and what thanks do we get? You tell us we stink!"

Lodren leaned his head to one side and, not wanting to appear obvious, sniffed his clothes. "OOH my, good gracious! Grubb… I think Queen Faylore has a point, we are a bit… ripe," he said, giving a little cough.

"You speak for yerself, stinky, I smell as nature intended. If I was meant to go in water, I'd 'ave fins and gills. It's not good for ye, getting covered in water."

"Like it or not, Grubb, you are going to bathe before we move from this spot. Even if I have to drag you into the river myself," warned Faylore.

"Sorry, Your Majesty… not a chance," replied Grubb, shaking his head. Faylore stepped toward him, but seeing the intent in her eyes, Grubb transformed into Wilf. He started to laugh. "I don't think you can drag me now," he said.

Watching the scene, Lodren looked around him. Walking a few steps away, he whispered to one of the young Thedarian girls, who pointed him in a direction. Faylore now had hold of one of Wilf's arms and was trying with all her might to inch him toward the river bank, unsuccessfully. Lodren ambled over to them, a smile on his face. The tussle between Faylore and Wilf continued and neither saw Lodren tapping his reclaimed hammer on his open palm. Faylore gave one final attempt but as she tugged at Wilf's arm, her foot slipped and she fell unceremoniously on her… well, you know.

"You are impossible, Grubb," she shouted. "You can't expect to meet royalty looking and smelling like that!"

Wilf, throughout, had not stopped laughing, but now his attention turned to Lodren who, hammer in hand, was giving him a strange look.

"Bath time!" exclaimed Lodren, twitching his eyebrows, a sudden air of glee in his voice. Without warning, his right arm swung the hammer. There was a dull thud as the flat side struck Wilf full in the chest. The hammer blow threw him into the air, directly toward the river and with a loud 'splash', he landed right in the middle of it. He immediately let out a roar and began to thrash about, flapping his arms up and down as if he were drowning. However, when he stood up, the water level barely reached his waist. Faylore fell about in hysterical laughter and Lodren, dropping his hammer, began to wade, still fully clothed, into the water, following his friend's reluctant lead.

Along the riverbank were numerous tents and shacks, all fashioned by the careful manipulation of the foliage and vegetation that grew there. The branches of bushes had been twisted and large, roughly-woven pieces of fabric were used to adorn them. The Thedarians had found that this was not always necessary, as in some places the foliage was dense enough to provide a natural shelter. A gentle nudge here, a push there and the occasional slender vine to tie it in place was sufficient to produce a habitable, although temporary, comfortable shelter. They milled about, exchanging pleasantries and greetings but could not hide their confused interest in the new strangers who, still arguing, were now bathing in their river. Thus it was that sometime later, as Lodren and Grubb exited the water they were beckoned by a young female Thedarian. She never spoke as she pointed toward the entrance to one of the rudimentary tents before them. Lodren bowed and gave the girl a little smile as he approached. Grubb simply frowned at her. His mistrust of all strangers, regardless of race or gender, quite apparent.

Lodren nudged him, grabbed his arm and pulled him into the tent. "Well, I'll be..." he said in amazement.

Minutes later, after a little squabbling that could be heard from outside, the pair emerged looking far more presentable than when they had entered. The Thedarians had seen that they had been through some tough scrapes and their clothes bore the scars of them. It was an easy task for them to make a couple of outfits by adapting clothes that would normally fit a Thedarian child. They gave up on the sleeves on Lodren's outfit and simply detached them. As they stood in their perfectly fitted attire, offers of haircuts, beard-trimming or shaving were offered, but all were declined.

"My, don't you both look splendid!" Faylore exclaimed as she approached them.

"Not too bad at all is it, Your Majesty?" asked Lodren, giving a little twirl.

"It ain't natural, getting' all wet like that. I'll probably catch something nasty from that river and die now. It's washed all the oils and things from me skin, I just know it has," grumbled Grubb.

"And the lice and the ticks," laughed Lodren. "*And* the fleas, *and* the natural layer of mud from under your fingernails."

"I did not 'ave fleas, nor nothing else 'orrible. I was fine as I was."

229

"Well, it's done now, Grubb, and I must say, you look very handsome in your new clothes. Green really does suit you." Leaning forward, she sniffed Grubb, "And you smell divine. Spring flowers, if I'm not mistaken."

"One of them stupid girls kept splashing me with something. I smell like a flower basket," he protested. "It's not right for a Vikkery to smell like a flower basket. What would me friends think of me…"

"We *are* your friends, you pillock!" exclaimed Lodren.

"You know what I mean. I mean Jared and Hannock, and the wizards. They'd think I'd gone soft in the head."

"What! You mean you *haven't?*" asked Lodren, sarcastically.

Grubb took a playful swipe at him.

Their conversation was interrupted as a procession of Thedarians approached in silent, solemn ranks as an official greeting. They bowed to Faylore, offering the respect that one should when facing a queen.

"Welcome back, Queen Faylore," said the girl leading them. "You have been greatly missed."

"That is most kind, Seenara," replied Faylore, taking the girl's hand. "It is good to be home. May I introduce you to my friends?" The girl turned slightly and smiled. "This…" continued Faylore, "… is Lodren the Nibby and Grubb the Vikkery. Gentlemen, this is my sister, Princess Seenara."

Seenara bowed to them in turn, and they to her. "Our mother is looking forward to seeing you, Your Majesty," said Seenara, turning to Faylore.

"How is Father?" asked Faylore, her expression turning to one of concern.

Seenara glanced at their guests and stepped closer to Faylore. "Physically, he is in perfect health," she whispered. "Unfortunately, his mind is more confused than when last you left."

"There is no need for you to whisper, Seenara. My friends and I keep no secrets from one another. Father is simply sick, it is nothing to be ashamed of."

"Anythin' I can do?" asked Grubb, holding out his hands and wiggling his fingers.

Seenara gave Grubb a confused look. She had never known a Vikkery before.

Faylore placed her arm around her sister's shoulders, "Grubb has a healing touch..." she explained, "... but I fear that even that would not be enough to help Father."

"If ye change your mind, Faylore, just give me a nudge and I'll do what I can," said Grubb. "Always willin' to give it a bash."

"And if there's anything he especially likes to eat, I'll be more than happy to cook it for him," Lodren added.

"We have people who cook for us, thank you," replied Seenara, slightly offended at the slur on Thedarian cuisine.

"Not the way that Lodren prepares meals, Sister dear. Wait and see. He's a wizard when it comes to pots and pans."

"You mustn't speak of wizards, Faylore," urged Seenara, nervously. "That's what started this whole mess."

Lodren and Grubb gave one another a fleeting glance, although intrigued by Seenara's last comment, they held their tongues.

"He's not a real wizard, Seenara," Faylore assured her sister. "It's just that his meals are so delicious, they seem magical."

"I do not require any magical meals, thank you. Traditional Thedarian meals are good enough for me," replied Seenara, frostily.

"As you wish, Sister," said Faylore, hugging her sister. "Come, let us go to our parents."

The procession, with Seenara at its head, turned and moved away. Faylore gestured to her friends, and Lodren and Grubb tagged along at a suitable distance. "She don't like wizards, does she?" whispered Grubb.

"Maybe they had some bother with one of those bad ones. You know, *Karrak's lot*," replied Lodren, in similar hushed tones.

"There's plenty of 'em by all accounts. Let's keep our ears peeled," suggested Grubb. "We might find out later."

"In that case, don't be your usual self and start asking stupid questions."

"Me?" asked Grubb, acting innocent, "I never say a word."

Lodren sighed as they both quickened their pace in order to keep up with the long-legged Thedarians.

They followed the procession through the quiet meadow. The Thedarians were so light on their feet that their steps were silent, allowing the slightest sounds around them to be heard. A lark song from above; the croak of a frog or toad over the bubbling of the narrow stream and the buzz of a dragonfly as it whizzed past them.

The toil of their arduous journey seemed to be sapped from them as they walked, and both Lodren and Grubb felt invigorated by their surroundings. They crossed a small bridge spanning the stream, a bridge formed by the natural knitted roots of the trees at its banks. Clearing it, they entered an avenue of straight-trunked trees growing like columns on either side that led to a clearing a few hundred yards ahead. Standing in its centre was an elegant Thedarian woman, and by her features, it was obvious that this was Faylore and Seenara's mother. Faylore bowed to her mother and then flung her arms around her. Her mother seemed quite taken aback by the show of emotion and gently pushed her daughter away. "Faylore," she urged. "It is most unbecoming for a queen to behave in such a manner. Please, contain yourself."

"Forgive me, Mother, I am just so happy to see you."

"I do not know where you are learning these bad habits, my daughter, but you must remember who you are. You are the Queen of Thedar and must set an example to your people."

"Exactly, Mother…" replied Faylore, grabbing her mother's hand, "… and I intend to. I intend to show them how much I love and care for them, as I care for my friends. Meet them, Mother." Without waiting for a reply, she tugged her mother forward, "This is my dear friend Lodren the Nibby, Lodren, this is my mother, Erenthas."

Lodren bowed as Erenthas looked him up and down, "Charmed," she said haughtily.

"And this…" continued Faylore, "… is my dear friend Grubb." Grubb also bowed but, not being one for ceremony, it was half-hearted.

"A pleasure," muttered Erenthas.

"Yeah. Sounds like it!" grunted Grubb.

Erenthas glared at him as a few of the Thedarians stepped forward. *How dare he insult the Queen Mother.*

"Hold your positions," snapped Faylore. "Mother! These are my friends, my *guests,* and as such, friends and guests of Thedar. They shall be treated with respect."

Erenthas, for whatever reason, had been uncharacteristically hostile toward Lodren and Grubb. "I apologise," she said. "Forgive me."

"No bones broken," said Grubb, "I can be a miserable sod meself sometimes."

"What he means is…" chipped in Lodren, quickly, "… no problem at all, thank you for receiving us into your home so graciously."

In an attempt to ease the tension, Faylore ordered refreshments. Drinks were brought and her family and friends relaxed as they made themselves comfortable on cushions that had been scattered on the ground around them. They chatted amongst themselves, but it was not long before their conversation became gravely serious and Erenthas was informed of the danger now threatening their world.

"You had him in your sights!" exclaimed Erenthas. "How is it that you missed? You are one of our best with a bow."

"He is a sorcerer, Mother. My arrows were incinerated before they could strike. If not for Grubb's distraction and Lodren's hammer, we may have all perished that day."

Erenthas smiled weakly at their guests. "I thank you for that," she said, gently.

"No bother," grunted Grubb. "It was just a shame stumpy wasn't a bit closer. That 'ammer of 'is would've finished the job if 'e 'ad been."

"If that was supposed to be a compliment, thank you. I think," replied Lodren.

"If you were to find this, *Karrak*," began Erenthas, "why would you…?"

"IT'S THE SECOND ONE, NOT THE FIRST! REMEMBER, THE SECOND. NOT THE SECOND, THE SECOND, NOT THE FIRST," bellowed a voice from behind them.

A haggard Thedarian man appeared amongst them. He turned from one to the other in no particular order, pointing his finger and shaking his head. "Remember…" he continued, as his warning became a whisper, "… the second, not the first, but not the second, the second." Although, obviously passionate to get his meaning across, he was making no sense and the smile that remained on his face throughout proved that Koloss, the once-proud King of Thedar, was far from sane. Erenthas lowered her head, in sorrow more than shame, if that were possible for a Thedarian.

Faylore rose and took the man's hands. "Father, it is I, Faylore, your daughter," she said, quietly.

"No, no, no! The second," Koloss continued. "He'll be here soon with the first. It's the second, not the second." His eyes darted frantically around. He had no perception of reality, it seemed, as he pointed at shadows and continued to shake his head. He began to laugh. "It was the old man… but he was a young man, not an old man… but he was an old man," he rambled.

Faylore, Erenthas and Seenara were more concerned, obviously, with Koloss' wellbeing than his meaningless rants and were attempting to calm him, but Lodren had heard something different. Nudging Grubb, he leaned across. "You don't think he could be talking about Karrak, do you?" he asked quietly.

"Why would he be on about Karrak? 'e's as mad as a frog with its bum on fire."

"Listen. The second? Karrak's the second son, and he's not old, he's young, but he disguises himself as an old man so nobody recognises him."

"Might be, I suppose. It could just be a coincidence."

"I would have agreed with you a few years ago, Grubb, but with all we've been through I don't believe in coincidences any more. Especially when it comes to Karrak."

"We'll 'ave to be careful what we say though, we don't want to upset anyone. We'll talk to Faylore when we're alone, alright?"

"I didn't know Faylore had another sister, did you?"

"Of course I did, Lodren. Tells me everythin', Faylore does. Ye know what a chatterbox she can be!"

"There's no need to be sarcastic, Grubb. I just wondered if she'd mentioned her in passing."

"No. I didn't know she 'ad another sister. Mind you, they 'aven't mentioned Jendilomin either, 'ave they?"

"Do you think they know about her and the forest nymphs?"

"I don't know if they know about 'er, the nymphs or that she was as barmy as 'er old dad."

"Keep your voice down, Grubb! And don't say things like that, you never know who's listening."

"*'ere*! *What if it's a family thing*? What if all the royal family go barmy eventually? Faylore could be next."

"Of course they don't, you stupid Vikkery. Her mother's fine, isn't she?"

"For now maybe, but who knows? Before long…" Grubb stuck his tongue out of the side of his mouth, crossed his eyes and pretended to screw his finger into the side of his head.

"You'll get another taste of my hammer if you keep this up, Grubb, and I'm not joking."

CHAPTER 15

"Alright, so it's decided, we begin our hunt for Karrak at first light tomorrow," said Jared.

"It's a long way to Merrsdan, Jared," said Emnor. "It's going to take weeks and we can't use magic to shorten our journey. For one, Hannock's body would never take the strain, and secondly, if the scroll is to be believed, Karrak would surely detect our presence as we drew nearer to his location."

"I'd rather you didn't discuss my body, thank you very much," said Hannock, pulling at his tunic.

Emnor rolled his eyes, "I was merely stating the fact that if we were to use relocation spells, your organs would become so dehydrated that it may give you heart failure or something equally as fatal."

"And you can leave my organs out of it as well!"

"Oh, do shut up, Hannock," said Jared. "This is the serious part, remember."

Hannock grinned. "By your leave, Your Highness," he said, and gave an exaggerated bow.

"He's right, Cap'. You'd be shrivelled up like a prune in a few days," whispered Drake.

"You've used that spell on me more than once and I was fine, why should a couple of more times do any harm?" asked Hannock.

"It's called *cumulative effect*," replied Drake.

"Which means what exactly?"

"Each time a mortal body is transported, it absorbs magical energy, but with each *consecutive* spell, it absorbs a greater amount than the previous time. Once is fine, twice isn't too harmful... but three or four, or even more, could be fatal. It dries you out from the inside. You can retrieve enough moisture from water the first couple of times but after that, you'd be pushing your luck if you were re-located more than once a month."

"Sounds nasty," said Hannock.

"It would be," said Harley. "You could dry out so completely that the flick of a finger could cause you to turn to dust."

"Jared, if we are to begin our search, we will need horses. We cannot walk all the way to Merrsdan," suggested Hannock.

"Are there any villages nearby, Emnor?" asked Jared.

Yello interjected at this point. "There is," he said. "At least there was one, not too far from here. I could take a couple of the lads and find out."

"No," replied Emnor, sternly. "We can plot a course that can take us through it. Even if you were to go ahead, you'd have to wait for us to catch up."

"Aren't we overlooking a couple of things?" asked Hannock. "The small matter of your father, who is incapable of travel. Not to mention the two Dergon we have locked up downstairs."

Jared sighed and gently banged his fist against the side of a cart, "The situation with the Dergon is simple enough, but as for my father, I am unsure of what to do."

"So you mean to execute the prisoners?" asked Yello.

"No," replied Jared, "*I mean to release them.*"

"What!" exclaimed Hannock, "Jared, you can't. They slaughtered hundreds of our people, butchered them. You can't just let them go."

"They can be another distraction for Karrak. It will take them as long to reach Merrsdan as it will take us, maybe less. If Karrak's attention is focussed on them, it may give us an edge."

"Or, if they get ahead of us," snapped Hannock, "They could lie in wait and ambush us again!"

"They have seen our strength, Hannock, six wizards and we two. I saw the rage in Ramah's eyes and it was not directed at us. He yearns for his revenge on Karrak, nothing else matters to him."

"Seven wizards," chirped Drake. The whole assembly turned to face him. "Well... six and a half, I suppose. You're not that strong yet," he added, winking at Jared.

"Do not forget, Jared, you also have two Gerrowliens on your side."

Jared turned to face Lawton, "Forgive me, my friend. I did not feel it right to assume your involvement in our mission."

"See, there it is. *Our* mission. We've come this far with you, we may as well complete the journey," Lawton placed his hand on Jared's shoulder. "To the end," he added.

"Are you in agreement with your friend, Poom?" asked Jared. "Will you be joining us?"

"What! Leave fat boy to his own devices and miss out on a good scrap?" laughed Poom. "You did hear him say *two* Gerrowliens? Of course, I'm with you. Just point the way."

Jared, Hannock, Emnor and Yello, flanked by the Gerrowliens, headed down the steep, stone staircase. Reaching the Dergon's makeshift gaol, Emnor unlocked the door and steered everyone inside. Ramah and Korbah immediately sprang to their feet. Poom and Lawton lurched forward and roared at their captives. Jared held up his hand and the Gerrowliens stepped back, still growling quietly.

"We mean you no harm, Ramah," said Jared. "My decision is all but made, but I shall need your word of no further hostilities toward us before I can make a judgement."

"If you look for apologies or a whimpering plea for our lives, you are mistaken, Borellian! You shall receive neither. We will not beg for our lives. Kill us and have done with it. If we cannot have our revenge on Karrak, our lives are meaningless anyway."

"So you maintain that your only goal is the destruction of Karrak?" asked Emnor.

"I do," sneered Ramah, "Karrak will die by my hand if I live through this day."

"Do I have your word that in no way will you involve yourself, or any other, with myself or my company?" asked Jared.

"I care not for you and yours, Borellian. Release us and never again will our paths cross. On that, you have my word."

The Dergon were led to the courtyard. Yello stepped forward. "Where shall I take them?" he asked, volunteering to transport them from Reiggan.

"Nowhere," said Emnor, suddenly. "I will remove them from here. You should rest, my friend. Don't worry, I'll only be an hour or so," and with that, he placed his hands on the Dergon's shoulders, and vanished.

"He goes on as if I'm a decrepit old fart!" exclaimed Yello.

The boys began to laugh, as did the Gerrowliens.

"He *goes on* as if he were your best friend, *because he is*. That's why he wants you to rest," said Jared, slapping him on the back. "Now do as he asks and *rest*. As he said, he'll be back in no time."

"I can't rest just yet, Jared. I have a suggestion on what to do about Tamor."

"Oh really?" asked Jared. "What's that then?"

"A seclusion spell," replied Yello, quietly.

Their conversation was not a secret, therefore it was no surprise that the boys overheard. "Oh, YES!" exclaimed Drake.

"I've read about those. Can we watch?" asked Harley, excitedly.

"We do not even know if Jared will agree to it yet, Harley. Hold your horses, boy."

"Why wouldn't I agree?" asked Jared. "Is it dangerous?"

"Not at all, dear boy," replied Yello, clearing his throat whilst mischievously avoiding eye contact. "Do you think that I would put your father at risk?"

"What do you mean!" exclaimed Drake, "I read about a bloke once who ended up like a pound of crispy bacon when it went horribly wrong."

"Firstly, Drake, that was a very long time ago, and secondly, I knew the fellow who performed that spell. He was bloody hopeless. Couldn't even boil water in a flask with a look. As a matter of fact, he was drawn to stop him from ever using magic again," snapped Yello.

"What do you mean, he was *drawn*?" asked Jared.

"Oh, Jared, you should see it. It's awesome," interrupted Drake. "A load of the elders form a circle around a wizard and suck the magic out of him."

"That's enough, Drake!" yelled Yello, "We do not discuss such things."

"No, Master Yello. My apologies, sir," Drake replied hurriedly, lowering his head.

"It's the idea of my father being reduced to crispy bacon that I'm more concerned about, Yello. Is there the slightest chance of that happening?" asked Jared, sceptically.

"None whatsoever, Your Highness. I could conceal your father as easily as you conjure that fireball you're so fond of."

"How does it work? Does it make him invisible or something?"

"It's far better than that. It conceals him in *time*," replied Yello.

"How can you hide someone in *time*?" asked Jared, now looking very confused.

"You've witnessed me freeze time, as I did when the Dergon were captured, yes?" Jared nodded, "Well, all I have to do is reverse time around someone and they're taken into the past, only by a few seconds of course. If anyone were to search a room where they stood or lay, they would remain undetected, because, in reality, that person would not exist in our time."

"If this works, and forgive me but I am a little dubious, how would you return them to the present?" asked Jared.

"You simply focus on the point where you left them, it's the area that is affected, not the person, you see?" replied Yello, confidently.

"And what if, somehow, that person has been removed from the area that was affected?"

"You'd be stuffed! Probably never find them again. But stop worrying, it's never happened before. At least I don't think it has," Yello replied, stroking his beard.

"Let's wait until Emnor returns, shall we?" suggested Jared. "I'd like to hear his thoughts on the matter."

"Oh, he won't want to get involved," replied Yello. "He was never interested in any type of magic that involved time."

"But he's the head, sorry, he *was* the head of the Administration. Surely, he'd know all there was to know about any type of spell?"

Yello laughed, "You'd think so, wouldn't you? Problem is, he was useless when it came to the simplest of time spells. When we were young students here, he tried to stop time around one of our classmates and botched it up. Poor fellow was only affected from the waist down, he couldn't walk properly for two days. Looked like he'd got two branches tied to his legs."

"All the same, I'd still like to hear his opinion," insisted Jared.

"Oh, don't be such a wet blanket, Jared. I'm not going to risk hurting your father after bringing him all the way here now, am I?" Poom cleared his throat and looked across at Yello. "I mean, after *we* brought him here, of course," Yello added.

Jared had his reservations, but the old wizard had proven his loyalty on more than one occasion and he was sure that he would never put his father at risk. "You're sure he'll be in no danger?" he asked, slowly.

"You have my word, Your Highness," Yello assured him.

Jared sighed. "Lead the way," he said slowly. "And yes, if you feel you need to watch, you may accompany us," he added, glancing over at the boys.

"We'll stay here, thank you," said Lawton, as Jared glanced at him. "We're not really interested in wizards' hocus pocus."

Jared nodded and turned to follow Yello and the boys who, in their eagerness, were already headed indoors. Hannock, who had remained silent throughout, followed them inside.

They entered the room where Tamor had been housed to find him still sleeping peacefully, unaware of both his surroundings and his planned concealment.

"Still out like a light," stated Drake. "Has he even stirred while you've been watching him, Alexander?"

"No, he hasn't even breathed heavily. Just lies there without so much as the twitch of a finger," replied Alex.

"Do you think he dreams at all, Jared?" asked Harley.

"I don't think he'd be having *dreams*. *Nightmares* perhaps, but no, not dreams."

"If he'd been having nightmares, Jared, I would have known. Who would know a person's reactions to nightmares better than I?" Alex said, quietly. The way he said it was a little disturbing. Admittedly, he had been through an ordeal when he was younger, having had no father's guidance, *but what would prompt such a statement*? Realising what he had said aloud, Alex turned to face the assembly. "You know what I mean, nightmares about being threatened and bullied when I was a child?" he added with a fake laugh.

"Yes, I suppose that would give you nightmares," said Jared, patting Alex gently on the shoulder.

"Come on, let's get on with it!" urged Xarran. He had witnessed most forms of magic, but never time manipulation, as it had always been frowned upon by the Administration. He himself had been frozen in time along with his friends and the Dergon. Now he had the opportunity to witness

246

someone being *hidden* in time by one of the masters. His impatience was getting the better of him, aggressively so as his voice changed, his words sounding more like a challenge than encouragement.

To Yello, time dilation was nothing spectacular and he waved his hand toward Xarran in dismissal, "Just wait a minute, dear boy. One does not simply just zap someone into the past. It takes time and preparation."

"What sort of preparation?" asked Jared, quizzically.

"Well, we need to apply the tonath oil for a start!" exclaimed Yello, amazed that nobody in the room seemed to have ever heard of it.

"What exactly is tonath oil?" asked Jared, giving in to the fact that this was something that he would not understand easily.

"It's a plant extract," Harley suddenly replied. "You have to apply it to the skin before the spell can be cast."

"Very good, Harley. How did you know?" asked Yello.

"I *am* Emnor's apprentice. It's my *duty* to know these things, Master Yellodius," replied Harley, pompously.

"Don't you '*Master Yellodius*' me, you little pipsqueak! You'll get my foot up your a…."

"Can we get back to the subject, please!" Jared was in no mood to referee a slanging match between two wizards, regardless of their ages. "Why do you need to apply the oil?"

"He'll be excluded from time, Jared. If he were left there for a century, he wouldn't age a day. Magic, however, dehydrates the mortal body and the oil will help to counteract that dehydration for… ooh, let's see, *coincidentally*, about a hundred years. However, if you don't apply the oil, he'll end up looking like a week-old kerrand fruit, and you wouldn't want that, would you?" asked Yello.

"Obviously!" replied Jared. "But I don't envisage him being hidden for the next century, either!"

"Of course you don't. An example, dear boy, just an example. Stop getting your drawers in ruck. He'll be fine until we bring him back in a couple of months or so. Now, where's my bag?"

"You left it in the courtyard," replied Drake.

"Do me a favour, could you?" asked Yello, winking at Drake, "Save my old legs and nip up and get it for me would you?"

Drake rolled his eyes and sighed, "Back in a minute."

Hannock strolled slowly across the room and leaned down so as to whisper in Yello's ear, "You do understand..." he began, "... that if this goes wrong and the king is harmed in any way or perhaps dies due to your incompetence, and please don't take this too personally, that you will be next?"

Yello smiled back at him, "I promise not to resist, dear boy. As pathetic as that hatpin of a sword you rely on is, you can run me through like a pig destined for the spit. Deal?"

Hannock backed away. His loyalty to the crown had never wavered, and his warning had been no idle threat.

The door opened. Drake entered the room, having retrieved Yello's trusty bag. "Here you go," he said.

"Thank you, Drake. Jared, I think it only proper that you do this," suggested Yello, attempting to hand Jared a small glass bottle.

Before Jared could reply, Hannock quickly stepped forward, snatching the bottle from Yello's grasp. "Jared is heir to the throne of Borell, not a valet. I shall apply the oil, thank you," he said haughtily.

Removing the stopper, he sniffed warily at its contents, "Now there's a surprise!" he said. "Normally, I end up regretting volunteering for *anything*. This stuff smells quite pleasant." Pouring some of the oil carefully into his cupped palm, he rubbed his hands together briefly before smearing it gently across Tamor's face, neck and hands. One would have expected this to embarrass Hannock slightly, but far from it. Hannock was proud to be caring for the man who not only was his king, but was also as close to him as his own father. His self-appointed duty completed, he stepped away from Tamor. With a half-hearted smile, he nodded at Jared. "Your wizard may commence, Your Highness."

"I'm not *his* wizard, you berk," snorted Yello. Raising his hands and closing his eyes, he began to chant quietly. A faint grey mist was forming around Tamor. Small electrical discharges snapped and popped within it, minute sparks and flashes were giving it the appearance of a miniature storm cloud. Tamor's body began to fade. It was fascinating to watch as suddenly he became completely transparent, causing the boys to gasp.

Yello's voice remained constant with not a hint of emotion detectable, despite the fact that the tiny storm cloud around his subject seemed to be growing more torrid. Yello opened his eyes, they had turned milky-white. The group were mesmerised by his trance-like state as he continued to chant. Tamor's body became virtually invisible until, with a blinding flash, he disappeared completely. The air pulsed and the scene became still, but there was no trace of Tamor to be seen. Yello staggered a little, obviously the spell was more arduous than he had revealed. Jared grabbed his elbow to steady him and the old wizard turned slightly to face him, his eyes now clear and normal in appearance.

"Well?" asked Jared, an unmistakeable urgency in his voice. "Did it work?"

"Of course, it worked!" came Emnor's reply from behind him. "He's been performing those types of spell for centuries. Your father is still there, Jared, safe and sound, but a few seconds ago…" Emnor screwed up his face, "… no matter how one says that, it never seems to make any sense, does it?" He smiled. "But you understand my meaning. Tamor will be fine, *is* fine. He *is* and *will be*, fine," he added.

They made their way upstairs, leaving Yello to place protective hexes and runes around Tamor's chambers. Reaching the courtyard, Emnor gazed into the sky, the failing light giving way to the twinkle of the first stars of the night and the lower edge of the red moon. "This is why we stand against Karrak. We fight for the freedom that allows us to witness such beauty in our world."

"And should we fail, Emnor, what then?"

"We shall not fail, Jared," Hannock assured him.

"And why is that, dear friend?" asked Jared, despondently. "Do you have a miraculous solution to our plight? Are you going to challenge my brother to a duel, man to man? Can *you* defeat him, Hannock, because I know I can not!" Jared was becoming agitated.

"Why would you believe that, Jared?" asked Emnor, frowning. "Is something troubling you?"

"You've all got it into your heads that I have the power to stop Karrak. Where did you get the idea from? A dusty thousand-year-old scroll, that's where. We saw what Karrak is capable of, and now he's even stronger. How can I possibly defeat him? There were five of us last time and we barely survived. Hannock, you lost an eye and almost your life and what did I do? Hurled a couple of fireballs at him, that's what. I can't even beat a twenty-something-year-old wizard, let alone someone as powerful as Karrak."

"So that's what this is all about," said Hannock, laughing. "You got your backside kicked by Drake and you don't like it," he added, pointing at Jared.

"Preposterous!" snorted Emnor. "Jared was merely toying with the boy, weren't you, Jared? You were toying with him, weren't you?"

"*I... couldn't... beat him*!" said Jared, emphasising each word. "Drake's little more than a child and I couldn't beat him."

"I think you could have. If you had really wanted to, that is." Drake had appeared unnoticed and now stood behind them, smirking. "Our dear prince has a little problem, you see... *he likes me*."

"What does that have to do with your wizard's duel?" asked Hannock.

"I, kind of, took advantage. The Heart of Ziniphar helped me," replied Drake, looking a little guilty.

"How could the Heart help you?" asked Jared. "I'm the one wearing it."

251

"Oh, what a silly old fool I've been!" exclaimed Emnor, suddenly. "It's obvious!"

Drake's smile kept on getting bigger. "Simple enough to work out really," he said.

"I'm glad it's obvious to you two. Any chance of letting *us* in on your little secret?" asked Hannock.

Emnor smiled, sighing as he cast a glance toward Drake, "The Heart of Ziniphar is around Jared's neck and therefore has to protect him."

"Yes, Emnor. I know that," said Hannock, impatiently. "The question is: *why couldn't Jared kick Drake's backside in a fight*?"

"Because, my dear Hannock, the Heart not only protects Jared from others, it protects him from *himself*."

"That makes no sense. He's hardly going to beat himself up!"

"Do you know something, Hannock?" asked Emnor, a little exasperated. "You can be a bit of a prat some days."

Drake rolled his eyes, "*Some days*?"

"If Jared were to really harm Drake, he would never be able to forgive himself. The Heart of Ziniphar obviously sensed his feelings of friendship. Whilst wearing it, his spells will be tempered, allowing no real harm to come to his friends by *his* hand."

"You see, soldier boy. *I'm* Jared's new best mate!" teased Drake.

"Just one thing, Drake," Jared reminded him, holding up the Heart of Ziniphar. "Remember, I can take this thing off."

Emnor laughed, "Drake, find something worthwhile to do or go to bed. We have an early start tomorrow." With Drake out of the way, Emnor returned his attention to Jared, "Are you alright now, Jared? You seemed most concerned about facing Karrak."

"If the Heart of Ziniphar is only for protection, how can it help me defeat Karrak?" he asked in reply.

"It is not merely for protection, Jared. We've been over this before. It's for enhancement. If you need extra power to defeat anyone that intends to do you harm, that power will be drawn from the Heart. It will never allow any harm to come to you. It may even act independently if you are in the gravest of danger."

"And Karrak has its twin sister. So tell me, Emnor, how will it help in the final battle? If there *is* to be one. Will it, along with its twin, be destroyed, as my brother and I are prophesied to be?" asked Jared, cynically.

"The only person, if he can still be referred to as such, who will not survive all of this will be Karrak. I'll *squeeze* the life out of him with my bare hands if I have to!" sneered Hannock.

CHAPTER 16

"My lord. I do not understand. *Why all*? Why not some, or even half?" Darooq could not disguise the look of horror and panic on his face as he glared at the countless corpses strewn around the chamber.

"They were mine to do with as I wished, and I wished them all dead," replied the shadow lord.

"But they were here to serve you, my lord. Their lifeless bodies can no longer be of service."

"Perhaps to you, it would seem so. But bear witness to my power, Darooq."

Karrak drew himself to his full height, his arms outstretched, a stance that Darooq had witnessed so many times before. A black mist oozed from his open palms and began to enshroud the scores of cadavers that littered the floor. Darooq was not a virtuous man. He himself was guilty of many atrocities, but he had never sunk so low as to attempt necromancy. He had feared it, in all its forms, and now witnessing this shadow lord performing the art made him realise why. Minutes passed as he morbidly studied the scene that unravelled before his eyes.

At first there was nothing, just the black mist swirling eerily around the limbs of Karrak's victims, but then the twitching began. The fingers of the corpse closest to him began to move, a gentle quivering that soon turned to a violent shiver. Darooq inadvertently retreated slightly. The remaining bodies began to display similar movements as the rasping breath came from their dry throats, rasping that became deathly groans. Heads began to turn and limbs were outstretched, grasping blindly for anything that may help them rise from the ground. Bodies writhed and jerked awkwardly.

The undead creatures, now gaining strength, drew themselves to their knees before lunging clumsily to their feet. Their skin was taught and dry. Their eyes sunken, lifeless and grey. One by one they turned to face Karrak, groaning with the voices of the damned. Darooq was shaking uncontrollably. *Why had Karrak done this? What use could he make of this undead horde?*

"Behold! Look upon my legion of damned souls, Darooq. Are they not magnificent? Nothing shall stand before them and survive. They shall not be moved by sentiment, slowed by painful wounds or hindered by malnourishment. I have lingered here long enough. The time for me to rule this world is almost here, and this is the beginning of the spearhead that I shall drive through the heart of it."

"A... and ... am I... to suffer the same fate as these... my lord?" asked Darooq in a shaky voice.

"If that is what you wish, Darooq. Tell me, *is that what you want*?"

Darooq shook his head. "No... my lord," he replied.

"Then save yourself, Darooq. Continue to serve me and I may yet spare you their fate."

"Anything you ask, my lord," Darooq replied quickly, dropping to his knees.

"Look upon the beginnings of my army, Darooq. They cannot easily be destroyed. However, they are still only flesh and bone. I shall not allow them to be decapitated by my enemies simply because they are so cheap a resource. You must arm them, Darooq. Give them weapons, dress them in armour. After all, it may be some time before I find any more suitable… *recruits*."

"Master, where will I find armour enough for so many? There is little of it left here in Merrsdan. Should I perhaps search further afield?" Darooq was, once again, thrown against a wall. Karrak floated toward him, stopping inches away from his face.

"Do not take me for a fool, coward. Do you believe that I would allow you to escape so easily?" he hissed, his foul breath causing Darooq's eyes to burn.

"Master!" exclaimed Darooq. "I have no wish to leave you. It's just that I could acquire what is needed far more swiftly from elsewhere than if I were to attempt to forge such a great amount by myself!"

Karrak paused, stroking his clawed finger across Darroq's cheek with enough force as to graze it slightly, "You have three days, my friend, no more than three," he whispered. "Whether you choose to venture abroad or fashion the weapons and armour yourself is your choice. Delay me any longer, and you might be making an extra set of armour for yourself, understand?"

"Yes, my lord," Darooq replied, nodding nervously. "I shall begin immediately. May I ask, if at all possible and merely to avoid suspicion, should I purchase what is needed with gold from the treasury of Merrsdan?"

"I, unlike you, care little of people's suspicion. More and more you prove your cowardice. I have no need of gold or jewels. Take it if you believe it will make your task easier. Purchase, steal or murder, but make sure you succeed," whispered Karrak, gripping Darooq's face. "And should you attempt to betray me, remember this. When I capture you, and I will, I shall skin you alive and feed you to my pets one piece at a time."

Karrak released him and Darooq fell heavily to the ground. Wiping the blood from his cheek, he watched the shadow lord glide away effortlessly before disappearing through the solid stone wall. Darooq rubbed his head as his heartbeat slowed. *Would it be easier just to end his own life?* It was obvious that Karrak would never allow him to leave, *so why continue to suffer his torment?* Karrak was right, he was too much of a coward to commit suicide. He stared at the undead souls ahead of him. *Was this to be his inevitable fate? Would he join Karrak's legion of undead?* The beasts in the pit began to howl and bay causing the tears to well in Darooq's eyes. Wiping them away quickly, he rose to his feet. He had proven himself a coward. At least, for now, he was a live one.

***

Karrak drew the golden platter toward him on the marble altar. Holding his arm above it, he sliced into his wrist using the same claw with which he had grazed Darooq. But it was not a mere graze he wished to inflict upon himself. The dark red, almost black, blood flowed freely onto the golden platter forming a shallow pool. He leaned forward and gazed into it, his black eyes momentarily flashing red beneath his cowl.

A vision began to form in the depths of the murky pool, swirling and shifting until, as clear as if he were in the room, Jared's face could be seen. He was talking to someone, but Karrak could not make out whom. He waited until the image swirled yet again and he could see the face of an old man, perhaps a wizard, a wizard that Karrak did not recognise. It was actually Yello. Karrak became agitated. They were plotting something, but he was unsure what. His sorcery allowed him to watch, but not to hear. More visions, another wizard, some younger men and then, HANNOCK. Karrak roared at the top of his voice. He swiped the platter from the altar splashing his blood across the floor and swept out of the great hall.

***

Lodren and Grubb sat huddled together in one of the many atria of Thedar, a whispered conversation transpiring between them.

"So, do you think she has?" asked Lodren.

"I suppose she must 'ave," replied Grubb.

"So why have we never seen it? She's never so much as mentioned it, if she has."

"So ask 'er then, if it bothers you that much."

"I can't do that!" replied Lodren, astounded by the mere suggestion. "That would simply be rude. I've got a good idea, *you* ask her."

"Oh, so it's rude if you ask 'er, but not if I do!" exclaimed Grubb. "I know some days I'm not the sharpest knife in the drawer, Lodren, but even I can see straight through that one. *Grubb's always grumpy and rude, once more won't hurt.* Well, I ain't askin', so there. You want to know. Find out for yerself."

"Oh please, Grubb, I desperately need to know," pleaded Lodren. "I'll cook your favourite meal for you, anything you want, just name it."

"Now there's a tempting offer," said Grubb, scratching his beard in contemplation. "Whatever I want you'll cook it, no matter 'ow difficult?" he asked, frowning at Lodren.

"Anything, I promise. All you have to do is ask Faylore one question," replied Lodren, gripping his friend's arm tightly.

"In that case," said Grubb, placing his arm as far around Lodren's shoulder as he could. "You can go away to your fire, get some fresh water, *and boil yer 'ead. I ain't doin' it*!"

Lodren stamped his feet in frustration, "What *do* you want then? There must be something I can do to change your mind?"

"You've got more chance of seeing me kiss Karrak's backside! I said 'no' and I mean 'no'."

"I wish one of you would have the courage to ask me. It's so annoying when one's friends feel that it would appear unseemly to ask a simple question of one so close to them." The Vikkery and the Nibby suddenly became petrified.

Slowly they raised their heads to see Faylore. She was perched high above them in the trees swinging her legs like a bored child. "Well?" she asked. "Can neither of you now remember the burning question? Lodren, you sounded as if your very life depended on its answer, have you nothing to say?"

"Well, erm, Your Majesty, what a lovely surprise. Another beautiful morning, isn't it?" Lodren began nervously. Faylore raised an eyebrow at him. Attempting a weak smile, Lodren continued, "It's, erm, well, we were just wondering…"

"Don't bring me into it, ye stupid Nibby. I wasn't wonderin' anythin', *you were*. I told ye I wanted nothin' to do with yer daft question," snorted Grubb.

"No, no, perhaps you didn't, but we, erm, we were discussing it nonetheless, weren't we?"

"No, *we* weren't. You wanted me to ask the stupid question for ye and I told ye to boil yer 'ead. That's as much of a discussion as we had, remember?"

"Yes, yes, you did say that. But in my defence…" Lodren stammered.

"Will you just ask me the blasted question, Lodren, before I put an arrow in your rear," snapped Faylore, causing the Nibby to physically jump with shock.

"Yes, Your Majesty, of course, Your Majesty," he answered, fumbling with his tunic, "I was just wondering, as you are a queen, something of which there is no doubt…"

"Get on with it."

"Sorry, Your Majesty," Lodren took a deep breath. "Do you have a crown?" he asked, sheepishly.

"*That's it*? That's the question that has been tearing you apart, you silly Nibby?" Faylore laughed. "Why in the world would you fret so much over such a trivial thing?"

"Because if you have, he wants to see you wearing it. Not all the time of course, just the once. You know what a prat he can be at times," announced Grubb.

Lodren had lowered his head and was shuffling his feet in embarrassment. "I'm not a… I'm not one of those that you said, Grubb. I just thought that even if you do have a crown, it couldn't make you any more beautiful than you already are."

Faylore swung gracefully down from the treetops and landed silently in front of Lodren. She placed her hand on his bowed head and leaned forward, kissing him gently. "Yes, Lodren. As Queen of Thedar, I do have a crown."

Lodren looked up at her and smiled. "Can I see it?" he asked, his eyes wider than ever.

"Of course, you may, but I shall not pose in it for *you, or* any other. Only on ceremonial occasions will it be placed on my head," she replied.

"Is that the law in Thedar then?" asked Grubb. "Can you only wear it for special occasions?"

"Oh no, not at all. I can wear it whenever I choose," replied Faylore.

"So why don't you?" asked Lodren, slightly confused.

"Simple, my dear Lodren, it's absolutely ghastly!" she laughed. Her friends' mouths fell open as they looked across at one another in disbelief. Faylore continued, "It was crafted many thousands of years ago, long before any of my people had considered that there may, one day, be a queen of

261

Thedar as opposed to a king. They must have taken every gold nugget they possessed to make the thing, it's *huge*. I think it would be equal in weight to you, Grubb, perhaps even after your transformation, and I am not referring to your splendid golden hawk persona. It is the ugliest thing I have ever had the misfortune to lay my eyes upon. I believe it is supposed to be the effigy of a dragon. To my eyes, the only way it could possibly resemble one is if one were to drop a mountain on the dragon first and then stick the remains back together with mud. It really is that hideous!"

Lodren and Grubb were now chuckling at Faylore's description of the Thedarian crown. "Now we know why ye won't wear it unless ye have to," laughed Grubb.

"Why not have your people make you a new one?" asked Lodren. "Something more delicate perhaps. Surely, if it is made for you by your people, it would still be the true crown of the Thedarian Queen?"

"It has been discussed but my father always refused to allow it to be changed. His belief was that the first crown actually possesses the spirit of a dragon, fabled to appear and defend us if ever we were in dire peril."

"Faylore…" Lodren began slowly, "… forgive me for asking, but was this before your father went… how should I put it, a *little strange?*"

"I'm not sure I like my father being termed as 'a little strange' Lodren, but in answer to your question, yes, centuries ago in fact."

"Oh well, it was just an idea. How terrible to have such an ugly crown on such a beautiful head," said Lodren, blushing slightly. "But can we still see it?" he added excitedly.

"Go on, Faylore, give us a look. It can't be that bad," sniggered Grubb.

"If you insist," sighed Faylore. "Follow me."

"Where do you keep it?" asked Lodren.

"For some strange reason, it is kept locked away in the hall of history. Goodness knows why. I'm sure no one would want to steal it. It's *so* ugly."

"You know what some people are like though, Faylore," said Grubb. "They'd pinch anythin' that wasn't nailed to the ground."

They proceeded through the lush forest, the sparse fallen leaves rustling as they walked. Lodren glanced into the trees and saw that their every step was being watched. Thedarian scouts were perched high in the trees, making their presence no secret to the queen's guests. Guests, invited or not, would never stop any Thedarian from attending to his duties and Lodren noted that each one held a silver longbow, and each bowstring already housed an arrow. A few paces behind Faylore, Lodren reached across and tugged gently at Grubb's sleeve.

"I know, I've seen 'em too," whispered Grubb. "Don't make any sudden moves and we'll be fine. They're only following orders, after all."

"But what if one of them slips?" hissed Lodren, nervously. "One of us could end up with an arrow in him by accident."

"The only way an arrow would strike you, my dear Lodren, is if it were intentional. They are my most skilled archers, they do not make mistakes," announced Faylore, without turning. "It may be a surprise to you, but a few of them are almost as skilful as I."

"But nowhere near as modest, eh, Faylore?" asked Grubb, sniggering.

"Modesty has nothing to do with it," replied Faylore, turning to face him. "It is a plain and simple fact," she added.

"How far is it to the hall of history, Faylore?"

"Not far. We shall be there in a few minutes. Please be silent whilst I speak with the guards, they will not allow you to enter without persuasion."

"But you're the queen and it's your crown. Don't they 'ave to do what you tell 'em?"

"The hall of history is only entered by the royal family and a very select few. No outsider has ever crossed the threshold. If it is allowed, you two shall be the first."

"Sorry, Faylore, but I find it strange that you 'ave to ask permission to show two friends your own crown. You're the queen!" exclaimed Grubb.

"It's Thedarian law, Grubb, and has been for a thousand years. There is an ancient tale of a member of our royal house being bewitched. An evil sorcerer commanded that he obtain the crown and hand it over but his plan was thwarted somehow. In order for that to never happen again, the law was changed so that the crown could never be removed from the hall unless there were at least two members of the royal family present."

"Sounds like a load o' crap to me. Anyway, we aren't taking it out, we're only 'aving a look." As soon as the words left his lips, an arrow struck the ground in front of him.

Faylore squatted down and placed her finger gently under his chin. Pointing upwards, she whispered into Grubb's ear, "My scouts also have excellent hearing. Mind your language in front of the queen, some of them may find it disrespectful."

The three reached a small clearing. There was nothing unusual about the scene. The same lush green grass, small shrubs, and tall hedges that provided a little shade if one wished to rest from the bright sunlight that pierced the canopy high above. Lodren blinked a couple of times, *had he seen something that Grubb had not*? Faylore had paused and was smelling the scent of the wildflowers that grew in abundance all around them. Lodren took the opportunity to amble off nonchalantly to the side of the clearing. He halted and began playing with his hammer, swinging it like a pendulum. Quite by accident of course, it slipped from his fingers and flew to the side of him before landing with a thump a few yards away.

"Aaarrrghh...!" came the scream as a Thedarian scout became visible, hopping up and down on one foot whilst trying to hold the other. It *had* just had a very large hammer dropped on it. "You fool!" he roared. "Why don't you watch what you're doing with that thing?"

Faylore ran across to help the injured guard as three more appeared from various trees and bushes. "Lodren, how careless of you," she said. "You are not usually so clumsy."

"I'm so sorry, mister guard sir," said Lodren, insincerely. "It just kind of slipped."

Grubb could barely keep a straight face. It seemed that Lodren was also being influenced by the Vikkery's mischievous nature. "Let me 'ave a look, see if I can help a bit."

On inspection, Grubb discovered that the Thedarian had actually suffered a broken toe and, feeling slightly sorry for him, sat him down. He held his hands above it for a few minutes, his magic touch bringing much pain relief to the guard. "There you go," he said. "Good as new. Ye should probably stay off it for a day or so though, just to be sure."

"That wasn't very nice, Lodren," said Faylore, dismissing the guard, who glared at Lodren as he left. "You knew he was there."

"How could I know he was there, Faylore? He was invisible," protested Lodren.

"Don't act innocent with me, Lodren. Any repeat of that sort of behaviour and you'll be sent back to Jared with a Thedarian escort. See how you keep up with them when they're in a rush," Faylore stormed off to speak to the remaining guard.

"That was a crackin' shot, Lodren. I'm proud of you," whispered Grubb.

"They can be so annoying. The younger ones anyway. Noses stuck in the air, thinking they're better than everyone else. Anyway, it wasn't that good a shot," he chuckled, "I was aiming for the other foot."

CHAPTER 17

A heated debate ensued between Faylore and one of the remaining guards that lasted for a good ten minutes. After raising her voice a little and threatening to have the guard re-assigned to a new and not-so-pleasant post, she turned and beckoned for Lodren and Grubb to follow her. She advised them to stay directly behind her. Her friends followed without question but became a little nervous as she grew closer and closer to the thorned branches of a hedgerow directly ahead of her. Just as it seemed she would be shredded by the inch-long barbs, something strange happened.

The branches of the hedge began to shrink, they began to wither and disappear back into the ground until there was a clear gap four feet wide, which enabled them to pass straight through. *But through to what?* Lodren glanced behind him and shuddered as he witnessed the ominous hedgerow re-spawning rapidly. Beyond was pitch-black, and as Faylore proceeded, she was suddenly engulfed by the darkness. Lodren and Grubb took a deep breath as if they were about to be immersed in water and followed, closing their eyes instinctively. As they inched forward, the sound of the rustling grass changed to a muffled padding as if they were now walking on the most luxurious carpet.

Lodren opened one eye, just a crack. Grubb, already ahead of him, was standing beside Faylore, his arms stretched out to his sides. Lodren looked down to discover that what he had at first thought to be carpet was, in fact, a deep layer of dark green moss. It was dry and springy, unlike moss one would expect to find in a damp cave or growing on the limbs of an aged tree. He padded forward and stood by his two friends. Looking up, he gasped. A chamber, of which he could see no end, sprawled before him. Row upon row of shelves that stood from floor to ceiling stretched as far as the eye could see, each completely covered with tomes, scrolls or a mixture of both. His eyesight, now becoming accustomed to the dim light, revealed the true extent of, what he now realised was, the Thedarian hall of history. "Wow!" he whispered.

"I'm terribly sorry, it is a little dusty," said Faylore, apologetically. "The air in here is so dry, you see. It has to be or the scrolls and books would simply rot."

"Don't you dare 'pologise. I've lived in some nice caves and caverns in my days but this, well this is something a Vikkery would be really proud to call home."

"Oh yes. I almost forgot that you prefer living in caves, Grubb. I'm afraid, however, that no Vikkery or any other will be allowed to call the hall of history his home."

"I wasn't suggestin' anythin' like that, Majesty," Grubbed assured her. "I suppose we all 'ave our dream home. Somewhere like this would be mine, is all."

"Your Majesty," whispered Lodren. "Where's the crown?"

"Good question, Lodren, wish I knew the answer," giggled Faylore.

"What? You mean, you don't know where it is?" exclaimed Lodren.

"Of course I know where it is, you silly Nibby, it's in here... somewhere," replied Faylore, shrugging her shoulders.

"This place is huge! Where do we start looking?"

"Anywhere you like, Grubb, you're the one who wants to see it," replied Faylore, seeming quite disinterested.

"I told ye before, it's '*im* that wants to see it, not *me*," said Grubb, correcting her. "Why do ye always 'ave to poke yer nose in, Lodren? We could be outside in the fresh air. Faylore told ye what it looks like, it's ugly. Come on, let's just go."

"Faylore said I could see her crown and that's exactly what I intend to do," said Lodren, adamantly. "If you want to leave, then *leave*. I'm staying until I've seen it!"

"Oh, just to help you, Lodren," said Faylore. "When you get close, the crown will call you."

Lodren tipped his head to one side. "The crown will *call* me?" he asked.

"Yes. Not with words of course, it cannot speak. It's more like a whistling, a whining, you'll know it when you hear it," she added.

"So, you're not coming with me?" asked Lodren.

"No. I trust you. You're not going to rob me, are you? You're not going to run away with my ugly crown?" she asked, playfully.

"I'd never dream of stealing *anything*, *especially* your crown, Faylore!" exclaimed Lodren, not realising that she was joking.

"Oh, that's a shame," she sighed. "Looks like I'm stuck with it forever then. Well, don't just stand there. Off you go."

Lodren shuffled away, his feet disturbing the cold, dry mist that drifted sparsely between the thousands of bookcases. He paused occasionally, picking up a scroll and glancing at it quickly or flicking through the pages of an interesting colourful tome. The air within the hall was surprisingly crisp and clean, as clean as it was in the expanse of the forest outside or above. He had lost all sense of direction now. He sniffed the air. *Surely not? Was that the smell of smoke?* No, too faint for that. Maybe the smell of ashes? *Who would be foolish enough to run the risk of lighting a fire in such a place?*

He followed the scent. Still no sound of the whistling song of the crown, of that he was sure, but the burning smell was getting stronger. He weaved in and out of bookcase after bookcase, only to be greeted by a scene identical to the one he had just left. More bookcases, more tomes and scrolls and the ever-present dry swirling mist. One more step and then, *crackle*. He looked down. Raising his foot, Lodren discovered that he had stepped on the remnants of a burnt scroll. Sadly, only the edge of it had survived and the remaining text was indecipherable. *Who had done this?* Faylore said that the only people allowed to enter the hall were the royal family and a select, chosen few. He had to inform Faylore.

Forgetting all about the crown, Lodren attempted to head back to where he had parted from Faylore and Grubb. *Was this the right way?* Aisles, bookshelves, scrolls and tomes, it all looked the same. It was not long before he realised he was somewhere he had not been before. Turning yet another corner, he was aghast at his discovery.

Not one or two but dozens of scorched remains of both scrolls and tomes, volume upon volume now reduced to ash. *What would Faylore say? Would she think that he was responsible?* Of course she wouldn't, *what reason would he have for such wanton destruction?* But first he had to find his way back, and then how would he be able to find this area again? His mind raced. *Which direction should he head in...* and *why won't that blasted whistling stop?* His head shot up. The crown, he suddenly realised. The crown is singing. *Maybe it could help him get back to Faylore?* He followed the whistling.

Although clear, it was obvious that the crown was still a long way away. On and on he trudged, every aisle identical and the song not increasing in volume. He felt as if he had been following it for hours. It seemed that not only had he lost his sense of direction, he had also lost all track of time. Briefly, he thought of calling out in the hope that one of his friends might hear, but stopped himself, not wanting to appear incompetent or childish. He was positive that if his calling out were successful, he would forever be at the mercy of Grubb's tireless teasing. Suddenly, the whistling song sounded louder. He hadn't moved forward or back, but was convinced that he was right. Louder and louder it grew until, rounding yet another corner, he faced a huge glass cabinet that bathed its surroundings with a deep, golden glow.

There, on a central glass shelf, sat the Thedarian crown. Nervously, he approached the cabinet. Tentatively, he stroked the glass with his fingertips, pondering whether to open the heavy doors in order to study the crown in more detail. Faylore had not said that he was not allowed to touch it. After all, *what harm could it do?* He had no intention of stealing it, although he did wonder how he would look with it adorning his massive head. No, he mustn't think such things. Holding it was one thing but it would be completely inappropriate for him to try it on. Gingerly, he reached for the brass doorcatch.

"Leave it alone! It doesn't belong to you!" barked the voice, suddenly.

Lodren jumped back, alarmed by the voice that had suddenly snapped at him. "I'm looking, that's all! I wasn't going to steal it!" he said nervously in his defence. He reeled around, looking for the source of the voice. "Queen Faylore brought me here. She said I could view her crown, ask her yourself," he continued hurriedly, his eyes darting from bookshelf to bookshelf, still unable to see his accuser.

"Are you telling the truth?" asked the voice quietly, "You wouldn't lie to me, would you? I don't like liars, the young man was a liar. The old man that was a young man. He was a liar."

Lodren stepped forward, "Koloss, is that you? I mean, *Lord* Koloss, is it you?"

Koloss suddenly peered from behind one of the bookcases some distance away. "I'm not Koloss," he said. "Who is Koloss? I am Peneriphus. I am Danzeez. I am Solinar."

"No, sir," whispered Lodren, not wanting to upset the obviously confused Koloss. "You are Lord Koloss, father to Faylore, Queen of Thedar."

"Never heard of her. Don't you think I'd know if I had a daughter? I am Peneriphus, King of Thedar and the treasure before you, the treasure *you* would steal, is my crown."

"Now see here…" protested Lodren, gripping his hammer tightly, "… I know these are Thedarian lands and that you are of royal blood but I can assure you that I am no thief. I came here to look at the crown and it was with the express permission of the Queen of Thedar. That was my only intention."

"In that case, why did you feel it necessary to open the cabinet? That is what you were about to do, is it not?" asked Koloss.

"Yes, I'll admit it, I was going to open the door, but only for a closer look. Nothing more," Lodren confessed.

"It never crossed your mind then, perhaps, to try it on for size?"

Lodren studied Koloss as he approached. His stance was not aggressive, but Lodren still felt a little uneasy. His inquisitor had proven himself to be quite mad in their previous meetings, but now seemed most lucid, despite his belief of being somebody else. "Of course not!" blurted Lodren. "Have you noticed the size of my head? I have far too many brains inside my large skull for that titchy crown to fit it."

"Oh!" replied Koloss, with a completely different tone. "That's alright then. If you took it, you see, the second might find it and we don't want that. The second wouldn't care, far too arrogant. But if the second were to obtain it that would be something entirely different. Beware the second…" Koloss stopped talking abruptly and scratched his head as if he had lost his train of thought and started humming to himself instead. He wandered over to one of the bookcases and began flicking at the scrolls arranged on one of the shelves. Finding one of interest, he unrolled it and scanned quickly through the text. "Interesting," he mumbled to himself before throwing it to the ground beside him. He crouched down as Lodren watched him intently. Koloss put his hand in his pocket and took out a couple of objects that Lodren could not see properly, but it was not long before he realised what they were. Koloss banged them together, producing a bright spark amongst the cold mist. Suddenly, the scroll erupted in flames. The items he had produced were, of course, a flint and a stone.

Lodren dashed forwards and immediately began stamping on the burning scroll. "What are you doing?" he yelped. "You'll burn the whole place down around us."

"But I have to," replied Koloss, confused by Lodren's reaction. "To protect the crown. It must be burnt. Beware the second, we cannot let him have power over the dragons."

Lodren stared at Koloss. *What was he talking about? Who did he mean by the second* and *what had any of it to do with dragons?*

Koloss turned away and resumed his search for scrolls on the nearby shelves. Lodren stared at the back of his head for a moment before glancing down at his hammer. He closed his eyes momentarily, trying desperately to think of a more suitable way to deal with his predicament. He had to stop Koloss' destruction of any more scrolls or tomes. "I'm really sorry about this, Koloss. Faylore, I hope you'll forgive me," he mumbled under his breath. Stepping up behind Koloss, he held his hammer up with one hand and half covered his eyes with the other. He gritted his teeth and scrunched up his face. With the slightest of twitches, there was a dull thud and Koloss fell backwards into the free arm of the Nibby. "He's going to have a really bad headache when he wakes up. Thank goodness Grubb will be there to get rid of it... I hope."

He placed Koloss gently over his shoulder. Time to find his way back to his friends. Looking over his shoulder, he found he was still enamoured by the sight of the crown. Unable to resist, he approached the cabinet once more, this time opening the door without hesitation and reaching in to take the crown from its resting place. He felt a strange sensation, a combination of incredible power and pure contentment. He held the crown aloft. The dim light that was reflected by it seemed magnified.

Lodren spun it around on his finger, but regardless of how he held it, the light constantly pointed in one direction. He walked forward into the area that was bathed in a golden glow only for the light to transfer to a different location. *Strange*, thought Lodren. There is no direct light source down here, *so how can the reflection change?* The Nibby continued to follow the light from the crown. *Could it actually be guiding him toward an exit?* It was not long before, either by design or coincidence, he found himself nearing his friends. Looking up, he saw Faylore. "Hello," he called, waving cheerily to her.

Faylore ran to greet him. A grave look of concern swept across her face as she noticed the body of her unconscious father draped over the shoulder of the seemingly carefree Nibby. "What happened to him, Lodren?" she breathed.

"Oh, he's alright," replied Lodren, smiling. "I'm afraid I had to calm him down a bit," he added, juggling his hammer.

"You struck my father with *that*?" yelled Faylore.

"I'm afraid I had to. Had to stop him trying to burn the place down. I'm not as good as you with your little green darts," he chuckled.

"Lodren! This is not funny!" she snapped.

"No, I agree entirely, Your Majesty. Neither is all that stuff your father said about the second and the crown and that he was Peneriphus and a few other names I've never heard of. Oh, and he was talking about the dragons. Wish I could make some sense of it all though. Anybody hungry?"

"What! Ye disappear for six hours, come back with the queen's father across yer shoulder, waffle on about dragons and such and now all ye care about is yer belly? What on earth has gotten into ye, ye daft Nibby?" stormed Grubb.

"Six hours? No wonder I'm hungry. Come on, I'll put some dinner on," replied Lodren.

"Did ye not hear a word I just said, Lodren? What reasonable explanation could ye have for knocking out the queen's father, ye gormless git? Worst of all is that ye don't even seem to care. Speak up, what's wrong with ye?"

"Calm down, Grubb," said Faylore, coming to Lodren's defence. "It's not his fault. He's entranced by the crown."

"He's what? Entranced? What do ye mean, *entranced*?"

"Only the reigning king or queen is allowed to handle the crown without suffering any effect. It's a defence that was imbued during its creation. I suppose it was to protect it from being stolen. Well, that's the only logical reason I can think of anyway."

"But Faylore, I've never met anyone who's as much of a goody-two-shoes as him, he'd never steal anything," said

Grubb, pointing at Lodren. "If he was any kinder, he'd be walkin' around naked 'cause he gave his clothes away."

"But the *crown* doesn't know that, does it? And it *is* still in his hand," she replied.

"I hadn't even noticed it. Why didn't I see it before?" asked Grubb, looking a little perplexed.

"Part of the same enchantment, my friend. Lodren no longer realises he's holding it and anyone close to him is unable to see it," she informed him. Lodren was grinning inanely at them.

"That makes sense," said Grubb. "If 'e doesn't know 'e's got it, 'ow could 'e pass it to somebody else? And if *they* can't *see* it, 'ow can they take it?"

"Exactly," said Faylore as she reached forward and took the crown from Lodren's grasp.

"Shall we go then?" asked Lodren, "Faylore, how did you get hold of your crown? I left it in the glass case before I headed back with Koloss."

"Don't worry about it, Lodren," she replied. "I'll tell you later. Come along, follow me." Before turning, Faylore placed the crown on a large table. "It'll find its own way back to its case," she announced, wagging her finger at it as if it were a mischievous child.

Lodren and Grubb cast one another a quick glance, Lodren raising his eyebrows, blissfully unaware of the full conversation that had taken place whilst he was slightly enchanted. He shrugged Koloss a little higher on his shoulder and followed Faylore.

Exiting the hall of history, they were immediately intercepted by the guards. Seeing the unconscious body of

Koloss over Lodren's shoulder, they leapt forward. "Stand aside!" bellowed Faylore, "Lower your weapons."

"But, Your Majesty, your father?" asked one of the guards in haste.

"Yes, *my father*. You were supposed to protect the hall of history, yet somehow my sick father managed to avoid you all and enter unseen. How dare you challenge anyone? You should be ashamed. If a sickly old man can pass without challenge, why are you here at all?" she asked, sternly.

Your Majesty it is beyond me. He must have…"

"I do not care what he may have done! What I do know is that he managed to slip past you undetected. The vastness of the hall could have swallowed him permanently. It is doubtful that he would have found his own way out and even more doubtful that he would have been discovered before he starved to death. Do you believe that any Thedarian would have suggested searching there once his absence was noticed?"

The guard had lost his nerve and was looking to the ground. "Perhaps not, Your Majesty," he replied, quietly.

"Perhaps not," repeated Faylore. "Take my father to his bed and have him made comfortable, then report to your superior for re-assignment. It seems that guarding the hall of history is beyond your capability."

Koloss was immediately placed on a litter and borne away by the guards.

"Honestly," said Faylore, angrily. "Have my people become so incompetent that they cannot notice an old man shuffling past them? A raving old man at that. I know he is my father but you have witnessed what he's like. You always hear him well before you see him."

Lodren rocked back and forth from heel to toe. "I'm afraid it's worse than you think, Your Majesty," he mumbled.

"What was that? Do speak up, Lodren. We have no secrets from one another."

"Alright. But I'll warn you now, Faylore, you're not going to like what I have to tell you," he replied. He explained to Faylore how he had lost his bearings before discovering the ashes of the scrolls and tomes before encountering her father and discovering the crown. The hardest thing was telling her how he had seen Koloss actually setting one of the scrolls alight, right before his eyes.

"How many scrolls had he destroyed?" she asked, concerned. These were written histories of her people, and, as such, were still sacred to many of the elders.

"I'm not sure, Faylore. I saw at least a couple of dozen, might even have been as many as fifty. They were mostly ash so I couldn't tell you honestly. And I was only wandering around. There could be more in other areas I never reached," replied Lodren.

"Why would my father do such a thing?" she asked. "He protected our archives more than anyone else. Why would he feel it necessary to destroy them?"

"When he surprised me…" Lodren began, "… he seemed to think I was trying to steal the crown. Then he said something about not letting the second get the dragons. Well he said 'the second, but not the second.' You know, what he was saying before, the second, not the second. I don't know

279

what he means by that, but he seemed most concerned about the dragons."

"Did he think they were in danger?" asked Faylore. "Should we be protecting them?"

"He said we can't let the second *get* the dragons. I have no idea what he meant by it, I'm sorry, Faylore. To be honest, he scared me a bit."

"*You? Scared*? When you've got that whoppin' great 'ammer in yer 'and? Don't make me laugh," snorted Grubb.

"You can scoff all you like, Grubb," Lodren retorted. "You didn't see his eyes."

"That's only 'cause 'e's a bit barmy," blurted Grubb without thinking.

"And of course, let us not forget…" interrupted Faylore, "… the father of the Queen of Thedar!"

"I meant no disrespect, Your Majesty," said Grubb, bowing graciously. "But ye have to admit, he has lost a few of his marbles since you last saw him."

"Maybe, Master Grubb. But I would never have put it so crudely."

"Perhaps your mother could shed a little light on the subject," suggested Lodren.

"Good idea," replied Faylore. "Come on, no time like the present," and she marched away rapidly, Lodren moving as fast as his legs would carry him and Grubb transforming into Wilf to do the same. Realising that Lodren was losing ground almost immediately, Wilf scooped him up as he passed and popped him on his shoulder.

"Thank you, Wilf, most considerate," said Lodren, smiling as he surveyed the scene from his new vantage point.

"We all need to 'ear what her mum 'as to say. If she '*as* anythin' to say o' course," replied Wilf. Lodren noted that this was the most he had heard Wilf speak. It was, in fact, only the second time he had *ever* heard him speak.

Making enquiries as to her mother's whereabouts, Faylore approached her father's chambers and slowed to a more sedate pace. Her friends were directly behind her, and realising they had reached their destination, Wilf lowered Lodren carefully to the ground before transforming back into Grubb.

Without invitation, the three entered Koloss' chambers. Erenthas sat at her husband's side, caressing his hand gently as he slept. She did not hear them enter.

"Good afternoon, Mother," said Faylore.

Erenthas jumped at the sound of her daughter's voice, "Oh, my dear! You gave me quite a start. I was deep in thought."

"I do not wish to intrude, Mother, but I have news and hope that perhaps you may answer a few questions," replied Faylore.

"Can it not wait? Can you not see that your father is unwell and needs my attention?" She turned to face Lodren and Grubb. "I am told that his condition has something to do with your so-called friends!" she snapped. "Tell me small one, what do you know of this?" she demanded, immediately pointing at Grubb.

"'ang on a minute, what ye pointin' at me for? I ain't done nothin'. It's 'im you should be pointin' at," replied Grubb, gesturing toward Lodren.

Erenthas' gaze turned to Lodren, who immediately panicked and went on the defensive. "I didn't want to do it, Your Highness. Is that what I'm supposed to call you?" he babbled, "It's just that he frightened me, sneaking around and hiding, asking questions from the shadows. Then, when he came out so I could see him, he started burning things. That hall is so dry I thought he'd burn us all to death, so you see, I had to do it."

"Had to do what exactly?" asked Erenthas, slowly.

"Well, I kind of bopped him on the head a bit," replied Lodren, scrunching up his face in anticipation of Erenthas' reaction.

"What!" she roared. "You struck a member of Thedarian royalty? I'll have your head for this, worm. Guards, arrest this *thing*. Place it in irons until its execution!"

Guards rushed in from all directions. Faylore leapt in front of Lodren, sword drawn and arm outstretched. "The first one to place a hand upon him dies," she bellowed, "I am your queen, my word is law. Step away or die by my hand." The guards stopped dead in their tracks, each dropping their weapon to the ground before taking a knee before Faylore. "You are dismissed," she growled.

"Faylore, what do you mean by this? Your father is assaulted and you protect the treason of the guilty party? You would stand in the way of justice?"

Faylore sheathed her sword. She took her mother by the hand, "Mother, you do not understand. If Lodren says he had no other choice, then it is the truth. He is a gentle soul and does not have it in his heart to commit any crime, especially one as grave as that of which you accuse him. He would lay down his own life to protect mine. Look into his eyes, Mother. Do you not see it?"

"I'm so sorry, Your Majesty," muttered Lodren. "It was just that... he's so big and I didn't have time to think. When he started burning things... I wouldn't hurt him really... honestly. I w w w wouldn't hurt anyone if I c c c could help it," he said, tears welling up in his eyes.

"Shut up, Lodren!" exclaimed Grubb, "Yer makin' a fool o' yerself. You've said sorry and Lady Erenthas 'as forgiven ye. Now shut up witterin' on."

Faylore leaned down and firmly slapped Grubb on the back of his head. "I suggest that Lodren is not the only one who should shut up right now," she hissed through gritted teeth. It took a while, but after plying Lodren with honey tea to help him calm down, Faylore gave her mother a detailed explanation of what had happened in the hall of history. Occasionally, she would pause to allow Lodren to tell his part, having witnessed it first hand, although there was still much sniffling and tear-wiping as he searched repeatedly for his handkerchief. "So as you can see, Mother, I am most perturbed by the situation."

"But I cannot see why he would want to destroy things in such a way. Why, until recently he would stay in his chambers from dawn 'til dusk. He very rarely answered when spoken to."

"How long has he been well enough to move about so freely, Mother?"

"Two months, maybe three. It started just after Jendilomin came home."

"Jendilomin!" exclaimed Faylore and her friends, in unison.

"Yes, *Jendilomin*. Why do you sound so surprised, my dear? She *is* your sister. This is her home as well as yours," Erenthas replied innocently.

"Yeah, but she never turned you into a tree, did she?" snapped Grubb.

Erenthas looked confused, "Turned me into a tree? How could my daughter turn me into a tree? She is not a witch or wizard, she is a Thedarian. We do not hold with the use of magic."

"Bloody 'ell, this just keeps gettin' better," mumbled Grubb under his breath.

"I may be old, you little pipsqueak, but there is nothing wrong with my hearing. What do you mean by that?" asked Erenthas, raising her voice slightly.

"I've just remembered," said Lodren, rising from his seat with a nervous laugh, "There was something very important I meant to do. Should have taken care of it hours ago, actually. Would you excuse me, only…"

"Sit down, stumpy, yer goin' *nowhere*!" snapped Grubb. "If I've gotta be 'ere, so 'ave you. PARK IT!"

"Oh dear," sighed Lodren, slowly lowering himself back down. "We managed to get past one lot of unpleasantness and now here we go, straight back into another."

"Did Jendilomin arrive by herself, Mother?" asked Faylore, tentatively.

"She arrived by herself, but I do not believe she travelled here alone. The scouts reported that she was accompanied by… *ghosts*, as far as they could tell. Jendilomin crossed the river by herself, parting company with the strangers on the far bank before climbing into a canoe. The most unusual thing, other than the fact that Jendilomin was in the company of ghosts, was that they all appeared to be children. Apparently, none were tall enough to reach half your sister's height, but they did not appear threatening in any way."

The three companions exchanged brief glances. "Forest nymphs," sighed Faylore.

"Don't be silly, Faylore. There is no such thing. They are a myth. I mean, a being that exists solely to protect the trees, it's absurd."

"Absurd as it may seem, my Lady, they *are* real. Not only have we seen them, we've been set upon by them. As Grubb said," added Lodren, "they turned us into trees, Queen Faylore included. If it hadn't been for Emnor and the other wizards, we'd still be stuck there now, made of wood and leaves."

Amazed by his revelation, Erenthas turned her attention to her daughter once more. "Does this mean that not only have you been risking your life travelling the wilds, but that you have also been consorting with wizards?" she asked, flabbergasted.

"You say it as if it were a bad thing, Mother. To associate with them is *not* a bad thing. They are good people, as are my friends here," replied Faylore, gesturing to Lodren and Grubb. "We are not simply united in order to protect only our people, we are united to protect the entire planet."

"What *are* you talking about? And what does all of this have to do with Jendilomin? How could she possibly turn people into trees?"

"How did she seem, Mother?" asked Faylore, trying her best to avoid the questions her mother was asking, "Did you notice anything unusual in her behaviour?"

"Faylore, you know that Jendilomin has always seemed a little preoccupied and distant, unlike you and Seenara, who were always up to no good with your inquisitive natures. I could never find you when you were children. You were always disappearing into the forests on some fanciful adventure. If it weren't for the scouts keeping a close eye on you, we would have never known your whereabouts."

"Yes, Mother, but that was a long time ago. Where is Jendilomin now? And why did you not mention that she was here when we first arrived?"

"She prefers her own company and asked that she be left in peace," replied Erenthas. "But you still have not answered my question. *What has happened to make you suspicious of your sister?*"

"My apologies, Mother, but the answers must wait," replied Faylore. "It is imperative that we speak to Jendilomin *now*. Where can we find her?" she asked.

"Somewhere around the small copse that lies slightly to the west of the city," replied Erenthas.

"Where Seenara and I used to play as children?" asked Faylore.

Erenthas nodded, "You should find her easily enough. But take my advice, allow some of the guard to accompany you. There is a strange feel to the place of late, the air seems heavy and thick."

"'Ere we go again," mumbled Grubb, nudging Lodren and pointing at his hammer. "Don't forget to bring that with you, sounds like ye might be needing it," he advised. Offering their respects to Erenthas, they left her company. Once Grubb thought they were out of earshot, he spoke again, "Do ye think she's up to 'er shenanigans again, Faylore?"

"Not really, Grubb. She's by herself now. You heard what mother said. The forest nymphs didn't even attempt to cross the river. They must have gone home once they parted company with Jendilomin," she whispered.

"You *think* she's on her own, Faylore, but what if she's not?" asked Lodren. "What if someone *has* seen something and is too frightened to mention it?"

Faylore had been asking herself the same questions during her conversation with her mother. Unfortunately for them all, they were questions she could not answer. "All will be revealed no doubt, Lodren. For now, we can only hope that it is all innocent coincidence."

"Yeah. It'd be good for somethin' to be a coincidence for a change," chirped Grubb. "But, let's be honest with each other for a minute, we've never been that flamin' lucky so far, 'ave we?"

"There's a first time for everything, I suppose," grinned Lodren, gently tapping Grubb on the shoulder.

"Are we goin' to take your mum's advice and take a few guards with us?" asked Grubb, hopefully.

"Of course not, Grubb, we always work alone. You know that," replied Faylore, smiling at him.

"We're goin' to get shot at again, or blown up or roasted. If she turns me into a tree again, Faylore, I swear I'll…"

"Oh, do stop moaning, Grubb, you know you love the thrill of adventure," interrupted Lodren. "You wouldn't still be here if you didn't. You'd still be in your cave, eating by yourself in the dark and if that's what you want, well, off you pop! Go on, don't let us keep you."

Grubb frowned at Lodren, "Stop goin' on at me, ye stupid Nibby. Save yer breath, we've got things to do!" Lodren knew that it was wrong to make fun of Grubb, but on this occasion, he had been unable to resist and a smug smile was now firmly planted across his face.

They ventured into the forest, Faylore confidently leading the way. It was not long before they approached the small copse. As they did, Faylore slowed her pace, steeling herself for any nasty surprises. The air seemed cooler here and Grubb shivered slightly. Whether this was due to the temperature change or simply apprehension would never be known as it went unnoticed by the others. "It feels a bit... *creepy* in 'ere, don't ye think?" he asked, quietly.

"Maybe a little," whispered Faylore. "Seems peaceful enough. The sun is still shining and the birds are singing. It is a different atmosphere to that of Cheadleford and *that* can only be a good thing."

"Oh yeah?" snorted Grubb. "Calm before the storm if you ask me."

"Nobody *asked* you," noted Lodren. "Nobody *ever* asks you. But it never stops you, does it, misery guts? Can't you just be a little optimistic for a change? Look," he said, "No monsters, no hissthaar, no Dergon trying to shoot us, no zingaard trying to eat us and no glamoch trying to trample us. What more could you wish for?"

"A bloody great castle with us inside it. Well, maybe not you, I'd leave *you* outside. They could shoot ye or stamp on ye or eat ye, then 'opefully they'd leave the rest of us alone."

"It's nice to know who your friends are, isn't it? They're the ones who always think of others before themselves. I swear you get grumpier by the day, Grubb. It's a good thing I'm not like you or I'd take my hammer and squash your grouchy head."

"Come on then," roared Grubb, transforming into Wilf. "Give it your best shot. I'm gonna rip your 'ead off, stumpy."

Lodren planted his feet firmly into the ground and raised his hammer, curling his lip with disdain as he faced the huge Wilf. "You take one step and I'll flatten you into the ground," he shouted.

Faylore, alarmed by the aggression being shown by her friends, leapt between them, arms outstretched to keep them apart. She was astounded when Lodren actually swung his hammer *at her*.

"You stay out of this!" he bellowed. "If it wasn't for you, we wouldn't be in this mess, and as for him," he added, nodding at Wilf. "*He's got it coming.*"

Luckily for Faylore, Lodren's wild swipe had been half-hearted, allowing her to easily avoid his hammer. Lodren and Grubb circled one another as they traded insults. Lodren was spinning his hammer, his breathing becoming more like a growl and Wilf's claws were clearly visible as he flexed his long fingers. It seemed there was nothing that Faylore could do to prevent the impending duel.

"THAT IS ENOUGH!" came a high-pitched screaming voice from behind them. "Behave yourselves! You are acting like children squabbling over a favourite toy. Desist immediately. I am Jendilomin, Princess of Thedar, *and I command it!*"

She suddenly ran between them and before either could move, she wrapped her arms around Wilf and began to hum. A fine lilac mist surrounded them both as she stroked Wilf's cheek before turning to face Lodren and repeating the process. Seated on the ground, Wilf began to transform until he was a very calm Grubb. Lodren dropped his hammer and he too sank down, a silly smile on his face. Jendilomin turned to her sister. "It is so nice to see you, Faylore," she laughed. "I trust you are well?" she added, grabbing her sister's hands.

Faylore was both shocked and pleasantly surprised to see her sister, but initially, she was unsure of what to say. "I am well, thank you, Sister. Where did you come from? What just happened? Are my friends alright?" she asked, glancing from Lodren to Grubb and back again.

"They will be fine in a few moments. What about you, are you alright?"

"Perfectly fine. Jendilomin, I don't understand, they are the closest of friends. What would make them turn on one another so fiercely? Did you have anything to do with it?"

"Of course not!" replied Jendilomin, indignantly. "Why would this be any of my doing? You are the warrior of we three sisters. You are the one who carries your weapons of war. Your longbow, your dagger and your sword are with you always and yet you accuse me of wanting to harm these beings."

"Of course not, Sister, but after your behaviour with the forest nymphs, I am sure you must understand my scepticism?"

Jendilomin looked puzzled. "Are you quite well, Faylore?" she asked, seeming *most* concerned. "Are you suffering with a sickness, or a fever perhaps?" she added, feeling Faylore's brow.

"No, of course not!" Faylore replied, brushing her sister's hand away, roughly. "Why would you ask such a thing?"

"Your friends are obviously affected and I feared that you were suffering from the same delusional state. *Forest nymphs*? They are nothing but a myth."

CHAPTER 18

"So tell me, Emnor, how far is this village you mentioned? Merra, Merra…"

"Mellanthion, Jared," said Emnor, correcting him. "About five miles as the crow flies. But as we are not crows, you can double that distance."

"Are we certain to find a horse trader there?"

"As I said before, Jared, Harley acquired a pig for me there once, but that was some time ago. If the village is still there, we should be able to purchase what we need."

"That, unfortunately, is something we must face whatever our destination. These are dark times for us all, Emnor. To have to consider whether a place still exists before setting your course for it is something that has never been a concern before."

"I have to agree. If Karrak can eradicate all life from a city as large as Borell, a small village in the wilds would be an easy target."

"Our only hope is that Mellanthion is too small and insignificant to be of any importance to him," replied Jared.

"For the moment, it may be. But it is only a matter of time before his gaze falls upon every member of the free world. In his mind, they must serve him or die."

"Looking on the bleak side, gentlemen," said Hannock, "what are we to do if this 'Mellanthion' has been destroyed?"

"We must think positive, Captain. Mellanthion will be there. Our route to it, however, will be difficult, I suggest we focus on that for now."

"It can't be that difficult, surely? Faylore and the two little fellows would have taken this route to begin with," suggested Hannock.

Emnor smiled at Hannock, "My dear Captain, none of us are as fleet of foot as a Thedarian. For instance, have you witnessed one of them climb a tree? As for the others, Lodren is nomadic by nature, and the Nibby are a hardy breed who love nothing more than climbing sheer rock faces. Then of course, there is Grubb; a Vikkery, a shapeshifter, who can transform into an eight-foot-tall four-armed creature and has no difficulty climbing. That, of course, is if he decided not to simply transform into a raptor and soar above any obvious obstacles."

"Some people have all the luck, don't they?" laughed Hannock. "But you have to admit, Emnor, none of them have my charm or good looks."

"Or your modesty," muttered Drake.

"You're getting to know him quite well, aren't you, Drake," laughed Jared, turning to face the young wizard. "Harley, you've visited Mellanthion before, what's it like? I mean, do you have any idea where they obtain their livestock?"

"I don't know much, I must admit. I know that there are farms on the outskirts of the village, so I presume that they must breed the livestock on those. I saw sheep, goats, pigs obviously and an abundance of fowl. As for horses, I only saw a few pulling carts. I don't remember seeing any that were saddled, but I wasn't really paying that much attention. *I was there to buy a pig.*"

"So you have no idea where they get the horses from?" enquired Hannock.

"Not for certain, but there were a few in a paddock. Some of the villagers were attempting to put bridles on them, as I remember, but they didn't seem keen on the idea and kept bucking and kicking as soon as anyone got close," replied Harley.

"You know what that means, don't you?" said Hannock, winking at Jared.

"They're *wild* horses!" exclaimed Jared. "The villagers were trying to break them in. If we're unsuccessful with purchasing horses, we can catch our own."

"Which may be a better option, to be fair. Our coin is beginning to run a little low, Your Highness. I mean, we haven't exactly had the chance to nip back to Borell to visit the treasury, have we?" said Hannock.

"Do you know something, Hannock? The last thing on my mind of late was the thought of not being able to afford any supplies we may need."

"No. It must be a hard life knowing that if you run short of money you simply have to give the order and someone will refill your pockets with gold," murmured Alex, giving Jared a disdainful look.

294

"Oooh, did I sense a little bit of jealousy there, Alex?" laughed Drake. "It's such a shame we can't all be born rich."

"Even *if* one is born into wealth but is never allowed to see so much as a single gold coin," Alex added, a look of disgust on his face.

"What are you talking about, boy? Hold your tongue unless you wish to explain yourself!" snapped Yello.

Jared stared at Alex, squinting slightly. *What was he saying? Was he trying to tell them something, but lacked the courage to come straight out with it?*

Alex suddenly gave a little laugh, "Had you going there, didn't I? Sorry, I couldn't resist. It's a story I heard when I was a boy. An evil uncle had his nephew kidnapped as an infant because he stood to inherit a large fortune, or something like that. You know the sort of tale. The boy grows up poor but ends up coming home to claim what is rightfully his."

"Your storytelling is in poor taste, Alexander, and your timing even worse. I suggest you think about what you're going to say before you open your mouth in future," advised Emnor.

"It was a joke, that's all. A joke! Nobody seems to mind when Drake plays jokes on everyone, why should it be different when I do it?"

"You are forgetting one thing," said Hannock, putting his arm around Alex's shoulders, "DRAKE'S AN IDIOT!"

***

The group had departed Reiggan Fortress at daybreak by the 'back door'. Now, only the faintest outline of the wizard fortress could be seen in the distance. They carried the supplies they had thought necessary, slung in makeshift packs on their backs as they trudged slowly between the abundance of boulders and rocks that littered the mountainous terrain. A fine dust rose from their feet with every step, the red tinge quickly beginning to settle on the skin of their exposed hands and faces. The water they had brought was proving to be far too little. With every thousand yards they covered, one of them needed to pause for a drink. Apart from Yello, Hannock was the most travelled of them and he suggested that they wrap their faces with rags in order to keep them from breathing in the choking dust. Taking a blanket, he tore it into strips and handed one to each member of the party, hoping that his idea would aid in the conservation of what little water they had. It was hard going and, as expected by Emnor, it was not long before Yello called for a brief stop. He rubbed his leg and began to rummage through his pack to find the pain-relieving Abigail's Mercy.

"Would you prefer to take one of the boys and go on ahead, Yello?" asked Emnor.

"No, no, I'll be fine. Just a few minutes to rest my leg and we can carry on," he assured his friend.

"We could do with Grubb being here. He could probably help with the pain," suggested Hannock.

"Oh, I don't need any help with the pain," chuckled Yello. "There's plenty without anyone's help."

"No! What I meant was…"

"I know what you meant, Captain, and I thank you for it. I'm afraid, even if he were here, our Vikkery friend would be able to do little for an old wizard like me. A battered body such as mine can only be patched up so many times. Alas, there are no more spaces on which to place them. What you look upon, Hannock, is no longer a body, just a pile of patches," said Yello, smiling at him. "But I will not cheat and go on ahead, I will keep my place with the rest of you. If I fall behind, you must not wait for me. I'll catch up one way or another."

"I thought Karrak was a lunatic," said Hannock, helping the old wizard to his feet. "But he's not half as mental as you."

***

The day passed slowly and, as he had predicted, Yello began to fall behind. One of the procession would pause occasionally and look to their rear to make sure that they had not lost him completely, only to witness him stubbornly hobbling as fast as he could in order to keep pace. They were not completely unsympathetic to the determined wizard's resolve. After a whispered conversation, Harley had deliberately slowed his pace and was now at Yello's side. They discussed their adventures to date. Harley took the opportunity to raise a point with which he was concerned. "Master Yello?" he began inquisitively.

"There are no masters here, Harley. Just you and I. Call me Yello, the time for masters has passed. It passed with the destruction of Reiggan. Plus, it makes me sound so bloody old. And if you say that's because I am, you'll get my staff

297

across your backside," he said, attempting to smile but managing only a grimace. "Now, what's on your mind, Harley?"

"I'm not sure I should say anything to be honest. It's just that, something's not right. There's nothing in particular that I can say that I've seen or heard, but…"

"But, you're worried about Alexander," interrupted Yello.

Harley stopped and turned to face him. "How did you know?" he asked, surprised at Yello's intuitive reply.

"Do you think that you are the only one who has ever had a friend who began acting strangely?"

"I suppose not. But have you heard the way his voice seems to change? One minute he's the Alex I have known for years and the next his whole demeanour changes. He seems bitter, angry, malicious, as if he has a hatred for everyone around him."

"Yes, I have noticed. But I have also noticed something, it seems, you have not."

"Which is?" asked Harley, with a look of concern.

"Whether it be an offhand comment or a verbal attack, it is *always directed at Prince Jared*."

***

"This is preposterous, Lawton. I do not believe I have ever travelled as slowly as I have today. Look at them, they can barely take a step without stumbling over themselves. And as for him back there, well, I just can't understand why he's allowing himself to struggle so. Why don't we just rush him? If we grab him fast enough, we can be back here before the silly old duffer has time to even *consider* retaliation." Poom was lying at the peak of a shallow rock face as he studied and berated his fellow travellers. The Gerrowliens, having feline genetics, were finding the route as easy as they would level ground. They were, however, becoming a little frustrated as they waited and watched their slightly less nimble friends attempting to negotiate the rocky terrain.

"He's a proud man, that Yello. Reminds me of myself a bit. Oh, obviously he's nowhere near as handsome or light on his feet, but he does have high moral standards, values friendship and has an honourable character," said Lawton.

"So, in what way does he remind you of yourself?" asked Poom. "The fact that he has gone grey?"

"Go on then, Poom, go and grab the old wizard and bring him back here. I'm sure he'd appreciate your help. Try not to shed too much fur on him though. You know how it falls out in tufts when you move a bit too quickly."

"At least I *can* move quickly, fatso," replied Poom calmly, slapping his stomach to show that he, unlike Lawton, carried no excess bodyweight.

"That's because you're more streamlined than I, my friend. No fur to catch the wind and slow you down. The air simply slips over your smooth skin. Let's face it, you can see enough of it," sniggered Lawton.

"Are we going to fetch the old boy or not?" snorted Poom, deciding that he was losing their war of words and quickly returning to the original subject.

"There you go again with this '*we*' nonsense. It's your idea, Poom. If you want to try, I say 'go for it'."

"What if he doesn't like the idea? I don't want to upset him. After all, he's not a bad old stick, is he?"

"I'd leave him to it if I were you, Poom. He can use magic if he needs to."

"Most of this lot are alright really. Except for that one," Poom said, pointing. "The cub."

"You mean the one that sneaks off and talks to himself?" asked Lawton. "Yes, he is a bit of a strange one."

"Do you think any of the others have noticed? They tend to keep their feelings to themselves most of the time, and I can't tell what they're thinking by looking at their faces. If only they had fur. It would make it a lot easier."

"What, that he's a bit barmy? I don't know what you've been watching, Poom, but I'd say they're all a few sticks short of a campfire; one who walks on a gammy leg when he could use magic but instead chooses to use a magic staff as a walking stick; old 'one-eye' Hannock, who doesn't care what happens as long as he gets to kill Karrak; Emnor, who tries to protect them all like a demented schoolmaster; and Jared, who tries to maintain his regal stance, despite the fact that his kingdom lies in ruins and his father lies comatose. Then, of course, there is the Nibby who walks around with a stupid smile on his face all the time; the Vikkery who is the complete opposite and the Queen of Thedar who has her nose stuck so far in the air it's a wonder she doesn't get it caught in a tree. And you think they'd care about a cub who talks to himself?"

Poom had a huge grin on his face that showed his pointed canine teeth, "I know. I like them too. They're all mental. But the young one, *he's up to something*. I don't know what it is yet, but I'll find out."

"You'll forgive me if I don't hold my breath, won't you, Poom? It's just that your track record does tend to leave you a little predictable."

"What do you mean, *predictable*?"

"It's simply that no matter what the situation, your solution ends up as being one of two things, namely, run it through with a spear or if there is no spear available, tear it apart with your bare claws."

Poom opened his mouth to speak. Thrusting his finger in the air and ready to protest, he paused, wracking his brain, "No... no... not always! There was the time, no, that's not a good example. Ah, what about when, erm... oh no, that was a spear. I don't always attack what I don't understand, Lawton! There have been times when..."

"The only time you don't attack is when you're asleep, Poom. It's in your blood, you idiot, you can't help it. Just promise me you won't slaughter anyone who is supposed to be an ally. All we have at the moment is a suspicion. He might just be a loony, surely you wouldn't run a spear through him for that? On second thoughts, don't answer that. If you do manage to find anything out, which I very much doubt, speak to me before you act, alright?"

"Alright, alright, stop going on! Shall we go and grab Yello now?"

"We shall go and ask him and *I'll* do the talking. If he accepts, all well and good. If he refuses, however, we shall return without question. If you agree to my terms, Poom, I will accompany you. However, if you refuse, you can go by yourself."

Poom nodded and within a matter of moments, he and Lawton stood facing Yello and Harley. "How are you coping, Yello?" asked Lawton.

"How does it look like I'm coping, you stupid cat? I'm in bloody agony. I swear if I could get my hands on the wizard who did this to my leg, I'd shove this staff somewhere he'd never retrieve it from," he growled, still managing to mix in a forced laugh.

"I wouldn't blame you, but a spear would do the job a lot better. I'll lend you mine if we manage to find him, I'll even hold him down while you…" Poom's speech stopped abruptly as Lawton glared at him.

"Yello, please allow us to help you," implored Lawton. "With each step you take, the others are taking three. It will not be long before you are unable to make up the lost ground. We could carry you quite easily, but without the others witnessing it. If we stop slightly short of their position each time, they need never know."

"They cannot know what doesn't happen, Lawton. I'm fine. Somehow, I'll catch up with you all," smiled Yello.

"And if you fall out of earshot and are attacked, what then?" asked Poom.

"I may be old, my friends, but I am far from defenceless. Don't you worry, I can take care of myself."

Lawton leaned forward and spoke quietly, not wanting Harley to hear, "What of the boy, can you also protect him? You can barely stand, Yello. This boy may be an accomplished wizard but he has none of your experience. Could you forgive yourself if he were badly wounded, or killed, simply to preserve *your* pride?"

Yello pursed his lips and glanced across at Harley. "Can you still see the others ahead?" he asked.

Harley stretched up on his tiptoes. "Just about," he replied. "It won't be long before we lose sight of them though."

"Good," said Yello. "Use your relocation magic, Harley, catch up with them. Go now. No questions, there's a good fellow."

Harley looked at Lawton. The Gerrowlien nodded as Poom stepped forward and placed his hand on Harley's shoulder. "Go on lad, he'll be fine. But not a word of this to anyone," he said. Harley stepped back, closed his eyes and vanished.

As gently as he could, Lawton leaned forward and easily lifted the wizard onto his shoulder. "I suggest you hold on tightly, Yello. Try not to pull the fur though, I don't want to end up as bald as him." Before Poom could protest, Lawton sprinted away.

It turned out to be an agreeable arrangement between them as the day wore on. Poom would attempt to cause a distraction tearing around so quickly that the others found it difficult to identify which Gerrowlien had actually passed them. Lawton would then take the opportunity to sprint off to retrieve the flagging Yello who, as dusk approached, was almost completely exhausted. "Here," said Lawton, "Take some water. Go on, you have not taken any for hours. We can't have you dehydrated as well as lame."

"Thank you, my friend. I do feel like a bit of a fraud though. The others are having to struggle on unaided, yet I have to rely on you to carry my haggard old carcase so that I don't get left behind."

"You did the same for King Tamor. And I'm certain you would again if he, or any one of us for that matter, needed your help. Plus, you weigh less than a one-year-old Gerrowlien cub and most of all, *I need all the exercise I can get*. I'm getting tired of Poom harping on about my weight. Some days I could happily tie him to a tree and leave him there."

"No, you couldn't, and you know it. He may be a little excitable and over-zealous but you know there is no way that either of you can do without the other." Lawton grunted as Yello passed back his water flask. "We need to find more water, Lawton. What we have will not last until we reach Mellanthion. I don't understand why the ground is so arid, there has never been a layer of dust here before and I should know, I've spent hours out here in the past."

"You have travelled these paths before?" asked Lawton.

"I wouldn't say *travelled*. Back when I was a student, which was obviously *a long time ago*, I used to sneak out of Reiggan Fortress when I grew tired of listening to the old masters. A lot of what they had to say was fascinating, but occasionally we'd be stuck with one of the boring ones who'd drone on about the importance of being able to find the right leaf to alleviate the pain from a bee sting. Emnor and I would come here and practice what we found more interesting, *fire and ice spells*. We'd duel out here for hours on end. Lost track of time more than once I can tell you. Then it all got spoiled."

"Did someone inform the masters of your whereabouts?"

"Oh no, much worse than that I'm afraid. *We grew up*!"

"You are not that different from Gerrowliens, if you don't mind me saying?"

Yello raised his eyebrows.

"We are raised as warriors from birth," Lawton continued. "One of my earliest memories is of being taught how to hold a spear. Shortly after, I met Poom. We were always competitive as cubs," he laughed. "He was faster and studied fighting techniques with every waking moment, whereas I was stronger and studied the intricacies of a battle rather than the skills of single combat. We argued constantly but always remained the best of friends. It seems that you and Emnor share a similar bond."

"If we were to compare one another, Lawton, I would be likened to Poom. Crash headlong into affray and damn the consequences. Emnor is like you, bide your time and achieve a better end with far less fuss. I could never see the fun in that. He was always pulling me out of the fire, sometimes literally, when we were in our prime of course. Oh, what a spectacle we made, robes flowing as we charged headlong into battle, fire raging about us as if the world itself were about to be engulfed. Listen to me…" he said smiling, "… rambling on like an old man missing his glory days. My days are nearly done, Lawton. Soon it will be time for the likes of Harley and his friends to replace us. I mean, look at me. Hobbling around like an old, lame warhorse, what use can I be if we go into battle?"

"I feel the same some days, I have to admit. Then I watch Poom doing something stupid. I'll rephrase that, *something else* that's stupid. Then I realise why I must go on. We may not be all that we once were, Yello, but only time can give us wisdom and that is something that only the likes of you can teach your young wizards. There are only two left who possess the knowledge of the ancients as far as we know. You are one, Emnor the other. When you doubt your worth, remember that fact. If you are not here to guide the young ones, they shall become easy prey for the likes of Karrak."

"It's like talking to Emnor," said Yello, smiling at the Gerrowlien. "What you say makes so much sense, but with a cantankerous old sod like me, it always sounds like a lecture," he laughed. "Come on, let's catch them up. Give me a hand, would you, I can barely stand."

CHAPTER 19

Alex had, once again, managed to slink away from his compatriots and now hid behind a large boulder. He rocked back and forth, his head clutched tightly in his hands, his mind tormented by the voice that only he could hear, the voice of his long-dead half-brother, Theodore.

"Ha ha ha, they're on to you, Brother. They're watching every move you make. They know you're up to no good, that you're plotting and scheming inside that twisted, sick mind of yours. What *is* your plan, Brother? Come on, you can tell me. Who can I tell? I can't tell anyone, can I? Because you murdered me. Caved my skull in by smashing me into a wall again and again. Join me, Brother, end your torment. Take your own life instead of plotting to take theirs."

"Leave me, I have no intention of taking their lives. Only one must die for me to have my revenge. *He* did this to me. So proud of who he is, so proud of *what* he is. His pride will be his undoing. Only when the light leaves his eyes will he know what he has done, and to whom," hissed Alex, his voice barely a whisper.

"Oooohhh look. You're doing that thing with your eyes again. Look at that, they're as black as coal. Are we getting angry again? Poor little Alex. Poor little, hard done to Alex. What are you going to do? Will it be tonight? Will it be now? Or is this another one of your idle threats?" Theodore teased.

"The time is near. The time to let them know who I am, to show them that he is not all that he seems. I'll show them all that he cares for no one but himself. He will betray them in a heartbeat, of that, I am certain. Who would know better than I? After all, I have already been a victim of his pompous pride. I *will* witness the light leave his eyes."

"So it's another one of your spineless rants," sighed Theodore. "Who is *he*? Who do you want your revenge on? ANSWER ME, DAMN IT!" he bellowed.

Alex glared at the apparition of Theodore. "You will leave me in peace," he hissed, throwing out his arm as if to strike someone with the back of his hand. Theodore's spirit began to laugh as Alex began his strike, but his laughter turned to a yelp as somehow he was thrown backwards through a small boulder. It was a strange sight, even stranger than seeing the full form of a disembodied spirit. Theodore now stood with his legs hidden inside the boulder. The look in his eyes had turned to one of alarm as he realised that Alex could now actually, somehow, make physical contact with him. "You will goad me no more, spirit," said Alex, thrashing out an arm, without leaving his hiding place. Theodore's ghost suddenly fell to the ground.

"Please, Brother!" he pleaded, "It was a joke, nothing but a joke. I'm sorry, I needed your company. I'm so lonely. Others like me hide, they cannot accept what they are. You are the only to whom I can speak."

"And when you speak, all you do is taunt me. You tell me to end my life. You tell me that I am worthless and would be better off joining you in the land of the dead. You only care about yourself. *You're just like him.* Why should I be surprised? After all, we are of the same blood, are we not, *Brother*?" There was an evil look on Alex's face as he held out a hand toward Theodore. The face of the spirit began to contort as if it were in great pain. It held its arms to its sides and dropped to its knees, writhing until, with a puff of grey smoke, it disappeared with a scream of agony and frustration. Not once had Alex raised his voice above a whisper. He tilted his head to one side, smiling at the ground where the spirit of Theodore had been. His eyes cleared as he turned away. Drawing his cloak tightly about his shoulders, he moved to re-join the others. He had barely exited his hiding place when he came face to face with Harley.

"What were you doing back there, Alex? Why were you hiding?"

"I wasn't hiding, I needed to be by myself for a few minutes, that's all."

"What for?" asked Harley.

"Well, you see," began Alex, "we happen to be in the middle of a mountain range if you hadn't noticed. Now you may not believe what I am about to tell you so I suggest you brace yourself." Harley moved closer to Alex, waiting for his revelation. "Somebody forgot to leave instructions to build any privies along the route. You may want to take it up with Emnor, maybe he could make some arrangements to take care of the problem," he whispered. Slapping Harley on the shoulder, he brushed past him.

"I don't understand…" began Harley, then, "Oh! Right, erm, yes, well, on we go."

Poom suddenly appeared before Lawton, having leapt from the rocks high above him. "Good news!" he announced, "I can smell water."

Lawton sniffed the air, "I think you're right, Poom. I can smell it too."

"What do you mean, *you think I'm right*? I'm always right. I'm better than any tracker or scout that you could find this side of the planet! Did you know that once, when I was only a cub, I was part of a scouting party and we hadn't had any water for six weeks…"

"Six weeks!" exclaimed Lawton, sceptically. "Poom, if you hadn't had any water for six weeks, you'd be dead."

"Well, it may have been five. Anyway, I was the youngest, and old Perbrin, you remember him, don't you? Big scar down his left cheek…"

"POOM! Let's just see if we can find the water, shall we?"

The Gerrowliens were largely ignored by the others whenever they travelled together and today proved to be no exception. They bounded ahead, ascending the rock face with ease. A few glances were cast their way as they climbed, but before any inquisition could be made by any one of their fellow climbers, they were too far ahead for the questions to be heard. Poom sniffed the air. "Definitely this way," he said.

"Indeed," agreed Lawton. "But something doesn't smell right. Not sure exactly what, but I'm sure we'll find out soon."

They resumed their search, but soon slowed their pace as they caught a strange scent. Before either could comment, they heard the growling voices far ahead of them. They dropped to all fours and stalked forwards silently. Reaching a small ridge, they peered over the edge warily. The barren rock offered very little in the way of camouflage. Below, they spied three massive beasts. They were a species the Gerrowliens did not recognise, all similar in appearance except for the colour of their fur. The black one had the carcase of a glamoch clutched in its huge, clawed hand and was tearing lumps from it with its razor-sharp teeth. It seemed wary of the intentions of the others and guarded its meal as it leaned away from them.

"So, you're not the sharing kind then?" growled the blue.

"Would you?" asked the black in reply. "If you want to eat, I suggest you speed up a bit. This one's mine, I found it, I killed it and I'm eating it."

"Why did we believe him?" asked the brown. "He said if we guarded this place, he would provide enough meat to keep us fed forever. Instead, I'm having to tolerate you scum on my territory. What's more, we haven't seen him for three days. It's obvious he lied, you two will have to go."

The black, the largest of the three, stood to its full height. "There's nothing I'd like more than for us to part ways," it snarled. "However, I'm not the one who'll be leaving."

"Oh, trust me, you *will* be going. Like I said, *this is my territory,*" sneered the brown.

The blue spoke gently, "And if we split up now what do you think he'll do to us? Use your brains, if you've got any."

Poom nudged Lawton. "What are they?" he mouthed.

Lawton shrugged his shoulders. Their appearance seemed familiar but he was adamant that he had never seen their like before. The reason for his partial recognition of the humongous beasts, he believed, could only be attributed to the description of them being related to him by another. His thought was fleeting and he returned his focus to the strangers.

"He'd have to find us first, wouldn't he?" snarled the black. "If he's as powerful as we think, wouldn't he have far more important things to contend with than the three of us?"

"Not that one. He'd hunt us down for the fun of it. And what was that thing he had with him? It was like no wolf or dog that I've ever seen," said the blue.

"He must have made it himself. After all, who knows what these magical types are capable of. I found one of our kin in a cave not far from here. He'd been dead for a long time, his head smashed in by who knows what. I looked at his pelt, looked like he'd been burned, and no normal fire can damage our fur. It might have been *him* what did it!" said the black.

"This is why our kind stay apart!" growled the brown. "You've been snooping around in my territory. You probably would have killed me in my sleep if you'd have found me that way."

"It was a cave, you idiot. They have more than one entrance, you know! Mind you, you're right," sneered the black. "I *would* have killed you in your sleep. There's not that much meat on you, is there? You'd have only kept me going for a couple of days."

They circled one another as they growled and snarled.

"This isn't going to get us anywhere. I think we should wait for him to come back, and when he does, we kill him. There are three of us, he won't see it coming until it's too late. If we grab a part each and all pull at the same time he'll be torn apart and *we* get fed," suggested the blue.

"So, defeating a magic man is that easy, is it?" asked the black. "I've got a better idea. You two try pulling him apart and I'll watch. Then, when you're both dead, whatever food he brings will be all mine, *and so will this territory.*"

"So, there's nothing we can do but guard these gulleys as we agreed. He'll come back soon and bring the food that he promised and I suppose he'll have his pet with him. All we can do is wait. If we *are* lucky enough to find anybody sneaking about, at least it'll be a bit more for dinnertime."

"Providing you don't get there first," said the brown.

The wary threesome moved away from one another. The black, having sated his hunger with the glamoch meat, lay down and covered his eyes from the light as he prepared for a snooze. Brown and blue, now a safe distance away from one another, turned their backs, each preferring to ignore the other's presence.

Sliding away from the ridge, Lawton pressed his finger to his lips before crooking it at Poom and beckoning him to follow. When they were safely out of earshot, Poom turned to face his friend "So, you have no idea what they are?" he asked.

"I've heard a description of something similar, but I can't remember what they were called," he replied, feeling a little perturbed. "Whatever they are, they're not friendly, that's for sure."

"And they're working for Karrak by the sounds of things," suggested Poom.

"What makes you think they're working for Karrak?" asked Lawton.

"Those things said they were working for some sort of magician, or *magic man* as they called him. A magic man who has a strange beast with him. 'Not a wolf nor a dog'. That can only be one of those things he's been turning the villagers into."

"Aren't we getting clever in our old age?" mocked Lawton, causing Poom to curl his lip and wobble his head. "It doesn't prove that it's Karrak though, does it? We know he wasn't alone when he attacked Reiggan, so it could merely be one of his followers."

"It doesn't matter who it is," said Poom, "Karrak or follower. If we find him, we kill him."

"Agreed, but only if we meet by accident. Our first priority is finding water for the group. Without that, they won't survive much longer. What do you think is causing all that dust?"

"Why do you keep asking stupid questions?" asked Poom. "As a matter of fact, *why do I*?" he added. "The answer is always the same. We dodge around answers all the time, but we always end up with the same one: *it's something to do with Karrak.*"

Lawton chuckled, "You're right, of course. Now, noses at the ready. Let's find this water."

Their search was not in vain. Despite both of them suffering slightly from not only the dust, but the stench of the strangers in the gulley, they soon discovered a shallow pool of water. Poom leaned over it but stopped well before he could lap at its surface. "Great, that's all we need!" he exclaimed.

"What's wrong, old friend? I thought you'd be overjoyed with yourself, finding it this quickly."

"Ordinarily, I would be. I would, however, be more overjoyed if it wasn't stagnant!"

"Oh, come on!" exclaimed Lawton. "Can't we have just a little luck for once?" He leaned down to the pool and sniffed. "Rotten as an old potato," he mumbled.

"So what do we do now?" asked Poom, dejectedly, "They're all going to die if we don't find fresh water."

"We'll have to find the source of this pool. It hasn't rained for days so it must be coming from higher on the mountain."

Poom rolled his eyes, "Shall I lead the way?"

"Oh, go on then, just for a change." Lawton glanced over his shoulder in the direction of their friends. The hour grew late and he had witnessed them beginning to set a camp as he and Poom had left. Yello was only a few hundred yards behind them and he was sure that the stubborn, old wizard could cover the short distance unaided. His heart sank a little. If he and Poom were unsuccessful, *would all be lost? Would the wizards have the strength that they needed to perform relocation spells?* Dehydration was a side effect of such magic, and in their current dilemma, it could prove to be a fatal one. He turned and sprinted after his lifelong friend, determined to succeed.

***

"Where do you think you're going?" asked Jared.

"Just erm, stretching my legs," replied Emnor. "Feeling a bit stiff," he added, stretching his arms and back. "I've obviously been neglecting to get enough exercise of late. If I don't keep moving, I think I might seize up. We can't have that, can we?"

"Oh, in that case I suggest you limit your walk to one around the campfire," suggested Hannock. "It's important to keep the muscles warm, you know? Stops any cramps."

"Thank you, Captain, but I'll be fine. I'm feeling a little warm actually, must be the dust."

"Emnor, just how stupid do you think we are?" asked Jared. "We've both known you for over twenty years and what a crafty git you can be. You're not going for a walk. You're going to use a relocation spell so that you can study the scroll, aren't you?"

"You see the thing is, Emnor, we can tell when you're lying," said Hannock.

Emnor shook his head slightly, trying to look as innocent as possible. "Nonsense!" he blurted.

"Do you know how we know when you're lying, old friend?" Jared asked quietly.

Emnor maintained his look of perplexity as Hannock leaned toward him and whispered in his ear. "Your lips move," he hissed.

"What is this?" snapped Emnor, feigning indignation. "Can an old man not go for a walk without being accosted and interrogated by royalty and military? I wonder why I fight these battles if this is the regime we are to adopt upon our victory!"

"Oh, shut up, you silly old sod," snapped Yello. "You know they're onto you so shut your face and sit down. We don't have enough water for you to be using relocation spells. You'll die of thirst if you keep it up."

"So you're in on the conspiracy too, Yello. I would have thought that you would protect my name against such outrageous allegations. I would not, under any circumstances, jeopardise our mission by putting myself or any other at such risk and you damn well know it. Why would I need…"

"Stick a sock in it, you soppy old git! You've been caught. We care about you and we won't allow you to risk it, alright?" Hannock said, addressing the head of the Administration as if he were a ten-year-old.

"If you kick the bucket, how are we going to know what the scroll says should we desperately need it in a few days, or next week, or next month? You are our greatest hope of defeating Karrak and therefore, the one who must always be furthest from danger, do you understand?" snapped Jared. "From now on, I want to know where you're going and why, before you attempt anything. We need every member of this group to survive in order to face Karrak. I am the closest thing Borell has to a king until we figure out a way to cure my father, and I have a feeling we'll all be needed for that as well. You'll bloody well do as you're told for a change, Emnor, or I'll have you arrested."

Emnor glanced across at Hannock who, despite looking a little dishevelled, tried his best to adopt an official stance. Turning his gaze to Jared, he bowed his head. It appeared his greatest pupil had, at last, become the man he was destined to be. "As you command, Your Highness," he replied, smiling.

"Now that's out of the way, we must decide what we are to do," said Jared. "This dust is not natural. Firstly, it's far too thick and secondly, the mountain would have to be crumbling around our ears for there to be so much of it."

"And what's more is the fact that it seems to hang like a mist. Look, you can see it drifting. If it were natural, it would eventually settle," added Hannock. "Could it have been set here as some sort of barrier? A trap to hinder any who decided to attempt to travel along this path?"

"I believe that is precisely what it is," replied Emnor. "I also believe that whoever laid it here would be more than pleased with how effectively it works."

"What we all think is that Karrak or one of his cronies put it here. Is that not so?" asked Yello.

"If that's the case, why not bring down the side of the mountain and block the route completely?"

Emnor glanced up at the sudden question from Drake, "What purpose would that serve, my dear boy? If you began to drain a river simply to catch one fish, the fish would surely follow the flow of water as it ebbed away. But place a net in the water and it is inevitable that, sooner or later, the fish will swim into it."

"So it *is* a trap then? Whoever laid it, wanted *us* to die of thirst?" asked Drake.

"Not *us*, as such. Anyone unfortunate enough to fall into their trap. If they had brought down the side of the mountain, whoever looked upon it would simply head in another direction," replied Yello, beating Emnor to the answer.

318

"So, why not set the trap by the main entrance to Reiggan?" asked Drake. "Surely that would work?"

"The entrance of Reiggan would be too obvious for a trap to be laid, and far too exposed," replied Hannock.

"Perhaps I should have thought about that question a bit longer before I asked it," said Drake with a smile.

"You're a grown man, a young man admittedly, but in order to learn, one must question things. Just make sure there aren't too many questions though, I'm still a bloody good shot with a crossbow, and a bolt in the backside really stings, I've been told."

Drake stuck his tongue out childishly at Hannock.

Harley joined them, closely followed by Xarran and Alex. "Master Emnor, I was thinking, perhaps a relocation spell might not be as harmful to someone…" He stopped short of finishing his sentence, casting furtive glances at his former classmates.

Emnor leaned forward, placing his elbows on his knees as he had done so often in the past, "Go on then, spit it out, Harley. *Someone what*?"

"Someone *younger*!" said Xarran. "I apologise, Master Emnor, it was my idea." He placed his hand on Harley's shoulder and steered him aside in order to face Emnor and the others. "Alex and I feel that we aren't contributing to this mission at all, sir. We carry a few essentials and do our share of the work but are never asked our opinion. You called Drake a man, Hannock. Do you even realise that both Alex and I are actually older than he is? What's more, do any of you care? We are treated as if we are children and we're not. You think we need your protection, trust me, *we don't*. If Alex and I were allowed to use a relocation spell or two, the

319

likelihood of our finding water would be increased substantially. If we stay as we are, our supply of both food and water will be exhausted in no time and we shall all die anyway. Or hadn't you realised how much our pace slowed as the day drew on? Not to mention the fact that, without the aid of the Gerrowliens, Master Yello would now be miles behind us, if not dead. Forgive me, Yello, I mean no offence."

Yello burst out laughing and looked across at Emnor, "Hah!" he exclaimed, "Remind you of anyone?"

"Unfortunately… yes. Yes, it does," replied Emnor, wiping his hand across his face.

"You and I when we stormed into Stumfort's office because he wouldn't allow us…"

"Alright, Yello!" Emnor said quickly. "I don't need reminding, I'm not that old yet. And I'm sure our friends don't need to know what we got up to as youngsters."

"Oh, how wrong someone can be," uttered Hannock, trying to make his voice as deep and sinister as possible.

"Xarran," began Emnor, "I understand your frustration, and please forgive me when I say that your exclusion from any decision making is not deliberate. However, I will admit that, to a degree, I may have been a little over-protective. As head of Reiggan, it is my duty to provide a safe environment for anyone in my care and as such…"

"We are no longer in Reiggan!" bellowed Xarran. "We are on the mountainside many miles from Reiggan. Your great wizard fortress lies in ruins. The lives of both your friends and mine snatched away prematurely by an evil that has no equal. Yet you still believe that you can protect us? We helped to cremate hundreds! Not one or two, Emnor, hundreds! What will it take for you to realise that we want our revenge as much as any of you? Our minds are made up, Master. Our time has come, we *are* and *will* be involved in the endeavours of this party to put a stop to Karrak's madness, from this day forward. Accept it or not, it is your choice," Xarran stormed away.

Alex turned slowly and began to follow him. Without looking, he paused momentarily, "Apologies, gentlemen. You may not like what he has to say, but you cannot deny that he is correct."

"That was unexpected," mumbled Hannock as the two younger men exited. "They're strange when they get to that age though. Not exactly a boy but a long way from being a man and unable to control one's emotions."

Jared glared at him, his eyes wide, "You're a fine one to be lecturing someone about controlling their emotions!" he exclaimed. "I've lost count of the times you've lost your temper and flown into a rage, and I mean recently, not when you were *his* age."

"I'm a soldier, Jared. The position sometimes requires a little more than harsh language," replied Hannock, smugly.

"Can we be serious for a moment?" asked Yello. Hannock's childishness was becoming far more tedious than usual. The pain from his leg was increasing and his stock of Abigail's Mercy was desperately low. "Are we going to allow them to do this?"

"I don't see that we have a choice. It seems their minds are made up. All we can do is come up with the closest and most likely area for them to search. If they find it on the first or second attempt with a relocation spell, they should be fine. However, beyond that, they'll be risking their lives. It may sound a little dramatic but, I'm afraid it's the truth, if they fail, we all die!" replied Emnor.

"Not all of us, old boy," added Hannock. "Don't know if you've noticed but the Gerrowliens did a bunk ages ago. Either they are searching for water or they have lost faith and left us to our fate."

***

Xarran stared at the ground, his brow furrowed. He had never behaved like this before.

"That was a very noble speech, Xarran. You should be proud of yourself."

Xarran turned to face Alex briefly, but turned his back on him once he realised who had spoken. "It didn't feel noble. I can't understand why I said it, Alex. To be honest, I wasn't even thinking it. I don't want to start jaunting all over the place in search of water. I don't even know the area! Why would I volunteer for a suicide mission?"

"You must have been thinking it subconsciously. Your emotions obviously took over and got the better of you," replied Alex.

It was dusk and the failing light added, to the plumes of dust that rose as Xarran paced back and forth, allowed Alex to retreat slightly into the shadows. He studied Xarran, a leering smile on his face as his eyes flashed black.

"Don't do this to him, Alex, I beg of you, leave him alone."

322

Alex glanced across at the ghost of his brother. "Be quiet!" he mouthed.

"But he's your friend, Alex, he's done nothing wrong. I don't know what you're doing to him, but knowing the way you have changed, it's bound to be something bad." Alex tilted his head slightly to one side. Theodore clutched his chest and began to cough. He started to wretch as a black smoke poured from his mouth. He fell to his knees, "Stop! Alex, please stop! How are you *doing* this? How can you kill me again?" With great effort, the spirit seemed to wrench itself free, leaping to its feet before turning and running, screeching in fear as it dissipated into the darkness. Alex smiled once more.

"I've made my mind up. I'm going to tell Emnor that I was being far too hasty, he'll understand. There's no way he wants me to go anyway, you heard him say so yourself."

Alex glared at Xarran, "Oh dear, showing yourself to be the coward you really are? What would your dear, adventurous father say? I'm sure he'd be most disappointed with his brave little boy."

The look on Xarran's face showed his anger at having been called a coward. Alex held up his hand and continued, "I'm afraid I can't let you do that, Althor. I have a few questions to ask and it's far too dangerous for me to go looking for the answers by myself. I'm taking you along as my bodyguard. Not to mention the fact that you'll back me up on anything I care to tell the old ones when we return. That is, you'll tell them *exactly* what I tell you to tell them." Xarran did not reply. He had a blank expression on his face.

A few moments later they were joined by Drake and Harley. Harley had a look of concern on his face but Drake, being Drake, piled into his friend without hesitation. "You're

323

mental, you are! What gives you the right to speak to Emnor like that? They all think you've lost your marbles, you know! It wouldn't surprise me if they were placing bets as to how long you'll last before you shrivel up from dehydration or get killed and eaten by something nasty. And why are you taking him with you?" he asked, pointing at Alex. "No offence, Alex, but you're hardly the type to get stuck in if you're in a punch up or something worse," he added. "Well, don't just stand there, Xarran, say something!"

"He's probably waiting for you to take a breath so that he can get a word in," muttered Harley.

Drake took an exaggerated intake of breath and held out his arms toward Xarran, awaiting his reply.

"If I hadn't made such a fuss, Emnor wouldn't have allowed us to go. Surely, you realise that, Drake? And before you start ranting again, the reason Alex is going with me is because we two are the most expendable."

"Of course you're not expendable, Xarran, and neither is Alex. In fact, none of us are, according to Emnor," protested Harley.

"We have covered half the distance we should have today, Harley. That means that the route that should have taken four days to cover is now going to take at least eight. In just one of those days, we have used almost half of the water we brought from Reiggan. None of us is sure of our position and the longer we wait to do something about it, the worse off we'll be. We're all tired, Emnor is ancient and Yello is only one step away from being crippled for life. So tell me, genius, *do you have an alternative plan?"* It was Xarran's turn to await a reply.

"When you put it like that..." began Drake, "... I can't see another option. How is it I always lose to you when we argue, Xarran?"

"Oh, that's an easy one to answer," replied Xarran, *"You're thick!"*

CHAPTER 20

Darooq's heart skipped a beat as, taking his eyes from the beast that loyally followed him, he caught sight of the pulsating red glow that had suddenly appeared at the end of the dark passageway. It was the light from the Elixian Soul. The supernatural gem now possessed the body of Karrak, he had become the shadow lord. He bowed low as his master glided swiftly and effortlessly toward him. Stopping immediately in front of him, Karrak's deep voice rasped menacingly. "A day has passed, Darooq, and I see no weapons or armour adorning my army."

"Apologies, my lord. I am unfamiliar with these lands and sought maps and charts within the libraries to aid me in my quest to find equipment."

"And did you find what you were looking for within those libraries?"

"Yes, my lord. There is a sizeable village that is protected by a fort. It may take me a few days to procure everything needed for your army, but I am confident that my journey will be successful."

"Two days, Darooq, your deadline is now reduced to two days. Why is this beast at your side? Do you not realise that this one is my own personal pet?"

"I do, my lord. The beasts are driven to devour one another as there is no longer food for them. Believing this to be your favourite, I thought it best to keep it out of harm's way. It seems weak and old. I am not sure that it would have survived much longer had I left it with the others."

"You are a poor judge of character, Darooq. The beast that stands at your side is probably the most cunning, devious, ruthless creature you will ever have the misfortune to meet. It knows a cruelty which even I admire and would tear out my throat and yours if it were given the remotest chance. The strongest of the pack will survive, and this one is the strongest of them all," Karrak gave a chilling, guttural laugh. "You have two days, Darooq. Return successful within that time, if you do not, pray that I never find you whilst you are still alive. However, even then you still would not be safe."

Darooq bowed, Barden cowering behind his leg as Karrak glided away and disappeared into the darkness.

Making his way into the daylight, Darooq leaned down and patted Barden gently before taking a firm hold on his collar, "Sorry boy, but if I allow you to escape, our master would probably roast me alive. Take solace, at least for now you are free of any punishment." With a wave of his hand, he and Barden vanished.

***

Within the blink of an eye, they reappeared on a broad makeshift dirt road. It was well used, showing the evidence of fresh tracks caused by the cartwheels that travelled it regularly. Darooq reached down and petted Barden again, "That wasn't too bad, was it, boy? Listen to me, I'm talking to a…" looking down, he curled his lip, "you're not even a dog, are you? Come to think of it, I have no idea what you are, or who you were for that matter. What I *do* know is that you must have offended Lord Karrak in some way. Who's a good boy?" he laughed. He shrugged his shoulders. The creature seemed to be smiling at him, a hideous smile admittedly, but still a smile. "We'll be alright for a couple of days at least, boy. He shouldn't beat either of us if we do a good job for him."

They followed the track for a few miles until, up ahead, they saw movement that could only mean that they were nearing their destination. Darooq thought it best to attempt to disguise Barden. Wrapping a shawl around him, he decided that should anyone enquire as to the breed of his dog, he would spin them a yarn of the dog having suffered a horrendous accident as a pup, perhaps having been run over by a cart. He looked down at Barden… *two carts… ten carts*, he thought. He was developing quite an attachment to the ugly, downtrodden beast.

He entered the village. Not the smallest of men, he still went unnoticed by the villagers. They were far too busy with their trade or gossip to pay attention to a travelling stranger and his pet. Darooq was in no rush and ambled between a throng of tents set at the edge of the village by various travelling merchants, hawkers and those who were not much more than beggars. He paused occasionally, pretending to show interest in an item, its owner trying desperately to enter into a bartering session with him. But he had no real interest

328

in any of the merchandise he was offered, he was too busy listening carefully, listening for the sound of the only thing he needed, the sound of a hammer striking an anvil. He was searching for a smith. It would have been illogical, and possibly suspicious, for him to storm into town and ask directions. The gentle approach, he thought, would glean far more results. Mingling with the crowds, he continued his search, then he heard it... *clink*.

Darooq approached the smith and, with a slight bow, smiled at him. "Forgive me, smith, I am a stranger in these lands. Tell me, how highly you would rate your work with the forge?"

"Is that how you begin a conversation where you come from? Walk up to a complete stranger and insult his skill!" Although there was a sharpness to his tone, he didn't seem overly insulted at Darooq's question. "Does it matter what I think, friend? Would a craftsman not tell you that his workmanship was second to none, whether it be true or not? I do not judge my own craft. If you want an honest opinion, go to the tavern. There are warriors, mercenaries mostly, who've had need of me in the past. Ask 'em what they think, although not one of 'em will part with coin enough to afford 'em new weapons or armour. Repair, repair, repair, it's all I ever do for 'em. I can't complain though, if they bought new, I'd be out of pocket in the long run," he winked at Darooq, knowingly tapping the side of his nose with his index finger, "An old sword blunts and breaks much faster than a newly forged one."

Darooq had met many merchants like him before. He may have been skilled at his trade, but what better way for the smith to increase his profit than to insult his other patrons for being tight-fisted. His smile remained as he eyed the smith. "May I ask your name, smith?" he asked.

"They call me 'ammer'. Been called it since I was a lad. Real name's Ben, but if you shouted me in the street with it, I'd probably ignore ye. I've been wielding one for nigh on twenty years now, an 'ammer that is, so the name just stuck after a while."

"Pleased to make your acquaintance, Hammer. I would like to talk business with you. I need one hundred suits of armour and the same number of swords, the bulk of both, in two days from now."

"Now why didn't you say so in the first place!" replied Hammer, laughing with mock glee. "Tell you what, I'll 'ave it ready by this afternoon. I'll even wrap it all in a giant flyin' carpet, 'ow's that?"

"Do not mock me, smith!" growled Darooq, glaring at Hammer. "Few who do so survive to tell the tale! I am no fool. You will be well rewarded for your efforts should you choose to accept, but failure is not an option if you do." He threw a bag of gold coins against the smith's anvil. The bag split, spilling the coins all around Hammer's feet. He dropped to his knees, snatching them greedily from the ground.

"All I'm sayin', sir, is… well, a hundred… in two days. It's a lot, sir. It can be done, but I'd need some 'elp!" he replied.

The smile had left Darooq's face as he watched the smith, who was still grovelling on the ground to make sure he had not missed any stray gold coins. As he reached for one, Darooq placed his foot on the back of his outstretched hand, grinding his heel into it. Hammer winced in pain but

330

did not attempt to pull his hand away as Barden moved closer until he was directly in front of the smith and began to growl, the stench from his rancid breath causing Hammer to wretch. "I suggest you begin immediately. Hire your help, there is plenty more gold where that came from. Remember, complete this task and there will be more opportunities for you in the future, and with even greater rewards. The armour needs to be strong and serviceable. The swords a basic, straight blade but perfectly honed. I shall return tomorrow to check on your progress. Work all night if you must, *it would not serve you well to disappoint me*. Now… where is this tavern you mentioned?"

Hammer rose to his feet and, rubbing the back of his hand, pointed toward the fort, "It's at the side of the fort, sir. You might want to be careful what ye say around them soldiers though, they bully anyone who gets near the fort. An' if you go into the tavern itself, expect a fight. The place is always full of 'em an' they tend to kick the crap out of anyone who dares to go in there. They act as if they own the place, an' the poor bloke who does, never makes any coin out of it, they never pay 'im for any of the ale an' other stuff they drink."

The smile returned to Darooq's face, "So, they like to fight and bully people, do they? Oh my… they're going to love me then," he sneered. He glanced down at Barden, "What do you say, beast, shall we go and introduce ourselves?" Barden began to growl quietly.

Darooq headed toward the tavern, a determination in his gait that showed his intent. He had suffered at the hands of Karrak for what seemed like an age, and a chance to vent his frustration was at hand. The mental and physical torture he

331

had suffered had become almost unbearable, and he knew that soon, his only release would be his demise.

If he was going to die, he was determined to take as many as possible with him on the journey to the abyss. He would not be as sadistic as Karrak. The ones he took with him would be those to whom such an end was deserved. The cruel, the violent and the vicious would be his unwilling travelling companions. As he walked, all emotion drained from his face as he pictured in his mind the events that were about to take place. Perhaps ridding the world of a few of its barbarous inhabitants could offer him a little redemption for all the innocents that had been slaughtered by Karrak? But he was not foolish enough to believe this. He had willingly joined with Karrak, and if things had gone to plan, maybe, he now would be the one wielding the power over throngs of innocents. He reached the doorway of the tavern and opening it slowly, he stepped inside.

"Can't bring that mangy thing in here," bellowed the barkeep. "You'll have to tie it up outside. Animals carry all sorts if diseases on 'em, kill people without even trying, they do."

Darooq stared at the barkeep, "My hound stays with me, or would you prefer that I take my custom *elsewhere*?"

It was almost possible for anyone to read the barkeep's mind. He could not afford to lose a single paying customer, Hammer had informed him of that. His eyes darted to the table in the centre of the room that was surrounded by at least a dozen, scruffy-looking unwashed guards. A few of them laughed at him, as his retreat was almost immediate, "Well, take a table at the back and make sure it behaves itself or you're both out. Understand?"

Darooq nodded once and began to cross the room. Barden stayed at his heel.

"That's it, you show him who's boss. Can't even keep his own customers in check. You're bloody pathetic, you are," bawled one of the guard as he hurled a pewter tankard at the barkeep. Luckily, it missed its target, smashing a bottle behind him instead.

"Alright, gentlemen," said the barkeep becoming flustered. "There's no need for any unpleasantness. Remember what happened last time?"

"I think I do," replied another one of the rowdy, uniformed men. "Although, I was very drunk at the time. I remember beating the living daylights out of a few of the villagers and then arresting them for causing a riot." He roared with laughter, as did his friends.

"But they didn't do anything. You tripped one of them up deliberately and then accused him of kicking you," said the barkeep.

"As I said," repeated the guard, "I was *very* drunk."

The barkeep turned his attention to Darooq, "What can I get you to drink, sir? Perhaps an ale? We do have a nice selection of wines, or perhaps some mead."

"You call that cat's water you serve, *wine*?" shouted the outspoken guard, "I could pee better than that stuff tastes."

"Well, why don't you do that? And leave me to take my refreshment in peace," hissed Darooq as he glared at the guard.

"Did you hear that, boys?" the guard asked confidently of his friends, although Darooq could see in his eyes that he was unnerved. "Seems this one wants to keep us company.

Looking for a nice little free bed and board in our gaol, I think. I suggest you keep a civil tongue in your head, stranger. This is our town and we don't like it when outsiders come here thinking they don't have to obey the law."

"And what laws do you uphold?" asked Darooq quietly. "The laws of the land or the laws of the highest bidder to fill your pockets, wretch?" he added with a sneer.

"Now, now, sir, let's not have any trouble or I'll have to ask you to leave," urged the barkeep.

A few of the guard were now on their feet, hands firmly on the hilts of their swords. One took a step toward Darooq but retreated rapidly as Barden began to snarl. "I am sure, innkeeper, that you would rather lose the patronage of such scum as these than that of a paying customer. After all, I'd wager that what I alone would spend in one sitting would outweigh what a gaggle of freeloaders would part with in an entire day."

The barkeep's hands were now visibly shaking. He had witnessed on more than one occasion what the corrupt guard were capable of, and nine times out of ten, their actions were unprovoked. They were the town bullies. More a gang of murderous bandits than a military unit. People had banded together in the past in order to stand up to them, and each time, those people had mysteriously disappeared.

"Do you want to know something, stranger?" asked the guard, "I knew you was trouble as soon as you walked through that door. I'd know a criminal from a mile away."

"Of that I am sure," replied Darooq. "Must be all those years seeing your own reflection."

The guard laughed again, but it had turned to a nervous laugh, "You really do like making trouble for yourself, don't you? You sit there as cocky as can be, thinking we're scared of you just 'cause you're such a big fella. Well, you're wrong. There's more than a dozen of us, we're not scared of you. Not one bit," he grabbed for his sword.

As he rushed forward, Darooq flicked his fingers as if he were shooing away a fly and the guard was blasted across the inn, taking some of the other guards with him. Barden flew into the air and with one sideways jerk of his head, he tore the throat out of another. The air was suddenly filled with flame and lightning as blood splashed across tables, chairs, walls and floors. The screams from within the tavern could be heard halfway across the village, but they lasted for just a few minutes before an eerie silence fell not only over the inn, but the entire town.

The door to the inn opened. Darooq stepped out into the afternoon sun. There were bloodstains on his robes and the jaws of the hideous beast that he seemed to care for so dearly. The large sorcerer closed his eyes. A blue hue that began at his head travelled down his body, shrouding both him and Barden. When it dissipated, not a trace of blood could be seen.

He turned and looked back into the tavern. The bodies of the entire troupe of guards lay dead, strewn across the room. Some had obvious wounds, whereas others seemed physically untouched, but the looks of horror on their faces told a completely different story. Darooq waved his hands toward the scene. A green haze appeared from nowhere and drifted silently over the corpses. They began to hiss and bubble, their skin resembling a joint of meat sizzling over a spit. The seething mist dissolved the bodies, literally melting them into the wooden floor.

After just a few minutes, not a single trace of the carnage that had just taken place remained. Darooq smiled at the barkeep as he threw him a purse of gold. "A good red wine, please, and water for my pet," he said politely. The barkeep nodded, aghast. "Then we shall have a discussion about the fort on the village outskirts. Who runs the place, and how best should we rid ourselves of them?" The barkeep gulped.

CHAPTER 21

"Lodren, have you, by any chance, seen my father?"

"Of course I have, Faylore! He's the mad one who keeps shouting at everyone, don't you remember? *The first this, the first that. Not the first, the second. But not the second, but the second.* Ring any bells yet?" It was unlike Lodren to be so curt, but his frustration was showing.

"Sarcasm really doesn't suit you, Lodren. Honestly, the bad habits you are learning from Grubb are becoming most tiresome."

"What bad habits? Do you mean speaking my mind?" Lodren sighed, "I'm sorry, Your Majesty," he said quietly, "It's just that we've been here ages now, and although it was lovely to meet your family, even Jendilomin, now that she's not all mental about turning everyone into a tree, I can't help worrying about Prince Jared and the others. They might need us. We're weeks away from them and if they need our help, we'd never be able to get to them in a hurry."

"Nonsense!" Faylore replied, adamantly. "We could return to them within a day should the need arise."

"Within a day?" asked Lodren, surprised. "How?"

"Never you mind. Save to say, if there were such urgency, we would be at their side almost immediately. Now, back to my first question: *have you seen my father?*"

"He was around this morning, Your Majesty. He was talking to Grubb, funnily enough. They actually seemed to be having a conversation, but I couldn't hear what was being said. Have you asked him if he's seen Koloss?"

"No, I came to you first. Imagine the response I'd get from a grumpy Vikkery if your reaction was anything to go by. He'd probably be ripping at me with his claws by now," she replied with a gentle laugh.

"Oh no! He'd never do anything to hurt you, Faylore! He can be a miserable so and so at times but he'd never raise a hand against you, I can promise you that much."

"I'd have said the same bond exists between the two of *you,* Lodren. Yet, only a few days ago, you were ready to tear one another to pieces."

Lodren pursed his lips, "Yeah… it's a good thing your sister was around. That could have ended up getting nasty. Do you know, I still don't know how it started or what it was about? Strangest thing is, I can't remember much about it either."

"Jendilomin thinks there is something in the soil itself, something that has tainted it. Explanations, however, on that subject, will have to wait. I need to find my father."

Lodren joined Faylore in her search and it was not long before they came across Grubb. He was sitting on the ground with his back against a large tree, idling his time away by playing with the silver dagger that Hannock had presented to him. His target, if you could call it a proper target, was the side panel of a hay cart. He would draw back his arm and throw the dagger, but he was so bored that he couldn't even be bothered to get up and retrieve it properly. Leaning forward, he was transforming one of his arms into one that they were more used to seeing attached to Wilf. Even with the transformation, this was a bit of a stretch, tell-tale by the grunt as he sat forward far enough to reach. It was quite apparent that he had been practicing his knife-throwing routine for some time, as the side of the cart was looking decidedly splintered.

"I don't know what that cart said to upset you, Grubb, but it must have been bad. I'd stop now if I were you, I think it's dead," chuckled Lodren.

Grubb glanced across at his friend, "Get stuffed!"

"Oh dear… you're in one of those moods, are you? That's not going to help us, Faylore."

Faylore ignored Grubb's mood, "Have you seen Koloss recently, Grubb?" she asked politely.

"No I 'aven't. And I don't care if I never see 'im again!" he snapped. "Tried to be nice to 'im I did. You know, 'cause 'e's your dad and a bit barmy, and what does *he* do? Insults me, tells me I'm not a proper Vikkery just 'cause I do things differently than the rest of my kind. Well, 'e can get lost and stay lost for all I care!"

Faylore stood wide-eyed at Grubb's sudden outburst, "I have no idea what you're talking about, Grubb," she said, crouching down in front of him, "What do you mean, you're not the same as the rest of your kin?"

Grubb was never one to show his emotions, but Faylore could see the tears welling in his eyes as he stared at the ground, "Mocked me, Faylore, *he mocked me*. Said I was a joke and that I should be ashamed. Said it was no wonder I left my family, 'cause they'd laugh at me. Just 'cause I'm different."

Faylore attempted to comfort him but Grubb would not allow it. Shrugging her away, he stood up swiftly and took a few paces away from her whilst wiping his tears away with his sleeve. "Well, I might be different, but none of 'em can do what I can! They can't heal cuts and bruises like I do. I'm not ashamed, I'm better than all of 'em."

Lodren was most uncomfortable with the tense situation. It was not the fact that Grubb was ranting and stamping his feet as he walked, it was the fact that his friend was in emotional pain. He knew that no matter what was said, or by whom, it would not ease his suffering. He did not know what Grubb's secret was but it was obviously most distressing for him. Not being able to help his friend after all that he had done for *them* was heart-breaking. Walking determinedly up to his friend, he slapped him on the shoulder, "I know you're not one for cuddles and things, Grubb, so I'll simply say this. Should you ever need to talk to anyone, someone who's not judgmental and offers only loyalty and friendship, I'll be right here. Do you hear me? *Right here,*" he said adamantly, pointing at his feet.

Faylore smiled at Lodren and then turned her gaze to Grubb, "I need you, my friend. Help me find my father, please?" she asked.

Grubb took a deep breath in order to pull himself together, "Can you lot not manage without me for one day?" he asked, putting on a false, grumpy mood. "*Carry me stuff, heal me wounds, save me life.* Honestly, will I never 'ave a moment's peace?" he grumbled, smiling at his friends. "Come on then. *Let's go and find yer mad dad.*"

The three wandered around the forest for some time, searching various caves and copses the former king was known to frequent before his illness, but to no avail. They heard a voice in the distance calling Faylore's name, a female voice, it was Jendilomin. They found her in a clearing not far ahead, but she was not alone. The guard that Faylore had rebuked when they had found their father in the hall of history was beside her, looking decidedly sheepish. He bowed as she approached.

"What is it, Sister?" Faylore asked. "Has something happened?"

Jendilomin turned to face the guard, "Tell Her Majesty what you told me."

The guard kept his head bowed, too fearful to look his queen in the eye, "Your Majesty, I cannot say how... it is impossible. He could not have passed without being detected, but somehow he did. Please, accept my humblest apologies. I understand that you will be angry with me... but I have done nothing wrong."

"Stop babbling and tell me what has happened!"

"Your father, Koloss, Your Majesty," he began nervously, "somehow, he has re-entered the hall of history."

Faylore went into a rage, "You were given strict instructions to prevent him from entering. How could you allow this to happen, again?"

Jendilomin raised her hand to calm her sister, "Majesty," she said quietly, "It appears that during his previous visits, our father may have been dabbling... with magic."

Faylore could not disguise the look of horror on her face, "He would never be so reckless! Even with his illness he would know that he would put his very life at risk!"

"It may, however, explain his rapid mental deterioration. We have held true to our laws regarding the use of supernatural forces, Sister. If our father's judgement was impaired due to his illness, its use would only exacerbate his symptoms. It would, *literally*, drive him insane."

Grubb marched forward, grabbing Lodren's tunic as he passed him, "Come on," he ordered. "We've got a king to save."

"Wait a moment," urged Jendilomin, "he could be dangerous."

Grubb transformed into Wilf and lifted Lodren onto his shoulder, "Maybe," he growled. "But so can we," he added, reaching up and patting Lodren on the head. Faylore and Jendilomin followed quickly and were directly behind them as they reached the door to the hall.

"I didn't like this place the first time we came here," whispered Lodren, leaning down to Wilf's ear, "I've got a nasty feeling I'm going to like it even less this time."

"Don't you worry, me friend," growled Wilf, "I'll be right here," he said, pointing at his feet and giving a deep, grunting laugh.

They closed the door gently behind them. Pausing for a moment, they listened intently, hoping to hear anything that may reveal Koloss' whereabouts. There was silence. Lodren looked down at the royal sisters, "Any ideas?" he asked hopefully.

"The aisle of royal remembrance?" asked Jendilomin, looking at her sister quizzically.

"By that, I presume you mean dead kings and the like?" asked Lodren, scrunching up his face in disgust.

"Don't look like that!" hissed Faylore. "It simply means diaries and scrolls of the ancient royals. Not the cadavers of them, you daft Nibby."

Lodren breathed a sigh of relief, "Thank goodness for that. For a minute I thought we'd be greeted by a load of dead people trying to keep us out."

"You have a very vivid imagination for one so small!" said Jendilomin, who could be very tactless sometimes.

"I think we should split up," growled Wilf. "Me and Lodren go one way, and you two go the other."

"Not bloomin' likely!" objected Lodren, hurriedly. "Wherever Faylore goes, we go. We're not splitting up. It always goes wrong when people split up. Or haven't you read any adventure stories?" He looked down at Wilf, "Stupid question, forget I asked it. Anyway, *we stay together* and that's the end of it."

They searched the hall of history as methodically as they could. It was vast, but after many hours, they found no trace or tell-tale sign of Koloss. As more and more time passed, both Lodren and Wilf felt that they must have covered most of its expanse by now. "How much of the hall do you think we've covered, Faylore? We should find him soon?" asked Lodren, hopefully.

"We should finish searching this level by tomorrow. If we're not successful, we'll be able to leave and come back the following day equipped to start the descent to the lower levels," she whispered in reply.

"*Lower levels*?" asked Lodren, his eyes wide. "How many levels are there?"

Faylore looked at Jendilomin, who leaned forward and whispered to her sister. She turned to face Lodren, "Twenty-eight," she announced confidently, "We think! There may be one or two more that have been forgotten. Well, don't look so dumbfounded, *it is centuries old after all.*"

"That means we could be down here for weeks!" exclaimed Lodren.

"Shut yer face, Lodren, you're only trying to cheer me up. It'll be like being back in the caverns again. I haven't been in a good cave for years, not since you lot piled in when I was having me dinner. Do ye remember?"

"Yes, unfortunately I do. I also remember the wolves and that zingaard that wanted to have us for supper. Nothing good comes out of dark places," said Lodren, becoming a little anxious.

"Thanks very much," growled Wilf, "I come from a dark place and I've always looked after *you.*"

"Alright, alright. Present company excepted, I should've said. But, most of the time, there's only bad things in the dark."

"I suggest you keep a tight hold on that hammer then, Lodren. Not that it'll be much use against ghosts," chuckled Wilf.

"Ghosts! What do you mean, ghosts?"

"Take no notice of him, Lodren. Grubb, stop teasing him," said Faylore sternly, trying her best not to laugh.

"Anyway, there aren't that many ghosts here. We hardly ever see them, and when we do, they leave us in peace. The worst they do is give a nasty scowl."

"You're not helping this situation, Jendilomin," advised Faylore.

"Perhaps not, but I am telling the truth," she replied.

"L-listen," gulped Lodren, his eyes darting from side to side nervously, "let's forget about the ghosts for a minute, shall we? If they're as harmless as you say, they shouldn't be a problem. The thing we should be focussing on is the fact that with this hall having so many levels to search, we could be down here for months."

Wilf transformed back into Grubb. Holding his arms in front of him, he balled up his fists, "Pack it in!" he exclaimed in glee, relishing the idea of being underground for so long. "You're getting me all excited."

"You won't get excited if a ghost takes a dislike to you, Grubb. You'll scarper just like anyone would."

Grubb rolled his eyes. Tilting his head to one side, his chin low to his chest, he sighed, "Lodren, haven't you realised yet? *Everyone* takes a dislike to me sooner or later, and guess what, *I don't flamin' well care!*"

Faylore laughed at them both, "I think we should make a start. Follow me, we'll try down here first."

***

"What is it? I've never seen anything that woolly before."

"I don't think it's wool, Poom. I think it's actually hair!"

"It can't be, it must be fur."

"Well, whether it's fur or hair, it's got far too much of it for its own good if you ask me. How can it see where it's going with that lot over its face?"

"Well, it can see enough to find water, I think. Doesn't look as if it's dying of thirst."

"No, it doesn't. Doesn't sound like it either. Why is it making all those strange noises?"

"If anyone asked me, I'd say it was… *singing.*"

The Gerrowliens had come across yet another strange creature they did not recognise. They watched intently as it strolled around, pausing occasionally to poke amongst bushes as if it were searching for something. It was one of the hairiest beings they had ever seen. Clumps of its matted coat became entangled on the smaller branches of the bushes, leaving them adorned with tufts as if it had been purposely decorated.

"I'd hardly call that singing, Poom. Sounds more like it's in pain," Lawton whispered.

"If we follow it, it's bound to lead us to water eventually," suggested Poom.

"This is so embarrassing! When has any Gerrowlien not been able to find a water source by himself?"

"When an evil sorcerer casts a spell that leaves an unnatural dust clogging the air, that's when, Lawton. I can't even smell myself."

"No, Poom, I can't smell you either. We should be grateful for small mercies, I suppose."

"I suppose... hang on a minute! Are you saying I smell?"

"Not at all, Poom, not at all. I'm just saying that maybe you should give up the practice of licking yourself clean. With your bad breath, it doesn't help your scent. Try a little water occasionally, that may help."

"Happy to oblige, *fatty*. I don't know if the sun baked what little brain you have left but it's the one thing we're a little short of at the moment!"

"Keep your voice down," Lawton hissed. "You'll scare it away."

The creature paused, glancing around nervously, unsure of what it may have heard. Looking directly toward where the Gerrowliens lay, it backed away slowly and hid in the shadow of an overhanging rock face. It sniffed the air, tilting its head to listen. Its fears seemed to settle quickly, as it ventured into the daylight once more before scurrying away. The Gerrowliens followed, their footsteps silent as they pursued their quarry. The beast travelled blissfully unaware of its followers until, after a few miles, giving one more glance over its shoulder, it disappeared into a gap between two bushes that grew beneath a rocky outcrop.

The Gerrowliens watched with interest, Poom pinching at his nose and shaking his head, "I think I smell water."

Lawton was literally slapping himself in the nose, "Work, you stupid thing!" he moaned. "That damned dust has killed my sense of smell completely, I can't smell anything."

"I'm sure of it, the water's in there," insisted Poom. "We'll have to go and take a look."

"And what if there are more of those hairy things in there that don't want us to drink any of it?"

"I have my spear, and you have yours. Anyway, if there's too many of them, you can sit on them, can't you? Nobody would survive that."

"Oh, ha ha, very funny! You mean if the smell of *you* doesn't kill them first? Or you could bore them to death with one of your war stories."

Poom glared at Lawton, "Are we going in there or not? We could stay here and die of thirst if you prefer. I know we're getting on in years, but you really have become a cynical, miserable old git recently."

Poom never waited for a reply and within seconds was standing in front of the bushes through which the beast had scrambled. Inching his way between the branches, he was surprised at how far he was having to travel and had no idea when he would be clear of them. This, combined with what seemed to be a complete blanket of hair that had been shed by the beast, or beasts, perplexed him greatly. Undaunted, he continued until, a few yards ahead, he could see a glimmer of light between the claustrophobic veil of matted hair. He peered through. The cocoon that had been produced around the entrance had muffled the noise beyond, but now he could hear the unmistakeable sound of running water. He waited until his eyes became accustomed to the light and was amazed by the scene.

He was looking into a large cave through, what seemed to be, the only entrance. The cave had no roof, allowing the sunlight to stream through and a small waterfall trickled down the wall to one side, forming a natural pool at the foot of it. Poom clicked his tongue quietly against the roof of his mouth then ran it across his lips that, even for a feline, felt dry and chapped. For this to happen in the matter of only a day made him realise the desperation of their situation. He stared long and hard at the pool and then turned his attention to the occupants of the cave. He could see the one that he and Lawton had followed, but it was not alone.

There were at least two dozen of his kind with him and Poom was surprised at how friendly they all seemed to one another as, one by one, they rose from where they were seated, to hug the new arrival. Through the facial hair, he could see bared teeth, but this wasn't a sign of aggression, they were smiling!

The beast they had followed was steered toward a rock and made to sit before one of the others pushed something into his hands, grunting as if it were some kind of offering. It held it to its nose and bared its teeth once more before raising it to its mouth. Then Poom realised what it was, food. Not just any food, *it was fish!* If Poom's mouth had not been so dry, he was sure that he would have started drooling.

What was he to do? Should he attack the strange beings and steal their food? Would he have enough of a chance to gather some water before he was outnumbered? Studying them, Poom realised that they were harmless. He could not, in all good conscience, harm another being that showed no aggression toward him and was sure that the race he now gazed upon were nothing but peaceful. He placed his spear on the ground and pushed his way through, staying low to the ground so as not to startle the gathering.

The first one saw him and let out a yelp, causing the rest to back away and cower against the cave wall. Poom held

349

out his hands in front of him, trying to reassure the cave dwellers that he meant them no harm. "Stay calm, it's alright," he said quietly, "I'm not here to harm you. I just need water, that's all. *Water,*" he emphasised, pointing firstly to the pool, then to his mouth. There was a slight drop to the cave floor and Poom dropped silently, still holding his hands out to pacify the alarmed occupants. He made his way across to the pool and, uncharacteristically, cupped his hand in order to scoop the water to his lips. Uncharacteristically because cats hate getting wet, even their hands, or more traditionally, paws.

The individual they had followed seemed to understand that all Poom wanted was to drink and began to nudge his fellow cave dwellers. It realised that Poom meant no harm. He picked up the flat rock on which was placed the fish that he had been presented with. Sneaking slowly forward, he held it at arm's length toward Poom. Poom took it slowly and nodded in thanks before his host scurried away, still slightly unsure of their uninvited guest. Poom raised the fish to his mouth, surprised by the fact that it was not raw. How had they managed to cook the thing? There was no fire in the cave nor remnants of an earlier one.

Poom's host bared his teeth as the Gerrowlien began to eat. It stretched out its arm and made a fist, but its thumb was in the air. *Where had it learned to do that?* It was actually communicating with him, as primitive as the communication was. Poom suddenly realised that he had left Lawton behind, and he had now been in the cave for some time. *Should he go and fetch him perhaps?* "Sod him," mumbled Poom, under his breath. "He can stay outside and stew in his own juice for a while, may make him a bit more appreciative of my efforts."

CHAPTER 22

"We're getting a little off track, don't you think, Jared? Does it matter where the Gerrowliens have gone? All we know is that they *have*. What we need to concentrate on is what *our* next move will be," insisted Hannock.

"Don't want to go over your royal head, old chap, but Hannock's right. The Gerrowliens have gone and both Xarran and Alex have buggered off to who knows where in search of water. That leaves the six of us to either wait here until they return or die of thirst if they don't, which I, for one, have no intention of doing."

"There's only one option open to us then, Yello, we resume our march and hope they catch up with us later," said Jared.

Emnor tried to be the voice of reason, *again*, "March!" he exclaimed. "What do you mean, march? We can barely stand through trying to conserve what little water we have, three of us anyway. We may manage a convincing stumble for a couple of hours but Yello's leg would halt him in his tracks within minutes. We should wait here. Xarran and Alex will return, I have total faith in them. As for the Gerrowliens, they have proven more than trustworthy. I do not believe for one second that they would abandon us. Whatever they're up to, I'm sure it's for the good of us all."

"You should listen to him, you know. He's got more brains than the rest of you put together." They looked up to see Poom lying on the rocks above them, four large water skins swinging from his hand, "Who needs a drink?"

They were astounded. Not one of them had heard him approach and now craned their necks, looking behind him. They were, however, bemused by the absence of Lawton.

"Where's the big fella?" asked Hannock.

"Left him behind with our new friends. He's getting far too fat to keep up with me so I decided it would be quicker to bring the water by myself." He descended swiftly and handed a water skin to each of his friends, "Drink as much of it as you need, there's plenty more where that came from."

This was the only invitation they needed and they gulped the refreshing water. Poom paid no mind to the fact that a large quantity ran over their dusty faces and was wasted on the dry earth.

"You found a river then?" enquired Emnor. "Or was it a stream?"

"Ooh, better than that," replied Poom, smiling. "Well, kind of, I found a waterfall. Only a small one, I admit, but it runs into a shallow pool within a cave. Keeps it nice and cool. That's where I met our new friends."

"Don't you mean *we*?" asked Hannock, a little confused.

"Oh, you mean old grumpy nuts? No, he hasn't met them yet. He couldn't fit through the entrance to the cave, barely got through myself. Might have been easier if there wasn't all that blasted hair clogging it up."

352

His friends were puzzled by his last comment, all except Yello, who had a slight smile on his face. "Don't suppose they introduced themselves to you, did they?" he asked.

"No, I don't think they have a language. Not like our common tongue anyway. They do seem quite partial to singing though, if you could call it that."

"And they kept hugging one another, I presume?" asked Yello, chuckling.

"How did you know that? Have you met them before?"

"It seems that you have gotten closer than I ever have, that's for sure. They're *gibbonites*, Poom. They communicate with song, at least with one another it seems. I've studied them for decades, but every time I try to approach them, they scarper. Mind you, I'm glad you've found some. I could do with some of that spare hair of theirs."

Poom stared at the top of Yello's head, "You have plenty of hair, why do you need theirs? Listen, if you're thinking of hunting them, I will not allow it. They are as peaceful a species as I have ever witnessed and…"

"I have no intention of hunting anything, Poom!" Yello announced loudly, interrupting the Gerrowlien's rant. "I simply need some of the hair that they *shed*, I do not need to remove their skins, you stupid cat!"

"Are you sure?" asked Poom, gripping his spear tightly and glaring at Yello.

"Positive! Put down the spear, remember what happened the last time you tried that with *me*?"

Poom lowered his spear, "Glad to hear it… and yes, I do," he replied, grinning.

"Right," began Jared. "Where's this waterfall? Can we make it on foot?" he asked.

"Not advisable, Jared," replied Poom. "Those… *gibbonites*…" he said glancing at Yello for approval of his pronunciation. Yello nodded, "… were not the only beasties we came across on the way."

Hannock sighed, leaning back on a rock and dropping his head, "Should have known it wasn't going to be that easy. What now, giant lizard people? Four-headed monsters with razor sharp teeth? Or perhaps something simple like a stampede of swamp beasts?"

Poom opened his mouth to answer, then realised what Hannock had just asked, "*Swamp beasts*? There's hardly any water out here, you berk. How could there be a swamp, let alone any beasts living in it?"

"Alright, maybe I was a little too precise," replied Hannock, realising how stupid his last question had been. "Just tell us what you saw," he sighed.

"This one's been out in the sun too long, Jared. He's getting as bad as the fat one," laughed Poom. "*Anyway*, about ten-foot-tall, big claws, covered in hair. Three of them, different colours. Overheard them talking about someone who had some sort of hound as a pet. They seemed terrified to abandon their post for fear of what he might do to them. I've never seen them before, but I think you have," he said, sticking out his bottom lip at Jared whilst leaning on his spear.

Jared glanced over at Hannock, they both recognised the description, *zingaard*. Without a word being spoken, Hannock nodded at him. "Where's a Thedarian when you need one?" he asked, grinning.

354

"Can we avoid them?" asked Jared.

"Shouldn't be a problem. Yello and Emnor will have to use magic though. No offence, gentlemen, but you're not exactly light on your feet," replied Poom.

Emnor gave Poom a sardonic glance, "You could say that," he replied. "Or you could say that it would not be advisable for three gormless zingaard to stand in the way of, what may be, the two most powerful wizards on the planet."

"Oh, I say!" exclaimed Yello. "The two most powerful wizards," he echoed. "But what Emnor forgot to mention was the fact that we are also the angriest wizards on the planet. There is only one who would lower himself enough to deal with their kind, and if they are in his service, they are fair game."

"I presume you have no intention of trying to avoid them then, old friend?" asked Emnor.

"You presume correctly, Master Emnor. My intention is to fry them in their own fat," replied Yello with a growl in his voice that impressed even Poom.

"We'll make a Gerrowlien out of you yet."

***

They crouched behind the rocks where Poom and Lawton had secreted themselves earlier. The wizards had relocated, bringing Poom with them despite his many protestations. Jared had done the same, his closest friend Hannock at his side. Hannock trusted him with his life, and this was to be another testament to the fact. "Are you sure you can do this?" he kept asking, "I've seen you do it by yourself but is it the same if you tow somebody along for the ride?"

Jared's reply was simply, "Shut it, Hannock. Stop being a baby and drink your water."

Arriving a few hundred yards from where they needed to be, they had sneaked in undetected in the hope of hearing any conversations between their newly discovered foe. They watched, straining their ears, but not a word passed between the zingaard. After half an hour, Yello had seen enough. Tapping Emnor on the shoulder, he indicated that it was time to face their enemy. They each took a sip of water, stood next to one another and vanished. Appearing a split second later, they startled the beasts who immediately charged toward them. The one that had been lucky enough to feed earlier, grabbed a leg bone from the glamoch carcase and hurled it at Emnor. With the slightest flick of his wrist, it was blasted to the side, striking one of the others full force in the face. It yelped in pain but its pace was barely hindered. The two wizards held their staffs aloft and bellowed in unison, "*Perranghorra!*"

There was silence. The zingaard were frozen in their tracks and Emnor and Yello turned to face one another. Shaking hands with one another, Yello asked a question, "Which one do we kill first?"

"I'm not really fussed," replied Emnor. "You choose. As a matter of fact, what's your least favourite colour? That may help you decide."

"Don't really like brown," said Yello. "Mind you, I've never been partial to blue either."

"That's settled then. Kill the brown one and the blue one and we'll question the black one."

"Question? I thought we were going to torture it," said Yello, sounding most disappointed.

"I thought we'd agreed, old friend. If one of them answers our questions, there'll be no need to torture them."

"You've taken all the fun out of this adventuring lark, you know. It was much better when we were children!" groaned Yello.

"Now don't go getting your robes in a tangle. None of them have agreed to co-operate yet. You might still be able to have some fun."

Jared and Hannock watched in amazement as Hannock leaned in to whisper, "Do you think they were actually like this when they were younger?"

"I sincerely hope not. With the powers those two possess, you'd need to change your breeches, even if they were joking," replied Jared, doing his best to curb his laughter.

"We only tackled one of those things and there were five of us. Look at their eyes, they're terrified."

"They're frozen solid, Hannock, completely defenceless. Wouldn't you be?"

"We need to speak to whichever one of you is the leader," announced Emnor. "You will be released in turn and offered one chance. We shall ask the questions, you shall give the answers. If you do not, you will be of no further use to us and will be put to death. If the first to be released co-operates, we shall release you all, and you may go on your

357

way, unharmed. *Any sign of aggression will mean your instant death.*"

Jared and Hannock, seeing no reason to remain hidden, joined the wizards. Poom, however, was not impressed and lay flat on his back, his head drooping over the edge of a rock with his tongue hanging from the side of his mouth, "Why not just tell them you're going to eat them whatever happens?" he mumbled, snarling with laughter at his own humour.

Studying the immobilised zingaard, Emnor noticed that the brown one seemed the most nervous of the three. It would be the perfect choice to be questioned first. With a gentle wave of his hand, Yello released it from the spell and it fell forward with a thud, causing a dust cloud to plume into the air around it. They were a stupid, vicious race, but wary of reprisals for an unsuccessful attack, the brown zingaard remained where it fell. "You won't get anything from me," it said, growling deeply at its captors. "You may as well kill me now."

"As you wish," replied Yello, raising his hand and conjuring a fireball. He launched it without warning, deliberately missing its mark. It struck the ground, the sparks splashing onto the beast's fur. "I will not miss a second time, beast," he added, conjuring another.

The zingaard scampered sideways from the inferno, slapping at the smouldering patches on its legs, "Wait!" it shrieked. "Wait! Stop. I don't know nothing!"

"That's good. Very good. If you *don't know nothing*, it follows that you do know something."

By the looks in their eyes, Jared could tell what the other zingaard were thinking. The black one was as scared as the

358

brown and was willing it to give the answers that the wizards required. The blue one, however, had a completely different look. Rage burnt within its glare and Jared was sure that, if released, it would tear its kin apart before allowing them to divulge any information. The questioning from Yello and Emnor continued and with each syllable that left the lips of their prisoner, the fire in the eyes of the blue zingaard burned brighter.

Jared's mind wandered from the interrogation. He could no longer hear what was being said by any party involved. His mind strayed to the memory of his dear friend Faylore, torn open and nearly dying by the hands of one of these ferocious beasts. He began to approach the fiery-eyed blue zingaard, unnoticed by his friends. Now standing directly before the beast, he held out his hand. A slender blue flame appeared, quite unlike any fire spell seen before. As perfectly honed as the finest blade and pointed at the tip, Jared waved it back and forth, its movement mesmerising the blue zingaard.

Suddenly and without warning, Jared thrust it into the chest of the beast, taking care not to drive it too deeply. He did not want his captive dead, at least, not yet. The beast roared in pain as Jared began to draw the flame downward. The flesh and bone of the zingaard's body was being sliced with surgical precision. With each inch the blade travelled, Jared drove it a little deeper. No emotion showed on his face as he tortured his victim. The roar had turned to a screech as the life-blood of the zingaard began to gush onto the arid ground. Having reached its stomach, Jared changed direction, cutting across and spilling the beast's intestines.

Hannock watched the prince in horror. Never would he have believed that his closest friend could be so sadistic but

Jared was not yet finished. The zingaard, having succumbed to the pain, had passed out, but it had never been Jared's intention to retrieve any information from this one. With a sneer, he punched his way through the offal that protruded from his captive. Rooting around, he found his target. With a loud grunt, he tore his hand from the gory scene. Clutched in his palm was the heart of the zingaard. Turning, he glared at the brown beast. "Emnor," he said quietly, "Ask your questions."

Some time later, three dead zingaard lay on the ground. Emnor cremated the bodies with Yello's help and the youngsters were instructed to bury the remains.

"I don't think they were talking about Karrak," said Jared. "They referred to him as a *dark-skinned* sorcerer. The rumours we have heard recently have been of a *shadow lord*."

"Do you think it could be Barden?" suggested Hannock. "Maybe Karrak has realised he needs help and has raised him from the dead?"

"We don't know for sure that he *actually* killed Barden. And why would his skin be dark?" asked Yello. "He was always such a pasty-faced old git."

"With all due respect, I don't care what any of you say. I think we have a new player in this game of ours," said Hannock, adamantly.

"I love the way you offer respect, *right* before telling us we're wrong. It's just so… *you*!"

"I know, Jared, but you have to admit I'm right this time! Barden was, I don't know, a million years old. This new fellow though, he only sounds about our age. Plus, the fact that he's huge, apparently. Barden was a weasel of a man."

"In more ways than one, I can assure you," agreed Yello.

"How do we know if anything they told us was the truth? They could have been lying. What if they realised we were going to kill them anyway after 'captain carve up' here did away with that big one. Bloody good plan by the way, Your Highness."

Jared's actions had not been mentioned. Yello did not feel that this was the right time to discuss them. "They were telling the truth alright, I guarantee you that."

"How, old friend?" asked Emnor. "How can you *guarantee* it?"

"We were kind enough to give the one some water, weren't we?" said Yello, reaching for his bag and ferreting inside, "Well. I took the liberty of adding a little…" Looking quite smug, he held up the bolinium root.

***

"If I'd have asked you to come along of your own free will, you'd have refused. You were the one who craved adventure, remember? *My father* the adventurer, *my father* the discoverer, *my father* who has the sun shining out of his backside. It's all you ever say. What about *your* expeditions, *your* discoveries? Surely, your old man has done enough to make him famous forever? It's your time, Xarran. Make your mark in history and surpass everything your father, and others like him, have done before."

Xarran shook his head, "That still doesn't forgive what you did to me, Alex. You should never subject anyone to mind control, however honourable your motives!" he replied sternly.

"You're right, Xarran, I apologise. My motives weren't completely altruistic I have to admit. The world famous Xarran Althor and his faithful lifelong assistant, Alexander Hardman. Oh well," he sighed. "Can't blame a fellow for dreaming. It was the only chance I had of fame really, I'll never manage it by myself. Come on, let's go. We'll have to tell them we failed when we get back of course, but don't worry, I'll do it to save you any embarrassment."

"Hang on a sec', Alex. Let's not be too hasty," replied Xarran, pondering over their situation. "We've only just arrived, although I'm not exactly sure *where*. We may as well have a poke about as we're already here. We have plenty of water to last the day, may as well make use of it. Better to die trying than not try at all, eh?"

Alex continued with his praise of his cohort, "That's the Xarran I know. Brave and noble, putting others' needs before his own. You're going to be *so* famous when you're older that you won't be able to go anywhere without people nudging each other and saying things like, *that's Xarran Althor, he saved the world* and, *is that who I think it is? How blessed we are that someone as famous as him should grace our village with his presence.*"

Xarran blushed, "Oh, do shut up, Alex."

"Are you forgetting the mission we're on? We may only be searching for water, but without it, we could all die. If we fail so will the mission to stop Karrak. *To impede upon on his progress, above all, is our goal,*" Alex laughed, striking a heroic pose.

"I think you may be putting a little too much importance on our role in this affair, Alex. We're water carriers, for goodness sake! It's a job that was given to the worst pupils in Reiggan. Can't do magic but want to be involved with wizards? Be a water carrier or a…"

"An apprentice?" interrupted Alex. Xarran gave him a confused look, "You know what I'm saying, Xarran, don't pretend that you don't. You're ten times the wizard that Harley could ever be. But who does Emnor choose? Harley! Nice, polite, 'I'll do anything you say master' Harley. His face fits and yours doesn't. The masters knew your potential and were afraid to allow you to investigate the extent of your powers. Harley was always weak, Emnor felt sorry for him and gave him a leg-up by making him his apprentice."

"How can you say such things?" asked Xarran. "Harley's always been one of our closest friends."

"I'm not saying he's a bad person, Xarran. He's just not that good a wizard. It's fine having hangers-on as children, there's always a weak one in the group, but we're men now and we have to show the elders that we can stand on our own. They've taught us all they can and I am deeply grateful to them for that. They're old, Xarran, ancient, and they won't live forever. We must learn to defend ourselves. What happens if they face Karrak and he destroys them? We'll be next, if we're lucky. If not, *who knows* what he could turn us into?"

"You sound as if you've been thinking about this for some time, Alex. Have you a plan in mind perchance?"

"Of course I have, you plum! I'm going to follow your lead. You're the one who has grown up with tales of death-defying adventures and the like. All I had was beatings from

363

the big kids in the village. How would I even start to plan an adventure?"

Xarran pursed his lips, suddenly looking far more mature than his years. "Right, first things first. If we come across anything dangerous, I'll take the lead and you copy what I do. If, however, what I do proves unsuccessful..." he squinted his eyes at Alex, "... we scarper."

"What are your orders, Master Althor?" Alex laughed.

"Well," said Xarran. "Water always flows downhill, right? So, we go downhill." He made the first move and Alex followed, willingly.

***

"Four days!" exclaimed Lodren, "Four days we've been in here and we haven't even had a sniff of him."

"I know. Great, isn't it? All dark and gloomy. Apparently, the deeper you go, the damper it gets. Ooh, I can't wait for that lovely, musty smell to fill my 'ead."

"If you don't shut your face, Grubb, my hammer's going to fill your head! Honestly, the longer we stay in here, the more you act like a kid in a sweet shop."

Grubb looked confused as he stared at Lodren, "What's a sweet shop?" he asked.

"Oh my days!" muttered Lodren, mopping his brow, "I despair, I really do."

"Come on, Lodren, it's not that bad," said Faylore. "We've not found Father yet, but we've not seen anything else either."

"Why did you have to say that!" exclaimed Lodren. "I'd forgotten there might be ghosts and things down here, and now you've gone and reminded me!"

"There are no ghosts in the hall of history, Lodren," Faylore said, trying to calm the panicking Nibby. "They're simply tales to keep out any trespassers."

"You know that's not true, Faylore. You've seen them yourself, many times in fact." Faylore nudged Jendilomin sharply in the ribs to silence her. "What was that for?" she exclaimed.

"Will you please be quiet?" hissed Faylore, "You're only making it worse for the poor fellow."

"Right! That's it, I've had enough. I'm going. I need to feel the sun on my back. We Nibby are not meant to be underground, I'm not a *famper*."

"Oh, I love those little things!" exclaimed Jendilomin. "Their little wiggly blue noses and their pink fur. They're adorable."

"And they tunnel underground, something you'll never see a Nibby do! We're made to be outside in the fresh air and that's where I'm going."

Grubb started to chuckle, "Good luck with that *Loddy*. Remember the way out, do ye?"

"Don't you worry about me…" he realised what Grubb had said, "… and my name is Lodren, *not Loddy.*"

Faylore placed her hand on his back to reassure him, "Lodren, you can't go by yourself. What say we give it two more days and if we don't find my father by then, we'll all leave together?"

"But that's another two days, Your Majesty," protested Lodren, rocking from side to side.

"I know that, Lodren. I just said it, *two days,*" repeated Faylore.

Lodren shuffled his feet. He hated being put in a predicament, but being underground was totally uncharacteristic of a Nibby, "I'm sorry, Your Majesty, but I can't. If I stay down here another two days, I'll go mad."

"What? Madder than ye already are?" chortled Grubb.

Lodren grabbed his backpack and, slinging it over his shoulder, marched off into the darkness. He hadn't gone far before he looked over his shoulder to see the glimmer of light given off by the lanterns being carried by his friends. "Suppose that's that friendship over," he mumbled, "Grubb won't care but I bet Faylore will never forgive me. Suppose I'll just go back to being on my own."

"You don't have to be alone," came a sighing voice. "You can stay with us. We shall be your true friends, *forever.*"

Lodren gulped. Turning toward the sound of the voice, he was greeted with something he had not expected. Facing him, an ethereal light shining from their transparent bodies, were three ghosts. Lodren's mouth fell open as he gazed at their grisly forms. They had, in life, been Thedarian. By the look of the ragged remnants of their robes, they had been of noble houses, but now only appeared as ghoulish. Small pieces of rotting flesh partly covered their skeletal faces as they stood before him, their teeth bared due to decades of decay.

Lodren began to babble. "That's, m-m-m-most k-kind, b-b-b-but I. Well… you see…" Turning as fast as he could, he

366

sprinted back in the direction from which he had come only moments before, "WAIT FOR ME! FAYLORE, GRUBB… WAIT FOR ME!" he bellowed.

Faylore, Jendilomin and Grubb paused and turned to see the panic-stricken Nibby hurtling toward them. He slid to a halt on the dry floor, placing his hands on his knees whilst trying to catch his breath. "I can't do it, Your Majesty. I can't abandon you in this place, it wouldn't be right. I'll stick with you no matter what," he said quickly, holding Faylore's arm and glancing over his shoulder repeatedly. "I think we should move on, don't you? We'll never find your father at this rate. Come on, Grubb, hurry up. Do you want me to carry that for you? There we go, we can travel a bit faster now. Lady Jendilomin, would you care to lead? Me? What's wrong with *me*? Nothing at all, just keen to help find Koloss. The sooner we find him, the sooner we can get out of here. Grubb! Will you please hurry up!"

It was obvious to them all that Lodren had seen or heard something that he was most uncomfortable with. "We'll go in front, Lodren. You bring up the rear," suggested Grubb.

"N-no, you bring up the rear, Grubb. I'll stay with Faylore. I can't protect her properly if I'm back there, can I? I'll stay in the middle and keep her safe. Can we go a bit faster, please?"

***

As luck would have it, the following day, as they descended into yet another level of the hall of history, they heard voices. Approaching cautiously, they saw a robed figure with his elbows resting on the edge of a desk,

367

pondering over numerous scrolls set out before him. Faylore raised her bow silently. She crept ever closer, as she had distinctly heard, as had the others, more than one voice. *Where were the stranger's allies?* Lodren nervously took a step back and accidentally bumped a small bookcase with his backpack. Having not even felt the bump, it toppled over and crashed to the ground, spilling its contents across the floor. Faylore drew her bowstring tighter as the alarmed stranger spun around. At the sight of Faylore, he gasped with relief, "My word, you scared me half to death! What are you creeping around in the dark for? Could you lower the bow please? It is a little disconcerting."

Faylore instantly lowered her bow, "Father, what are you doing down here? Mother is worried to the point of distraction. What were you thinking? More importantly, how have you survived? Did you bring provisions with you? How did you manage to avoid being detected by the guards?"

Koloss raised his hands in an attempt to halt Faylore's string of questions, "Shush, shush, young lady. I am afraid you have me at a disadvantage, have we met before?"

"Of course we have, I'm your daughter, as is Jendilomin," replied Faylore, gesturing toward her sister. "You have been missing for almost a week, you must be half-starved," she continued.

"Miss, if I had a daughter, or daughters, do you not think that I would remember? My mind hasn't completely gone. I mean, there has been the occasional comment about my forgetfulness but I can live with those. *Peneriphus, you'd forget your head if it wasn't attached* or *Peneriphus, put some breeches on, you'll catch your death of cold.*"

Jendilomin stepped forward and took her sister by the arm. Nodding at her, she addressed Koloss, "Please forgive me, sir. Did you say your name was *Peneriphus?*"

"That is correct," he replied. "Is there something I can do for you, miss?"

"Peneriphus? As in *King* Peneriphus of Thedar?"

"But of course, do you know of another? Ladies, I have important tasks that I simply must attend to. Please, if you would be so kind, take your leave. One of the maids will escort you from the palace once you have concluded your business, good-day."

"'e's as mad as a bag o' nuts," chortled Grubb.

Lodren always tried his best not to encourage Grubb, but even he had to stifle a snigger.

"This is no laughing matter. Our father believes himself to be a king who lived over a thousand years ago. I fail to see exactly what it is that you find so amusing about that?"

"Not 'im… *you*. You should've seen the look on your face."

Faylore scowled at them before returning her attention to her father, "Erm, excuse me, King Peneriphus," she said with an enquiring tone.

"He's probably around here somewhere, but you won't get any sense out of him."

The words had been spoken by Koloss, but his tone of voice was now completely different. The first voice was gentle and had a pleasant, kindly tone, whereas this one sounded harsh and impatient.

"I beg your pardon, sir. Could you kindly repeat that?" asked Jendilomin as politely as she could.

"I am King Kallambar and I am not in the habit of repeating myself!" he roared suddenly, "Guards, guards! Take these impudent interlopers away. Perhaps a couple of weeks chained in the dungeons will teach them some manners!"

The smiles had gone from the faces of Lodren and Grubb. The first voice, calm as it was, had amused them. The second had done the complete opposite and both seemed slightly nervous. Lodren clutched his hammer and watched as the skin on Grubb's arms began to bubble, a sure-fire sign that he could morph into Wilf at any moment.

The Thedarian sisters crouched down with their friends and tried to explain, which was difficult as they didn't really understand what was going on themselves. "There is a legend," began Faylore, "a legend that all Thedarian kings when in advanced old age, see flashbacks. Actual memories of those who have ruled before them. It seems that our father has reached that time in his life."

"Ooh, you must be really happy then? You can ask all the questions you wanted to know about your family history. Who was nice, who was nasty, those kind of things," said Lodren.

"Yes. Unfortunately, there is also a major problem, once this happens," said Jendilomin, solemnly, "It also means that our father is close to death."

"What!" exclaimed Lodren, "How close? Months... weeks?"

Faylore leaned her head sideways as a tear rolled down her sparkling white cheek, "Hours," she replied. "Perhaps only minutes. But at least we shall be with him, my sister and I."

Each minute that passed seemed an eternity. To be facing the inevitable loss of a loved one was the worst torture that anyone could possibly endure. All that Faylore and Jendilomin could do was wait. Over the next few hours, Koloss' conditioned worsened as the voices that spewed from his lips became too innumerable to count. Some were morose, some fearful, others completely manic. Koloss' body twitched and jerked as each memory, or possession, changed. Voice after voice would beg or plead for life, others would scream profanities and threats toward any who would not come to their aid by saving their lives. The sisters sat either side of their father, each holding a hand, when suddenly he seemed very peaceful. Opening his eyes, he smiled at his daughters.

"Faylore... Jendilomin. My beautiful girls have come to visit their old father. How blessed I am," he whispered.

"Father, rest. You must be exhausted," urged Faylore.

"Nonsense! I'm not exhausted, just dying... that's all," he said, blinking slowly.

"You're going to be fine, Father. A few days' rest and you'll feel better," said Jendilomin, fighting back her tears.

"Of course I will, but for now, I have some news for you. It's about this Karrak fellow." He began to cough as he finished his sentence. This was the first time in a long time that there had been any clarity from the lips of the former King of Thedar, and for it to be regarding Karrak was a bit of a shock to them.

"What do you know of Karrak, Father?" asked Faylore, taking her father's hand. "Did you learn something from the scrolls?"

Koloss had closed his eyes. It seemed his time had come, "Stop the son. You must stop the son… dangerous… end of the world…" he whispered with his dying breath.

CHAPTER 23

"I'll order him to show it to me. He can't refuse, I am a prince after all," chuntered Jared.

"Absolutely!" agreed Hannock. "But I wouldn't upset the old coot if I were you. He's never been answerable to anyone, even your father. He might turn you into a glamoch if you upset him," he laughed.

"This isn't a joke, Hannock. We'll be facing Karrak before long and I need all the help I can get."

"Well, I don't!" replied Hannock, raising the golden crossbow, "I have all the help I need right here."

"If Karrak has become this 'shadow lord' as the rumours suggest, you won't get near enough to use *that*."

"Don't you think? Well, maybe I'll throw stones. Perhaps a few select insults would throw him off guard."

"Cut it out, Hannock! This is serious! Look at what he did to you last time, or do you no longer feel the cold of the golden eyepatch that presses against your cheek?"

"On the contrary, Your Highness, I feel it every day, whether the day is cold or hot. It is what drives me. It reminds me of why we are here and gives me the strength to continue. It gives me purpose; purpose to find the one that rendered me blind in one eye and took half of my face; purpose to hunt him down like the animal he has always been; purpose to have my revenge by piercing his skull with a golden bolt." A fire raged in Hannock, his voice rasping as he glared at the ground.

Jared stared at his friend. Nothing would cause Hannock to show any form of leniency should they one day confront their enemy. Should their luck hold, Karrak would die, and they would both live to tell the tale. But, for the first time, Jared was beginning to doubt their abilities. He cleared his throat, "I think we're getting a little side tracked, old friend. What are we to do about insisting that Emnor…"

"You could simply ask me, Jared. However, insistence is not always the way to achieve one's goals when dealing with a wizard. You should know that by now. After all, you *are* one."

Jared turned to face Emnor. He raised his finger as if to emphasise the point that he was about to make, but on opening his mouth, paused momentarily. *Did Emnor just refer to him as a wizard*? The thought had never crossed his mind before. But it did make sense, after all, he had been a student of Emnor's for decades. *Had he now learned enough to be considered a wizard by the Head of the Administration*? "Ah, there you are, Emnor," he began, "I know you may not agree, but I feel that the time has come for you to reveal…"

"Yes, you're quite right of course, Jared. Let me know when you're ready and we'll take Captain Hannock along as well," interrupted Emnor.

"What?" asked Jared, looking slightly confused.

"You feel that it is your right to consult the Peneriphus Scroll, and I completely agree with you. I'm just surprised you haven't asked to see it before now."

"So you knew? All this time you knew that I needed to consult it yet omitted suggesting it?"

"I do not believe that you *needed* to see it before now, only that you *wanted* to. And who am I to suggest what a prince of Borell should or shouldn't do?" replied Emnor with a smile.

"You're a crafty old sod, you are," laughed Hannock. "Tell me, is there anything we may think of in the future that you don't already have the answer to?"

"I have no idea what you mean, my dear Captain. I cannot predict the future, only deal with events as they unfold. The scroll, however, can give us a much better idea of what those events may be, *before* they unfold."

Jared and Hannock followed Emnor as he headed to a slightly secluded spot, pausing briefly to grab a couple of water skins.

Yello gave them a nonchalant wave as they passed, not bothering to look up from a tome he was studying. He never questioned Emnor and knew that if he was needed, he would have been summoned.

Emnor turned to face Jared and Hannock, "Just one thing," he said, "we must speak only to one another, do not be distracted by the guardians, whatever they may say. Ready? Place your hands on my shoulders. Here we go."

"Wait a minute, what guardians? Only talk to one another..." But Hannock's sudden protests and questions were cut short as they vanished.

The whirling sensation ceased and Hannock realised that they had reached their destination, wherever it was. He squinted but could barely make out the silhouettes of his friends as they were in almost complete darkness. "Didn't you think it a good idea to put lights in here, Emnor? The occasional torch or brazier would have been a good idea. Other than that, I like what you've done with the place," he hissed.

"Shut your face, Hannock."

"So sorry, Your Highness. Only I do have a penchant for being able to see where I'm going."

"Please be quiet, Captain. I have to be sure that none of the guardians are too close. The light will attract them if it's too sudden and trust me, we wouldn't want that."

"We wouldn't?" asked Hannock.

"No, Captain, we *really* wouldn't," replied Emnor in a whisper.

"I don't like the sound of that, but at least I could defend myself if I could see where they were, these 'guardians' of yours."

"Give me a moment," Emnor raised his staff ahead of him and it began to glow faintly, illuminating a winding path ahead of them. "Follow me closely. Remember, speak to no one."

"What do you mean, *speak to no one*? We're the only ones here, you loony."

"I'll ignore that, Captain, but be careful. *You don't want to be in here alone,*" Emnor warned him.

"Where is *here*, exactly?" asked Hannock.

376

"*Everywhere* and *nowhere*," replied Emnor, cryptically.

"Oh, that makes perfect sense. Why didn't you just tell us that before?" hissed Hannock testily.

"It's a construct of my mind, Captain. It's an amalgamation of my darkest memories, but as it does not exist in a physical realm, its location cannot be found by others."

"Forget I asked," sighed Hannock. "Let's just find that blasted scroll and get out of here."

"That's a good idea, but perhaps it has been hidden during your absence," came a soft voice from the darkness.

Jared recognised the voice. It was Faylore. He was about to call to her but Emnor clamped his hand across his mouth before he could speak, shaking his head vigorously.

"Do not call to it, Jared," he urged. "It is not her, merely a trick by the guardians. Believe nothing that you see or hear in this place, we can trust only one another."

Jared nodded and Emnor removed his hand. "I have to be honest," he admitted. "It had me fooled, I could have sworn it was Faylore."

"And the guardians know that," Emnor told him. "They can read your mind. The very second you speak to them directly, you will be at their mercy."

"Why have you made it so dangerous, Emnor? Surely, only you can enter this place, why such an elaborate security?"

"To protect me from myself, of course. If my mind were being controlled by an outside force, I would not remember how to defend myself in here. The scroll must be kept hidden from all, whatever the cost."

"Sounds a bit over-the-top to me," muttered Hannock.

"Maybe, Captain. But better that than Karrak obtaining it. Come along, we have a long way to go yet." They seemed to follow no obvious route as they followed Emnor. Occasionally he would make a deliberate 45-degree turn to his left or right, despite there being no walls to guide him. It was at the point of one of these turns that they had their next encounter with the guardians.

Stepping carefully, Jared felt his foot brush against something solid on the ground. Looking down, he saw the familiar shape of a hammer, Lodren's hammer to be precise. Raising his head, he noticed that a campfire had suddenly appeared in the darkness and sitting beside it tending to his pots and pans was Lodren.

"Where have you been?" he called, waving to them. "Dinner's nearly ready. Haven't seen my hammer by any chance, have you? I'd lose my head if I wasn't careful."

None of the three answered as their mouths fell open. The figure of Lodren hadn't seen the zingaard approaching from behind him. It snatched him up and held him in the air by one leg, defenceless as it prodded him with its huge fingers. "Help me!" he yelled. "You're supposed to be my friends! Help me! It's going to eat me!"

The zingaard held him aloft and opened its mouth, revealing its pointed teeth. It groaned in anticipation of its long-awaited meal as it released Lodren from its grasp.

The entire scene turned to mist, nothing more than a gruesome vision.

"I can't take much more of this!" said Hannock, rubbing his head. "How sick are you to come up with stuff like this? It *is* your mind that's creating it all, isn't it?"

"*Certainly not!* I merely created the guardians, the scenarios are entirely their own, used to prey on your darkest fears."

"Well, it works a little too perfectly for my liking," said Jared, shaking his head. "I almost charged at that zingaard, it was so realistic."

"Thank you very much, Jared. How kind of you to say," said Emnor, pompously.

"It wasn't a compliment, you bloody idiot! Hurry up, find the scroll!" Jared exclaimed.

Hours passed, Hannock could bear it no longer, *"How much farther is this bloody scroll, Emnor? Is there something you're not telling us? Have you forgotten where you've hidden it or something?"*

"Not far now, no, and no."

Hannock gave him an exasperated look, *"That's it? That's all you have to say?"*

"I answered your questions, Captain. What else is there for me to say?"

"We've been tramping around after you for hours now and so far we've witnessed Lodren being eaten by a zingaard; Faylore smothered by forest elves as she was turned into a tree; Grubb being torn apart by wolves, and King Tamor being roasted alive by Karrak. If I should see one more of those visions of yours, I don't think I'll be able to hold back."

"Ah!" exclaimed Emnor. "I see the problem. You're feeling left out. And I shall remind you once more. They are not *my* visions."

"*What*?"

"The visions are the creations of the guardians to…"

"I know all that claptrap, that's not what I'm talking about. What do you mean by, *I'm feeling left out*?"

Emnor pouted and began stroking his beard. *How could he explain to Hannock without insulting him*? It seemed a little diplomacy was needed. "The thing is, and I shan't beat around the bush with you, Captain. There are many kinds of people in this world, most, very similar in their behaviour. You, however, are quite unique. The things you have seen are a statement to your friendship of others and your concern for their wellbeing and for that, you must be commended. On the other hand, you have a pride that radiates. Your very stature gives that away. It is only right that you would expect to see yourself within at least one of the visions, as a protector or saviour, perhaps."

"And this is your idea of, *not beating around the bush*?" asked Hannock, folding his arms.

"Absolutely, my dear Captain."

"*Nothing you said makes any sense!*" exclaimed Hannock.

"Let me give it a try, shall I?" suggested Jared.

Hannock shook his head, not in refusal, more in confusion. "Why not? It's bound to make more sense than what *he* said!"

"Here goes then. The visions are to illicit a response, that's why they show our friends in danger, understood?"

Hannock nodded.

"The problem is that you're such a big-headed git, all you want to see is *you* being the hero, charging in to save them. I've known you all my life, Hannock, and I can honestly say, I have never known *anyone* who spends as much time looking at their reflection as you do."

"So you think I'm vain, simply because I take pride in my appearance?" asked Hannock in a surprised tone.

"No I don't *think* that at all, Hannock, *I damn well know it*. Now shut your face and let's crack on, shall we?"

Emnor was telling the truth. Within a few minutes, they were facing the only wall that had been visible throughout their time in this perplexing construct. Emnor stroked at the bare rock, as if trying to find some way of penetrating it. He mumbled under his breath as he found what he was searching for. A faint crack of light appeared in the centre of the wall, but rather than opening like a hidden chamber or doorway, the rock simply melted away and oozed to the ground like molten lava. The light became brighter and there, secreted in the small alcove, lay the Peneriphus Scroll.

"We have two choices, Jared. Study the content of the scroll here, where it is safe, or risk taking it with us so that it is readily available to us at any time."

"Take it with us!" said Hannock, adamantly. "Anything that means we don't have to come back *here* again," he added, looking about him.

"Thank you, Captain, but my question *was* posed to Jared."

381

Hannock nodded his head vigorously as Jared glanced at him.

"I'm going to have to agree with Hannock on this occasion, Emnor. We don't have the time to keep returning here each time we wish to consult the scroll."

"As you wish, Your Highness. In that case, I relinquish it into your safe keeping," replied Emnor, handing it to Jared. "Keep it safe, Jared," he whispered. "We cannot allow it to fall into Karrak's hands. You must promise to destroy it before ever allowing that to happen."

"Let's just hope it predicts any steps that may be taken by Karrak, *before he makes them,*" said Hannock.

"We've survived so far without the use of the scroll," sighed Jared.

"We still have to get out of here though," noted Hannock, "I wonder what gory delights the guardians have in store for us next?"

"Nothing at all," announced Emnor. "Once the scroll has been removed, their part is over. No more visions, no more voices, just a darkness in which only your own imagination can scare you."

"In that case," said Hannock with a sigh of relief, "can we get out of here?"

Emnor led the way and eventually instructed them to place a hand on his shoulders once more. In a split second, they were again bathed in sunlight. The three blinked as their eyes became accustomed to it, each seeing a blurred figure strolling slowly toward them.

"*A mind prison*?" exclaimed Yello. "You've lived for over a thousand years and that's the best you could come up

382

with?" he laughed. "And what's more, you've been gone for fourteen minutes. I can remember when you could retrieve anything you'd hidden within five. Then again, you weren't a crusty, old codger back then."

"Thank you, Yello. How good of you to point that out. And I am not *crusty*, I bathe at least once a fortnight."

"Alright, I'm only joking. Did you retrieve the scroll, or have you just read the highlights?"

"Your nose is going to get stuck somewhere you don't want it to if you don't stop poking it into other people's business," chuntered Emnor.

"It is my business, you silly old fool. If Karrak comes after it, I'll be just as much a target as anyone."

"Can we just go somewhere quiet and read it? That is why we… *fourteen minutes*?" said Jared.

"Sorry?" said Yello, raising his eyebrows.

"You said we were gone for fourteen minutes."

"Well, approximately. Now don't you dare say that Emnor's getting slow. I'd like to see you do better when you're over a thousand years old," replied Yello.

"We were in there for hours, not a few minutes!"

"No, Hannock. It merely *felt* like you were in there for hours. It's not real, remember?"

"Whatever you say, Emnor," replied Hannock. It seemed that he was never destined to understand the intricacies of magic. "Shall I read it?" he asked. "No? Alright then, just a thought. Lead on, Jared."

Faylore, Jendilomin, Lodren and Grubb had almost completed their ascent from the hall of history and were now less than a day from returning the body of the former King Koloss to his wife, Erenthas. Very little was said as they travelled. Faylore and Jendilomin remained silent through grief, Grubb and Lodren through the respect they felt for the queen and her sister. Grubb had insisted, as politely as he could, that he would carry Koloss' body, an easy task for him once he had transformed into his alter-ego, Wilf. After wrapping Koloss in a cloak belonging to Faylore, Wilf gently lifted him with as much care as was possible. Lodren did his best to persuade the sisters to eat, but was never so insensitive as to insist. He suggested that they rest for a while. "Would you care for anything, Your Majesty? A small bite to eat or a drink perhaps?"

Faylore managed a weak smile as she shook her head but her sister did not hear Lodren's repeated question as she knelt, staring deep into the ground.

Wilf placed Koloss on the ground and began to shrink as he headed toward Lodren. "It's a shame, *it ain't fair!* Look at 'em Grubb. Their little hearts are broken an' there's nothin' we can say to 'em to 'elp."

"Give them time, Grubb. That's all that can help them, I'm afraid. Time, and being there when they need you," replied Lodren.

"But look at 'em, they don't *need* us," insisted Grubb, becoming more upset.

"Not right now they don't, Grubb, but they will eventually, and we *will* be there for them when that time comes. Just you wait and see," replied Lodren, placing his arm around his friend's shoulders.

The solemn procession continued without queen or princess eating so much as a morsel or taking a sip of water. As the day drew to a close, they exited the hall of history to face the heartbroken Erenthas, and the devastated people of Thedar.

Koloss was buried two days later in a traditional Thedarian ceremony. Lodren and Grubb were relieved to see that Faylore and Jendilomin were beginning the healing process after the loss of their father.

"The one thing I don't understand is why they put him back in the ground," said Grubb. "If that was the plan all along, why didn't we just leave 'im in the halls where we found 'im?"

"We brought him back so that his people could say their farewells. You don't leave the body of a king where you found it, you dope."

"They could've gone down there to say 'bye. It was a lot less cramped 'n' all."

"It's the way the Thedarians do things, Grubb, and that's all that matters. Stop going on about it, it's done now."

"Yeah, I suppose so and Faylore and… 'ang on a minute, can you see what I can see?"

"I'd have to be blind not to. What is he doing here? I thought they never left their home!"

Even if he were blind, Lodren would have felt the ground tremors as the impressive dragon, Thelwynn made his way toward them. Lodren and Grubb were delighted to see him and waved frantically as they ran toward him.

"Thelwynn, over here. How lovely to see you. Fancy you visiting us here. To what do we owe the pleasure?" asked the excited Nibby.

"'Opefully 'e realises what a real pain you are an' 'e's gonna sit on ye," laughed Grubb.

"I do wish that the purpose for my visit was a pleasant one. Alas, I bring grave news. Where might I find Queen Faylore? I must speak with her urgently."

"Whatever is the matter, Thelwynn? Are you alright? Are the rest of the dragons alright? Speak up!" urged Lodren, almost beside himself with worry.

Word had spread rapidly about the arrival of a dragon, and before long, Faylore was seen approaching them. "My lord, Thelwynn. Welcome to Thedar. Please forgive me, we are in mourning for the loss of our father."

"News came to me of your father, Your Majesty. May I offer my sincere condolences?" said Thelwynn, bowing graciously. "But I am afraid that you must leave immediately, your friends are in grave danger. I have news. Karrak is preparing for his final attempt at domination. I heard the mountain's breath. It says 'the *seconds* are soon to meet'."

"What *seconds*? What does it mean?" asked Faylore.

"I am unsure, my lady. It is difficult for me to translate into your words. All I know is that your friends need your aid. You must not tarry."

"Right!" announced Grubb. "Lodren? Up on me shoulders when I change, Faylore, you take the lead."

"I am afraid, Master Grubb, that even you would not be swift enough to reach your friends quickly enough. Even as your other persona," breathed Thelwynn.

"My other what?"

"Your other… oh what's the use? He means as Wilf," snapped Lodren.

"Why didn't 'e just say that then?" replied Grubb, wobbling his head.

"There is only one way for you to reach them, Your Majesty. You must ride upon my back," announced Thelwynn.

"My lord!" exclaimed Faylore, "I could never ask you to lower yourself to such a thing. You are a skylord, royalty of the clouds and as such, beneath such things. You are no mere beast. Thank you, but I cannot."

"Now we don't want to insult him, Your Majesty. He volunteered after all, wouldn't be offering if he didn't want to do it," babbled Lodren as he dashed about grabbing a few things he deemed essential. "We are his friends after all, and he obviously wants to help. Hurry up, Grubb, don't dally."

"Lodren!" snapped Faylore, stopping the Nibby dead in his tracks, "You aren't, perchance, accepting his offer simply because you want to ride on a dragon's back, are you?"

"Oooo… Your Majesty, *how could you say such a thing*? I can't believe you'd think something like that about me. I mean… really!"

Faylore folded her arms and stared at him, "It's the truth though, isn't it? You want to ride on a dragon's back?"

"Oh, yes, yes, yes, more than anything in the world. I'm sorry, I can't help myself. They're so beautiful, so majestic in the air as they soar and glide and swoop," he replied, jigging up and down and dancing with excitement.

"Lodren," sighed Grubb, "yer such a pillock at times. Get yer stuff ready. *We're goin' dragon flyin'!"*

CHAPTER 24

Yello had joined Emnor and the others as they unrolled the scroll. They puzzled over its content as they attempted to interpret the meaning of the script.

"It doesn't actually tell you *anything,* does it?" said Hannock, scratching his head.

"One becomes used to its meanings after a while, Captain. But I understand your confusion. The scroll is very old and not written as it would be now," said Emnor.

"To be precise," added Yello, "It's not actually 'written' at all."

"You mean the words magically appear by themselves?" laughed Hannock.

"That's exactly what they mean, Hannock," said Jared.

"It's not important how the words appear. What is important is that we understand what it is suggesting. It is not a set of instructions, more *hints* as to what *could* transpire."

"*Could*?" asked Hannock. "So, whatever the scroll predicts can be changed?"

"They are not predictions, Hannock. The scroll seems to evaluate the possibilities of all outcomes, and shows the most probable," advised Emnor.

"So it's a 'best guess' thing then? Nothing set in stone, as it were?" asked Jared.

"A crude way of describing it, but accurate all the same," smiled Yello.

"Well, what are you waiting for? Start reading," suggested Hannock.

As the four studied the scroll, the words before them would change, occasionally shuffling themselves around the page or vanishing completely, only to be replaced by a different text a few seconds later. Just as something seemed to become clear, the words would shuffle once more and change their train of thought drastically.

"Every time we seem to be getting somewhere, the bloody thing changes again!" exclaimed Hannock. "We'll be here forever at this rate!"

"Patience, my dear Captain, *patience*," implored Emnor. "This happens every time. Give it a while and the words will settle. Once they do, they'll give a hint as to our next possible course of action."

"Exactly! *Possible course*, we may as well burn the thing!" said Hannock. "Every step we take is hindered in some way. You're always saying *we must hurry*, *we don't have time*. Then we waste hours and sometimes days with useless crap like this!"

"Hardly useless, Hannock," said Jared. "It's your impulsive nature, friend, to charge in, head down. Who knows? Studying the scroll for five minutes could save us days later."

"I hate sitting around whilst Karrak is up to *who knows what*, Jared. We should have found him by now."

"And we shall, and soon. But as Emnor said, you have to have patience."

"Oh dear," muttered Emnor as he lifted the scroll suddenly. "That's not good, not good at all."

"What is it, Emnor? What does it say?"

"*The meeting of the seconds is inevitable,*" replied Emnor, almost in a whisper.

"Then there's to be some sort of duel? It's the only time that one would require seconds," suggested Hannock. "But a duel between whom? Jared and Karrak perhaps?"

"I do not think that it is referring to seconds in a duel, Captain. I think it is something far more dangerous," said Emnor. "Jared, could you answer a question for me?"

"Anything, ask away," replied Jared.

"I know that Karrak was never married, but did he have any children you know about? A son, perhaps?"

Jared paused. The intimate affairs of House Dunbar were not something that he was comfortable discussing, especially when it came to the indiscretions of his younger brother. He cleared his throat, but found that he could not look Emnor in the eye. "Erm… there were a couple of liaisons I am aware of, bar wenches to be truthful. I'm not proud of the fact, but I paid them well and relocated them. They would want for nothing in their new homes."

"*Children*, Jared. *Were there any children*?"

"Both women were with child when they departed Borell, each claimed that Karrak was the father. I have no idea what became of them after that, it was open blackmail. All either of them wanted was to be paid and neither had designs on being involved with House Dunbar," replied Jared.

"Then I know what the scroll is suggesting," announced Emnor. *"The second son and the second son are destined to meet. Should they join forces, nothing and no one will be able to prevent their rise to power."*

"You mean Karrak has a son?" snapped Hannock. "Jared! Why didn't you tell me? We are the closest of friends. Surely…"

"And you are captain of my father's guard!" snapped Jared. "Do you really believe that I wanted to keep it from you? I was under strict instruction from my father. My loyalty to House Dunbar comes above all else, as does yours."

Emnor placed the scroll before Jared, "We must find Karrak, preferably before this meeting takes place. We alone must become the bane of Karrak."

***

Karrak haunted the halls of the great castle of Merrsdan. Undead guards stood around, motionless and devoid of all thought or emotion. He barely glanced at their rotting flesh as he drifted from room to room, his mind consumed by his hatred of all living things. His insanity had grown to the point where the only thing he cherished was The Elixian

Soul. He would talk to it and stroke it as if it were a pet nestled in the chest plate of his armour.

His perception of time, however, remained unaffected. He was enraged that Darooq was now overdue, as was his favourite torture victim, Barden. He could sense neither of them and concluded that, for now, they were far enough away to render them safe from his reach. *Would Darooq attempt to flee? Did he believe that he would be able to travel far enough to elude his master, taking his new pet with him?* No, Darooq was not that naïve. He would return soon with pathetic excuses for his delay, and this at least would give Karrak the reason to further torture his only loyal follower.

***

The shadow lord tilted his head suddenly, he sensed something, something unknown to him, *someone* unknown to him. Slowly, he glided along the passageways, pausing occasionally to get a better sense of who he was about to face. There were two of them.

Strangely, and for the first time, the shadow lord felt anxious. *Why would he feel this way? Who could be powerful enough to unnerve the great Lord Karrak?*

Entering the courtyard, he saw no one, but he *was* getting close. He could sense their immense power. *Why was there no commotion, why were the intruders not being attacked by his mindless guards?* He had created them to protect his castle but they remained as immobile as they always were. He threw his hand up and one was instantly incinerated. *Useless*, he thought as he watched it burn and fall to the ground without a murmur or scream of pain. Only then did he see the intruders.

At the far end of the courtyard stood two young men. They did not flee as he approached them, much to his surprise. *They are little more than children*, he thought. But by their attire, he could tell that they were wizards, one radiating a power that he knew could rival his own.

Neither of the young men spoke as Karrak stood before them. One had a confident, almost arrogant look of disdain on his face, the other was oblivious to his surroundings.

"So, this is how the world wishes to defeat me? An inexperienced child sent to face the destroyer of this world. Do your allies believe that I will take pity upon you, child? Do they think that I will allow you to live through this confrontation due to your lack of years? If that was their hope, I'm afraid that they were mistaken. My only concern is not *whether to kill* you both, but *how*."

Karrak laughed as he circled the two young wizards, leering at them in a vain attempt to intimidate them.

"Come, boy!" he bellowed. "Do you have nothing to say before your execution?"

The voice that replied was not spoken aloud, it was inside Karrak's head.

A deep threatening voice that resembled his own, "What would you have me say, shadow lord?"

Karrak backed away in alarm. How could anyone enter his mind? He was not only powerful enough to prevent this, he was also still wearing the Order of Corrodin.

"I know, what about this?"

"HELLO FATHER!"